THE MYSTERIES OF
CAMP MYTH
UNDER THE THRONE

WRITTEN AND ILLUSTRATED

BY: SIMONA C. HUSKA

THE MYSTERIES OF
CAMP MYTH

UNDER THE THRONE

SIMONA C. HUSKA

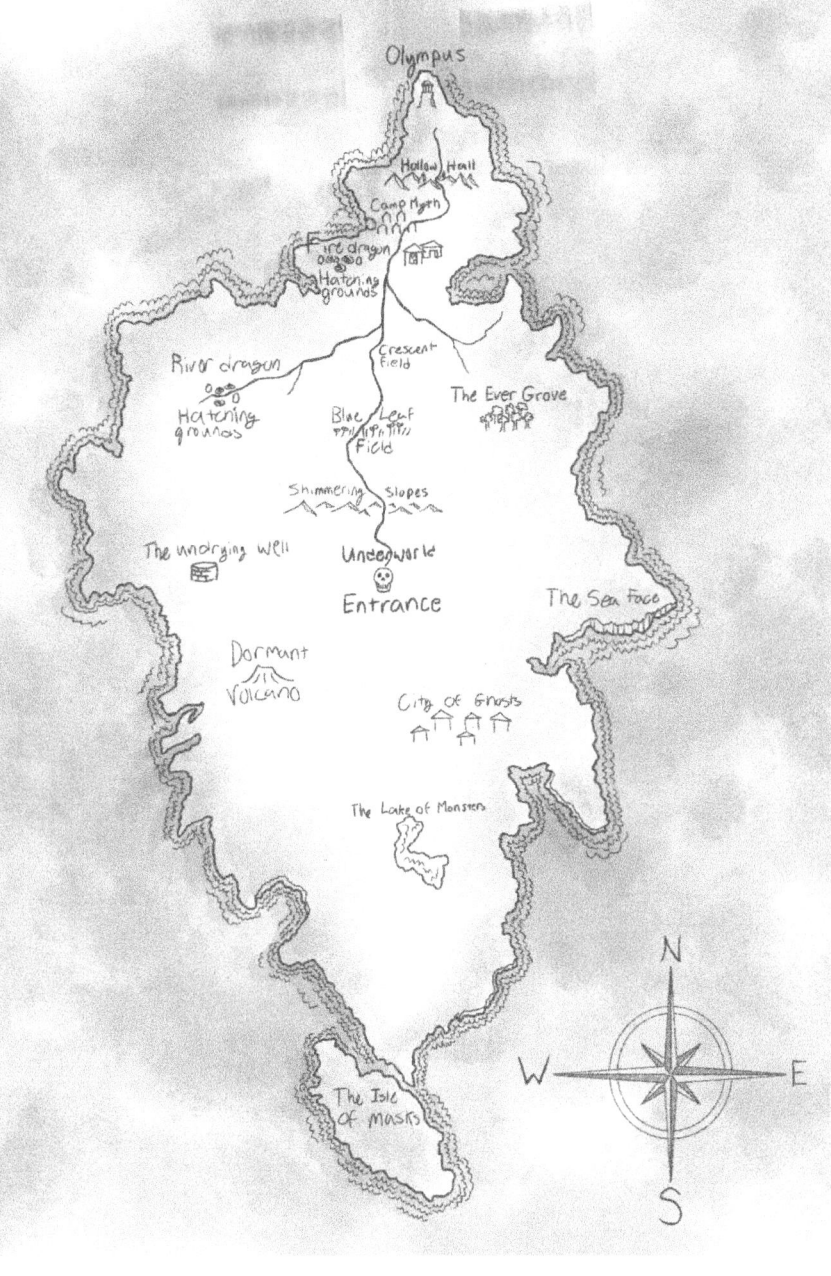

DEDICATION

For my parents and sister whom I love very much: Thank you for never sending me on a deadly quest.

TABLE OF CONTENTS

PROLOGUE

'You are late." A cold voice spoke out of the cursed mirror.

"Apologies, my lord." The gifted one bowed deeply.

The cold, raspy voice then asked, "Do you have it?" She held out the jewel-encrusted iron helmet.

"I was nearly caught, my lord, stupid skeletons," She muttered angrily.

"Do the spell," The cold voice purred.

The gifted one plucked a ruby off the helmet's surface and placed it into the seeing bowl. She swirled the water with her finger.

"Show me the one that will make him fall," She recited. The water whirled with color. "Give me the power to see her toll, in my blood, my tears, my sacrifice, give me the sign to start the pit's rise."

The thing in the mirror smiled eerily as the image of a girl with a pale freckled face, curly red hair, and vivid green eyes filled the water.

CHAPTER ONE

I ACCIDENTALLY MAKE FRIENDS WITH A SWORD WIELDING KID

I'M Klotho Marina, and my life is absolutely nuts-even at the age of eleven. Now, if you see yourself in these pages with the hints that I give about not being like other kids, get the cheapest ticket to Maine (okay maybe not the cheapest one, unless you don't want to be sitting in a puke-covered seat with shoelaces to strap yourself in), and head for the island! If you're one of us, you'll see it off the coast. Doesn't matter how you get there, you could swim, surf, take a boat, a catapult, a giant dog with flippers, a crashing plane, whatever! As long as you get there, you'll be safe. Or, as safe as you can be when you're a gifted one. Our eyes give us away. They're always special in some way. For example, mine are an unnaturally bright shade of green.

Enough rambling, let's get to the story. This all happened the summer after fifth grade.

"All-school Dodgeball? Seriously? That's what they came up with? It's the last day of school! We should be having fun!" A kid in my class grumbled as our gym teacher announced the reason the gym had a line of ugly gray duct tape separating the sides of the gym. How they managed to keep kids from tearing it right off the ground, I had no clue.

It's been an awful day till now. Someone had spilled cranberry juice all over my new shirt, (of course it was white) and my drum set got dented by some idiot sitting on it.

Good start, I thought as one whizzed by my head and caused me to duck at the last moment. Just as I stood back up, thinking I was in the clear, a blue dodgeball sailed at me and hit me squarely in the face.

The force of the ball knocked me over like a falling tree. I fell flat on my butt and rubbed my now sore nose. The ball thankfully didn't have any rocks inside, but getting smacked in the face with a public-school dodgeball is still getting smacked in the face with a public-school dodgeball and it does hurt.

"TIMBER!" Lily Stanley, the one who maybe hid rocks in the dodgeballs last year, yelled. She snickered to her villain side-kick Megan Pruddy. The P. E. teacher promptly called to Lily that she was out.

There's a strict rule, no headshots. She glared at me as if it were my fault that she'd aimed for my face. The game continued and I eventually got pelted. I had no problem going to the side to sit down away from the absolute war-zone that the gym had turned into.

When I went home that day, I collapsed onto the couch in our small living room and whooped with delight. We lived on the thirteenth floor of an apartment in Minnesota, the state where snow falls in October, and people go to the beach more to skate than to swim.

"You better start packing your things." My mom walked into the room with a grin. Her black hair was swaying across her shoulders, and her electric blue eyes were wide with joy.

"What do you mean?" I questioned.

"We're going to Maine!" She flashed our passports in my face. She was so happy it was contagious, and her smile made its way onto my face.

"Is dad coming?" I asked, secretly hoping that he wouldn't. Nothing against my dad, I'm really grateful to have him, but when it comes to trips, I would rather be with just my mom.

She shook her head. "Nope, this is a girls' trip."

Yes! I thought as I ran to my room to pack. I managed to fit a bunch of clothes, a hair brush to wrangle my curly red hair, my tooth brush, shampoo, conditioner, a pillow, and a blanket in a blue duffle bag.

The next day, mom and I spent the majority of the day on the plane and at the airport trying to find our way around. We spent the first two days at a hotel and did sightseeing until lunch, on the third day and then we hit the beaches.

During the week, I noticed a boy named Sam and we hung out by the pool and the beach. He had blonde hair, tanned skin, and rusty brown eyes that looked metallic. He was pretty nice, which was surprising considering what most of the boys in my fifth-grade class were like.

"So, there's this cool island that we'll have to take a boat to get to. Wanna go see it?" Sam asked, as I slathered my freckled face in sunscreen. He pointed at a green mass in the distance.

I thought for a second. "I could ask my mom," I replied. I was a bit hesitant. Sam was very new to me, but I was sure I'd be fine.

I walked over to my mom. She was laying on her towel in her bikini, her electric blue eyes hidden behind shades. "Hey, mom?"

"Hmm?" She didn't look up from her book.

"Sam just asked if I wanted to check out an island off the coast, can I go with him?" She pulled off her shades and sat up. She looked out across the ocean at the green landmass that was the island that Sam had pointed at.

Her face was normal and unemotional but her eyes held a look that I had only ever seen in movies, it was the 'the time has come' look.

Odd, I thought.

She snapped out of it. "That sounds fun, but change into proper clothes and tennis shoes, and don't stay for too long." She laid back down.

"Thanks! I'll be back soon." I rushed off to Sam. "She said it was fine, but I need to change," I told him.

I ran to the very gross bathrooms to change, and when I came back, Sam was waiting next to a boat. He switched out his flip-flops for tennis shoes with a mysterious brown stain on them.

"Ready?" He gestured to the boat. I wondered how he got one without an adult deciding that an eleven-year-old should operate heavy machinery, but shrugged it off. Maybe the people of Maine were more relaxed than Midwesterners.

"Yup." I climbed into the boat and sat down, laying my hand on the railing, just in case.

"WHY DID I THINK THIS WAS A GOOD IDEA?" I screamed over the wind as the boat sped across the water. My fingers gripped the railing so tightly, I couldn't feel them. The ocean sprayed me with salty mist.

"IT WAS A GOOD IDEA!" Sam yelled back with an impish grin on his face.

I looked back behind me to the receding coastline, and Lily's poison-green eyes and ginger hair looked back. Except, no, no way. Her hair curled and writhed around; it was a nest of snakes. She was swimming behind us at not-at-all-okay speed.

Wait, swimming? Out here? And snake hair? That can't be right, I thought to myself. I forced myself to let go of the railing with one hand and wipe my eyes in case it was a mirage.

Yup, she was there alright. But there was no way, she couldn't have swum that far. Right?

"Umm, Sam..." I started uneasily. He looked behind us, caught sight of Lily, and his tan skin paled. He made the boat go even faster, and I shrieked at the sudden burst. I smacked my hand back onto the railing to avoid getting pulled out of the boat by force.

I'd always found the ocean terrifying.

Next thing I knew, we'd skidded onto the black of this island and we were scrambling to get onto dry land.

The second that we got out of that boat, Sam and I sprinted into the woods. I made the mistake of looking back to see Lily running after us. I tripped, fell on my face, scrambled upright, and threw myself over a log. I heard Lily's new snake hair hiss and I chucked something at her to hopefully keep her at bay. My heart pounded in my chest like an off-tempo drum beat. And even though my throat and legs hurt like nothing else, I kept running.

We had been sprinting for about two minutes through the thick forest, jumping over logs and ducking under branches (I had no clue how we'd managed that long) before stopping. I panted like a dog; my throat was raw, and my heart was about to beat through my rib cage. I fell to my knees in the brush and heaved in gulps of air, glancing back frantically in case the two had followed us. When my panting finally calmed down, I took in the scenery around us.

We made it to a crystal-clear river with moss-covered slab-like cuts of rock jutting out from the ground. The thick trunk of a fallen tree bridged the trickling water.

"I think... we lost them." Sam was finally able to get out the words through his panting. I gazed at the forest around me, taking in my surroundings. My throat and lungs burned like I had been breathing nothing but acid. I hardly noticed. The trees had the greenest leaves I had ever seen and some of them almost looked metallic.

There was a willow tree with silver hand-sized flowers that were shaped like bluebells, and flowing in the water were water lilies with petals that looked like moonstone, mostly blue, but shimmering with other colors.

"Yeah," I said absentmindedly, awestruck by this beautiful area.

"Um hello? EARTH TO KLOTHO!" Sam said. His yell shook me out of my stupor.

"Oh right." I snapped back into focus. "*Now, WHAT THE HELL IS GOING ON? WHERE ARE WE? WHY DID YOU BRING ME HERE? WHAT THE ACTUAL HELL IS THAT THING THAT LOOKS LIKE MY BULLY—*"

My question was cut short by a hiss. My heart roared in my ears and panic rose in my throat. I whipped my head around.

Lily!

Sam and I ran onto the log, slipping on the wet surface, but Megan was on the other side, waiting for us.

We were surrounded.

Suddenly, Sam's ring turned into a three-foot-long copper sword.

"YOU HAVE A SWORD?!" I screamed. My voice was going to get hoarse if I kept screaming at this rate. My blood pressure must have been through the atmosphere. I was terrified and confused, and panicking, and all of that. Mainly terrified.

"KLOTHO! NOT THE TIME!" He slashed at Megan, making her hiss and leap back.

"WHAT AM I SUPPOSED TO FIGHT WITH?" I backed up as Lilly came forward, about 900% sure that I was going to die. My knees shook like the earth during an earthquake.

"I DON'T KNOW! FIND SOMETHING IN YOUR BAG!" Sam yelled, clearly panicking himself.

I rummaged through and found a nail file.

Good enough, I thought quickly to myself.

Lily lunged at me, so I threw my hand forward and tried to stab her in the eye, but I ended up poking her eyebrow instead. She hissed and flinched away, but then giggled to herself at my weapon of choice.

She lunged again, claws out and ready to slice me to bite-sized bits. My shaking hands dropped the nail file into the water, leaving me with nothing to defend myself with. I jumped back and tried to stab her, but my foot slipped, and I tumbled into the river below.

I hit the water bum first with a smack. The cold water rushed over me as the back of my head smacked into a log, and everything went black.

****

I woke up under that willow tree with silver bluebell-like flowers hanging off of some of the branches. My head felt awful, sore, and aching. My legs didn't feel much better, and I was sopping wet.

"Sam? Sam, where are we?" I pushed myself into a sitting position even though my arms hurt, and looked around. How long had I been out? I remember hearing that if someone gets hit in the head, they could get permanent brain damage. I looked over to my right, Sam was trying to build a fire.

He glanced over at me. "We're on the north island." He said, "If I didn't take you here, they'd come for you eventually. She'd kill me if I let you die."

I started to freak out. My breaths were short and quick and my voice reached a yell, "Sam, I need to get off the island! I can't stay here—"

"Shhhhhhhhh!" He hissed, "Do you want to get eaten by monsters?!"

"No! But—"

"But nothing! There's twice as many monsters on the mainland! You have to stay here!" Sam interrupted.

"The what? Monsters? What's going on? This place, why does it change anything? Who really are you?" I was beyond confused. I crossed my trembling arms, waiting for an explanation.

"I can't tell you anything yet. I'll explain when we get where I need to take you. For now, we need to find a place to set up camp," Sam muttered. I didn't have anywhere to go, and no survival skills, so I followed Sam.

We walked silently; the sounds of the forest weren't any different from what I'd heard back home. Chirping birds, rustling leaves, mosquitos. I itched a spot on my thigh where one bit me. The sweltering summer sun beat down on us, and I wished I had a hat or more sunscreen.

Finally, we found a small gap in the trees. Sam set up a tent while I found sticks for a fire. I carried my small collection to Sam, who stacked them up into a pyramid shape. Both of us were silent until the fire had been set.

"Why did you start a fire?" I asked quietly. I glanced around in case something had heard me, "It's hot out."

"It'll keep mosquitos away, and help dry you off," Sam added a stick to the little plumes.

He stared into the burning pile of sticks. "I'm sorry. I can't tell you anything. If I could I would, believe me, knowing now will get you in a lot more trouble than you're in now." Sam seemed genuinely sorry, and I wanted to believe him but... I'd just met him the day before.

"It's okay," I lied, "At least I won't have to deal with Lily."

Sam looked at me, confused. "Who's Lily?"

"One of my bullies. She was the snake-thing that attacked me. She filled a ball with bricks one year and a kid almost dislocated his arm trying to throw it. There's no evidence that it was her but we all know she did it." I explained.

"Well, at least she won't be able to throw her pebble-filled balls at you anymore." Sam snickered.

I burst out giggling before a sound caused me to stop.

Footsteps. Not just any footsteps, running footsteps. The tempo matched the one my heartbeat rose to.

"We need to go," Sam whimpered, his eyes widening. He tried to drag me upright but I was frozen in place.

He managed to pull me out of my trance. "Come on!" He hissed, finally wrenching me upright.

We ran as fast as our legs could take us. I was only looking straight ahead, even while my legs were getting scraped up by bushes and fallen branches when the ground disappeared from under my feet. My idiot self hadn't noticed the small drop-off, I'd say 'cliff', but it was only about an eight or nine-foot drop, and it appeared to have some sort of bushes at the bottom. I could have landed it even if I hadn't been prepared, just one problem, the bushes I saw were thorn bushes.

I flopped through the air and landed hard. The shrubs broke my fall with their prickling agony. I felt those blasted plants tear through my skin. When I finally landed on the floor under the bushes. I looked at my arms and felt immediately sick when I saw they were cut and bruised and some strange black liquid was smeared on them.

"KLOTHO!" Sam screamed. Blood pooled under my legs, and flowed down my arms like little rivers of red. I smelled something sweet in the air and started to feel light-headed. The bushes had what looked like little white beads attached to them, and several of those beads had opened up, letting out that scent.

I heard a girl's voice, echoing through the forest with enough volume to give an old lady a heart attack. "SAMUEL OLIVER STEFANS!" She sounded ready to fling him out of an airplane. Though, I wasn't as concerned with her as I was with not passing out.

"Klotho, hang in there—"

I didn't hear the rest. I blacked out.

Chapter Two

A Twenty-Foot-Bearded Guy Gets Roasted By An Angry Twelve-Year-Old Girl

I felt a pair of hands gripping my wrists, followed by a cool sensation that made the stinging in my arms disappear. I heard voices swirling around the room, bits of tangled conversation. I heard the girl who had yelled Sam's name screaming at him. I heard a woman saying she was worried, someone else put their hand on my arms but didn't say a word and a boy asked a question.

I sat up as fast as I could. Someone next to me screamed. That shrill scream was followed by a thud and I jumped out of the bed and fell on my face. I scrambled upright and ran to the corner, preparing to run and hide for what might come next.

A boy was lying on his back on the floor. He had black hair, midnight blue, monolid eyes, and milky skin. He had a scar on his neck and he was wearing a dark gray T-shirt, jeans, and black tennis shoes with white laces. He had a white square-shaped crystal that appeared to have a crack snaking down the middle of a leather cord. He looked over at the corner, his fearful expression softened when he looked at me.

A girl marched into the room.

"Ethan! What are you doing? You blundering fool! You scared the poor girl!" She had silky, shoulder-length black hair, light brown skin, and upturned ice-blue eyes. She was wearing a navy-blue tennis dress, leather lace-up sandals, and gold-rimmed glasses. She had a necklace kind of like his, although her crystal was shaped like a splatter of water, and changed colors as I looked at it.

"Sorry, Anne," Ethan said, scrambling to get up.

"Don't say sorry to me! Say sorry to her!" The girl called Anne retorted. "I'm so sorry dear, he's an idiot."

"Sorry. I didn't mean to startle you," Ethan apologized, standing up. He was taller than I was by maybe an inch.

I nodded shyly. "It's fine, where's Sam?" I asked. I looked around the small room, trying to look for Sam as if he would appear out of thin air.

"Facing the wrath of Simone," Ethan shuddered.

"Good," Anne growled, placing her hands on her hips. "At least that'll teach him not to take young gifted ones to the island after just meeting them like he did to Klotho." Anne shook her head.

I looked at her in surprise. Hold up, he knew me before the beach? And how did she know my name? Then it occurred to me that Sam probably told them.

"What are you two talking about? Where am I? Who's Simone?" I asked nervously. The way Ethan shuddered made me think that this Simone girl might hurt Sam.

"Simone is my friend; Ethan is terrified of her-"

"I am not!" Ethan retorted quickly.

She looked at him skeptically.

"Suuuure, anyway, Sam and Simone's butt heads a lot because Sam hardly listens to her, and he's been begging her to bring you to camp for like half the week. But she's been telling him that he needs to wait," Anne explained.

"And why is she involved in this mess?" I asked.

"She's the assistant director of Camp Myth and basically runs Nikephros Academy," Ethan told me. "Without her, the entire island would be run by a sleep-deprived Medea, and you don't want that, believe me," Ethan explained, shuddering again.

"Wait, back up. Camp? Academy?" I was so confused. "What the heck is going on?"

Anne sighed in exasperation. "Oh for goodness sake, did Sam tell you *anything* about why you're here?"

I frowned. "Not really..."

"Ugh! If Simone doesn't end up killing him, I will!" Anne snapped. "This island is a place for kids like you, me, and Ethan. Gifted ones. We each have three powers, and a Greek god chooses to watch over and guide us. Our eyes always give us away, since they're always unusual. Yours are too bright to be normal, mine turn silver in cold weather, Ethan's change with the weather, Sam's are metallic, and so on."

The logical part of me told me they were pulling my leg. "So, I'm a magical kid with weird eyes?" I asked.

"That can see through the Veil," Ethan added.

"The what?"

"The thing that keeps humans from seeing monsters and magic and stuff," He explained.

"Okay, I'm a magical kid with weird eyes that can see through the Veil." I rolled my eyes.

"You don't believe us," The two of them said at the same time.

"Well of course I don't! What you're telling me is crazy," I said.

"Do you want proof?" Anne asked.

"Yes, please!" I said. '*This is going to be good,*' I thought.

13

She sighed, and her colors shifted so that she matched the patterned carpet, she was nearly invisible. My jaw dropped.

"You-you, you just, how? You know what, I'm not even surprised anymore," I told myself, "How do I sign up for this camp thing?"

"Later, you need to change and shower." Anne dragged me to a small bathroom with a closed-off shower and set down a stack of clothes on the counter.

She left and I washed my hair, lathered my body, and scrubbed myself until I was squeaky clean. I wrapped the towel around myself and looked at the clothes that Anne had stacked neatly on the bench. A short-sleeved t-shirt with black and white stripes, blue jean shorts, what I hoped were clean socks and underwear, and a pale straw hat with mini yellow cloth roses sewn onto the ribbon around the ribbon trim.

Once I'd changed, I emerged back into the room right as the door to the cabin thing opened and Sam stepped in, he was whiter than me and clearly shaken.

I gasped at the sight of him. "Sam! What happened? Are you okay? You look awful."

Anne giggled while Ethan just stared, seeming to brace himself.

Sam glared at them. "Simone is *mad*, she was ready to flay me alive and dip me in acid before Medea reminded her that we don't skin campers. She sent me to come get you."

"Medea? Like the Ancient Greek sorceress?" I asked. I was mildly interested in Greek mythology, but I'd never done any super in-depth research. I did know that the sorceress Medea poisoned the princess her husband was cheating on her with and let the resulting mob kill both of her kids.

"Yup," He replied. "And she basically raised Simone, so she's always on her side."

14

I cocked my head to the side. "I guess that makes sense." I paused. "She didn't actually hurt you, did she?"

Anne gave me a proud smile. "You ask good questions." She told me. Ethan looked at Sam and Anne, and then sighed in a way that said 'Here we go again'.

Sam huffed and crossed his arms irritably. "Well, she thinks she's in charge of everyone—"

"She is!" Anne and Ethan said at the same time.

Sam went on. "And she's acting like if we do something that we aren't supposed to do, it'll cause problems for her—"

"It will!" Anne and Ethan interrupted again.

"My point is, she doesn't let people take good risks." He glared at Anne.

Anne shot him a matching scowl. "Yeah, because the 'good risks' that most campers want to take are *dangerous.*"

Ethan muttered in agreement.

Sam rolled his eyes and focused his attention back on me. "Well, you need to go see her." He pulled me out of the room and started walking outside.

The river wound around the grounds and into the forest on the far side of the camp. The dew-covered grass soaked my socks. At least 100 small cabins were in a group about 40 feet from the forest. Another tree line was in the distance, directly opposite of the one that I had probably come from. There was even a lagoon in the distance, an archery range, an old shack, an outdoor auditorium, a greenhouse, a giant marble building that looked kind of like the Parthenon, and canoes lined part of the lagoon's beach. I saw a group of kids by the lagoon, splashing in its bright blue water. I couldn't tell much since they were so far away but it looked like one of the kids was lying on the bank and it looked like someone with a lot of brown hair was standing over the kid.

"What's going on over there?" I asked Sam.

"It looks like someone's in trouble." he pointed out, "And where there's trouble, there's Simone."

Sam and I ran to the river bank. A girl with red hair braided down her back was lying on the river bank, her face twisted in pain. Blood soaked the side of her shirt; she was breathing heavily.

The girl kneeling next to her had her arms hovering over the girl whispering incoherently. Glowing tendrils of iridescent greenish-teal light wrapped around her hands and forearms like the northern lights.

She pressed her hands on the injury and kept whispering in that mysterious language. The redheaded girl's side began to glow the same iridescent greenish-teal as the girl's hands, and the tendrils of light seemed to flow into the red-haired girl's side.

The wound closed, but the shirt was still torn open.

"Th-thanks," the red-haired girl stood up shakily.

"No problem, Iria. Tell your cabin head that you need to go to the infirmary to get properly fixed up, I've stopped the bleeding for now but it won't last long." The girl replied. The red-headed girl nodded and ran off.

The magical one turned around, "Oh, Sam, and Klotho?"

She was taller than me by three inches.

The girl had wavy hair that fell to her mid back, parted in the middle and dark chocolate at the roots of her hair fading into caramel brown. She had pale skin, and her eyes were bluish-green with a bronze ring around her pupil. She was wearing a short-sleeved black button-up shirt, high-waisted jean shorts, and midnight blue ankle boots with a bronze heel. The crystal on her necklace was cut geometrically with tiny crescent moons on the sides and it was translucent with black tendrils snaking around it, and iridescent blue was splattered all over its surface.

She stood with her back straight and her weight set comfortably on one foot. She looked regal and powerful. Her dead-inside eyes flicked up and down, tracking my every move.

"Hello. I am Simone, assistant director of Camp Myth, and assistant principal of Nikephros Academy," she said.

I tried to school my expression into something a bit more formal, but I probably just looked like an idiot. "Um hello, I would like to register for Camp Myth."

She nodded. Her silver ring turned into a clipboard, and she checked off a box with the pen clipped onto her shirt pocket. "Follow me." She started walking toward the tree line.

I looked back to see if Sam was following, but he wasn't. She took me into the woods and we walked in silence for about five minutes before I spoke.

"So... ummm, where exactly are you taking me?"
She jumped onto a log that had fallen across the river and began to cross.

"To your guide choosing. During the ceremony you will get your identification crystal and your murder tool—weapon, I mean," She corrected herself quickly, "You'll also find out what your powers are, assuming you haven't found out yet." She paused and raised an eyebrow at me.

"I don't know any of my powers," I confirmed. She nodded and continued to walk.

"In case you ever choose to stay on the island year-round, you'll get your locker and tower." She added to her explanation.

"What's a guide choosing?" I asked as I slipped and nearly fell into the river.

"Once you know your powers you will be chosen by a god who is willing, they will guide you," Simone explained.

"So… everything in Greek mythology is… real?" I asked. This was still a massive shock, so I apologize for my slowness.

"Well, kind of, all the gods and monsters are real, but so is a bunch of other stuff that isn't really from any mythology. Stuff is completely unique to the island. I've been told that it feels more like you're living in a fairy tale, but with Greek gods to watch over and criticize you, and you're constantly trying to either not die, or trying to keep that stupid Dionysus camper from downing the toilet water." Frustration coated her words. "But enough about me."

I snorted in laughter. She didn't realize it, but humor had eased my panicked confusion.

"Is healing one of your powers?" I asked, remembering how she saved that girl.

"No, that's one of the spells everyone can do, you just have to chant the rhyme. Healing spells are tricky, though, they only last a little while without the intervention of someone who actually has healing powers, or a plant that keeps the effect. You could get cut open and healed, only to have your guts fall right back out fifteen minutes later." She replied.

"And an identification crystal?"

She held the crystal on the long leather cord up. "It functions as the key to your locker, the dragon pavilion, and to your room, mine can get into other places, but you don't have to worry about that."

"Wait, a *dragon pavilion*?" I stopped dead in my tracks and glanced around as if one was going to jump out from behind a bush.

"You didn't see it?" I shook my head. "Huh, well, all kids over the age of ten get access, but don't worry, as long as you don't mess with them, they won't hurt you. Really, they're only here for the food."

She dragged me on and the trees split around us. A school building stood in the massive clearing, but it was unlike any school I had ever seen.

The walls were made of dark gray bricks, and ivy was growing all over the walls. Gorgeous stained-glass windows were on the six towers with colorful roofs. The six towers in question were massive and on the outer edges of the academy. On the right three towers, the shingles were yellow, pink, and red. On the left they were turquoise, green, and midnight blue. The other smaller towers had onyx-tiled roofs. The double doors were dark wood, and carved with elegant scenes and what looked like runes. It was beautiful, and even had a pond next to it, with rock spires framing the clear water.

"What is this place?" I gasped at the scenery.

"Nikephoros Academy." She walked to the doors and took off her necklace. Simone shoved the end of the crystal into a hole, turned it and shoved it in further. A click sounded and the huge doors opened.

The stone halls were lined with purplish-blue lockers. Each locker had an oddly shaped hole, like a keyhole, on it somewhere. I assumed that the holes were at every person's eye level.

"Do you have normal classes or magical ones?" I wondered.

"Magical ones, but we still have to learn things like math and history." Simone replied, "Though the history classes are usually super depressing and math is just legal torture."

"Dorms?"

"Depends on the tower, Lunarmist, is the tower that's furthest north, Brookstone is east, etc." Simone turned a corner and I smacked my hip into it despite knowing it was there.

"And how do you figure out which tower I'm in?"

"This way." Simone opened the door to a room. White walls, with a white table, sitting on it was a rectangular piece of glass.

"Put the glass up to your eyes, and blink slowly three times."

I did as she asked the piece of glass bumping my nose. When I opened my eyes after the third blink, I nearly dropped the glass, it had turned bright yellow. I set it down, scooting away like it was possessed.

"What does this have to do with anything?" I asked.

"It means your tower is Serin. Symbolized by clouds and the colors yellow and silver. The typical traits are, kind, empathetic, optimistic, and fearful," Simone explained.

"What's your tower?" I wondered.

"Lunarmist, the most common traits being, intelligence, wits, creativity, bravery, and secrecy." I could definitely see that in her. "And because whoever created it had no sense of subtlety; its symbol is a crescent moon with a cloud of mist half-covering it."

"What's next?" I asked.

She walked out of the room and I followed her down the classroom-lined halls. The halls twisted and turned, and we went down several staircases until we reached a door. Plain wood with the same odd keyhole as the doors of the school. When Simone put her crystal in instead of the door opening, the crystal shined a beam into her eyes. It scanned her eyes for a minute before the door creaked open.

"Why did it do that?" I wondered out loud.

"We can't risk gifted ones getting in without permission, they'll get lost and starve, the tunnels are hard to map and they all look the same, only Medea really knows the way through," Simone said grimly.

Simone led the way, I tried to remember the path, but she was right, the tunnels kept tricking me, every single one of them looked the same. At one point I thought we had hit a dead end, but we walked straight through the stone wall. The tunnels smelled like cool stone. It was really hot outside, but down here it was pleasantly cold.

The light in the tunnels was being emitted by glowing runes on the walls. The same set over and over again carved in a straight line through the middle of the wall. They gave off a blue light, almost too dim to see. It was an eerie look, but strangely beautiful.

"What exactly happened when you got to the island? How did Sam get you to go with him?" Simone questioned as we walked.

"He told me it was a cool place to visit, why?" I walked behind her, my footsteps echoing off the stone wall.

"Well, on the mainland monsters run wild, they also do so on the untamed parts of the island. Monsters can see our auras, he tried to bring you earlier, but I told him that he needed to wait. That your parents or guardians would lose their minds, but no, he didn't listen, and I had to explain to your terrified mom and dad that you are ok, and not dead in a ditch after getting ripped apart by a monster," Simone explained with no small hint of irritation.

My head spun; I hadn't even thought about that. My poor mom and dad, but I could see where Sam was coming from. Simone had said it herself; the mainland was more dangerous than the island. But jeez, couldn't he have at least waited to explain properly?

We turned and arrived at a brick wall. Simone took her crystal and tapped it with her nail in a distinct pattern. The crystal glowed an eerie blue. She took her necklace off and started drawing rune-like symbols on the bricks until the whole wall appeared to glow with magical writing. All of it except one circular brick in the middle.

"What do those do?" I pointed at the glowing runes.

"They'll open the door—don't touch them." She chided as I tried to trace one of the runes. She pushed her crystal into the circular brick in the center of the wall. It seemed to back into the wall before opening like a door to reveal a room. It had a large iron cauldron in the middle, a fancy book stand in front of that. Shelves of books and potion vials lined the walls.

As the brick wall/door closed behind us I noticed symbols carved on each of the walls. I stared wide-eyed.

Simone took a jug of clear liquid off one of the shelves and poured the entire contents into the cauldron. She swirled the liquid with a silver stick that had a hook on the end, it moved faster and faster until it turned into one of those water tornados.

She handed me the stick.

"Put your hand in the water, and wave the hook around until you feel something on the end." She instructed.

I looked at the liquid nervously.

"It's not going to kill you, just do it," She ordered, pushing me closer to the cauldron.

I gritted my teeth and stuck my hand in the liquid, it was freezing cold. I waved the stick around for what seemed like forever when I felt something catch on the hook. I couldn't see what it was, and I really hoped whatever had caught it wasn't my guide. I imagined a wriggling god hanging on the end of the hook and nearly laughed at the thought.

I pulled the stick out and it was glowing bright white, on the hook at the end was a crystal on a cord and a tablet with a cord through the top.

The crystal looked like one of those shells shaped like a unicorn horn. Simone picked up the tablet and read the runes scrawled on the front. "She shall control liquids, and storms, and will heal with her songs. Okay, Mrs. Fairytale princess." She added sarcastically about the singing power, grinning at me.

"Hey!" I felt my face go red.

"I'm just kidding, you have some pretty useful powers." She waved me off.

"What now?" I asked.

"Oh, jump into the cauldron." She said it as casually as one might say, 'Oh, we're going on this bus today'.

"You want me to do what?" I questioned, backing away from the cauldron.

"By Zeus's godforsaken family life, you aren't going to drown. You'll just get teleported to the Olympian throne room," Simone told me.

I took a breath, bent my legs, and tried to gracefully jump into the cauldron. But my legs went in, and my momentum made my chest smack the cauldron edge. I fell back and shrieked as the cold water spun and spun until I plopped onto a cold marble floor.

I looked around, I was in a huge and I mean *huge* room. It was the size of an auditorium. Why it needed to be *that* big was beyond me. Twelve 10-foot-tall thrones in a U around a central hearth. Everything was blinding white, which made it hard to look at.

"Ugh, he always does this!" Simone grumbled.

"What?" I jumped up at the assistant director suddenly beside me.

"ZEUS! GET YOUR DYSFUNCTIONAL FAMILY DOWN HERE *NOW!*" She screamed so loudly that I felt my hair vibrate, her demand made me question if she was fully there mentally. I was about to ask her who she was shrieking too, when colored winds swirled around the giant marble thrones. Sitting on the thrones now, were people, twenty-foot-tall people.

The dude in the middle had white hair, a cloud-like beard, pale skin, and sky-blue eyes. He wore a gray silk suit and black loafers. The man on his left-hand side had tanned skin, black hair, and a beard, and his eyes were turquoise like the sea. He wore beige Bermuda shorts and a floral-printed shirt.

Another guy sat directly at the white-haired guy's right. He had black hair, ghost-white skin like a corpse, black eyes, and he was wearing a black robe. Of all three, he looked the most intimidating.

The guy in the middle spoke. "Who have you brought us this time, Simone?" He sounded very bored.

"Klotho Marina, age 11." Simone reported and then added under her breath, "No respect for people's time," bitterly.

The man rolled his eyes. "Alright, anyone willing?"

"What are your powers?" A woman with intelligent gray eyes, dark brown wavy hair and olive skin asked me. She wore bronze Greek armor over a white dress.

"Um, I can control liquids, a-and storms, and I can heal people by singing." I stuttered. She regarded me with interest.

"Those might be good for war," A man with a war helmet on his head, tanned skin, and full armor said. He looked muscular.

I must have looked horrified because Simone stepped in saying, "Ares, she is *11* and will absolutely *not* be fighting any wars."

He looked disappointed.

"I'll guide her!" The tan guy said.

"Oh, no! I will!" The white-bearded guy thundered. They acted like children fighting over a toy.

"ZEUS!" Simone roared. They shut up so fast you'd think she had the power to squish them like cockroaches. "Poseidon claimed her already." She said sternly.

"What?" The one I guessed was Zeus, asked.

"I said that Poseidon claimed her first. Your heroes hardly ever live past 15, and your so-called 'advice' gets gifted ones into more trouble than they were in before! I can't stand another conversation with a kid's parents telling them their child died because they followed your advice! *And don't even get me started on your mating standards!* All they need is a pulse and they're good to go!"

Zeus looked star-struck. "Wel-well—"

Simone finished her assault of insults with, "Poseidon claimed first, he gets the hero." She said each word slowly and with emphasis like she was talking to a six-year-old

Simone's bold statement shocked him so much that he sat there staring for a good two minutes. She stood firm. "You'll move into the Poseidon cabin," she told me calmly. She grabbed my arm and we teleported back into the underground room.

Chapter Three

I Volunteer to Get Eaten By Monsters

ANNE led me to the Poseidon cabin before leaving to do something. It was right next to the Zeus cabin, where constant noises like thumping and banging came from. It felt like listening to a concert without music, but I would have to learn to live with it. I stood awkwardly, through the rows of bunk beds, which looked sturdy enough. Everything there was varying shades of turquoise. The sheets, pillows, blankets and even the walls, on which the paint was slightly peeling. An antique-looking chest rested in the corner; no idea what that could have been for.

Everyone in the cabin stared at me, some whispering to their neighbors. I just stood silently.

A boy in black Bermuda shorts and a blue-green t-shirt walked up to me. He had mahogany brown skin and eyes of deep purple. Although he appeared to be in his late teens, his physical build made him look like he could lift my dad over his head like it was nothing. For some reason, he wasn't wearing his crystal around his neck.

"Hi kid, I'm Elija, I'm the cabin head here." The boy spoke in a smooth, deep voice, "Your bunk is the one right in the middle there," he gestured to one right next to the wall in the middle of a row. The top bunk, with a shelf over it for my things. He handed me a piece of paper. "Here's your schedule. Make yourself at home."

I nodded in thanks and climbed up to the bunk. I set up my toiletries like the kids in the bunks next to mine had.

The tanned skin girl in the bunk right behind mine shut her book,

"Hey there, who're you?" She asked in an accent I couldn't quite place. She had short hair—such a dark brown it seemed almost black in the shadows. Her striking green eyes sparkled with flecks of gray and black around the edges, like a split geode. Her crystal was shaped like an elaborately carved key, totally white except for stripes of clear green crystal swirling around it. Her nose was small and round, and she was overall petite, wearing a camisole and circle skirt.

"I'm Klotho," I said shyly. "What's your name?"

"Oh, I'm Csilla, how do you like camp so far?" She smiled.

"It's nice," I replied.

"Let me see your schedule," she said, abruptly taking the schedule from my hands. "I can help you if we have dragon feeding together—" she was interrupted by a loud bell. Swinging her legs over the bunk edge, she jumped down. I tried the same but winced when my ankles prickled in pain.

Some campers grabbed quilted picnic blankets out of the trunk, before leaving the cabin and for the pavilion, "For dinner," Csilla explained.

When we arrived, I was shocked to see that there weren't tables or chairs, instead, kids sat in circles on picnic blankets around ceramic bowls with fires in them.

"Klotho! Over here!" Anne called. I walked over to their blanket and sat down awkwardly. "Klotho, meet Annalyn." She pointed to a girl with Tera-Cotta skin, shoulder-length black hair that curled softly around her thin face, a small splattering of freckles, and large doe-like brown eyes that had a strange glossiness, almost like glass. I noticed a scar on her nose and shoulder. She was wearing a white tank top, jean shorts, and sandals. She had two gold bracelets on her left wrist. Her identification crystal was shaped like a blooming flower, it was pearly white with green swirls.

"Hi," I said awkwardly.

I felt like something fell into my lap. I yelped and looked down. A ceramic plate with gold designs on the edges was filled with one of my favorite meals; chicken wings, rice, and vegetables.

I started, shoving food into my mouth, Simone giggled.

"Hungry, huh?"

"Aphum," I said, my mouth full of rice.

"Remember to scrape some into the fire, the gods get cranky when you don't feed them," Simone said, tossing a piece of broccoli into the fire.

"Alright, let's fill you in on camp news. Simone, care to do the honors?" Anne said.

"Well, the third group of kids searching for Hades's helmet returned, three campers got swallowed by the Zeus cabin toilet, someone vomited onto Kempolia's altar, and she responded by creating a cyclone in the lagoon so I had to get Zxypher to fish them out. Oh yeah, and one of the Allan brothers was turned into a fly for trying to strangle a new camper."

"Woah, woah, woah, back up. Swallowed by a toilet?" I asked.

Simone looked thoroughly annoyed. "The paperwork had me up until one AM, and you can probably imagine the conversation with their parents. 'Um yes ma'am, your child got flushed down the toilet, no they flushed themselves down, I would like you to test their cognitive abilities when they come back for the school year, alright thank you for understanding'". She said, pretending to be on the phone.

I almost peed my pants laughing.

"And, Hades? How does he just randomly lose his helmet? Did someone steal it?" I continued.

"That's what he suspects, but we don't know. He told me he woke up one morning and his helmet was gone." Simone made a 'poof' motion with her hands.

"You guys sent kids to look for it?" I asked, concerned about how they could lend the task to children.

"Three groups so far, they all came back empty-handed. We're sending another group of kids to interview him, I've already volunteered, I've gone to the underworld before and came back fine—"

"Simone! You came back practically on the verge of death!" Anne interrupted.

"Well, I'm alive, aren't I? Anyway, Medea says that I need a group. A camp meeting is going to happen tomorrow in the field, make sure to be there by ten," Simone informed me.

"How is Medea going to decide who to send you with?" I asked.

"She'll draw three names and they can accept or decline, though it's probably going to take a couple more names to get someone that wants to go. The underworld entrance has the fortune of being right in the middle of the island."

"Are you guys sure that it's not just under his bed or something?" I asked, what a waste of time it would be for everyone to go looking for it and Hades coming in saying 'Whoops, false alarm! It was just in a cupboard,'

"The first group was sent to comb the palace, it took them three days to search the whole thing, and they looked almost everywhere, so yeah we're sure," Simone said. "Any other questions?"

I shook my head just as I took the last bite–dinner time was over too.

When I got back to the cabin, I brushed my teeth and climbed back onto my bunk. I had nothing to do and was immensely tired, so I just wanted to go right to sleep.

"Is she alright?" Csilla murmured to the girl in the top bunk next to hers.

"Oh yeah, I heard she fell into a slumber-thorn bush, she might just need to sleep the rest off."

So that's what the thorn bush was.

When the sounds of the cabin died down, I finally drifted off to sleep.

The bell tolled, signaling my time to sleep was over. I rolled over and felt like I was in a vacuum for a millisecond, and then I heard a thumping sound accompanied by a sharp pain—that's when I came to my senses and realized I had fallen smack down on the floor. From the top bunk, onto the wooden floor.

Somehow, I had failed to notice that none of the bunk beds had railings.

"Klotho are you ok I heard a thud—oh," Csilla said.

Klotho, you idiot! How on earth did you not notice that? That's the most important part of the top bunk! I thought angrily.

"Yeah," I said, rubbing my side.

I followed the rest of the cabin to the amphitheater, before breakfast, where a large box stood on a small wooden stage. A woman with golden blonde, wavy, hair, which fell to her hips, stood there next to the box. Her pale skin, red lips, and deep black eyes accentuated the color of the long crimson dress she wore. She had a gold necklace, gold earrings, and a gold ring. Simone stood beside her.

"Hello campers, as you all know Hades's helm of darkness has vanished. We must send a group of four to interview him to get more details. Simone has already volunteered, so we just need three more to go with her." The woman, who I assumed was Medea, reached into the box and pulled out a slip of paper.

"Annalyn Dulfo," Medea's voice carried into the crowd. "Do you accept?"

"Yes," Annalyn called from somewhere in the crowd, she walked down the steps to stand next to Simone.

Medea smiled, "Thank you, Annalyn," she and the rest of the camp chorused. She pulled out a second slip of paper, "Samuel Oliver Stefans."

"I accept!" Sam yelled before Medea could even ask. He practically ran down the steps and nearly stepped on Annalyn's foot when he stopped.

"Thank you, Sam," she and the camp chorused, though her smile wasn't as bright this time. She reached into the box one last time, "Klotho Marina."

My face went beet red as everyone near me turned and stared. There was no way going on the mission would be at all helpful. I was about as useless as someone could get, but I wasn't about to refuse in front of this many people.

"Do you accept?" Medea asked, cutting through my train of thought.

"Yes-I'll-do-it," I spat the words out so fast they jumbled together.

"Apologies, Klotho, could we hear that again?" Medea asked kindly. I heard snickering and wished that I could hide in a hole and die.

"I accept!" I yelled as loud as I could, which wasn't super loud. I turned my gaze to the floor and scampered to the stage, refusing to lift my head to look at even Sam.

"Thank you, Klotho," Medea and the other campers chorused. "You four will leave for the underworld in three days, best of luck,"

"Best of luck," The campers repeated. We all went off to do the rest of our activities, but I went to the bathroom first to rein in my embarrassment.

Simone came up to me at lunch. "Are you really sure that you're ready for this? The island has monsters all over it, plus poisonous plants, and unpredictable trails. The last time I went I came back with three monster bites, five gashes, and I was vomiting from accidentally breathing in yellow morrow pollen."

I gulped nervously but tried to look brave. "Yeah," my voice caught.

"Nervous? Don't worry, everyone's nervous on their first mission," Simone said.

I sighed in relief, at least I knew my fear was validated.

"What time do we meet for the mission?" I asked.

"Seven AM sharp, if you miss it, you miss breakfast, and eating will be a top priority to get through before the mission starts," Simone said.

"Okay."

I didn't know what else to say, so I just went to the lagoon to swim. Csilla had taken me to the camp store to pick out a swimsuit, which I was able to buy with the little money I had on me. I waded into the cool water until my feet couldn't touch the floor. I realized this might be a good time to practice using my powers.

I tried to make a water current carry into the middle of the lake and ducked underneath. The water was surprisingly easy to see through. It was like looking through a turquoise lens. I saw fish of every color swimming around, coral, rocks, and gems lined the bottom of the lagoon. A group of nereids played with a dolphin nearby. They were unbelievably beautiful, with their long flowing hair, and large blue-green eyes. I resurfaced and gasped for breath.

I wanted to be able to breathe underwater so I tried to make an air bubble. I managed to make one about twice the size of my head, ducked under again and tried to breathe. I chickened out the first time, but I eventually couldn't hold my breath any longer and was forced to breathe. Air filled my lungs.

It worked! I swam deeper to get a look at the gap in the rock that led to the ocean.

It was further away than I expected. I tried to make the same gentle current to carry me there, but I guess my powers worked better when I was completely underwater because I was blasted nearly out to sea. I managed to stop right in the middle of the tunnel that led to the ocean, and I say 'tunnel', but it was really just a hole in the rock; it may have been two or three meters long at most. The tunnel-like-way entirely underwater, with only a four-foot gap, let me breathe. I thought I saw one of the shadows move but I assumed it was a fish and surfaced. I broke through the water and breathed in the fresh salty air.

The tunnel was illuminated by a dim teal-ish-blue light,

"Hey, Klotho."

I shrieked and spun around until I saw who it was. I sighed in relief, "Oh it's just you. Ethan, don't sneak up on me like that."

He giggled, "Sorry, I'm used to the girls always knowing I'm there."

I raised an eyebrow.

"Anne has magical glasses that she can switch to thermal vision, Annalyn can sort of talk to plants, Vega... well Vega might just have a sixth sense, and Simone just has to look around and she can see what I'm imagining." He explained.

This left me even more confused. "Simone can see what people are imagining?"

He nodded. "She can see the images in people's heads, kind of imagine them with them. All she must do is look at them." He told me.

My jaw fell open. "That's so cool! She must be great at catching kids who break the rules, like the perfect detective!"

He looked pretty surprised. "Wow, I didn't expect you to react like that, most people think it's creepy," he said.

I cocked my head to the side. "Why?"

"They think it's a privacy violation." He shrugged.

"Is it the kind of thing that she can control whose imagination she sees in her head?" I asked. If the answer was yes, I would totally get the idea, but if not... ok, well I still get it. You probably don't want anyone looking at your imagination.

"No, it just happens. On her tablet, it said that her power would always be working unless she wasn't looking at anyone."

"Can she hear anything?" I wondered.

"No, just images," he said.

"What are her other powers?" I asked.

"Well on her tablet it said that she can, quote, 'change form' and 'become unseen' so she can shapeshift and turn invisible, plus the whole seeing-people's-imagination-thing." He explained.

"What are your powers?"

"I can change the shapes of rocks, melt into shadows, literally, and teleport short distances," he said proudly.

"Neat, which god chose you?" I asked.

"Hades. Zeus tried to argue, but Simone screamed at him that Hades claimed first. I didn't know how she could have possibly gotten any scarier over the years but she just turned one of the Allens into a fly for trying to strangle an eight-year-old boy. I was watching. It. Was. Terrifying." He shuddered.

"And loud," Sam said, surfacing next to Ethan.

"Jeez, what is it with you two being so quiet?" I wondered.

Sam shrugged.

Anne saw us right at that moment. "Hey! Guys, be careful! You might get swept out to sea!" She screamed.

"We don't care!" Sam screamed. His voice echoed around the walls of the tunnel.

"Actually, I don't know about you two but I don't think I'd survive if I got swept out to the sea," I said. The waves slapped the rocks and I could feel the gentle pull trying to lead me out to the ocean.

Ethan mumbled in agreement, and I immediately dove under the surface of the water using my bubble trick, and swam as fast as I could, letting the currents carry me to shore.

The rest of my free time was spent in my cabin. I was open in there, none of the other campers seemed to like being inside for their free period. I was sitting on my bunk with a book from the camp library when Simone marched in, telling me I needed to pack.

"Gaaaah! Why is packing for a mission so hard? What am I supposed to bring? Should I bring extra clothes? Will one tent be enough or do we need four? As if I would get time to sleep or rest! Should I bring food? Water bottles? Matches?" I garbled. "Simone, you've got to help me!" I tripped over my own backpack and fell flat on my face at her feet.

"Everyone packs their own clothes, tent, weapon, and water bottle. Some extra stuff can be helpful, like matches, and a small sewing kit," She explained.

"I don't have a weapon, how am I supposed to get one? You told me it was supposed to appear at the guide choosing," I complained.

She waved my own bracelet in front of me. It was just a typical silver chain. No charms. No beads. It was quite boring looking.

"You want me to fight with a bracelet?" I asked.

"You really are as dense as a rock," Simone said, rolling her eyes. "No, genius, it transforms into your weapon."

I took it and wished I could see what it turned into. Suddenly the shape changed, turning into a three-foot-long bronze sword. The hilt had little jade chunks studded into it, and the handle had a black leather grip.

"Woah."

"Told ya," she said. "Oh, and you might want to get ready for the scavenger hunt. It's going to happen after dinner, make sure to get your armor on before then."

"Armor?"

"In the closet." She opened the wardrobe and pointed at the bronze armor set hung inside.

"And... how... do I put it on???" I searched for holes and spaces, figuring out the right places to position my arms and head.

She handed me an instruction manual and walked out.

CHAPTER FOUR

I GO ON A WEIRDLY INTENSE SCAVENGER HUNT

I finally managed to get my armor on, even if it did take me an hour to figure out how I was supposed to do THOSE STUPID SHOULDER PIECES. I finished just in time for dinner. When I came out, I saw about half of the pavilion wearing their armor along with me. Some kids had dawned protective suits over their armor, which was definitely strange. Sitting down was a process. It took me a solid minute to sit without getting my legs stabbed and cut apart by the leg plates.

"Still getting used to the armor?" Anne said. Her armor was also bronze. In fact, it seemed almost everyone's was.

"Yeah, who would have thought that metal could be so uncomfortable?" I asked rhetorically.

"You'll get used to it," Simone said, materializing behind me without making a sound. Her armor was iron and silver with runes carved into the edges of each plate.

"Easy for you to say, how long have you been at camp anyway?" I asked.

Her face darkened ever so slightly. "Eight years, I'm twelve. Do the math," she said.

"You've been here since you were four?" My mouth hung open. "Wait, you're twelve? I thought you were fourteen."

She sighed. "That sounds about right."

"So, how does this whole thing work? What are we trying to find?" I asked.

"Well, what's going to happen is that you're going to get paired with a dragon—"

"A what?!" My heart sped up.

"A dragon. Don't worry, we'll pair you with a nice one. Either way, you have to find clues in the forest to figure out what you're looking for. There are two teams, black and white." She handed me an obsidian pin to clip to the edge of my armor. "And you have to try and stop the other team from finding the clues and the objects first." Then she pulled out a neon orange scarf. It was so bright, it almost shone in the night sky. "Tie it around your arm or thigh."

"Why?"

Simone's face darkened. "You don't want to know."

I decided to take her word for it because I didn't want to exacerbate my anxiety any more—the dragon-pairing thing was enough for me. So, I changed the subject. "And you do this all with dragons?" I wrapped the scarf around my upper thigh, over the armor, and tied it tight in a knot, the bright colors were so bright they hurt.

"Yeah, they're great, they help you get around and can even help you find the clues," Anne told me.

Simone glanced at the clock in the ceiling, which I hadn't noticed until now, and vanished, reappearing on the platform at the back of the pavilion. She stomped her heel twice, creating two loud cracks against the marble platform. It echoed through the pavilion. Everyone went silent and looked over at her.

"All campers who are joining the scavenger hunt! Five-minute warning! Those who are finished can go to the dragon pavilion, and those who don't want to play can go have free time inside their cabins," She shouted from the platform, before vanishing again.

A good half of the campers stood up and split off to go back to their cabins. If not for the fact that I was already wearing a pin and had no clue how to get my armor off, I would have run right along with them.

I looked down at my empty plate. Maybe I could have gone, but the thought of actually going up to a live dragon terrified me, so I stayed put. Campers started leaving for the dragon pavilion, and when Anne stood, I followed her.

She walked to the dragon pavilion, which consisted of large marble platforms with what looked like massive nests spread around, the paths between these nests had grass and moss growing, as though the platforms were really just garden beds. The bottoms of the platforms, which made the roofs of the ones beneath them, had vines hanging down. The fourth level was the lushest of all of them, sprouting flowers that hung down over the third level, shading and hiding it.

An elevator column in the center holding them up. I saw what must have been at least a couple hundred dragons lying on the circulatory platforms. The dragons on the very top platform had gold scales. The other dragons hanging out on the top platform had airy blue scales. Various dragons hung out on each level, from having green and brown scales to red and orange. Even dragons with scales that shimmered with iridescence longed around on the lowest level, sunbathing.

There was a ten-foot-wide moat around the whole thing, with a stone bridge leading to the first level. Dragons in shades of blue, green, and turquoise swam around in the water. I couldn't see the bottom from where I was, but the moat must have been deep. I gulped at the sight of a brown and green dragon yawning, the sharp teeth gleaming with saliva.

"Who's pairing us with the dragons?" I asked Anne nervously.

"Some of the counselors double as wranglers, they have special training to handle dragons safely. I'm starting to go through that training myself," Anne told me excitedly. I tried to smile back, but my nerves shaped my lips into more of a nervous grimace. Thankfully, Anne didn't seem to notice.

About fifteen older campers lined up on the lowest level of the dragon pavilion.

"Everyone, get in line behind one of us," A girl with a long sheet of black hair, pale skin, and pomegranate red eyes with an outline of gold. She had a Scottish accent.

"Who's that?" I whispered to Anne as we lined up behind the girl. Other campers split off to line up in front of other wranglers.

"That's the Persephone cabin head, dragons love her," Anne whispered back. She shoved me in front of her, "You can go first since you have less experience."

I swallowed hard and stepped forward.

"Name?" The girl asked.

"Um, Klotho, Klotho Marina," I mumbled.

"Ah, you're the girl going on the mission. And a new one, let's see here," She looked me over, eyes narrowing. "How do you feel about dragons?"

"Um," I wondered whether I should be honest or not, "I don't have any experience with them."

"Ay, yeah I've been there, you got some kind of water power?" She gestured to my crystal. I looked down at it stupidly and fidgeted with it.

"Uh, yeah," I ran my thumb along the ridges of the shell shape.

"Then I'll hand you over to Coral. Come on, girl." She clicked her tongue at a bridled dragon lounging on a rock. She had blobby patterns of lighter teal on a body of aqua. Her eyes shone bright ocean blue. The dragons snorted but rose slowly and shook off before lazily coming up to me. She was twelve feet long and had a fin going down from a single horn on her forehead to the base of her neck. She had fins on each of her legs as well, and her claws gleamed in perfect cleanliness.

She reached her head towards me and I stepped back with a squeak. Coral reached further and sniffed me. My knees banged together. She snorted in what I hoped was approval.

"There you go, grab her reins like this now." The girl showed me to grab the reins right under her chin and to hold the rest. I shook like nothing else. "Don't be scared now, Coral won't hurt you. Just take her off to the forest and get looking."

"Thank you." The girl just nodded and called for the next person. I led—or rather Coral led me, off into the woods.

We walked together for a while while I glanced around, unsure of what I was looking for in the first place. I heard flapping wings just as Coral yanked me backward. One of the iridescent dragons landed in front of us with Anne on its back, she slid off and patted the dragon's shoulder.

"Find anything yet?" I didn't answer for a couple of seconds, trying to get over the other dragon's massive claws. This dragon had a pair of horns, each perfectly smooth and razor sharp. Its eyes shone pure yellow.

"No," My voice came out squeaky.

"Then let's keep looking, usually clues are like signs on rocks or trees. Easy to spot if you're looking for them." Anne led the way, and we went down into a dip in the ground where one side was just a bare trail, and the other half had a large boulder covered in ivy and moss. On top of that boulder was a plateau-like rock half buried in the dirt and grass.

We were just about to pass it when I saw a flash of white between the bits of ivy.

"Over here," I called out to Anne. She whirled around with her dragon and led the dragon over. I reached out and parted the ivy, revealing a piece of paper tacked onto the stone.

"Now that you've reached me, go in the glow for the final clue." Anne read out loud.

"What's that supposed to mean?" I asked just as Coral and the other dragon snarled. I jumped in startlement as Coral poked her head through the ivy, revealing a cave. A pond sat in the hollow rock, and the water glowed blue. It lit the cave rocks eerily. When I looked deeper, the water seemed to go down forever.

The dragons were snarling at Simone and Annalyn, who were walking, or in Annalyn's case trying to walk, with their dragons towards us.

"Anne, Klotho, hi," Annalyn clicked her tongue at her dragon, green and slender, and yanked it forward. The dragon moved reluctantly. Simone walked holding the reins of a dragon with obsidian black scales, each with a silver edge. Its horns were silver with an opalescent sheen and swirled around above its head. There was a circular scale between its eyes with a sliver of silver like a crescent moon. Its eyes were like moonstones set into its skull.

Both were gorgeous.

Both were terrifying.

"Did you guys find the clue yet?" Annalyn asked.

"We found one on the boulder outside the cave, but not the one that's supposed to be in here," Anne replied. "It said it was 'in the glow' which probably means the water, but before we look for it we should probably destroy the clue—"

A dragon with golden scales and a brown and green dragon burst in, campers on their backs.

"Too late." One of them, the girl on the golden dragon, said with a smirk. Her dragon's body radiated heat.

Coral took one look at this and apparently said nope, because she wasted no time diving into the pool of glowing water, dragging me along with her. I hit the water with a smack before Coral's reins tightened and I was pulled further down. The water was surprisingly warm, but I hadn't gotten in a breath. I panicked for a moment before Coral shoved me up into some dry pocket under the water. I gasped in the air still holding on to the reins before trying to slow my panting to listen.

I heard a muffled splash, then a vague shriek and struggling. Eventually, everything went quiet.

"Did you see anything that just happened?" Simone and her dragon materialized, with Simone beside me and the dragon beside Coral.

I yelped and jumped, smacking my skull into the roof of the cave. I winced and rubbed the crown of my head.

"No," I replied.

"I think it's safe now." She looked down at her dragon. "It's safe now, let's get out. Make sure to keep hold of Coral's reins." She swung her legs back into the water and turned into a blue-ringed octopus. She vanished, swimming away with the reins in one of her tentacles.

Well, that's a sight I never thought I would see, I thought. I swung my legs over, took a deep breath, and plunged into the water. I forced my eyes open and kicked myself up. The weight of the armor dragged me down, so I had to swim harder. The dragon followed me, thank goodness, and I broke the surface a little bit later.

I threw my arms over the edge of the water and pulled myself out the best I could. My armor clanged against itself and scraped horribly against the rock's edge. I looked around, no Anne, no Annalyn.

"Where did they go?" I asked, breathing heavily. My heart sped up.

"I don't know, sometimes people from the other team tie them up so that they can't progress further. They have to take them out of the woods and get them into a building, but it happens." Simone replied she was still dry which felt very unfair.

"Where would they be?" Coral slid out of the water and shook off. The droplets rained down on me and I flinched.

"My bet's on the library," Simone told me. "And it just so happens that I've found the clue in the water," she handed me a rock painted with fluorescent letters.

Find the key in Athena's favorite place, unlock the book with the prettiest face.

"So, it is the library, we need to get there fast," I told her quite obviously.

"Good thing we have these two with us." Simone patted her dragon's shoulder.

"Sorry, what?" There was no way I was going to get on a dragon. I was terrified of heights and flying on the back of a sharp-toothed killing machine—

"We're flying, I'll help you get on once we're outside," Simone walked out of the cave, and Coral dragged me out with her. Honestly, I was kind of grateful that Coral was there to make me move. My feet scuffed on the stone and the orange light of the setting sun came upon me.

"What you're going to do is throw her reins over her head, yup," She instructed. I grabbed onto the end of the reins, and threw it up and back. They got caught on the dragon's horn, and I couldn't reach up there.

"Uh..." I glanced over at Simone sheepishly.

"Oh, yeah that happens, you could pull down on the reins to get her to lower her head, or I could get that for you," Simone offered.

"Could you?" I didn't want to admit it, but pulling on the reins of a creature with its teeth way too close to my hand wasn't something I was in the mood for.

She nodded once before turning into a hawk and pulling the reins the rest of the way down. She turned back into a human and folded her hands together, bending her legs so that I could step up.

"Go on, grab onto her back and swing your leg over," I put my foot in her hands and managed to jump up and grab hold of the dragon's back. I pulled myself up, lying on my stomach and ungracefully pulled my right leg over to the other side. "Perfect, now just sit up. Straight back, we want good posture!"

I giggled nervously, but I pushed myself up and straightened my spine.

"There we go, we don't want your spine to look like a deformed tree trunk," I barked out a laugh as Simone turned into a bird, bringing the reins over her dragon's head. Instead of having to do the whole on-stomach-flail to get on her dragon, she just turned back into human form on its back.

"Show off," I complained.

She shrugged but didn't deny it. "Kick and click to take off. Oh yeah, and hold on tight, I don't want to have to scrape you off the ground as Klotho-mashed potatoes."

The thought of taking off drained the blood from my face and I nodded. My knuckles were white on the reins as I kicked Coral's sides and clicked my tongue.

Her wings spread, and she took off into the sky. I shrieked and tightened my legs. My heart beat hard in my ears and I was breathing fast.

The trees brushed the bottoms of Coral's feet, and she beat her wings once, sending us higher. Simone's dragon was faster, clearly made more for the air than Coral's. The undersides of its wings were splattered with pale dots like stars.

I made the mistake of glancing down, and my head spun at the sight. I was at least fifty feet off the ground, and seeing that firsthand made the blood rush from my head. I shut my eyes and breathed in with the wind whistling past my ears.

When I opened my eyes, we were flying over the camp and I could see the library building in the very center of the camp. We landed off to the side and I was able to get a good look at it. The Ancient Greek pillars that held the marble roof up were carved beautifully, the marble walls were plain and polished. Windows popped through the otherwise solid walls. It was huge, at least three stories tall. The amount of books that had to be inside was staggering.

No one guarded the doors, in fact, it was almost completely silent.

"Do we just walk in with two dragons?" My heart rate finally started to slow down now that we were on the ground.

"No, we'll leave these ladies out here." Simone slid from her dragon's back and patted her side.

I leaned forward and pulled my leg over Coral's side. I held on and slid until I couldn't anymore, then I fell with a yelp and landed on my butt in the grass. Coral stretched her wings, looked at me, then folded her legs underneath her.

Simone and I walked up to the double doors, she pulled on the handles and one of them swung right into me.

"Ow!" I winced away, rubbing my shoulder.

"Sorry, sorry," Simone hissed in sympathy.

"It's fine." I walked into the library, filled with massive shelves of books. Novels, textbooks, instruction manuals, everything you could think of and more must have been there. The shelves weren't separated by floors, instead, they had walkways with railings that people would need to climb rolling ladders to get to.

"You start looking for this key or a book, and I'll find Anne and Annalyn," Simone whispered.

I nodded and ran off to a section labeled 'Spells', figuring that if there was a book with a 'pretty face' anywhere, it would be there. I searched through the bottom shelf first, on my hands and knees. I stretched my back after the thirtieth book and spotted a book labeled 'Beauty'. I pulled out the thick volume and frowned when the cover was plain.

I heard footsteps and jumped, dropping the book. It thudded to the floor and fell open while I crouched down and peered around the corner. I saw a flash of armor, but it went to a different section. I breathed a silent sigh of relief, but when I looked down to close the book again, there was a lump in the pages. I opened it to the spot where the lump was and found a tiny key, no longer than an inch.

I gasped, then clapped my hand over my mouth and glanced back out from behind the shelf. No one, I didn't think. I picked up the key, shut the book, and slid it back in place. The book with a pretty face must have been nearby, but searching the utterly massive spell section was taking forever, and my heart sped faster with each click of the massive grandfather clock on the back wall.

I walked around to the other side of the first Spell shelf to look at the other side. On the tenth shelf, one I could just barely reach was a very thick book that seemed to have a gap between it and the other book in front of it. I pulled it down to reveal an old book with the 3D face of a woman with smooth golden skin. Her black eyebrows were thick and beautiful, and her eyes were shut with long eyelashes. The book had a thick leather strap keeping it shut, and that strap had a little lock around the clasp.

"Oh wow, you found it!" Sam said excitedly from behind me. I shrieked and whirled around.

"Oh, hi Sam, you scared me." My face heated with embarrassment.

"That's great, here, I can help you open it, books with that kind of lock are a pain." He reached out as if waiting for me to hand over the book. I was just about to hand it to him when Anne ran over with Annalyn.

"Stop!" She called, panting. "He's from the other team."

I glanced down at his pin for the first time, finding it pearly white, and started laughing.

"You almost tricked me!" I giggled, which made Sam crack up too.

"I guess I should have known you'd be warned," He shot a playful glare at Anne. I clumsily shoved the key into the lock and found a pocket with a little medal on a blue ribbon inside.

"Whooo!" Anne cheered, Annalyn clapped lightly, a small smile gracing her face. "Come on, let's get outside. We need to show you off to Medea."

Anne grabbed me by the arm and dragged me outside. She, Annalyn, and Simone successfully dragged me to the pavilion, where Medea sat with a black cat in her lap. She stood, the cat jumping off her and stalking away.

"Ah, I see we have a winner." She walked over to us and checked the book, key, and medal in my hands. "Congratulations, I'll be off at the bell tower to call the game off if you need me. Since you all are here, I recommend you go to sleep after this successful game." It was late already. The sun had gone down and the only light was from some lit torches on the pillars of the pavilion.

The four of them insisted on walking me back to my cabin since I was new.

"I was so close to tricking her," Sam complained, "but these two just had to step in."

Simone rolled her glowing eyes. "You're just upset that you didn't win."

"Guilty as charged."

As soon as I got out of my armor with some help from Annalyn, I collapsed onto my bunk and passed out almost immediately, sinking into restful sleep.

I was rudely awakened by the breakfast bell.

I groaned, got out of bed and got dressed in the cabin changing room. As I came to the dining pavilion, I noticed it looked a little different. It had scorch marks on the ground and on the marble pillars. I sat down with Annalyn, Anne, and Simone, and I started eating my breakfast. I looked around to try and find clues as to why the usually pristine dining pavilion was so beaten up. I saw hairline cracks in the marble and more scorch marks. Simone had dark circles under her eyes. The other campers were unusually quiet.

"What happened to the dining pavilion? It looks a little beaten up," I inquired.

"A baby sun dragon got loose and freaked out here. Medea and I stayed up all night trying to calm it down. The way its bridle was cut looks purposeful like it was made with a sharp object," Simone explained.

"Couldn't it have just been the dragon's claw?" I asked.

"No, the ropes we use can't be cut with dragon claws. Besides I can tell the difference between dragon scratches and weapons. Even in the dark," Simone said.

"You need to take a nap, Simone," Anne told her.

Annalyn nodded in agreement.

"I can't! I have a ton to do today! I'll tell the campers to expect crankiness 'cause I'm running on half an hour of sleep and pure spite." She aggressively stabbed her pancakes with her fork.

I checked my schedule. I had archery right after breakfast. The range was in a corner of the camp, surrounded by walls of gray-black rock with moss and lichen all over them. I went to the range and narrowly avoided an apple being flung in my direction. Why there was a random fruit hurling towards me, I had no idea, and I decided it would be better that way.

"Klotho!" Ethan yelled from one of the targets, "Hi!"

"Hi Ethan, where do I get a bow?" I looked around. I spotted a small box but there was no way that multiple bows would fit in there. I also saw a cave the entrance of which was covered by a black curtain with silver, gold, purple and blue embroidery.

"Over here." He led me into the cave. Hundreds of weapons lined the walls. He went over to a rack fully devoted to bows and handed me one.

"I think this should work for you." And he walked out.

I went outside and tried to shoot at the target. The bowstring was much tighter than I thought was necessary. And it took me several tries to get the string pulled back without the arrow falling off. When I was finally able to shoot, I completely missed the target and the arrow snapped against the walls of rock.

"Not your best activity, is it?" Annalyn asked.

I jumped a little. "No, I guess not. What about you?"

She shot a perfect bullseye as an answer.

I grabbed another arrow and tried to shoot again. I was really hoping that it would at least hit the target. It didn't. It instead flew completely off course and shot another kid.

I screamed and started panicking because the boy's blood was leaking out of the wound like I'd stabbed a paint bottle. He just pulled the arrow out of his arm and the limb healed instantly.

"That's Heroldus, he can heal himself," Annalyn explained.

I tried to say sorry but he didn't seem to hear me. The boy had dark skin, and hair cropped close to his head. His shirt was cotton and bright white, his shorts and shoes were both black, and his eyes were honey-like orange. His crystal was hidden inside of his shirt.

"He's also deaf." She added. She signed something for him and he did the same.

He signed something to me, and somehow, I understood what it meant:

'It's ok, just watch out next time.'

I nodded. "How-"

"He can make people understand other languages for a short time," Annalyn said helpfully.

"That's so cool, how does that even work?" I asked her.

She shrugged and opened her mouth as if to speak, but was interrupted by a bell. "Oh, it's changing time, you need to get to your next activity."

I checked the paper. Oh, this is going to end well.

I had training next; I had to work on my powers. It said on the paper that Simone was going to supervise, and a girl named Vega was going to help me out. I walked to the place that the map showed. That place is the pond by the academy.

Odd, I thought. I got there after following the map as closely as I possibly could.

When I arrived, I saw a girl with pale skin, long silvery-blonde hair in a braid and the purest pale blue eyes I had ever seen. They were almost fiery; they were so blue. Her gaze was far off and a bit unfocused. She was wearing a deep blue camisole with golden star patterns, and white jean shorts. Her crystal was silvery gray swirled with freshwater blue, dotted with white, and shaped like the moon, craters and all. She looked about twelve. She was barefoot and, wait, that can't be right, she was standing on the water.

"Hello Klotho, this is Vega Aaberg, she will be helping you learn to control your powers," Simone said. She was wearing a black camisole with high-waisted jean shorts with a gray and black flannel tied around her waist. Her hair was in a low-twist bun.

"Take off your outer feet and walk," Vega told me, gesturing to the pond. Her voice was far off and calm. I looked at her in total confusion for a second.

"Take off of your shoes and walk onto the water," Simone translated. So that's why she was here, to translate. I did as she said and was surprised to find that the water felt solid, like a wet trampoline.

I wobbled into the center of the pond. "What do I do next?" I asked her.

"Do what you know," she said.

I showed Vega the bubble, but I didn't have anything else to show her, so her just staring at me and waiting for more dragged on much longer than I would have liked.

"What about the motion of a river?" She asked.

"Current." Simone picked at her nails.

"Yeah, while I was swimming," I replied.

I nodded. She taught me how to make water feel solid and fuse my mind with the flow of the water. It took me several tries, and several times falling into the water before I got the hang of it.

She then told me to use it to slide around the pond. I went too fast and almost slammed into one of the rock spires. Simone turned into a bird to get to me and stopped me from becoming mashed Klotho by letting me fly into her instead. This was definitely going to be an interesting lesson if body-slamming the assistant director would be a regular thing.

The lesson kept going and by the end, I was pouring in sweat. Vega seemed oddly unaffected. She kept that far-off look in her eyes. Unfocused and off in the clouds somewhere. We all headed to lunch after that.

Once Vega was out of earshot I asked Simone, "What's up with Vega? She seems a little... off."

"That's just the way she is. Yeah, most people don't understand her, but she's a very nice person and has excellent ideas," Simone explained. We reached the dining pavilion to see Anne and Annalyn waiting for us.

"Hi guys," I said, sitting down.

"Hi, any news on the helmet situation?" Anne asked.

"None so far, Hades told me that if it was in the fields of Asphodel that we'd never find it. The fields of punishment are too risky for gifted ones to search, the isles of the blest are islands that no one can really get to. Elysium has been searched already." Simone informed us.

Something caught my eye about Annalyn, she seemed... nervous. Why would she be nervous?

Maybe she's nervous about the mission. I thought. Yeah, that makes sense.

Simona C. Huska

Chapter Five

Shenanigans

I woke up on the day right before the mission. I checked my schedule

after breakfast and saw I had sparring. When I checked who I'd be sparing with, my stomach dropped. *Aw crap, I'm dead.* I was supposed to spar with Simone, who had been here for eight years. Yay.

Yeah, this was not going to end well. I walked nervously to the sparring arena. I was fidgeting with my bracelet and trying not to vomit from nervousness as I entered the large stone walls to find that Simone was the only one there.

I swallowed hard. "Hi."

"Hello, so this is how it's going to work, I'll do a spell to count every time you miss a strike. Whoever has the least misses wins." She explained. She whispered a rhyme and a board appeared on the wall. It had our names glowing on it and underneath had a zero for each of us. My name was glowing turquoise, and Simone's was glowing misty blue.

"So do we just... attack each other?" I asked.

"Pretty much," Simone answered.

I gulped nervously.

"Don't worry, I'll go easy on you," Simone reassured me.

She turned her ring into her dagger. I turned my bracelet into my sword. She lunged at me and nicked my arm. I tried to return the favor but she dodged my strike. The number over my name changed to one.

She turned invisible, and I spun around, trying to predict where she might be. She tackled me from behind, and I tried to blow her away, but she turned into a bird and nicked my leg. I tried to swing my sword at the raven that was now flying around me, but I kept missing 1,2,3,4,5,6,7,8,9 over my name, and the misses kept going up.

Simone turned invisible again and reappeared much closer to me than I would have liked. She tried to stab my chest, but I caught her dagger with my sword. We struggled for a minute before she twisted the hilt of the sword with the blade of her dagger, and it clattered out of my hands. She pressed her knife to my sternum.

"Dead," she said, lowering her dagger and walking away.

I picked up my sword and stared at my reflection in the shiny blade. My curling red hair was even messier than usual, I had sweat and dirt and grime all over my face and hands. The places where she nicked me stung.

"You're really good," I told Simone as she offered me a towel and a bottle of water.

"Thank you. You're better than most new kids yourself." She replied.

I wasn't exactly sure what to say to that so I responded with an awkward· "Thanks."

I looked at the scoreboard. I had twelve misses. Simone had one.

"What now?" I asked.

"We go again." She said. She reset the board and got ready. "You strike first this time," She ordered.

I lunged at her but lost my balance and stumbled. She moved to the side and turned into a dragon with airy blue scales and silvery eyes. She opened her mouth and breathed out. I thought that I would end up baked, but instead, a very strong wind blasted me into the arena wall.

I shrieked like an idiot and ended up smacking into a chunk of the wall that had remnants of glue on it. Why on earth it had glue stuck on it, I didn't know. What I did know was that I was stuck on the arena wall and looking like a squashed fly.

Simone turned back into human form and laughed her head off. She was there laughing hysterically for a good ten minutes before she got me down. By that time, a good number of campers had come to see what the wheeze/cackling was.

Simone had to chip away at the stone to get me off of the wall. My shirt was ruined by the magical glue and I had to throw it out. My arms and legs were sore from being stuck and I got water splashed all over me when I left.

One of the campers had put a bucket on the door to spite me, but I hadn't noticed it. I had to get blow-dried by Simone's air dragon form.

I had a dragon feeding next, which almost made me faint out of fear.

Simone and I walked to the dragon pavilion and grabbed some live chickens from the coop.

"They're better for the little ones so that they can learn to hunt," Simone explained, handing me a flailing chicken as if she were giving me nothing more than a pencil. Along with my poultry, Simone handed me some protective gear to put on—a fireproof brown jumpsuit with brown fireproof protective gloves.

"Slide your crystal into the slot. It needs to remember your crystal shape." Simone said as we got to the dragon-sized elevator. Apparently, the dragons would slide their claws into the slot to get in.

"It's for the dragons that can't fly," Simone explained as we got onto the elevator.

The glass walls of the elevator gave me an even better view of the dragons. I saw one with brown scales flecked with green yawns, revealing sharp yellowed teeth.

I actually vomited from nervousness, I wiped my mouth with the glove and winced at the awful smell.

"On second thought, why don't you feed the babies instead?" Simone said, backing away from the puke on the ground.

"Yeah, I think that's a good idea," I said, still holding onto the brown chickens as they attempted to flap their wings.

Simone directed me to the baby dragon area. My hands shook as I entered the area where the baby dragons played. One of the smaller ones started walking towards me. It jumped up and licked my sleeve-covered elbow. I held my breath. I could hardly keep myself from screaming.

I let go of the chicken and after flapping its wing so hard it hit my chin, it sprinted around. Several sun dragons ran after it and pounced. As they tore it apart, I turned away, and a baby sun dragon leaped into my arms. The utter terror of having something that could easily burn or kill me made me scream, and I fell over. I hit the ground like a sack of bricks. A baby dragon with golden scales and yellow eyes sat on top of me like a puppy. It licked the side of my face, and its breath made me gag.

"Klotho! Klotho, are you okay? What happened?" Simone ran up to me and knelt down.

"I got knocked over, a little help here?" I asked, trembling with terror at the honestly pretty cute baby dragon on top of me. Simone nodded and picked up the sun dragon, which now regarded me with concerned golden eyes. I sat up, and Simone told me that she would finish feeding the dragons if I wasn't up for it. I entered the elevator and sat down. I took some deep breaths. When the elevator reached the ground, I bounded out and waited by the chicken coop.

When I sat down for lunch, I was still shaking.

"How was your morning?" Anne asked.

"Sparring was terrifying, and dragon feeding was even more terrifying. So terrifying," I summarized.

"What dragons did you get to feed?" Annalyn asked.

"The baby sun dragons," I said.

"Maybe you should try the baby crystal dragons. They only eat bugs and fruit, and they won't eat it if it's been on the ground for too long," Anne explained.

"Yes, but the crystal dragons are *very* picky," Annalyn countered. "The babies snap at you if you feed them too slowly."

"Maybe the sun dragons weren't so scary after all," I said.

The bell for changing time rang. I had wind training after lunch.

I walked all the way up a steep hill to meet Vega. When I got there, she was wearing a pale blue summer dress, it had floaty sleeves and a floral print. She wore silver sandals with tiny little bells on the bands. Her silvery blonde hair was still in her braid. Simone stood there out of the way.

"Hello," Her voice was still far away and light.

"Hi, um, what do I do first?" I asked.

"Are you scared of the sky?" She asked, ignoring my question. Scared of the sky? Huh?

"Are you scared of heights?" Simone translated.

I gulped, afraid of what she would make me do for the sake of training. "Yes," I wasn't proud to admit it, but lying would probably come to bite me in the butt.

"Then we'll fall upwards later," she said, her blue eyes flickering towards the sky.

"Flying." Simone sat down on the grass, and a sketchbook appeared in her hands.

My head spun. "*F-flying?*" Flying on the back of a dragon was terrifying enough; if Vega tried to make me use my wind powers to fly, I would probably end up splattered on the floor.

"Yes," Vega said absently. "Now, can you blow without your mouth?"

"She wants you to show her what you can do with the wind." Simone didn't even look up from her sketching. I nodded and tried for a small breeze, the wind licking me gently.

"Good," she said. "Can you make it spin around?"

A direction change, I guessed. I did as she said and the lesson went fine until she decided to let me try flying.

"Jump under the wind. Up you go." Vega's eyes fluttered around the sky as if following a bird. But when I looked up, nothing was there.

She's crazy, isn't she? I wondered.

I imagine the wind like a geyser underneath me, and when I jumped, I released the energy and it blasted my shirt and hair up. It didn't come close to lifting me.

"More air," Vega instructed. Finally, a regularly worded request. I tried to think of more underneath me. I pulled it around with my mind to the best of my ability, and when I released it this time, it didn't boost me an inch, but I shifted my shirt higher, so at least I knew I had the right idea.

I tried again and again, and each time it wasn't enough. Vega basically announced that it would be my last chance to try before free period, and I was determined to get it right. I collected the air, the wind and jumped, forcing it underneath me like a trampoline. I released the pressure, and... fell down the hill.

Simone helped me up and told me to just go wherever I wanted for free, period. I headed to the lagoon. I dove into the water and started swimming around. When I got to the edge of the lagoon, I saw a small cave. I had a bubble around my head so I could breathe, and for once, I felt like exploring.

I swam inside and found that it was an uphill slope. I climbed the rough rocks, and tried to avoid the small puddles in the misshapen stone. My hair felt heavy with water as I climbed up into the cave. I finally got to the top and saw that glowing moonstones and silver were lodged in the rocks.

As I looked around, I was transfixed. But not because of the beauty of the inside of the cave. No. The thing that made me freeze in place were tens of dragons. The same type Simone was walking with during the scavenger hunt.

The dragon's eyes were all closed. Indicating that they were sleeping. all of the dragons had slender snouts, and thin tails. They looked almost wispy. They were beautiful, but their claws were as long as a human finger, and sharper than any knife.

I made a tiny squeaking noise out of panic. The dragon closest to me's eyes opened. They looked like a moonstone embedded into their eye socket. The pupil was a black sliver. The dragon started to stretch its wings and stand. When its wings were spread, I saw the underside looked like a night sky. It was beautiful, but it didn't quell my fear.

My mouth hung open in terror as I struggled to figure out what to do. I didn't dare to breathe, but my heart pounded hard in my head. The dragon started walking towards me.

Run! My mind screamed, but I was frozen in place. The dragon nudged me with its tail, and the push knocked me gently into the water.

I regained my ability to think and swam out of there as fast as I could without becoming a Klotho smoothie on the rocks.

I surfaced by a large rock spire in the lagoon and tried to get the water to perch me on top, I ended up getting dropped into the water seven times before I managed to grab hold of the edge and yank myself up. This was only about seven feet up so I wasn't too scared of what could happen, even if my thighs hurt from smacking into the water. I would just use the water to save me if I needed to.

A raven landed next to me. "What's up, Klotho?" The raven turned into Simone. She was wearing a black one-piece swimsuit.

I immediately thought of the dragons sleeping in the cave.

"You found the moon dragons, huh?" She asked.

"I guess," I said, "One of them pushed me into the water with their tail."

"Oh, that's Caldera," Simone explained. "She's the one that I had during the scavenger hunt. She won't hurt campers; in fact, she actively protects them from other dragons and monsters. She's very nice."

"Well, she pushed me into the lagoon, so maybe she just doesn't like me," I said.

"All dragons have the ability to know a camper's powers just by looking at them. She saw your water power and figured that you would regain your focus once you got back into the water. Moon dragons are the most intelligent dragons on average," She told me, "Basically, she saw that you're a coward and wanted you out of her sleeping caves."

"Maybe that baby sun dragon should take notes," I joked.

"Ah yes, Klotho, the baby sun dragon that can't even understand its mom yet, much less your emotions regarding it," Simone responded sarcastically.

"Why must you do this to me?" I asked.

"Because." She then proceeded to shove me off the edge of the spire and turned me into a fish of some kind. I smacked head-first into the water and, right after impact, turned back into a human.

I saw someone surface next to me. I popped my head out of the water. It was Anne. She was wearing a blood-red two-piece.

"Simone threw you down?" She asked.

I sighed, "Do you know why she's like this?"

No response. I looked around. She had vanished. I felt a yank on my ankle that tugged me down underwater, filling my sinuses with a half-pound of salt water.

"I'm like this too. Get used to it." Anne said once I stopped sputtering.

When dinner came, the lightheartedness of the campers vanished into a sense of nervousness that I could feel wafting through the air. I sat down to see that Annalyn was missing.

"Hey, where's Annalyn?" I asked.

"She said that she forgot to pack and that she'll get food later," Simone replied.

Something about this excuse made my alarms go off. I heard the campers whispering about the mission since the meeting. There was no way that she'd forgotten.

Oh, quit it, Klotho, I thought; she's probably just forgetful; stop being paranoid.

"Any news on the helmet situation?" Anne asked.

"None so far; I checked with the groups that came back, and none of them found any leads," Simone replied. "Honestly, how hard is it to find a helmet radiating magic like a neon sign?"

Anne frowned. "Are you sure none of them missed something? Like a clue that they didn't notice before?"

"They let me check through the entire experience in their imaginations. Nothing," Simone grumbled. "Honestly, how hard is it to find a helmet radiating magic like a neon sign?"

Anne sighed. "That's frustrating, should I help Medea while you're gone?"

"She says she's got it covered, but you might want to watch the more rebellious campers for her," Simone responded.

"Are the Allans off the radar?" Anne asked.

Simone thought for a moment, then grimacing, said, "Keep an eye on them. Discreetly."

Simone vanished and reappeared on the elevated platform. She stomped her heel, and all the campers' heads turned to her. I noticed that some of the campers looked annoyed, and some were whispering to each other.

"Campers, the fourth group of gifted ones, will leave to interview Hades tomorrow." She paused for effect. "We wish them luck and hope the lord of the dead has any answers about this unfortunate occurrence." She stepped off the elevated platform, and I saw Medea come up to her and talk to her for a short period of time.

Suddenly, Annalyn sprinted into the dining pavilion, panting and sweaty. "FIRE DRAGON LOOSE!" She screamed.

This launched all the campers into a panic, and panic means chaos. I don't think I have to say that chaos with over a hundred kids in a single pavilion is bad news.

"EVERYONE TO YOUR CABINS! GET UNDERNEATH SOMETHING! AND WAIT UNTIL I SAY IT'S SAFE! WHATEVER YOU DO, DO NOT LEAVE YOUR CABINS!" Simone hollered. Everyone was running around screaming, and I got swept through the Demeter kids to their cabin.

I ran to the bathroom and got into an empty stall. I heard screaming and an earth-shattering roar. I waited for what felt like hours as the sounds of fighting filled the air. No one in the cabin made so much as a sound. We were all afraid of the dragon noticing us. Finally, a knock on the door followed by a reassurance by Simone that the coast was clear let me go back to my own cabin.

When I went outside, I saw some parts of the camp were still on fire. Simone had burns and scrapes all over her, and she was suspiciously hiding her left arm.

"What happened?" I asked, looking around.

"The fire dragon's eggs were threatened by a cloaked figure. Fire dragons are *very* attentive mothers. They will murder anything that so much as steps too close to their eggs. The Fire dragon panicked and went nuts towards the camp to find who messed with her eggs. I had to calm it down and put out all the fires it started," Simone explained with tightness in her voice.

"Are you ok? You look pretty banged up," my eyebrows furrowed.

"I'm fi-AAH!" She yelped as she accidentally brushed her left arm on her torso. Her arm was red and raw with burns. She gritted her teeth in pain.

"Do you need help?" I asked sheepishly. *Well, no crap, Klotho, her arm is burnt to a crisp.*

"I need to wait until I know all the campers are safe and in their cabins. That's the protocol for when a fire dragon freaks out," She explained. "The campers have to come first."

"You're a camper," I argued.

"I'm in charge, it's my job to keep the campers safe," She said,

"Is there a protocol for all the other dragon types?" I asked,

"No, we use the same one for all except the fire dragons. They're the most dangerous if they freak out." Simone explained.

We got to my cabin, and I asked her, "Do you need a healer? Or can you do the spell on yourself?"

"For this, I'll need a healer." She gestured to her arm.

"I have healing powers." I pointed out.

"You've never used them before, plus you need your rest for the mission. Go to bed." And she shut the door.

I laid in my bed thinking about what happened that day. Why would someone mess with the dragon's eggs? To sabotage the mission? Or... did they maybe want someone to not be able to go? Who would want that? Endanger the entire camp to get one person out of the mission? No, no one would be that cruel, would they?

Before I could contemplate this further, I closed my eyes and ordered myself to sleep.

Chapter Six

This Is A Disaster

Oh boy this is gonna be bad. I thought as I got out of bed. I changed and slung my backpack over my shoulders.

I had set my alarm early as Simone instructed, but I was already regretting it. I walked outside and to the dining pavilion. There was a table with a bit of food on it. I started eating and heard someone stumble up behind me. I looked back with half a muffin in my mouth to see Sam. He straightened back up and casually started eating cereal right out of the box. He was wearing a blue t-shirt with basketball shorts.

"Do you think Simone is coming? She was pretty beaten up from dealing with that dragon," Sam commented. "Maybe they'll have to postpone the mission."

"I hope she's ok. She's done this before, so she might be helpful," I said.

"Yeah, that's true," Sam replied. Annalyn walked into the pavilion and chose an apple to eat for breakfast.

"How are you feeling?" She asked. She was wearing a white t-shirt with a gray sweater, jean shorts and tennis shoes.

I yawned, "Tired. Why did we have to start so early?"

"Because," Simone said behind me.

I whirled around. She was wearing what she'd been wearing the day I came to camp. "We need to get an early start."

"Can't you tell we need our sleep? Even Klotho agrees with me," Sam whined.

"It is early," I murmured, even as my face burned Christmas red. "But it's not like we could fall asleep now."

Annalyn and Simone nodded in agreement.

We set off through the forest and just walked for *hours*. I was exhausted, and it didn't help that Simone and Annalyn walked way faster than Sam and I. We were following the river, it flowed south to where the underworld entrance was. By the time lunch came I was absolutely finished. I plopped down and drank half my water bottle before asking what we were going to eat.

"I'll catch some fish. Can you guys start a fire?" Simone asked.

We all nodded, and I was instructed to find some dry sticks. Once I had collected my share, I went to the river bank to watch Simone.

She had turned into a huge brown bear and jumped into the torrents of water. She was catching colorful fish in her jaws and throwing them onto a large black mat on the river bank. I stepped onto a rock to watch closer.

I was mostly interested in the fish. The ones that were swimming through the river were in every color you could imagine. I saw one that was teal and pink at the same time. Another was blue and green and purple with golden scales behind its eyes. I was mesmerized.

I wobbled around on the rock I was standing on and fell into the rushing current. I was so panicked that I didn't even think to use my powers. I just screamed as I was launched through the river. I went head-first into a rock, and everything went black.

Suddenly, I was underwater, but I could breathe. A man was floating in front of me. I recognized him as Poseidon.

"Hello, young hero," his voice echoed in the water.

"Um, hi." I waved. My voice came out all bubbly, as if I was speaking underwater. Poseidon's expression didn't change.

"Something very bad will happen on your mission. I do not know what, I do not know when. But it will happen. Be careful," he warned.

My eyes opened slowly, and I was immediately floored by a wave of agony. My head felt like it had been hit by a train. I was in the shade of a willow tree. I was lying on a mat. Annalyn knelt next to me. I felt my head. The skin didn't feel broken or anything, but I felt dried blood.

"How long have I been out?" I asked.

"About two hours," Annalyn replied. "We gave you some slumberthorn to keep you asleep so the pain would subside."

"Two hours!?" My vision swirled, indicating that yelling probably wasn't a good idea.

"You took quite the hit," Annalyn said soothingly.

"Yeah, you slammed head-first into a rock at full speed. You're lucky you're not dead," Simone grumbled, propping me up on the trunk of the tree and handing me a blue fish and something that looked kind of like a potato. I ripped a massive chunk of the fish off and chewed quickly before swallowing, though I felt some small bones left.

"You're really hungry," Annalyn observed.

I nodded in response, my mouth still full of fish.

"How do you feel? Does your head still hurt?" Simone asked.

I nodded to that, too, though it was slowly going away.

She pursed her lips. "Do you think we'll have to wait here until tomorrow?"

"I don't know, I think I can walk." I stood up and tried to walk. Unfortunately, my legs felt like Jello, and the only thing I could do was wobble around. "Oops, my legs are disagreeing with me. Very naughty legs. I think we should wait a little."

"I found the silverbells!" Sam loudly announced, walking over. He threw Simone's messenger bag at her head. She failed to catch it, and the bag hit me instead. The force knocked me over as I was already wobbly, and I gave Sam a good glare for it.

"Well done, Sam, you just knocked over an injured child," Simone rolled her eyes. She picked up the bag and rummaged through. She pulled out a silverbell and handed it to me.

"What am I supposed to do with this?" I asked.

"Pluck a petal and eat it. You'll regain the little balance you had before, and your head won't feel like it's been hit by a train," Simone explained.

At this point, my brain was kind of mush, so I didn't question it and did as she told me. The petal tasted like a fresh rose petal.

As soon as I swallowed, my headache vanished. "Wow, that really does work," I said, amazed.

"Are we good to keep going?" Simone asked.

"Now we are." I stood up again, and this time managed to stay standing. We kept going and the more we walked the more my head spun.

"Klotho, are you ok? You're looking a little green." Sam asked.

"I'm fi—," and I puked all over his shoes.

"Aww come on!" He complained. Thankfully he brought an extra pair, but one of those shoes had a small hole in it that would definitely keep getting bigger throughout the journey.

Simone handed me a tiny vile of pale green liquid.

"Drink it; I am not about to have you puke again," She ordered. I obliged because I still felt very sick and found that I couldn't feel anything incredibly different, but I wasn't about to puke anymore. It tasted like a sweet lime.

A few minutes later, Simone screeched and turned into a black hen. I saw a rat skitter into a bush next to her. I couldn't help but giggle.

"You're literally a chicken!" Sam laughed. Simone turned back and clearly decided that since she was no longer at camp, she no longer had to hold herself back because he turned into a caterpillar right at that moment.

I picked him up. "Is he gonna be ok?" I asked.

"As long as he doesn't slither off, yes. Can you hold him while we walk? I can't stand looking at worm-like creatures," Simone shuddered.

"What about snakes?" I asked.

"They have eyes; that thing doesn't. Or at least I can't see them."

Sam wriggled in protest, and I held Sam the caterpillar as we walked.

"How exactly does your shapeshifting power work?" I asked Simone.

"I can technically shapeshift into anything, but I mostly stick with living things," She explained.

"Can you change the form of anything?" I asked.

"I—" she thought for a second. "I don't know; I've never really tried."

"Wouldn't it be cool? You could do pretty much anything," I added. She nodded.

It must be cool to have a power you can shut people up with. I thought.

We stopped again at about seven o'clock to eat.

"What do we need to do? Is someone going to stay up and watch for monsters? How do you set up a tent?" I questioned.

"I'll stay up for the first watch. Annalyn, can you help with the tents?" Simone explained, "Then I'm going to start the fire, and get food ready."

Annalyn nodded in agreement. After getting the tents ready, I sat down and started eating. It suddenly occurred to me that Sam wasn't eating.

He was still a caterpillar at this point, and I felt bad about leaving him to go hungry.

"Hey, what about Sam?" I asked, pointing to him as he wriggled around on a log.

"I've got it," Simone handed him a leaf of some kind and he started to gobble it down.

"He can eat that? Won't he get sick?" I asked.

"The only thing that's still human in him is his soul and his thoughts. Other than that, he could eat or do anything a caterpillar could." Simone explained.

My dream that night was... nothing.

I was dreaming that I didn't have a dream. It was weird.

"GAAAAAAAAAGHHHHHHH!" I heard Sam screaming, seemingly in terror. I shot up and raced out of my tent.

"What's going on?" I asked.

"FIRE!" He screamed. He was right. flames curled off Annalyn's tent.

"Annalyn! Wake up!" I screamed. She shot out of her tent so fast I hardly saw her. She'd shrunk herself so that she was about the height of my ankle from the floor.

I heard giant footfalls; a giant blast of water was blown from an elephant's trunk. The elephant then turned back into Simone. The soaking ashes of the tent were swirling in the wind.

"What happened?" I asked, now wide awake.

"I don't know. I just woke up, and the tent was on fire," Annalyn fretted, "Where am I going to sleep? In a tree?"

"You can share my tent," Simone offered, "You two go back to bed."

Once everyone agreed that we were ok, I crawled back into my tent and tossed myself to sleep.

I was greeted by an odd dream. No, not a dream. A nightmare. I was standing in front of a deep pit. A giant crack in the earth. It was like a void; I couldn't see the bottom and cold mist was rising through the craggy rocks.

"Child," A deep voice coming from the pit said. It sounded indescribably evil. ***"Listen here, you are my signal. You will be my catalyst. Beware."***

I shook with fear. "But I'm just a kid," I whimpered. The voice laughed an ungodly noise that made me want to flee. However, most new things made me want to run from them. The laughter made the ground rumble. It shook so severely that I fell into the pit.

Down, down down, the air rushed past me, and I could almost feel the ground coming toward me—

I shot up in a cold sweat. I felt like I had left my stomach back in the dream. I crawled out of my tent and was blinded by the morning sun. The others were waiting for me.

"How did you sleep?" Annalyn asked the three of us guiltily, "You know, other than the fire and all that."

"Good," I lied. "What's the plan for today?"

"Walk to the old ferry station. We'll be able to get a small river raft and speed up our journey," Simone explained.

I gulped; I had a bit of history with boats. When I was little, I was in one, I fell off and nearly drowned, and another time we almost ended up going over a cliff in one, then of course there was the whole Lily incident.

As you can imagine, I was *not* stoked to get on another boat.

We'd walked for a long enough time that I was starting to wonder whether my feet were going to stay on or not. As we walked, the trees started to clear and get sparser. Finally, we entered what looked like a ghost town. The dirt paths had been taken over by weeds, and the mud cabin-like constructions were crumbling.

"Before we go any further, you all need to know that this is an old settlement on the island. Like, women belonged to their husbands old; it was taken over by monsters a century ago, and no one knows whether the suckers have left or not. We need to be completely silent," Simone whispered. We all nodded in agreement.

I made a special effort to not step on any of the sticks or dead plants, afraid of what the noise could attract. Annalyn and Simone had slowed down, to stay closer to Sam and I when we were walking through the abandoned settlement. We all stepped carefully over the rocky path. I tried to keep my steps to the areas with the least rocks, but it was difficult, and every step was deafening.

I did my best to breathe shallower than usual and listen extra well.

The entire settlement was silent. It felt like the place was holding its breath. The only detectable noises were the sounds of our feet hitting the floor, the small rustling of leaves, the creaking of long open window shutters, and my own shallow breathing.

We turned a corner, and I made the mistake of stepping on a stick. The snap echoed through the ghost town. All of us stood frozen, holding our breaths. We waited, and... nothing. We all let out a breath.

"There aren't any monsters here, we just psyched ourselves out," Annalyn said, relieved. We all waited again, and the silence was broken by all of us laughing.

"We're all freaking out over a bunch of old houses and an old well!" Simone wheezed.

"We're panicking over nothing!" Sam barked out.

As my own laughter echoed, I heard a hissing sound, and we all froze. They heard it, too. I stood totally still, and I couldn't move. I was so scared to look behind me that I just stood there completely still. Not breathing. Not moving. I felt a sharp pain in the back of my head.

Everything went black.

My eyes slid open, and I surveyed my surroundings. We were in a marble pavilion, the ceiling and the pillars around us were cracked and crumbling. Vines had taken over and there was a marble, ivy-, and moss-covered fountain in the center of the pavilion.

I was propped up on a pillar with my hands and feet tied. I saw Sam and Simone hanging over an empty cauldron by their hands, both looking extremely peeved. They had gags in their mouths. There were two people standing next to the cauldron. No, not people, *monsters*. They had scaly green skin and snake tails for legs.

"AAAAAAAAAAAHHHHHHH!" I screamed when I saw them. One turned around, her eyes were amber-brown and she looked like the monster-version of Peggy, one of Lily's villain sidekicks.

She smiled wickedly. "Hello, Klotho, fancy seeing you here."

Simone got her gag off somehow, and she started cussing out the monsters. She was delivering maximum emotional damage. I was gobsmacked. Out of all of the things that I hadn't expected on this mission, I had definitely not expected the twelve-year-old assistant camp director to start cussing out snake-women.

Even the snake ladies were staring at her in surprise.

"One of you, gag her!" Peggy yelled after Simone had ripped her a new one and made her partner snake-lady start sobbing.

Peggy's sobbing friend went up to her with a rope, but Simone kicked her in the teeth with her bronze heel and swung her entire body so that her heel cracked against the snake lady's head. She had been forced back and down by the force of the heel hitting her forehead. She was thrown into a rock, and her noggin collided with it.

The snake lady's head split down the middle, exploding in brain matter and blood. It spilled all over the otherwise pristine floor, red and pink. Her scaly fingers twitched one last time.

I almost vomited.

"Aaaarggghh!" Peggy roared, sounding more frustrated than sad. "She can't do anything right!"

I got my sword ready in case I needed to fight. My bracelet was still on my wrist, so I activated it while Peggy had her back turned. When she wasn't looking, I was able to see my way out of the ropes without stabbing myself.

I slowly stood up. I shoved my fear away and leaped at Peggy. I cut her arm but slipped on her partner's snake lady's blood. I hit the ground hard with my shoulder, the marble hard and unforgiving beneath me.

Peggy roared in rage and raked her claws across my left hip, making me whine in pain. I got to my feet and swung my sword at her.

I missed, and my sword slammed into a pillar.

She pulled my hair and scratched my neck.

Not hard enough. I screamed and threw myself back into the ground. I took her with me and got up as fast as I could. She was faster, though, and she leaped at me, ripping her claws across my side.

I gritted my teeth and tried as hard as I could not to scream.

I failed, and my shriek echoed across the pavilion. I shoved her off of me as hard as I could, but it was just barely enough. I rolled to the side and got onto my feet as the burning in my side was replaced by panic.

What am I thinking? What am I doing? *I can't fight! I can't even jump into the deep end of a pool without being scared! What made me think I could do this?*

I didn't have any more time to mull it over. She lunged at me, and I swung my sword in a random direction. It hit another pillar with a loud *clang*. I swung again, in her direction this time.

I felt my sword pass through something fleshy and hard in the middle. I had managed to lob off her arm, which hit the ground with a wet thud, and she let out a blood-curdling scream of agony. She stabbed the claws on her remaining arm into my shoulder and tore through my flesh. I shrieked in pain and swung my sword at her chest, managing a killing blow.

I fell over and breathed heavily in the air. I retched into the pool of blood underneath me.

"Klotho! Are you okay? Klotho, Klotho!" Simone fretted, rushing over to me to inspect my wounds.

My vision blurred, and my head spun from blood loss. I felt hands on my back and under my knees. I could feel myself being lifted and swayed up and down. My mind kept wandering to the monster-Peggy.

She was lying on the floor. The wet thud of her severed arm against the marble. Her partner's head split open on the ground. Blood and goop splayed out around her.

The world was a blurry-spinning mess. My head throbbed, and I was finally realizing why Sam had that grim look on his face when we got to the island. This is what it meant to be a gifted one. If you stayed at camp, you'd be dealing with dangerous games and activities. If you left camp to do some sort of errand, you'd get hurt fighting the monsters.

This is my life now, I realized. *I can never go back.*

I was set down on a spongy wooden floor. It felt wet under my back and I heard rushing water to my right. Someone's hands ran over my wounds. The burning got worse as my adrenaline faded, but I could hardly move. The most I managed was a small groan.

I was on the verge of passing out.

I felt that cool numbness spreading through my wounds. My vision started to clear and my head stopped spinning. I saw Annalyn and Simone kneeling over me, and Sam was standing off to the side.

"Where... ?" I didn't need to finish. I looked around, and we were by the river, on the ferry dock. The damp wood felt slippery under my hands as I sat up.

"We're going to take a ferry as far as we can before the river gets too dangerous. But first, I'm going to bandage you up; your wounds are going to split open again like a bad seam," Simone said to me.

She pulled rolls of gauze out of her bag and wrapped them tightly around my side and shoulder. She used some tape to stick a wad to my neck. The bandaging felt strange on clean, unwounded skin, but if it was to keep me from coming apart, then I'd deal with it.

"I don't want to strangle you," She explained. "You haven't done anything to warrant that yet."

I would have laughed, but all I could manage was a smile. Annalyn and Sam were already at the edge of the dock, and it was clear that they were just waiting for me. I stood up on shaky legs and wobbled over to the edge of the dock.

'Ferry' was a generous word for it. It was really more of a busted river raft that looked on the verge of collapse. It was made of deep brown wood, and it looked like it hadn't been used in years. The ferry was flat like a square plate and had a manual rudder on the back. It was tied to the dock by a rotting brown rope that looked about five minutes from snapping on its own.

The other ferries looked similar. Some had chunks taken out of them, and some had no rudder. One was literally split down the center and just begging for death to take it. Another had scorch marks and looked like it had been set on fire recently.

Annalyn jumped onto the least rickety ferry first. Sam went next.

"Are you going to get on?" Simone asked. My throat was dry. This stretch of it was calmer than where I had fallen, but it was still a several-foot drop from the dock. Now, in case you haven't caught on, I have terrible balance, and jumping onto a wobbly ferry from five feet up didn't seem like a great idea.

"Um..." She saw my hesitation, and without a second thought, she STRAIGHT UP SHOVED ME ONTO THE FERRY. I was stunned, and I screamed as I stumbled off the old dock.

I fell onto my stomach and yelled some random garbled nonsense about how you don't just push people like that. She ignored me and jumped onto the boards of the ferry with ease. Sam cut the rope, and we began our totally not dangerous cruise down the river.

Simona C. Huska

CHAPTER SEVEN

OH MY GODS,
THAT BETTER NOT BE A CLIFF

(SPOILER ALERT, IT WAS A CLIFF.)

WE sat on the floor of the raft as the river took us along. I was holding on for dear life as we made sharp turns and maneuvered around rocks. I had never been on a ferry like this one before, but then again, I had never been on a mission either. Different types of trees framed the river bank; I saw animals, too. Turtles and birds, fish in every color that the human eye can see, salamanders, snakes. I even saw some butterflies and some tiny river dragon babies. They had blueish-green scales with winding patterns of lighter blue.

The water was clearer than glass, and it almost looked like we were floating. The ferry was surprisingly smooth to ride on when we weren't swerving. I wanted to put my hand in the water, but I was too scared that I would fall off.

I was mesmerized by the plants; there was one with purple leaves and blackberries that were shaped like cubes. Another had blueish green leaves, like a succulent, with metallic golden fruit shaped like tear-drops.

I saw a bush with heart shaped leaves, one with multicolored branches. The plants all looked so beautiful with each other. I saw regular trees too. Maples, and birch trees. Ones that I had seen before but didn't know the names of.

This was the peaceful part of the ferry ride. See, remember how I described the moss-covered rocks in the river? Yeah, those caused some problems. We had to constantly swerve around them to avoid crashing.

The rudder of the ferry wasn't all that forgiving, so Sam didn't last long when he tried to use it. Simone took over, muttering something about noodle-arms. Sam, with his new freedom, was now attempting to stand while Simone turned the ferry around a particularly rocky area, and Annalyn told her which way to turn and how much.

"Sam, what are you doing?" I squealed as we took a sharp turn. The trees framed the river, and the dappled light warmed my arms and legs.

Sam stumbled and yelped, "I don't want to sit on that disgusting floor!" He ducked under a thorn-covered branch that would have probably ripped his face off otherwise.

He's ridiculous, I thought, *even Annalyn is sitting down.*

"Sam, you're going to get thrown off of the ferry! Sit down, or I'll confiscate your kneecaps!" Simone demanded as we swerved past a sharp rock.

"Gah!" Sam screamed as he was thrown to the side. He hit a branch and was almost yanked right off the ferry. I grabbed him by the arm and pulled him to the floor. I was only hanging onto the gaps between the slippery boards with the sheer brute strength of my fingers. Sam grabbed onto me, and I swore that by the next turn, my fingers would fall off and I would become a frizzy-haired human baseball.

"Hold on!" Simone yelled as we turned with the river's bend. I dug my nails into the wet wood and waited for the force of the turn to make my fingers feel like they were being strangled.

But no, what happened was worse. As the turn happened, the force was so strong that MY NAIL BROKE IN HALF. I screamed in pain and yanked my hand away from the gap.

Bad idea, I would soon realize as I was thrown to the side and nearly fell off the ferry. My entire pointer finger was covered in blood.

"What happened?" Annalyn turned around, and her eyes widened when she saw the state of my finger. Tears welled in my eyes. I always hated it when people were all like, 'Oh aRe yOu ScArEd To BrEaK a NaIl?' Yeah, don't you think that hurts?

Anyway, back on track, Annalyn was screaming, Sam was screaming, Simone was screaming, and I was soaking, yelling, jumping, and, you guessed it, screaming. The trees had vanished, and through my watery eyes, I saw that the river had dropped off. I thought that my eyes were just playing tricks on me until Sam and Annalyn started screaming at Simone to stop the ferry.

"I CAN'T! THE BRAKE IS BROKEN!" She screamed. The roar of falling water filled my ears.

Wait, THAT BETTER NOT BE A—

The thought was cut off when the ferry tipped over the edge of the waterfall. The bottom was rocky, and the waterfall was like a steep slide. I let out a screech of pure terror as the ferry fell off of the cliff. I thought that the swerving we were doing was bad, none of that could compare to being hurled over the edge of what basically amounted to a wet cliff.

The ferry flew into the air and we were thrown off it. I spun in the wind like a bird in flight for a minute before I crashed onto the cliff again. The water split and slashed at my face as I slid down the steep, rocky slide. I was screaming, but I couldn't hear myself over the roaring current. Annalyn looked pale with fear, and Sam was swearing louder than I'd ever heard him.

I tried to control the current to turn around but I wasn't advanced enough with my powers. I was able to make the water swerve my body away from rocks. I tried to do the same for the others, but it was harder.

Come on, Klotho, you need to do something! I thought as I dropped down the extremely steep slide-like waterfall. I willed the current to shift, and we were thrown onto the river bank.

I landed hard on my hands and knees, skinning my palms. The water had ripped off my bandages at what had to be the worst possible time because I could feel my wounds reopening. I had tons of bruises and cuts all over me. I lay down and tried to ignore the way all of my limbs started.

My clothes clung to my body, and my hair was heavy and wet. My curls stuck to my cheeks and the back of my neck. I felt the cool, hard ground against my back. The grass tickled my shoulders and arms.

Sam was, quite surprisingly, too shocked by our recent cliff-dive to complain. Annalyn was kneeling by a tree.

"Are you ok?" I asked.

"That was scary," Sam said quite obviously.

"I'm alright. Thanks to you, Klotho." Annalyn gave me a look of gratitude. Her hair hung around her face in dripping strands. She had a nasty cut down her arm, dripping blood onto the grass.

"I'm good too; get over here; your wounds are opening again." Simone gestured for me to sit down, and she opened her messenger bag, which she'd somehow kept. She pulled out a box labeled 'Remedies for stupidity,' sanitized my reopening wounds, and reapplied my dressings.

"You saved us, your powers really are useful," Sam told me.

"Uuuh, thanks," I replied, the morning sun burned my face. I spied the water in the pool under the waterfall, jiggling like something was about to pop out of it. "Did you see that?" I pointed at the water right after it moved,

"See what?" Sam asked, the water moved around and formed into a Naiad. She had long, straight hair, like the water that spilled over the waterfall, round, misty gray eyes, and a flowing dress made from water.

She was one of the most beautiful women that I had ever seen in my life. She stood knee deep in the water, looking peeved.

"You've gotten my water all splintery!" She spoke with an unplaceable accent.

My cheeks burned with embarrassment. "Sorry, we didn't mean to."

"Can you at least clean it up? Those splinters are going to get in my friend's stretch, and they aren't as forgiving as I am!" She demanded haughtily.

"I can try to clean it up for you," I offered as I waded through the water to get the pieces. I picked each splintered chunk of wood out of the water with Sam's help while Simone and Annalyn asked the Naiad about her friends, whether they were known to send people to the underworld the traditional way and whatnot. As I worked, I found a piece that looked like it could have been a brake for the ferry.

Odd, I thought.

As I got the last boards out of the water, the Naiad hugged me. Her embrace soaked my shirt again, but I didn't mind.

"Thank you. Most of the time, children like you tell me that it's my problem," the Naiad said gratefully.

"No problem," I said. "Thanks for not drowning us."

She giggled and vanished into the water. I waded back to shore to find Simone glaring at a large chunk of the ferry.

"Glorified tray," she murmured with almost unreasonable malice.

We moved on, walking along the bank of the river until the sun went up high in the sky, and my stomach growled. Thankfully, by this time, I was almost completely dry, and my wounds had scabbed over. I went off to get sticks for a fire and saw a bunch of broken branches in a trail. At first, I was suspicious. What could have made a trail like that? I shook it off.

Come on, Klotho, just get the sticks and go back to the campsite, I chided myself.

When I got back, Sam offered to teach me how to start the fire, and since I had nothing to do, I accepted.

"So, you build it to look like a pyramid, like this," He instructed, placing the sticks in rough pyramid shape. I noted that he used the really thin sticks and bark that I had collected. "Then you light the match and set it on fire." He handed me the match box and I tried to strike the match. Unfortunately for lucky-old-me, the match snapped in half instead of lighting like it was supposed to.

"Ok, well, that's not how you do it," I thought out loud.

Sam laughed. "No, here."

He took the matches away from me and swiped the edge of the box quickly. The end of the match burst into flame and he lowered it slowly onto the bark that he had put on the base of the pyramid. The shabby stick-pyramid was now a small fire.

Annalyn and Simone came back with berries, nuts, mushrooms, and fruit. Simone cooked while Annalyn reviewed the plan for the rest of the mission.

"We're going to follow the river until we get to the entrance of the Underworld. Then, we'll enter the Underworld and interview Hades. After that, there should be that set up of nymphs to send us back to camp," Annalyn explained. "We just need to make sure to keep away from the more dangerous stretches of the river. The more violent the waters, the more violent the nymph."

"Won't the Kindly Ones stop us when we get to the underworld?" Sam asked.

"We have permission, so they probably won't even come to check who's coming when we show up," Simone replied; the mushrooms sizzled on the stick we'd shoved them on.

"Who are the Kindly Ones?" I asked.

"They are responsible for the torture of the souls in the Fields of Punishment. They are also known as," Simone leaned closer so that she could whisper, "the Furies."

I gulped. "T-torture?"

"Yup, don't worry though, they're actually pretty cool when you get to know them," Simone reassured me. This didn't sit right with me somehow.

Wait a second— "YOU'VE MET THEM?!" I screeched.

"I've been to the Underworld, so yes, I have. Be quieter unless you want to be deleted from the land of the living like a badly written grimdark fanfiction," Simone hissed.

My mouth snapped shut.

We set off again after our short meal break. We wove around the trees to keep the river in view, and walked and walked until my legs ached, walked some more until I could feel my feet bleeding. And walked some more until the sun went down.

We set up camp, though my tent was wet and had bits of river weeds on it. Sam took the first watch, and I fell asleep.

I was back at camp, but something was wrong. The grass was yellowed and dead. Ash floated through the air. The cabins were on fire; the dining pavilion was in ruins, and the river had dried up. Dead campers littered the ground. I was horrified. I knew it was a nightmare, but it felt so real. I looked at the lagoon; the water was brown, and dead fish floated through the water. The sky was gray with clouds, and it was unbearably hot. The air smelled like burning plastic.

My breath quickened; I had never seen anywhere that looked like this. I was walking around looking for people, animals, any sign of life. *The dragon pavilion.* I ran over to the one place I swore that I would never go near again, but now I was desperate.

When I got to the pavilion, I didn't see any dragons; I saw dark blood and sharp teeth littering the grass. The elevator was still functioning, so I shoved my crystal into the slot. The door screeched open, and I jumped into the elevator. I gasped for air; it burned in my throat.

I sat down and felt something *squish* under my butt. I shot up and looked down. The severed head of a baby sun dragon was lying on the ground, its dead golden eyes staring at the ceiling. I screamed and leaped out of the elevator. I ended up on a higher floor of the pavilion. Severed dragon limbs were sprawled out around the floor. I gagged. I jumped off of the edge of the pavilion and made the wind carry me. As soon as I sat down on the ground, I ran. I pumped my legs until I reached the crumbling dining pavilion; I searched for a camper, or Medea, or anyone. I saw Mom face down on the ground. I flipped her over.

I sighed in relief. "Oh, thank goodness. Mom, what's going   " Her face was twisted into a silent scream, and her head was almost completely torn off. I gasped and stumbled back. I tripped and saw my mom's body. Her straight black hair was sprawled across the ground, and her stomach had been torn open like a package. Tears welled in my eyes.

"M-mom?" She didn't respond.

The earth started rumbling. The ground yawned open, swallowing everything like a giant mouth. I was right on the edge of the massive chasm. My mom's thin figure spilled into the giant crack, and I watched everything disappear into the dark pit.

I shot up in my bedroll, breathing heavily. My heart raced in my chest.

It wasn't real, it wasn't real. I sighed in relief. I looked outside and saw the stars splattered across the sky. The crescent moon shone above us.

Simone was outside; she was watching our campsite from the corner. Her eyes glowed through the dark campsite.

"Couldn't sleep?" She asked, turning her head towards me.

"Yeah, what about you?" I asked, hoping that talking would distract me from that horrific nightmare.

"I'm on second watch today." She flicked a lock of hair over her shoulder.

"Oh, what happens if something goes wrong and you guys are asleep?" I asked.

"Then either solve it yourself or start screaming bloody murder. The latter will likely result in me being very grumpy, but then again, when am I not?" She replied sarcastically.

I snorted. "You aren't that grumpy."

"If you think so, then I've hidden it well," Simone responded. "Seriously, my circadian rhythm has suffered more abuse than the dragon pavilion elevator; it's a miracle that I'm still functioning."

I giggled. "How exactly *are* you still functioning?"

"Spite," She replied. "How are you doing?"

"What do you mean?" I asked in an attempt to avoid the question.

"You were kidnapped by a very ugly snake woman and hurled off a waterfall on the same day. You know exactly what I mean."

I sighed. "I feel really bad about what I did to that monster." On one hand, she was trying to kill me. But on the other hand... maybe I should have found a more peaceful way.

"It was her or you, and if you didn't kill her, we'd all be as good as dead," Simone told me in some aggressive form of comfort.

"I didn't think that this would be so dangerous." I curled my legs to my chest.

"You'll get used to it. Missions are easier on the South Island, from what I've heard," Simone replied.

"There's a South Island?" I asked.

"Yup, if you live in the southern states, then you'll end up there. It's in the Bermuda Triangle."

"Are you guys friends or allies? With the South Island, I mean," I wondered.

She hesitated. "Technically, yes. But their leader, Kendra, isn't the nicest. By which I mean she's a bully, and anyone who challenges her leadership suffers for it." Simone sounded bitter and annoyed.

"How old is Kendra?" I asked, noting Simone's tenseness.

"She's sixteen, Ares has her, which explains some of her violent tendencies." Simone fidgeted her fingers more, or I think she did; I could hardly see a thing.

"What are her powers?" She must be pretty strong to spook people so badly.

"She can see people's weaknesses, create fear in people, and she can wield any weapon with decent skill," Simone listed off.

"Those sound... scary. Especially for a leader." I shuddered at the thought of having to live there.

Simone nodded. "She's a menace. She's impulsive, and she doesn't know how to differentiate between a joke and a misunderstanding."

"She once locked down the South Island because Medea and I told her to quit telling her lieutenant that he would never amount to anything. She thought it was a sign that we were going to come for her position, even though Medea wouldn't, and I was only ten at the time." Okay, wow, that lady must have been insane.

"Why would she do that? What kind of sociopath is she?" Her poor lieutenant, that kid was going to get messed up *badly*.

"I don't know. There are a lot of people who lack empathy in the world. Unfortunately, one of them happens to run Camp Legend. The southern camp." Simone said sadly.

"She doesn't treat the campers like that, does she?" I questioned worriedly.

"When they break the rules, their punishment is based on how much she likes them. One time, she tossed a girl into the middle of a lake, *knowing that the girl was afraid of water*. What did the girl do, you ask? She tripped and spilled juice on Kendra's shirt."

"That's awful! How is that girl still in charge?" I bet if I lived in a southern state, I'd avoid that place altogether.

"There's no one to keep her in check. I'm hoping that something happens to her so that her lieutenant can take over," Simone said. "You should try to go back to sleep, Klotho; you have the first watch tomorrow."

Simona C. Huska

Chapter Eight

My Friend Gets Swallowed by an Overgrown Worm

When we set off the next morning, we soon realized that we had run out of water. This wouldn't have been a problem, if the river was in easy reach, anyway. We had strayed away from it to keep from running into violent Nymphs, so by the time we finally got to a pond, my throat was drier than the Sahara.

"Ok, guys, don't drink the water yet; a camper accidentally fumbled a bottle of poison into the water a few weeks ago. I have a potion that can clean a little of the water at a time, but we shouldn't—"

Simone was interrupted by a burp. Sam was standing next to the pond with his water bottle in his hand.

"Sam!" All three of us yelled at once.

I started to freak out, "What does the poison do? Is he going to die?"

"Oh my gods! Sam, what was I just talking about, you blundering idiot!" Simone yelled.

"Oh, calm down, nothing's going to h—" he fell on the ground, and he started gagging. I backed away, a good call since he started projectile vomiting *everywhere*. I bet you didn't think you needed to see a fountain of puke today. The smell almost made me do the same, but unlike him, I was able to hold in my breakfast.

"UUUGH! I SWEAR THAT MORON IS GOING TO BE MY DEATH!" Simone complained she started shuffling through her bag, and she pulled out a jar of pale golden liquid. She unscrewed the cap and placed a metal straw into the jar. "Klotho, can you control the vomit and toss it into the bushes or something?"

"I can try." I focused on the vomit and imagined it collecting in a ball and tossing itself into the bushes behind Simone. It ended up just splashing back onto the floor.

"Great," Simone grumbled. "Annalyn, can you prop him up on that tree?"

Annalyn obliged and Sam was just barely conscious. He groaned.

Simone bent down next to him and shoved the jar under his mouth and the straw in his mouth, "Drink," She ordered.

"I want a bendy straw," He murmured.

Simone's face contorted into a look of frustration, which made me wish I had super-speed. She took the metal straw out of the jar AND BENT IT BY HAND. My mouth hung open in fear. Even Annalyn looked concerned for Sam's safety.

"That's a metal straw," Sam pointed out,

"I haven't slept in forty-three hours and I am not happy with you, don't test me," she said through gritted teeth. She shoved the straw into his mouth and I saw the golden liquid slowly retreating from the jar.

"It's too sweet," Sam complained,

"DRINK IT OR I WILL KILL YOU MYSELF!" She threatened. Annalyn squeezed my arm.

Sam clearly sensed danger because he drank the rest of the jar without argument. Once Sam was back to mostly normal, we collected some water and poured the filtering potion in. After our drink, we set off again. I was walking next to Sam when I heard something rustle in the bushes next to us. My head whipped around, but nothing was there.

"What?" Sam questioned.

"I thought I heard something. It was probably my head playing tricks on me." I said. Sam frowned.

As we walked, I kept hearing that rustling behind us. I ignored it, telling myself that I was just hearing things. I *was* known to be paranoid. I figured that it was just the wind and that it would go away. I was calmed by this thought until I heard a sharp crack. Sam and I whipped our heads around, and Simone and Annalyn turned with us.

The massive snake had green scales glittering in the dappled light and bright yellow eyes. I was paralyzed. The snake opened its mouth, revealing fangs with holes in them. They must have been made to secrete poison.

"Drakon," Simone muttered, "Here we go."

I heard her running footsteps as the snake lunged down, not at me, but at Simone. Her scream was stifled when the thing swallowed her whole.

"NO!" Annalyn screamed. My eyes welled with tears, and I couldn't make myself move. Annalyn screamed. The drakon still had a lump under its mouth that was very slowly making its way further down.

"What do we do?" I whimpered. Sam was staring in pure shock. It didn't seem real that the drakon could swallow the same girl who'd just bent a metal straw in her hands to cure a poisoned friend. It didn't seem real that it went so fast. The tears spilled from my eyes as I prepared to join her.

The drakon shrieked as the blade of a black iron dagger ripped through its outer scales. The dagger swiveled, slicing off the drakon's head.

"You didn't think I'd go down that easily, I hope," Simone said to our open-mouthed staring, an evil grin on her face. The severed drakon's head fell to the ground with a *squelch*.

"You're alive!" Sam yelled as he leaped back.

"Fortunately for all of you, yes, I am." She was covered in slime and drakon spit, but at least she was alive. Annalyn tackled her with a hug.

"You scared us so badly! Are you hurt? You didn't lose anything?" Annalyn worried.

"I'm alright," Simone insisted.

"Don't drakons have magical death spit?" I asked, I remembered hearing it somewhere.

"Yes, but they only choose to secrete it when their meal is running around," Simone explained. She then lay face down on the ground.

"Are you okay?" I asked.

"Yup, just give me a minute," She said.

Once she was done, we kept going, per Simone's insistence and ended up back by the river. Annalyn said that it was safe to follow it now since we had, at this point, passed the stretches with territorial nymphs. Simone dove in, scrubbing herself off so hard I was half worried she'd take off her skin. Once she was done, we followed the river for half an hour before we got to what looked like a massive bird's nest, made of long, green grass along with some drier grass at the bottom. Several eggs the size of my head sat in the middle, all in hues of red, orange, and yellow.

"Oh no," Annalyn whispered.

"Oh no, what?" I asked nervously.

"A fire dragon nest. Where there's a fire dragon nest, there are fire dragons," Simone responded quietly. With either perfect or awful timing, a massive dragon stomped through the trees to her nest. She spotted us immediately with her bright yellow eyes, her razor-sharp teeth bared in a snarl. The dragon's nostrils flared, and smoke plumed out. She spread her red-scaled wings and took a breath.

Wait, fire dragon. Deep breath. Fire.

"SCATTER!" I screamed and bolted away. Heat radiated from the area as the dragon roared. Fire blasted from her mouth and engulfed the place where we were originally standing. Sam hung on a tree, swinging, and desperately grabbing at the only other branch in reach to get up. Annalyn was hiding behind a bush, shivering like it was negative 30 degrees Fahrenheit.

The magnificent beast turned her narrowed eyes towards me.

I whimpered.

She looked harder as if trying to see my motives, stepping towards me. I stiffened. As she stepped closer, I shut my eyes, waiting for it to burn me to a crisp. But the moment never came. Instead, I felt something wrap around my waist. I opened my eyes and found the dragon's tail wrapped around me. She lifted me off the ground and placed me on her back. Annalyn, Sam, and Simone stared in disbelief.

"I think it's safe," Was all I could manage. Annalyn and Simone grinned at me. Simone was up in the tree right next to Sam's; she must have been invisible when I was looking before.

"Of course! Fire dragons can read emotions. That's why she let you onto her back. No wonder she isn't murdering us, you're a coward!" Simone swung down from her tree. I'd never heard anyone call me a coward and make it sound like a compliment, but here I was.

"Yeah, you were so scared of her that she took pity on you and decided to help us out," Sam added in amazement.

The fire dragon shifted and stood up. She spread her wings and took off. Simone pressed her hand into the back of the dragon's head, and her eyes started to glow. The colors in her eyes swirled around, engulfing her sclera and pupil, and the dragon changed direction to follow the river.

"What was that?" I asked.

"I've recently learned to show people my imagination, though I can only do it when I touch people. I call it transferring. All I did was show her where we're going," Simone explained as she shifted.

We flew for a long time. By the look of it, it was about two PM when the other dragon came into view, flying towards us. Another fire dragon. It was bigger than the one we were riding, and it looked *mad*. It was beating its wings and speeding towards us like its life depended on it. The dragon we were riding panicked and jerked up.

The world tilted to the side, and I screamed as we plummeted off of its back. I tried to make the wind swirl around us like the water when we fell off of the cliff. Instead of ending up safely on the ground, we found ourselves *swirling in a tornado*. My screams were stopped when I found myself in the center of the tornado. The wind swirled around me but I was unaffected. I was just floating in the air.

I'm controlling this tornado, I told myself. *It'll do what I say.*

I watched as Annalyn, Sam, and Simone were thrown around me by the high-speed winds. I was trying (and failing) to make the tornado smaller, but I ended up losing my focus and the tornado just vanished. We ended up free-falling from about 20 feet in the air.

My screams were drowned out by the wind as I plummeted towards the canopy. Sam was already hitting trees to my right, Annalyn was using the branches to catch herself, and Simone had managed to turn into a very frazzled raven.

My lucky self-managed to miss all the branches before crashing into a massive leaf on one giant bush that broke my fall. I smacked into the ground, groaning. My voice was hoarse from all my shrieking, and my side wounds had been ripped back open.

"AAAAAAAAHHHHHHHHH!" I heard someone crash through the trees behind me. I whipped myself up and turned around; Sam was on his knees behind me. He had sticks pierced through his shirt, and he was all scraped up. I breathed a sigh of relief, but when he turned, it revealed that the back of his neck was badly bleeding.

"Sam, are you okay?" I asked, concerned. The blood flowed down onto his shirt, staining the blue fabric black.

He reached up and touched the back of his neck, pulling his hand away with a hiss.

Annalyn set herself down with a tree branch. "Oh, my." Her perpetually glossy eyes widened. She walked up to Sam and leaned to look closer at the cut. Sam flinched when she prodded the area. "You'll be alright, just bandage it, and it won't cause you any problems," She decided.

Simone landed shortly afterwards and turned back into a human. She didn't waste time speaking, just pulled out the bandages and taped them to the back of Sam's neck.

"We've had a long day; I'm starving. Klotho, can you come help me find something to eat?" Annalyn asked. The two of us set off, and she started explaining which plants and mushrooms were good to eat.

"What about those silverbells? Are they edible for anything other than medicine?" I asked.

"Silver Willow fruits or galaxy buds are," Annalyn told me.

"What do they taste like?" I asked.

"They taste like a mix of pomegranates and pears," Annalyn told me, "and they look like purple and blue ombre crystals."

"This place is wild. Literally," I said.

Annalyn nodded. "It's great, well, other than the camp. Camp isn't the best place if you have the wrong powers."

"What do you mean?" I asked.

"A lot of the campers are super judgmental. One girl had mind-reading powers and blood manipulation. A group of the campers literally bullied her out of camp," Annalyn explained, a sad look crossing her face, but it wasn't just sadness, something else too, bitterness?

"That's... so sad," I said. "Didn't anyone do anything?"

"Simone and Vega tried, but the girl didn't know the people's names, and she had aphantasia." Annalyn stepped over a log.

"What's aphantasia?" I asked, promptly tripping over on that same log.

"It's when you can't imagine things," Annalyn explained.

"Ah." I wondered what it would be like to live my life without any images in my head. What it would be like to read a book and not be able to imagine the characters.

"Anyway, it's happened to a lot of campers. Some cases are worse, some are more backhanded, and it obviously depends on the camper getting bullied. Some are tougher than others," Annalyn said. "But I've noticed a pattern. Most of the campers getting bullied have some sort of mental power or telepathy."

"What's the campers' deal?" Mental powers were so cool I couldn't fathom ever bullying someone about them.

"I'm trying to figure that out," She assured me.

I didn't know what to say, so I just walked behind her in silence.

We continued up to what looked like a weeping willow. It looked like it had blue and purple ombré crystals hanging off the branches, just like

Annalyn had described, and they had tiny flecks of white, like stars, the leaves were more of a bluish green with a frost effect over them. It was beautiful.

"Woah," I said in amazement. "They're beautiful."

"Almost everything on the island is…" she mumbled something after that, but I didn't hear it. I was too mesmerized by the tree to inquire.

Annalyn told me that she would collect the mushrooms down by the trunk and that I could collect the fruit.

When we came back to camp, a raft was waiting on the ground. It had handles on the sides, and the boards were tightly tied together with vines. With some sort of frame under the main floor of the raft. Simone was loading our things into a compartment in the front of the raft.

"Woah, you guys built this pretty fast," I said.

"Thank you," Simone said. "You guys brought food?"

"Mushrooms and galaxy buds," Annalyn said proudly.

"Gimme! Gimme!" Sam leaped out of the bushes and snatched three of the fist-sized galaxy buds. He shoved three in his mouth at once and proceeded to chomp them into colorful pulp.

"Gods, Sam! Slow down. If you start choking, then I'm not going to do the Heimlich on you," Simone warned.

"I'm not gonna—hurk—" The fruit caught in his throat, and he started to choke.

I started freaking out, patting his back while trying to control the liquid in the fruit to get it out. As expected, I failed spectacularly, and the loss of the juice that I did manage to yank out didn't help him at all.

I wasn't able to get it unstuck and Annalyn was trying to use her plant powers on it, but unfortunately it didn't work. Simone came over, sighing.

"I thought you said that you *weren't* going to do the Heimlich on him," I pointed out.

She grinned evilly. "Who said that it would be the Heimlich maneuver?" And she socked him in the stomach.

I'll give it to her, the method definitely worked. The galaxy bud that was caught in his throat shot twelve feet into the air. However, she also made him puke out everything that he had eaten that day, and well, that wasn't great.

"Help us carry the raft to the river," She ordered.

Sam groaned, "But my stomach." He tried to make an excuse, but Simone wasn't having any of it.

"I just saved your sorry butt from a stupid decision that you made." She glared at him. "You're going to carry the raft." So, we picked up the decently heavy, nine-by-nine raft and set off for the river.

By the time we *finally* got to the river, the sun had almost completely set.

"Can we sleep while on the raft?" Sam asked, yawning.

"What?" The other three of us asked.

"You know, like, lay down, shut our eyes, sleep? The river will take us in the right direction." Sam shrugged.

"All of us?" I asked, and he nodded.

"Do you want to drown?" Simone asked as we set the raft down on the river bank. "Someone needs to stay awake to keep us on the right course, and you know, KEEP US FROM CAPSIZING."

"I'll stay awake to do it," He offered. This made me suspicious, but Simone and Annalyn agreed.

The rocking of the raft lulled me to sleep. Pure blackness ensnared my senses.

I heard a loud *crack*, like thunder, but so. Much. Louder.

The raft broke in half with a loud *creak,* and I was thrown into the choppy, fast-moving water. I was on full alert now; I needed to get out of the river before I drowned. I heard Sam scream.

What was left of the raft was on fire, but it was quickly put out by the pouring rain. Thunder clapped in the distance. I flailed around, trying to stay afloat. The water was so much colder than it was during the day. I was sucked under the surface; the current pulled me through the freezing water. My lungs begged for air, but my flailing didn't do me any good. I was tossed around like a rag doll. The wind and rain caused waves, and I was constantly being thrown up and down.

I focused on the way that the waves threw me up and used the momentum to pull the water with me. What resulted was me getting thrown out of the water and landing in a pile of mud.

I saw Sam's silhouette floating in the water and I used the same momentum to push him onto the river bank. Annalyn and managed to grab onto some long grass and pull herself out while Simone had transformed into a goose.

All of them coughed out water as I waited for them to be ok. Simone lit a lantern.

"Thanks, Klotho, you're really getting–AAAAHHHH!" Annalyn yelped in pain when Simone touched her arm. Upon closer inspection, it was burned badly. My mind raced for a solution. I wanted to say something to help, but I couldn't. And I felt sick, so I began humming to keep myself from vomiting. Everyone could definitely hear me, but none of them told me to stop as they fretted over Annalyn's wounds.

Then it started to get weird. Little yellow music symbols started to appear around Annalyn's arm, a new one for each beat I added. They glowed comfortingly, flickering in and out of existence as though they were only trying to form. Annalyn and Simone both gasped.

"Klotho, keep humming!" Simone told me, and I didn't dare to stop until Annalyn's arm was completely healed.

"Wow, my powers work pretty differently than I imagined." I had thought that it would just instantly heal.

"Huh, I guess I can stop feeling guilty now," Sam said. I looked at him with confusion. *Wait, he said that he would stay awake, did he fall asleep?*

Simone figured it out first. She lost it. She started screaming at him full volume. I was terrified, Annalyn and I hid behind a tree.

"YOU'RE TELLING ME THAT YOU FELL ASLEEP?" I had seen Simone angry before this, but not like this.

"Y-yes!" Sam said shakily, "But it wasn't my fault! Right before she fell asleep, Annalyn gave me tea from her water bottle; I didn't think it would make me so sleepy!"

"And you didn't think to refuse it?" She demanded, "Sam, you know tea makes you fall asleep!"

"I'm sorry, okay!"

There was an earth-shaking roar. The kind that could only come out of a dragon's mouth. Sure enough, a massive dragon stomped its way toward us. I was frozen in fear.

"RUUUUUUUUUN!" Annalyn blared. My legs obliged for me and I booked it away from the towering beast. I jumped over vines and sticks and logs, for the first time in my life I didn't trip at the worst possible time. As I ran my surroundings became a dark black blur. I heard footsteps next to and in front of me, but I was mostly focused on getting away from the roaring and crashing of giant claws.

I was still soaking as thunder rolled in the distance, and rain poured from the sky as though it came from a canister. Each droplet felt like a death toll. There was a bright flash somewhere high to my right, lightning.

My feet pounded the ground and as I leaped over a log, I found a crushing sense of dread overwhelming me. When my feet hit the ground, I realized why. I had lodged myself into a sticky mud. I had landed so hard that I had managed to get myself stuck all the way up to my ankles.

Simone and Annalyn had fallen for the same trap, and San landed right next to me.

"What do we do?" I asked frantically. The dragon roared behind me. If we didn't do something fast, we'd be dead in minutes.

"We need to get under the quicksand," Simone said, very much too calm for the current situation.

"What!?" Sam, Annalyn, and I shrieked.

"I know that it seems counterintuitive, but this has happened to me before. Under the quicksand, there's an underground passage; if we sink fast enough not to asphyxiate and die, then we'll have a place to stay until the morning," Simone explained quickly.

"Ok, problem number one, none of us can control quicksand!" Annalyn informed her.

"Klotho can dilute it with rain water, it'll make it thinner and easier to get through." Sam said excitedly, he smacked me on the shoulder to make his point more clear.

Why, oh, why do my powers have to be so useful when I don't know how they work? I asked myself.

"I can try," I told them. I closed my eyes and focused on the rain falling more into the quicksand. I made it soak into the mud-like sand, and made as much rain as I could without getting a headache.

I sank further down, to my waist, then to my elbows, the quicksand was getting more slurry-like by the second. Down to my shoulders, then to my neck, and I was completely shoved under.

My feet poked out as I held my breath. The grainy sludge slid over my face into my nostrils, making me choke.

More water, I told myself, *more water will help.* I focused more and I popped out underneath the quicksand. I fell about five feet and landed, covered in muck, in a shallow stream with a rock bottom. The water was freezing cold.

Annalyn, Simone, and Sam followed closely behind.

"Quick! Drain all the water out of the quicksand!" Simone ordered hastily.

I felt for every drop of water left in the muck and yanked on it with my mind. The massive blob trembled and exploded down over us, washing away the muck. I shivered. I was clean, but dang, that water was cold.

I looked around the cavern. Gray rods of stone hung from the ceiling and poked up from the floor. Stalactites and stalagmites, but what made me gasp were the hundreds of glowing crystals. They looked like clumps of blue glitter, some were a deeper blue, while others were pale like moonstone. Small bits of them were embedded in the stalagmites, and stalactites, I was standing next to a column that was full of them.

Chapter Nine

I Didn't Like Dragon Spit Anyway

I stared in awe. "It's beautiful," I breathed.

"Those," Simone gestured to the crystals, "are midnight jewels."

"I didn't know those existed," I said, not taking my eyes off the beautiful crystals.

"That's because they only form on the north island. Some say that if you hold one in the dead of night and close your eyes, it will tell you your fate," Annalyn informed me.

"Oh please, that's not true," Sam scoffed.

"Even if it isn't real, they're still pretty," I told him. "Now, how are we supposed to get out of here?"

"We follow the cave stream until we find a hole that leads to the surface," Annalyn said.

I heard a whoosh in the tunnel and felt a massive wave of water behind us. Judging by their faces, the others heard it too.

"FLASH FLOOD!" Simone yelled.

"WHAT DO WE DO?!" Sam screamed.

"RUN FOR IT!" I belted.

And I was sprinting again. Through a cave. In the middle of the night. After having just done the same through thick woods for heaven knows how long and shoved through quicksand. At least I was getting my cardio in.

After enough running to leave me completely breathless, we got to a wall. It was breaking apart and, oddly for a cave, made of wood. Simone and Annalyn were trying to get it to open with their weapons. I started slashing at it, but with every cut I made, the wood regenerated.

Then a massive wave smacked me from behind and sent me hurtling through the wooden wall. It splintered as the others were also, quite indignantly, slammed into it. The wave swept us away and blasted us to the surface. Warm morning air blasted my skin as I was thrown out of the cold cave. I slammed into the floor, and I heard several *crashes* in the bushes near me.

I got up, my hands and knees throbbing. Sam was sprawled out on the ground behind me. Annalyn was standing up rubbing her back, and Simone was stuck in a tree.

"I'm alive," I said, still not sure how to process what just happened.

"Yup, and I've been given the pleasure of being stuck in a tree. How lucky." Simone said sarcastically as she tried to slither her way out of the branches.

The bark of the tree was a regular brown. Very boring considering all the other trees I had seen. The leaves were a calming shade of bluish, frosty green. They hung like weeping willow leaves and they were shaped like hearts. Small, perfectly spherical fruits hung on the branches. They were pearly white.

Several of the fruits were knocked off the tree from Simone's flailing and fell to the ground. I picked one up to examine it. It was the size of a pearl. It smelled sickly sweet, and it was hard as a rock.

"What type of tree is this?" I asked, trying to get my nail to cut through the fruit's skin.

"This is a," Simone grunted as she broke the branch that trapped her. "Fogfruit tree." Just as she jumped down to the ground, I was able to break

108

through the fruit's skin. Quite unsurprisingly, white fog burst from the skin. It completely engulfed me, and as I tried to run out, the fog just spread.

"Annalyn? Sam? Simone? What's going on? Where are you?" I asked, frantically searching my fog-covered surroundings for my friends.

"Over here!" Sam yelled from behind me.

I walked in the direction of his voice; the fog had started to clear a little and I was able to see his silhouette now. My eyes watered and the sickly-sweet smell of the fruit's fog traveled up my nose.

His blonde hair and shimmery brown eyes came into view.

"What else does this fog do?" I asked, as my vision started to go blurry, I wondered if the fog was poisonous.

"It can make people go unconscious, it's like an anesthetic," Sam explained.

Oh well, that's great, I thought. It smells bad, and it can make me collapse.

The sickly-sweet smell was really starting to get to me now. I expected that I would have the lucky pleasure of passing out first, so you can imagine my surprise when Sam crumpled like a tin can. I didn't have time to contemplate his luck versus mine, since my brain went all slow. I bent down and tried to pick him up, but my arms felt like Jello, and my brain was so fogged up that I could barely manage to think at all. My eyelids started to feel heavy, and I eventually couldn't keep them open anymore. I coughed as the fog filled my lungs, and everything went black.

I woke up a while later, lying on my stomach. I felt something on my back. My arms had grass stains all over them. Sam and the others were still out cold. Simone and Annalyn had clearly found each other because they were lying near each other.

I sat up, and a weight lifted off me. I heard flapping wings and an angry *quack.*

I giggled to myself as I looked back at the duck behind me.

It quacked again, jumped onto my leg, and curled up. I felt like a Disney princess; the problem was that I kind of needed to check on my friends. I tried to push it off my calf, it quacked and climbed back up. I tried again and stood up.

"Sorry buddy, you can't hang out on me," I said apologetically. The duck quacked and flew straight at my face.

Its wings smacked my head as its clawed duck feet scratched my chest. I did what anyone else would do: I started screaming bloody murder. Its wing smacked my ear and I tried to push the bird away with my forearm. The bird screamed in my ear and dove at my face again. Its weight knocked me over, and I threw my arm out to break my fall.

The bird tried to bite me, but I stuck my arm out, and it bit that instead. Strangely enough, I didn't feel pain, just pressure. I yelled out as I tried to smack the bird off me.

"Klotho, what is going on? Are you seriously being attacked by a duck?" Simone asked. I had been too preoccupied with, you know, being attacked by a duck to notice that she was awake.

"HELP ME!" I yelled.

"Just pull out your sword," she told me as the bird went for another strike.

"No! I don't want to hurt it!" I complained.

"It's attacking you." She pointed out calmly.

"But it's a duck! It doesn't know any better!" I tried to say, the bird smacked my mouth and I tasted iron.

110

That awful bird proceeded to smack my face with its wings five times while quaking like an ungrateful turkey. I grunted and threw it as hard as I could, but that cursed duck came flapping back at me and nose-dived right toward my face. Its bill clamped onto my cheek and its tiny claws raked across my neck.

I grabbed its foot, mustered my strength, and chucked it into the sky. I then made the wind change directions to hit the bird and send it flying in the direction away from me. The blast of wind didn't last very long at all, but it was enough to deter the bloodthirsty bird.

I couldn't believe that I had just been attacked by a duck. My neck and chest felt strange; they didn't hurt, but I knew that my skin was scratched up.

"You ok?" Annalyn asked groggily, "I heard screaming and woke up."

"I was attacked by a duck; I'm fine, though," I said sheepishly.

"Sorry, by a duck?" Annalyn giggled.

"What did you do to make it so mad?" Simone wondered, crossing her arms.

"I didn't let it sit on me," I said, my cheeks flushing.

Once Sam woke up, we checked that we had everything with us, and went on our way. The feeling of not feeling pain was strange, more numb than usual.

"Hey, guys?" I asked.

"Yeah?" They chorused.

"What exactly did that tree do?" I wondered.

"It makes you unable to feel pain for a few hours, don't worry, we'll just be extra careful," Annalyn reassured me.

I was pretty excited, *no pain? That must be cool.* I soon forgot about it as the smell of leaves morphed into smoke. The trees started to get sparser and the ground looked scorched in odd trails. As if someone had burning grass all over their feet and just walked around like normal.

I was understandably alarmed. I thought there was a fire dragon nearby, and as you've read so far, I hadn't exactly had the best experience with the things. My steps faltered.

Sam noticed, "What's wrong?"

"Is there a fire dragon around here?" I wondered, pointing to the tracks.

He kneeled down, then shrugged. Simone and Annalyn stared at the tracks in concern.

"Those are dragon tracks," Simone said, confirming my worst fears, "But they aren't fire dragon tracks." She added.

I was confused. "What?"

"Fire dragon tracks don't burn the ground; only two types of dragon tracks do that: sun dragons and lava dragons. Sun dragon tracks would completely scorch the ground that they're standing on, and then some. So, these tracks would have to be lava dragon tracks." Simone explained. My growing sense of relief was squashed.

"L-lava dragons?" I stuttered.

She nodded.

"Should I be scared?" I stammered.

Simone took a minute to respond, "I'm not sure. Lava dragons are incredibly rare. Their eggs can only be hatched in a volcano. There is a volcano on the island, but it's been dormant for centuries."

"There's a volcano on the island?!" I shrieked. I looked around, expecting a random hill to explode and put me in the underworld *permanently*.

"A dormant one, yes. It's basically a glorified mountain, as far as I know, the chance it could erupt is so close to zero it's not worth worrying about." Simone waved away my worries.

I tried to shove my fear away, but the more I thought about it, the jumpier I got. I ordered my feet to walk in the same direction as Annalyn and Simone, even though they were walking in the same direction as the tracks.

As we walked the grass seemed to get greener and fuller. The plants in this area seemed to be thriving. We reached a small opening between the river, which we had been following, and an oxbow lake.

The opening was only a few feet wide, but several meters long. The amount of bushes and tall grass that occupied the path made walking through without tripping slow and annoying. Once the opening between the oxbow lake and the river got wider, the space between the two was larger than two football fields.

Long grass looped around my foot, and I tripped. I tipped over, right into the oxbow lake. I caught myself with my arm and screamed.

The water burned my arm. I yanked myself up as fast as I could. My arm looked red and raw. Normal water was *not* supposed to do that.

Sam sprinted over, "What's wrong?!" Sam shrieked when he saw my arm.

"That is not normal!" Annalyn yelled as she came over to see what was going on. The skin on my arm burned, and tears streamed down my face, blurring my surroundings.

"A rabbit could have told you that! The question is, what's wrong with it?!" Simone yelled sarcastically, clearly trying to mask her own worry.

Sam grabbed my arm and yanked me off the small opening in between the river and the oxbow lake, where the grass was shorter, and shoved my arm into the river. The cool water soothed the burning in my arm until I could hardly feel it anymore.

"Are you ok?" Sam inquired.

"Y-yeah, I think I'm fine." My voice trembled.

"What happened?" Simone asked.

"I fell into the oxbow lake and the water... I guess it burned me?" I said she looked confused.

"But that doesn't make any sense. Can I see your arm?"

I showed her how my skin had blistered and gone red, "it really hurts." I told her unhelpfully.

"No kidding," she muttered as she started rummaging through her bag.

"Do you have something that might help?" I asked,

"I'd better," She kept rummaging around through her things until she pulled out a small bottle of murky goop. It looked a bit like Vaseline. The label on the bottle said something in runes that I couldn't read.

"It's not a perfect solution, but it'll have to do," Simone said, making me wince as she spread the ice-cold balm on my arm. A sharp tingling followed.

Just as my skin started to turn back to its normal pale color, the ground shook.

I swiveled my head to a hole in the ground, about seven feet away from me. It was completely dark on the inside, except for two glowing orbs with black slits. Shadows curled around large plate-like scales, and glowing threads of orange and yellow light flared in between the spaces as the creature started to crawl out of its hole.

I was transfixed. Frozen. Simone's hand clamped around my arm and dragged me backward. I wished that the dry ground in between the river and the oxbow lake had more trees to hide behind, as what was, by far, the biggest dragon that I had ever seen crawled out of the hole.

It was at least twenty-three feet long from head to tail. Its scales looked like large plates of black rock, with veins of what looked like lava running in between the gaps. Its intelligent eyes were red and orange, like lava, and the scales on its face were slightly lighter, like ash. Its body looked strong and sharp, with a long snout and black claws. The horns looked like sharp cuts of obsidian.

The dragon snorted smoke out of its nostrils. Then, it's cheeks puffed up, for a second I was confused. Simone's vice-like grip on my arm tightened. Then it clicked.

If fire dragons breathe fire, I thought, *then lava dragons must—*

"*MOVE IT!*" Simone blared, she yanked me behind a large rock faster than I thought was possible, pressing me against it. I spotted Annalyn and Sam behind a tree.

"W-what's it g-going to do?" I stammered, my voice shaking so much I was barely able to form the sentence.

"Lava dragons can spit lava if they're warm enough. She's going to hack lava at us until we're all properly fried." She tried to hide her fear with sarcasm, but it was hard to miss the tremble in her voice and the shake of her knees.

"Why? Didn't you say that dragons are usually nice? Except for the fire dragons?" I questioned, "Also, how do you know it's a girl?"

"I said that some dragons are nicer than others!" She snapped, "I certainly did *not* say that they're 'usually nice'."

"But Caldera—"

"Is the exception! Not the rule, the fire dragon that let us ride her was an extremely rare case, and this dragon will *not* be as forgiving," Simone informed me. "As for how I can tell she's a female, they tend to have longer tails and forearms and have more slender builds."

A roar of frustration shook the ground, and something collided with the boulder. The massive rock shattered, and I was forced to dive out of the way as shards of gray rock flew in every direction. A glob of partially-hardened lava had flown into the boulder. It must have been sent with a lot of force to be able to do that to such a substantial rock.

The grass where I had been sitting was now black and scorched, and a small fire had started. As I looked around, I realized that the fires had been started all over the grass.

The dragon's eyes fixed on me. Its cheeks expanded, and I barely had time to leap out of the way as a glob of lava the size of my head hurled at where I had been standing. Annalyn had snuck up behind a tree *much* closer to the dragon than I would have ever thought about going, and without warning, the grass at the beast's feet wrapped around her legs and wings.

The dragon roared in anger and spread her wings, tearing the grass that Annalyn was trying to hold her down with. The dragon turned to her and blasted a chunk of lava that was almost as big as a car at her. She dove out of the way, using the grass to propel her into a tree like a rocket.

The lava scorched the ground instantly, sending the tree that it had landed next to, up in flames. The air was starting to smell like smoke. Sam was screaming bloody murder for someone to help him; the dragon locked her eyes onto Sam and her cheeks puffed up like a raging black chipmunk.

Sam froze in place.

"No!" I screamed. My instincts took over, and the water in the river splashed the dragon. Engulfing everything for a moment before stopping. Solidifying the water around her just like Vega had taught me. My arms shook with the effort and the beginning of a headache started at my temples. Her cheeks deflated, and she seemed to cough, if dragons could even do that.

I was frozen in place now. The dragon tried to shake off the water but I didn't let the water budge. The spaces in between the dragon's plate-like scales dimmed and the eyes stopped glowing, now looking like gray ash. Her eyelids drooped, like she was tired and before I knew it, the dragon laid down and closed her eyes.

"What?" Was the only question that I could come up with.

"Of course! Why didn't I think of that? Lava dragons can spit lava unless they're warm enough, and when they get to a certain temperature, they fall asleep, sort of like hibernation." Annalyn grinned.

"Well, whatever you did, you saved me," Sam said, crushing me with a hug.

"Um, no problem," I said, extracting myself from his grip.

"Ok, guys, cool, nice, but we have bigger problems. The dragon's body is blocking both of our exits," Simone pointed out.

"Can't we go under its wings or something?" Sam asked dismissively.

"Her wings aren't what's blocking the exits, that's her tail and her head," Simone snipped at him.

"Can't we just wade through the water?" Sam suggested, sounding a bit peeved.

"Did you even see what that water did to Klotho? Look at her arm," Annalyn pointed at me. I looked down at my arm and saw that it was completely healed.

"What? But I thought that it wasn't the perfect solution," I said, confused.

"Exactly, I used an antidote for *acid burns* on your arm. If the water was just unnaturally hot, it wouldn't have worked perfectly, but since it did work, we know that the water in the oxbow lake is acidic," Simone explained to me.

"So?" Sam asked.

Simone took a deep breath, "So, wading through the water in the oxbow lake will result in A: acid burns, B: extreme pain, and C: *literally dissolving our legs.*"

Sam looked frightened. I couldn't really blame him.

"So, how are we going to get out?" I asked, and then something clicked, "Wait, can't you just turn us into some sort of flying animal?" I suggested, remembering her shapeshifting power.

"Oh," Simone said, her cheeks going a bit pink. "Right."

I blinked, and suddenly, I was flapping my black wings and following Annalyn, Sam, and Simone along the river.

We touched down when we couldn't see the dragon anymore. By that time, the sun had turned into a smear of orange on the horizon.

"Ok, so what now?" I asked, happily back in my human form.

"We should look for some sort of shelter," Annalyn suggested.

"Good idea, Annalyn," Simone said.

We walked for about twenty minutes before we found what looked like a marble building. Half of the walls had crumbled, leaving only the pillars to support most of the building, the solid marble floor had moss and weeds growing in the cracks. I saw three large, electric blue, and purple, bee hive like masses on some of the pillars. But they looked different somehow. They seemed to crackle with energy.

"Hey, what are those?" I pointed to one of the masses. Annalyn, Sam, and Simone looked up.

"That's a lightning-bee hive. I think it's empty. They usually nest in the ground or in really, *really*, tall trees." Simone told me.

Sam walked over to one of the hives. He raised his sword and hit the beehive as hard as he could.

"Sam!" Annalyn, Simone, and I screamed.

"What? You said that it's empty." Sam said.

We all waited for a swarm of bees to come sting us to death. The beehive didn't move. Nothing happened. But just as I was about to let my guard down, the beehive emitted a loud *buzz* and what must have been hundreds of bees poured out.

Chapter Ten

A Water Park Tries to Kill Us

THEY were glowing such a pale electric blue that they were almost white. Their bright electric purple stripes and stingers made sure that they could be easily seen. I shrieked and covered my face with my arms as a barrage of bees attacked me.

At this point, the foggfruit had worn off, and I could feel every second of the electric bee stings. Every sting was accompanied by a small electric shock, the kind you get when you turn on a light in the middle of winter, except in at least fifty places, all over my body. And it didn't stop hurting afterward. My eyes started watering, and I tried to have the wind blow the bees away. It only seemed to aggravate them more. I shut my eyes as tight as I could and tried to let some of the water in the clouds above us come down as hard as I could.

I heard a loud thunderclap and the most rain I had ever felt in my life poured down on us. The semi-collapsed roof funneled the water in so that it felt more like I was being poured on by a bucket than anything else.

The bees retreated, but I was still aching and fried from their stings. The cold water soothed me, but it was quickly getting dark. Thunder clapped in the distance, and the rain wouldn't stop.

I looked over the group, Annalyn was just as soaked as I was, with red welts all over her and scorch marks on her clothes. Her hair stuck to her face and neck as she spat rainwater out of her mouth. Sam had tears streaked down his now soaked face. His hair was plastered over his eyes. He had the same red welts and scorch marks. Simone looked pretty much the same, save for the tears.

"What did you do?" Sam asked, sniffling slightly.

"I—I don't know," I stammered.

"She blew in a thunderstorm," Simone said, clearly annoyed.

"Klotho, can you try to slow it down? We lost our tents in the river, remember?" Annalyn asked me.

I tried to make the wind slow, but it didn't work, I tried to make the rain slow, with the same result.

"What do we do now?" I fretted.

"I remember this old building from the last time I went to the underworld, there's another old temple nearby, but if we run, we might not get too badly soaked," Simone suggested as she shook water out of her hair, only to be splashed by the leaking roof.

"I just want to get out of the rain, let's do it," Sam said begrudgingly.

Simone took the lead as we ran through the forest. The rain splattering in my skin, the thunder rolling like drums in the distance. The trees started to clear; the thinner canopy left us exposed to the large showers of dripping rain. My hair started to become more like a water-logged sponge than hair, and my clothes had gotten to the point where it would probably take days for them to dry.

When we reached the old temple, I was so exhausted I didn't even have time to process what it looked like. I just laid down on the mostly dry marble floor, and let my mind drift to sleep.

I was in complete darkness. Warm, snug, tight, strong, heavy, suffocating, trapped, darkness. I started to panic. I flailed like a drowning cat, but my limbs still moved like sludge. I screamed, but my force flickered out like a candle. I felt something crawling on my ankle when I shot up.

The temple around me was made of dilapidated marble. The roof had protected us from the storm that I had brought the night before. Now there was a thick layer of fog, keeping me from seeing very far outside.

I looked down at my ankle and saw a centipede. I screamed bloody murder like I had been stabbed. I shot to my feet and kicked the horrible little thing off me.

"Klotho, what the—" Simone screamed like there was no tomorrow and turned into a small red dragon, blowing white-hot fire around us at the hundreds of centipedes around us.

I started trying to manipulate the fog to splash the creepy crawlies away, failing miserably. Sam was screaming uselessly, and Annalyn had climbed onto the ceiling, how? I have no clue. Just when I thought it couldn't get any worse, Sam puked right next to me on a pile of centipedes, sending them scuttling back to their holes.

I was smashing the horrible little things with my sword clumsily. In a few minutes, what would have normally been a calm morning had us surrounded by flaming centipedes.

Simone had torched them enough to have us stuck behind a wall of flame.

"What now?" I asked, assuming that most of the centipedes were long dead.

"Uh, we run, obviously," Sam said.

"No, we need to put the fire out first," Annalyn argued, "if we don't it could start a wildfire."

"Annalyn's right, Klotho, do you think you can make the fog collect to put it out?" Simone asked me.

"I don't think I can do that. We could get to the river and use that." I suggested.

"Then let's get going," Annalyn said, she seemed anxious.

We rushed over to the river as fast as we could. Annalyn had insisted that she needed to stay to make sure that the fire didn't get out of control.

We reached the river and I willed a decent amount of the water to follow us. As we ran back the water kept soaking the branches and getting pulled off the blob by leaves. By the time that we got back to the temple the water was full of leaves and sticks.

I was worried that they were going to make the fire bigger, but I didn't have anything else, so I just used what I had. I splashed the trembling blob of water on the fire, which got a decent amount smaller, and then surged up to the twenty-foot-tall ceiling.

This is bad, I thought as fear pushed itself from my stomach all the way to my head and back. *OH CRAP.* My mind screamed.

My heart quickened as my mind raced for a solution; I thought I saw the temple ceiling moving, and I thought I heard the pillars screeching a bit. I barely noticed what everyone else was doing because my only thought was something along the lines of, AAAAAAAAAAAAAAAAAAAAAAAAAAAAHHHHHHHHHHHHHHHH HHHHHHHHHHHHHHHHHHHHHHHHH.

I started sucking water off the fog and throwing it at the fire. The only thing that I achieved was giving me a headache. And splashing the water in the wrong direction.

I could have sworn that the rocks that made up the ceiling were expanding. I thought they were going to collapse.

Sam screamed, "KLOTHO, LOOK OUT!" And yanked me back.

Turns out I was right about the whole collapsing thing because the temple ceiling fell only seconds after Sam pulled me away, snuffing out the fire with a deafening *bang*.

"What happened while we were gone?" Sam asked breathlessly.

"I didn't do anything, if that's what you're asking," Annalyn snapped.

"I wasn't asking that!" Sam argued.

"Well, maybe if you hadn't used that tone—"

"Both of you, cool it! We are going to go take a bit of a break from the serious stuff since you two seem so tense," Simone ordered, shoving them apart. "Off to the level four excursion with us."

"What is it?" I asked, following Simone and Annalyn through the forest. "Or, better question, *where* is it?"

"It's basically a natural water park; it's two pools connected by a series of waterfalls that can be like slides. It's a quarter mile south on the river," Annalyn explained, I grinned, though sliding down slopes made of rocks sounded utterly terrifying to me.

When we finally got there, I realized what she meant. The pools were pretty small, bigger than the average pond, but not by much. The hill was littered with rocks and the river was quite wide. The waterfalls that connected the two had trickling water flowing over the smooth rocks that they were made from. The water was crystal blue, and I could see fish and turtles swimming around.

I smiled. Maybe this could be a good way to relieve some tension.

I immediately jumped into the pool that was above the other, letting the water cool me. I flipped around in the water and waited for the bubbles around me to disappear. I didn't really enjoy being wet again, but it was better to be wet and cool than hot and damp.

I was sucked down the waterfall closest to the east side of the lake. It had been an even slope when I looked at it before, but as I slid down, it changed; it sloped up, and I screamed as I was thrown upwards and plunged into the water of the lower pool.

The water wrapped me up like a Christmas present and I started in awe at what I saw before me. The weeds at the bottom of the lake were in so many different colors I had a hard time telling which one was the prettiest. The fish that I saw at the bottom were also colorful; I was so distracted by the scenery that I barely noticed when the others all splashed into the water of the bottom lake. I saw beavers and salamanders, but I couldn't ignore what just happened.

Right at that moment, I accidentally breathed in the water and had to shoot up to the surface. I coughed and sputtered as the others stared at me.

"Did that just do what I think it did?" I asked when I stopped sputtering.

"The waterfall moving? It happened to me, too; I don't know if that's a good thing or a bad thing," Simone said. "I know that didn't happen when we last came here.

"What do you mean, 'if it's a bad thing?' It's cool!" Sam argued, Annalyn nodded in agreement. I frowned, it was pretty fun, but it was also dangerous. What if it moved in a way that would hurt us?

I squashed my worries and climbed up the rocks in between two of the waterfalls and went on a twistier one. As I slid, I felt it shift. The twist got more pronounced; it tilted up, then down, then sideways. I screamed bloody murder as I plummeted off the slide. It shifted again so that it was underneath me, and I slammed into the rock with my side. I yelped in pain, my entire side hurt.

The slide edge pushed me up, and I was thrown into the cool water below. I was so shocked that I couldn't bring myself to move. My side hurt so bad. I was just sinking like a rag doll filled with rocks that a dog threw into a lake.

The surface was only getting further away. I saw the silhouette of the others above me, and one of them dove down to get me. I was too surprised to move, swim, or do anything. I felt something underneath me. Hard, cold, rough, and flat...

Oh no, I thought as I was pitched into the air by the equivalent of a rock springboard. I screamed as I was hurled into the air like a frazzled, untalented gymnast.

I heard someone down below scream, too, but as I was thrown, I quickly realized that I had been chucked much, much higher than I had the first time. As I was contemplating falling back down to earth, waiting to get smashed into a Klotho pancake, a bird flew right into me. Beek first. Because my day wasn't bad enough already.

The beak stabbed my right arm really hard. I screamed in pain as I plummeted further down. Now, with a bird sticking out of my arm. I felt the wind whip around me.

Wait a second, I got an idea. I used the wind and pushed it up with all my concentration. I managed to make an air current that was shooting straight up from the ground. I floated in mid-air, suddenly very glad at Vega's lessons. The bird flapped a bit in my throbbing arm. I grabbed it by the neck, gritted my teeth, and pulled. It hurt almost as bad as when it went in, and it immediately started bleeding; I let go of the bird, and it was hurtled up by my wind current before flinging itself away and flying off.

I slowly started to lower the wind speed of the air current, and I floated back down to the pool. My vision was spinning, and I had a really, really bad headache. My arm was bleeding aggressively. The water around me started to smell like iron and turned red.

"Klotho!" All the others said as I heaved in breaths as I had just tried to sprint up Mount Everest while lying on my back in the water.

"What happened?" Sam asked, with a tone of clear concern.

"Your arm!" Simone scrutinized the bleeding limb. "By the gods, what did you do?"

"A bird flew into me," I mumbled.

"And you pulled it out?! Come on! Don't they teach you not to do that in mainland schools?!" Simone complained,

"In case you haven't noticed, Klotho is kind of bleeding here!" Sam pointed out.

"What do we do?" Annalyn fretted.

"I've got this. I have most healing spells memorized." Simone swam over to me and pushed me to shore; I didn't have the strength to move. My side touched the beach, and clearly, the others decided that this was good enough.

She placed her hands on my shoulder, where the bird's beak had stabbed me. She started to whisper something I could only hear strings of. I felt the same cool numbness that I had felt both of the other times that she had healed me before, but now it felt stronger. Her whispering slower, steadier.

When the light in the corner of my eye faded, my head no longer throbbed; my arm was only a little sore. I tried to sit up but my arms were still shaky.

"Next time something stabs you, don't take it out, for goodness sake." Simone shook her head and bandaged my arm in preparation for the wound to reopen.

A pathetic "Ok" was all I could manage.

"We should keep going. This place is clearly trying to kill us," Sam said.

We all nodded in agreement. I tried to stand up, but my legs wobbled like Jello.

"Ok, my legs are disagreeing with me, give me a minute." I leaned against a tree, waiting until I could fully feel my legs again. I saw something move in the water. I squinted and saw a head of lagoon blue hair bobbing around in the water solemnly.

"Who's that?" I pointed at the head bobbing around. She turned around right at that moment.

She had blue skin and blue watery eyes without pupils.

"Oh, you're the Naiad that lives here, aren't you?" I asked, a bit angry.

She nodded sadly.

"Why did you toss me around like that?"

Her eyes spilled all over her face with tears.

"I'm sorry for hurting you. I didn't mean to." She sobbed.

My expression softened, and I felt a small bit of pity for her. She looked so lonely.

"It's okay," I decided. "But you need to help us out a little before I fully forgive you."

"What do you need?" She asked me gratefully.

"We need you to give us a ride down the river. We're heading to the underworld," I told her.

She thought for a second. "I think I can arrange that."

128

She whistled an intricate, high-pitched tune. I was confused for a second, why was she whistling? The answer became very clear when four dragons surfaced. They were river blue and gray with patterns on their scales that looked like rushing water. Their wings looked more like fins and their snouts were sharp and sleek.

"River dragons," Simone breathed.

"I hope this helps," The Naiad said before turning into water.

I stepped into the water and walked to the first dragon slowly. I was shaking with fear. Dragons really scared me, but this was better than walking.

I stretched my hand out and touched the snout of the dragon in front of me. It had freshwater blue eyes, and one of her teeth stuck out of her mouth like a crocodile. I felt vulnerable. I was up to my hips in water and couldn't easily run away if I needed to.

The dragon's coo sounded almost like a growl. It swam in between my legs and lifted me up. I was sitting backward, and I yelled as it stood back up; it paused, giving me time to shift to the right position. I hung on to the dragon's back as it started to swim. The others had gotten onto different dragons. Annalyn seemed to be having much more trouble than the rest of us. Her dragon seemed to not like her very much, and she didn't seem to like it, so she sat very awkwardly as her dragon seemed to try and make her ride as bumpy as possible.

The dragon I was riding on the other hand, glided smoothly across the water like a snake. As we continued down the river, the sense that it would hurt me slowly trickled away, leaving space for something else. Amazement. *I was riding a dragon, again*! As we floated through the bends of the river I found a new appreciation for the dragons on the island.

They weren't scared of us even though all of us carried weapons, and the only ones that ever attacked us were after being provoked. They could wipe out the entire population of gifted ones on the island and have it to themselves, but they didn't. And they wouldn't as long as we wouldn't give them a reason to.

They had helped us, seemingly without question. As we floated down the river, I expected to feel a sense of calmness, but that wouldn't come. The rushing waters carried the sounds of singing birds and rustling leaves, which by all means should have been calming and soothing. But what I felt was dread. The sounds in the distance? Rapids. I didn't know much about riding on the backs of river dragons over rapids, but I was sure that it would not be a pleasant experience.

I heard the rustling in the trees get quicker, as if something was jumping in between them. Nervousness curled in my stomach. *What if we get attacked again?* I wondered.

"Hey, guys?" I asked, barely able to choke out the words. Regardless of whether humans can smell fear, we can definitely hear it. I heard it in my own voice. It shook with fear as I imagined us getting smashed to bits in the rapids.

"Yeah?" Simone replied with a bit of concern in her voice.

Chapter Eleven

Yet Another Cliff!

"Aren't the rapids close?" I asked fearfully.

Simone paused and listened for a second, her eyebrows squished together in concern. She heard it, too.

"I think that they'll stop there and let us off," She didn't sound very convinced herself.

What will they do if they don't let us off? I wondered.

As we floated back down the river, the sounds of the rapids ahead only got louder. I felt like I was being watched, and I could feel the tension in the group rising. The thought of ground through such dangerous waters was weighing on us.

The dragons didn't seem to notice, they just kept swimming. It was like they had done this hundreds of times. I could see the rapids now, the river roared and twisted around sharp rocks, the water white with bubbles. Fear washed over me as the dragons got faster. They didn't stop or go to shore, in fact, they pulled closer to the center of the river. They were heading right for the rocks.

"What are they doing?" I yelled, panicking as we got closer to the roaring waters. The current pulled at my feet, and I lifted them up to keep them out of it.

"They're going to climb over the rocks," Simone told me calmly.

"*They're going to what*?!" But it was too late to stop now. The dragon moved at incredible speed. It clambered up on a steep, sharp rock, nearly knocking me off in the process.

I clung onto the dragon's neck like a leech and shut my eyes as tight as possible. I was being jostled around so much that I would have thought I was being manhandled. The dragon's rounded claws scraped the surface of the rocks, making a sound like someone was sharpening a knife. I felt myself drop. I opened my eyes and screamed; we were plummeting straight towards another rock.

The dragon caught itself easily, and as I looked around, I realized that the others were far in front of us. What if they left us behind? All of them were brave, unlike me, but I was worried that none of them would be willing to go back through the river to get me.

I took a chance. "Can we try to go faster?" I whispered in the dragon's ear. *Stupid, it can't understand you!* I thought to myself aggressively. But to my utter shock, the dragon picked up its pace.

It slithered over the rocks using its tail for balance, and its wings to steady me. As we got closer to the end of the rapids, the roaring only got louder. I watched in horror as the dragons that the others and I were riding on inched closer to a drop-off in the river.

"Umm, guys?" I asked nervously, "Are you seeing what I'm seeing?"

"Hold on tight," Was all Sam said back as the dragons sped up.

I screamed as we were launched off the edge of a fifty-foot-tall waterfall. The dragon's wings spread and it glided across the wind even smoother than it did over the water. Quite a relief since I had expected to plummet from the sky and splatter like a bug onto the rocks that lined the bottom of the waterfall. This was one of those waterfalls that would have been completely unsurvivable if fallen from, and that thought made me shiver. How many people had died being hurled over this cliff?

"THIS IS TERRIFYING!" I screamed over the wind. As I was saying it a bug flew right into my mouth. I coughed and sputtered, yelling 'stop' and 'quit flying' as another one buzzed around my eyes. The bug didn't stop, but the dragon did.

It folded its wings in, and we plummeted toward the earth.

My stomach dropped and I screamed, "HELP!" As loud as I could. I heard Sam yell something but I couldn't hear it over the wind. Whatever Sam said, it saved my life. The dragon heard him and spread its wings again. My entire body was shaking with fear.

"Are you ok?" The dragon Annalyn was riding gilded right next to mine.

"No," I said, annoyed that she even had to ask. I had almost just plummeted fifty feet to the ground. Of course, I wasn't ok. "Why did it stop flying in the first place?" I asked her.

"You told her to, these dragons can understand basic commands," Annalyn explained.

"She wouldn't have been hurt by the fall. Dragons are very durable, but you would have gone SPLAT and become a grease spot on the forest floor. A very undignified way to die if you ask me," Simone told me, swooping in closer herself.

"Well, that's reassuring," I informed her.

"You're welcome," she said sarcastically; her dragon pulled away, and we were now gliding just above the river. The dragons set back down in the river and kept swimming; we had gotten to a wide enough stretch that the water was pretty deep.

Every so often I would see a shadow pass under me, making my heart race. *The more violent the waters, the more violent the nymph,* after all. But nothing had happened yet, and for all I knew it could just be some fish. This psyched me out enough that when I felt something brush my leg, I flinched away so hard that I fell off of the dragon. It twisted underneath me and pulled me back up, though her scales were now very slippery.

The dragon growled a bit with annoyance.

"Sorry," I said apologetically.

The others were way ahead of me. At least twenty feet. I took a deep breath, bracing myself to be jostled like a box labeled 'handle with care' in the back of a delivery truck. I gulped.

"Faster," I thought for a second. "Please."

The dragon sped up, she slithered through the water and slowly sank.

"Wait, what?" I asked as she went completely under the surface. I had managed to make an air bubble right before she pulled me under with her. The river was darker here than the stretches that I had seen before, the water murkier, the fish more scarce. Animals and plants, in general, seemed to have been sucked out.

It made me uneasy. The rest of the river was overflowing with life, so why did this part seem so... empty?

"Up," I tried to say, but my bubble popped, and water flooded my mouth and nose. I panicked because I was, you know, kind of drowning. The dragon I was riding took the hint and surfaced. I coughed and sputtered for a good two minutes, earning me a worried look from the others, who were now behind me.

"I'm fine," My nose is still burned from breathing in water. "Just breathed in some water."

"We should probably be getting out of the river soon. The dragons are getting tired," Simone told us, patting her dragon's neck.

"Yeah, this place is starting to give me the creeps," I admitted. Simone and Annalyn nodded in agreement.

Sam gave me a look, "Why? Nothing creepy about this part of the river. There aren't any animals to worry about and it's quiet."

"It's too quiet, and it's unusual for there to be no animals here," Simone countered. "I didn't pass this part of the river last time, I think I actually made a point to avoid it."

"Why?" Sam asked.

"I have no clue—" Simone was interrupted by my scream as I was grabbed around the waist and pulled underwater. I just had enough time to take a breath before I saw what had yanked me under.

A girl, no, a Naiad, had grabbed me. She had white hair, like the rapids, and her skin was the murky mix of blue and gray. She bared her teeth. Her pitch-black eyes boated into me, not anger, not rage, just pure *hate*.

"STAY OUT OF MY RIVER!" she started, pulling me closer to the bottom.

I flailed, kicking and punching her, but I was underwater, and none of them struck hard enough to deter her. I was starting to run out of air. Drowning seemed like it would be a peaceful death, but it hurt. As the last bit of air left my lungs, it hurt to not breathe in. This was her river. This was her domain. I could only stop her if I turned the water against her.

I pulled strength from every corner of my body and pushed the water from the bottom of the river up, begging in my scattered mind for it to work. The blast thrust us both off the bottom of the river and into the air, I shoved her off of me as fast as I could. She scratched my waist and arm with her long nails, trying to hold on. But we were on the surface; I could breathe now. I kicked her as hard as I could, and that demented Naiad tumbled back into the river with a hiss.

The others had gotten out already; they were screaming my name, the dragons next to them roaring and whining for me, too. I was about to crawl out of the river when harp nails clawed at my back. I screamed and threw myself up, the water giving me a helpful push.

I landed *hard* on the ground by the river, right into a mud pit, and with enough force to jam myself shin-deep in mud. Simone and Sam pulled me out as fast as they could. The Naiad ran up to me from the river and slashed my neck. I shrieked in panic, and the other joined in the fight.

"Stay off her!" Sam yelled as he tried to slash her with his sword. She dodged his strike, and he ended up with his sword embedded hilt-deep in a tree.

"Come on, Sam! Leave the poor trees alone!" Annalyn yelled at him, managing a good strike. The Naiad tackled her and scratched at her throat while screaming incoherently. I ran up behind her and threw myself into the Naiad.

I guess I could have just chopped her head off, but she was just defending her river, and I didn't want to hurt her. The Naiad came off Annalyn, and we both slammed right into Simone. She turned into a large river dragon and smacked the Naiad with her tail. She flew back into the river and screamed curses at us as we ran away.

"See? This is why you don't mess with Naiads." Simone said, out of breath.

"But we didn't mess with her! She just attacked Klotho for no reason!" Sam argued.

"I hate to say this, but for once, I agree with Sam," Annalyn relented, panting as she finally caught up to us.

"We imposed on her stretch of the river; some Naiads will take that personally. We just had the misfortune of meeting one that does," Simone heaved out in between her heavy breaths.

"Let's just find some food and keep going," I suggested.

"Good idea, I'm *STARVING*," Sam complained.

We had all split up to make less noise and left Sam at the campsite, which sat in a field of tall grass that tickled my knees, and the river went quite thin, almost hidden if not for the telltale rushing.

I set off trying to find an animal to hunt down and eat, though I was half sure I wouldn't be able to bring myself to kill one. Stepped quietly through the forest, watching for an animal to catch my eye. I saw a flash of brown. I whipped my head around. Sword at the ready.

I came face to face with a rabbit, it was cute with its brown fur, and long ears, and, wait a second. Wings? This furry little rabbit had wings, iridescent green and shiny.

"It's a fairy rabbit!" I thought out loud. The little rabbit looked at me with big black eyes. "Aww, I can't eat you." I walked up to the cute little rabbit and stretched my hand out to pet it, the rabbit pressed its face into my hand. The fur on its face was warm.

"You're really cute—" The rabbit's face stretched out, and its mouth clamped around my right hand. I screamed as loud as I could and swung my sword at the cute little beast. Its lengthened legs tossed it out of the way. Foaming at the mouth, it looked like a rabid dog with long ears and fairy wings. Hilarious looking back on it, not so much when it was trying to scratch my face off.

The fairy/dog/rabbit thing lunged at me, its claws outstretched and its mouth wide open. Revealing hundreds of thin, yellowed teeth. Its eyes gleamed with hunger. Ready to rip me apart?

My wrist was bleeding and slobbery. Useless if I wanted to fight. I jumped away. Unable to properly get my grip on my sword with my under-utilized left hand.

"Bad dog-rabbit-fairy-thing!" I sputtered. Swinging my sword around stupidly with my left hand. It bared its teeth at me. I didn't take any chances, I sprinted as fast as I could. When I stopped for breath it lunged again, knocking me over this time. Its weight pressed on my chest, and I did the only thing I could; I grabbed its head and screamed as loud as I could into its ear. Hoping to scare it off.

It responded by stabbing my stomach with its claws. Thankfully, they were only half an inch long, but I yelped in pain as the claws sank through my tattered shirt and into my flesh.

I swung my sword clumsily at the monster with my left hand. I hit it with the sharp edge but only managed to cut its wing off. It barked in pain and bit my shoulder in response. I had moved my head away from its initial strike, going for my neck. I swung my sword again, catching it in the shoulder and cutting clean through the short, thick neck. Its severed head fell onto my chest, and its body went limp.

My shoulder stung in spiky pain from the bite. My stomach hurt even more. I pushed its head off my body and sat up.

I picked up its corpse, nearly throwing up because of the bloody smell, and threw it away. I laid back down, my heart still beating through my chest. As I was looking up at the tree above me, I saw the first familiar fruit that I'd seen in days, a pear.

I shot up and looked at the tree, happiness spreading through my veins. The tree was tall but not impossible to climb. I jumped and grabbed a branch of the tree. I swung my body, trying to get my feet up to it. It took me several tries, but I managed it. I pulled myself onto the next branch, a thin one.

I was worried that it wouldn't hold my weight, and it bent when I put weight on it. It didn't matter; I was in reach of the pears.

I started pulling them down, using my shirt as a makeshift basket.

"What are you doing?" A critical voice asked from behind me.

I yelped and jumped a bit, falling out of the tree. The pears fell all around me, and I started frantically picking them up when I realized who the voice belonged to.

"Why are you alone?" She crossed her arms. Her smooth skin was light moca like a fawn; her hair was such a dark brown it almost looked black, and it was twisted into two braids that ran down her back. Bands of silver were wrapped around the ends, glinting like stars. Her eyes were large like fawn eyes and silver like the moon, glossy and almost glowing. She wore a short white dress and golden sandals. A quiver of arrows was on her back. She was one of the most beautiful women I had ever seen in my life. I was about three seconds away from dropping the pears and running. I got to my feet as fast as I could.

"Uh, ummm, I'm just—" my cheeks burned with embarrassment. I didn't know I was stealing, and considering my skin is whiter than printer paper, I likely resembled a tomato more than a human.

She chuckled, "I know why you're here, Klotho. I am Artemis."

My jaw fell open, and I dropped the few pairs I had managed to pick up. I wasn't sure how to act. It wasn't every day that I got to meet a goddess one-on-one.

The only words that came out of my mouth were, "Why are you here?"

"I have come to tell you that I've sent my hunters to aid your group for a short while. Go back to your campsite, and you will find them. I must go." And she vanished in a flash of light.

I, still starstruck, did as she said. When I finally got back to the campsite, I found a group of what looked like 30ish girls. They ranged in age from twelve to twenty and were all wearing some kind of tunic and usually a skirt, though there were some pants mixed in.

Several were chatting with Simone and Annalyn, Sam was sitting in a corner. Silver tents had been set up absolutely everywhere. The girls were sharpening arrows, talking, laughing. Fires had been set up everywhere too. The smell of food wafted through the air.

"Wow, Artemis wasn't kidding," I muttered.

Two girls looked at me. One had deep skin, with a black plume of hair. She had a scar on her lip and deep eyes, pools of darkness, but they weren't brown; they were... purple. I did a double take; I had never seen purple eyes before.

The one she was with had her wavy black hair in a long ponytail. Her eyes were such a pale pink that they were almost creamy, and she had a tan complication.

"Um, hello," I waved awkwardly.

"Artemis showed herself to you?" The one with the scar on her lip asked me.

"Um, yeah," I said sheepishly. I was afraid that they would give me a judging look, thinking, 'Really, this freak?'.

The girls smiled, "Then you must be quite special," The one with the scared lip said. "I'm Zuri." She had an unplaceable accent.

"And I'm Elena," The one with milky eyes reached out a hand for me to shake, and I gripped her hand sheepishly, shaking twice.

"So... what exactly did Artemis tell you about our group? She told me she sent you all here to help us out," I asked.

"Well, she did send us. She told us that you all needed a bit of assistance getting to the underworld entrance," Zuri explained. "Perfectly alright, but you are still far from the entrance, and she has told us not to bring you too far."

"Why not?" I tried not to pout, but my voice came out a bit whiny.

"It is your quest to complete; you must do so as independently as you are able." Zuri didn't seem to notice the whining.

"So, are you hungry?" Elena asked, looking at my arm full of pears.

"Yes!"

She gestured for me to sit down with them and handed me a wooden plate. It had some sort of meat and an assortment of cooked vegetables. I shoveled food down my throat at the speed of light.

The girls giggled as they ate their own food.

"When was the last time you ate?" Elena asked.

"A while ago, but we've been doing a lot of activity," I slowed down my lightning-fast eating. "Those dragons weren't so easy to ride."

"So, you've just been riding on the river dragons for the entire morning? I would have expected you to be much further," Zuri replied.

"Well, not the entire morning. We spent a decent amount of it at what is basically a natural water park," I told them.

The girls looked at each other; Elena was about to respond when I heard an earth-shattering roar.

Chapter Twelve

The Universe Really Wants to Set Me on Fire

I recognized the sound as a dragon and shot up, my sword springing into my hand. My wrist still hurt from where that bunny/fairy/dog thing had bitten me, but I didn't dare try to fight left-handed again. Not against a sun dragon, whose babies could probably scare me just as much as the mother.

The first dragon we ran into on this mission was at least helpful, the second one only needed some cold water to beat it. But what about this one? Its skin burned things, if I tried to splash it the water would just evaporate. Could it breathe fire? Or was it worse? As the dragon stomped into the field, the grass around it burst into flames, I could see the heat ripping in the air, feel it warming my arms and legs.

It had the golden eyes and golden scales of a sun dragon. I could have run away until I got to the coast of the island. But with my depleted energy reserves, I settled for the other end of the large field, which was quickly becoming more of a fire pit than a field.

Clearly this was a popular choice, the hunters along with Annalyn, and Sam, had also booked it away from the dragon. The grass caught on my legs, making me stumble and trip. I shoved myself back to my feet and took off again, wishing I had the speed of some of the huntresses.

The dragon's cheeks puffed up; my eyes widened in horror.

"TAKE COVER!" Simone's loud voice was nothing like the roar that followed her cry, the heat that followed, was enough to tell me that the dragon could in fact breathe fire. that was a sound I could feel in my chest. The beat of the sound made my heart pick up its pace.

I didn't have time to look at where Simone or the dragon was; I just jumped into the river. The cold water hit me like a shock, and I landed in the shallow bank on my hands and knees, sinking into the dark mud. My hand made sucking sounds, and I pulled myself out and waded further in, jumping, and kicking to get myself further.

This stretch of the river was only ten feet across and probably wasn't the deepest, but I swam to the middle, made a bubble around my head, and kicked as far down as I could. I curled up and waited, waving my arms to keep from floating back up. After a few minutes, the air in my bubble was already stale, but I didn't go back up, I was too afraid of what I would find.

My powers were having none of this, and the bubble around my head popped. I was forced to go back up for air, and my fears were confirmed. The field was almost completely on fire. A bunch of huntresses had followed my lead and jumped into the river, so were trying to fire their arrows at the dragon while staying afloat, a bunch more were fighting on the grass that wasn't yet on fire, but that land was being eaten up quickly.

The dragon blasted white-hot fire at the people that were jumping and flying around its head, all trying to get a good enough strike to make it leave us all alone. The dragon was as tall as a two-story house, with long, sharp claws and teeth etched in blood, so I have no idea what made me stand up on the river surface (Vega's trick again) and scream: "OVER HERE!"

I added to that stupidity by focusing a stream of water right at its head and missing spectacularly. Instead, the water splashed onto the dragon's stomach. The huntresses stared at me like I had gone completely crazy, and I wasn't so sure they were wrong. Terror bloomed in my gut at the realization of what I'd just done.

The dragon roared and spread its wings. It launched into the air, its massive wings sending hot wind into my face. I got a peak of its underbelly to see it was oozing blood. There was a now flaming tree sticking out of it, and yes, I do mean a tree.

"KLOTHO STOP!" Simone screamed, appearing back in her regular human form. She tripped and nearly fell into a plume of fire

"What do I do?!" I shrieked as the dragon whimpered and growled at me for blasting its injury. Its cheeks puffed out, ready to blow flames.

"USE YOU HEALING POWERS!" She screamed, running away from the dragon before it had the chance to bake her.

I started singing 'Itsy Bitsy Spider' as loud as I could.

"The itsy-bitsy spider went up the water spout,"

The dragon paused. Glowing yellow music notes appeared and flickered around its injury. It set itself back down, leaving it about three steps away from turning into a shiny flamethrower and taking a few decades off my lifespan.

"Down came the rain and washed the spider out,"

It looked down at its stomach. The scales on its belly had healed. It looked around at the damage and flew away like a coward. Though I can't really be talking, I'm a coward myself.

"Up came the sun and dried up all the rain,
So the itsy bitsy spider went up the spit again,"

It looked around at the damage and flew away like a coward. Though I can't really be talking, I'm a coward myself.

"Seriously? No apology? It could have at least said thanks," Simone blurted.

"What?" I asked, the water underneath me loosening at the oddity of her statement. I wobbled for a second and pulled the water together more.

"It just looked around, thought about eating you, and left," Simone sounded even more offended than I was.

"Before you all continue to be annoyed at the dragon, the field is on fire and so is the campsite," A girl in the water gestured toward the field, which was in flames.

"Right, Klotho blast it with water, the whole field if you can. Anyone who has hydrokinetic or pyrokinetic abilities help to try to stop the fire. Everyone else, stay in the river," Simone turned into an elephant and sucked up water in her trunk. I started blasting the flames with river water wherever I could, though I missed a couple of times and ended up splashing myself instead. Several of the huntresses turned out to have pyrokinetic abilities and were trying to get the fire to cut it out. The rest of them just waited in the river.

By the time all the fires were out the field was completely destroyed. Our campsite was even worse, the cloth just kept burning in the hunter's tents, even though they were magically fireproof. They tried everything, and I mean everything, to put it out, until one of the pyrokinetic hunters passed out from the effort. That was when the fire decided to stop. Of course, just our luck.

The hunters left right after we managed to put the fire out.

"What do we do now?" I asked. Walking was always an option, but my head hurt, and I was sluggish.

"We need to keep moving," Simone answered confidently, though not providing a solution.

"We can't possibly walk all the way to the center of the island!" Sam argued.

"Come on, Sam, it's been done before and it'll be done again. Let's get going, we've been here for too long as it is," Simone sounded ready to sling him over her shoulder and carry him if there was a need.

"Shouldn't we try to figure out a ride in case our energy gets depleted too quickly?" Annalyn suggested, "It doesn't seem like that long of a journey until we have to consider fighting and finding food, we've been going five days now and we're only a third of the way there."

"Oh, fine, let's go find something to take us for a while," Simone relented.

We walked for a long time, discussing what we could use to take us down the river.

"Wait, can't you just turn us into birds, and we'll fly?" I asked.

"Flying is just as tiring as walking, and you're holding yourself off the ground by flapping your arms like an idiot," Simone retorted.

"You do it all the time." I pointed out.

"I have been doing it for years, you've only done it once," She deflected.

"We could make a boat," Annalyn suggested.

"We can try. Annalyn, come help me find some wood, Klotho, can you find something to tie them together?" Simone requested.

"Hey, what about me?" Sam asked.

"You stay here so we know where to come back to. If you get attacked by a monster, scream. No running away." Simone sauntered off into the trees with Annalyn trailing close behind.

"I'll just stay here then," He grumbled and plopped down on the dirt.

I waved goodbye and set off, walking around the forest, looking for some sort of vines or thin branches. The trees seemed endless, and if it weren't for the land markers I had been keeping in my mind, I would have definitely gotten lost.

I found a bunch of ivy growing on something. I couldn't tell what it was, but I started pulling the ivy stems, or vines, whatever they're called. They were thin, but maybe if we braided enough of them, they could work. I had already collected a bunch of very thin branches, but that wasn't enough.

As I pulled down the ivy more, the large stone structure it was concealing slowly revealed itself. It looked to be a boat of some kind, with a round shape and a pole with a shredded sail standing from the center. I dropped everything and ran back to Sam, finding Annalyn and Simone already back with an unfortunate lack of sticks.

"I found something!" I panted, "It looks like a boat!"

"Really?" Annalyn's eyes widened. "A boat on land?"

"Well, yeah, it probably wasn't on land when whoever left it dropped it there—whatever! The point is that we can just carry that to the river and sail to ask Hades about his helmet," Sam and Annalyn glanced at each other, shrugged, and then looked up at Simone.

"What I'm hearing is that we won't have to haul a bunch of sticks around just for them to fall apart, let's go steal this boat before someone else can," Simone grinned. "Lead the way."

I excitedly led them to my discovery, managing to not trip over a root and fall on my face. Unlike Annalyn, who managed to trip twice.

We got to the overgrown boat, and Sam checked its seaworthiness (or is it river-worthy?), he announced that it was alright and set up the four of us to lift it.

"Alright, everyone has a hold?" He called out.

"Yes," the three of us answered back.

"Up it goes," Sam grunted as we heaved the thing off the ground. The roots of the ivy and grass wrapped into it were pulled out of the ground, snapping and tangling. I stretched out the arm going under it so that I could get a better hold.

"Which way?" Annalyn managed, trembling with effort.

"The way Klotho led us here," Simone replied, trembling less, but her voice was taught like a pulled rope. "Off with us."

So, we walked and crashed Annalyn into a tree. ("Ow!" She yelled) and walked some more. I stumbled and caused some old board to snap off and crash into Sam's head. I heard Annalyn murmuring quietly to herself, maybe some kind of self-encouragement.

"Sorry!" I winced in sympathy. Sam murmured, 'It's fine' back, and we kept going. Under my arm, the dirt and ivy shifted with each step. I hooked my fingers into it for a better grip. I could have sworn it struggled a little when I did, but I was too focused on getting my legs to cooperate with the others and the massive weight of the boat to say anything.

Finally, after what felt like hours and a lot of sweat, we got to the river bank. I leaned against the boat, trying to make my breathing slow and give my raw throat a break.

"This thing better hold up," Simone kicked it, and Sam winced.

"Don't do that," he told her, "We don't know how old this thing is."

"Well, speaking of age, we should get all the ivy and stuff off it. It might catch on something and stop us." Annalyn gestured to the bottom of the boat and how we couldn't even see the wood underneath.

I, too tired to argue, started helping her strip the ivy off with my fingers. I shoved my hand in between the interlacing vines and pulled back. The ivy fell down like a blanket; the smooth leaves tickled my skin. I pulled my hand from the ship, noticing how it was trembling. Maybe that was from the muscle it took just to get the thing here. I shrugged to myself and shoved my fingers back to the ivy stems, but this time, when I pulled, the ivy pulled back.

I shrieked as it wrapped around my forearms, the cries of the others following soon after. I kicked myself away or tried to, but the ivy held on tight. My sword appeared in my hands, but before I could cut anything, the ivy swallowed it up. Little bits of bronze showed through the leaves, just out of reach.

Sam and Simone cursed at the ivy, kicking at the boat until their legs were stuck, too. Annalyn struggled silently, twisting her wrists to try and break the stems. The ivy shot out and yanked her closer, lacing her arms to the side of the boat like she was giving an aunt she hadn't seen in years an involuntary hug.

I whispered in fear as the vines crawled up. I kicked at them awkwardly, only to have the vines hook around my ankles.

"Horrid—little—sentient plant bastards!" Simone whacked at them with a pair of sheers that was stolen from her by the very upset ivy stems. A long arm-like protrusion grew out of the leaves and smacked her in the face, causing her to swear loudly.

"Let us go!" Sam crowed, "We'll leave you on the boat, just let us go!"

"Yes!" Annalyn tried to wiggle her arms out of the prison the ivy had turned itself into, only to have the ivy pull tighter against her.

It seemed that the ivy wasn't convinced because it didn't release any of us. It only kept fighting.

"Simone, turn into something!" Annalyn cried out.

"I can't! The ivy will hold on!" Simone turned invisible, leaving the ivy grasping at what looked like air, but quickly turned back when that yielded no results.

I reached for my sword, the ivy yanking me closer to it anyway. A stem shot out and wrapped around my waist. I reached out desperately and got a hold of the hilt, I pushed down, the sharp edge of the blade ripping through the stems. The vine around my waist pulled so tight I couldn't breathe; I yanked my hands to my stomach, trying to pull it off, and unwittingly severed the base of the vine on my way there. I gasped and ripped at the stem that was once around my waist. I stabbed further with my dagger, nearly cutting open Annalyn when I swiped the blade underneath her arm.

Sam's sword slid up next to me, out of his reach but inside mine. I reached into it and snatched it. I tore the blade of Sam's sword through the vines, holding my legs to the boat, shooting up and falling right back to my knees when I realized I had failed to free myself completely. My wrists were still very much attached to the boat.

The vines flew out at me, engulfing me in their cut-apart embrace. I raised both of my arms, swiping through a massive swath of the ivy and leaving it tied around my arms like wings. I kicked myself back, dirt flying up from the ground and one hand landing in a patch of mud. Without thinking, I grabbed a chunk of the mud and hurled it at the boat. It passed several tails of ivy to the ship, making the rest of the ivy go still with shock. My chest heaved up and down with my quick breaths; my heart thudded hard against my ribs.

Annalyn kicked the side of the boat, managing to pin a small section of the ivy down. Unfortunately, the ivy quickly pinned her leg against itself. It squeezed until her rich brown skin went pale, and Annalyn cried out in pain.

I grabbed another chunk of mud and threw it at the ship. This managed to splatter all over the back of Sam's head since my aim was garbage. With all my ideas spent and my mud-throwing skills clearly not up for the task, I charged at the boat with a nervous screech.

I hacked at the vines coming towards me with unpracticed jerkiness, and the fact that Sam's sword was a bit different in shape and size than mine didn't help me. My palms were wet with nervous sweat, and my knees shook and banged together. I bet I looked like a wrench with severed plant parts stuck all over me, like a bad craft project.

"Klotho, find the co—" The vines gagged Simone before she could continue. They wrapped around her face, leaves sprouting out and poking one of her eyes. She made a grunting noise of offense.

"The core! Of whatever spell this—" Sam swiftly met the same fate, though with a noticeably more gentle gag. Maybe the ivy was also upset about Simone's swearing.

I had no idea what the 'core' was, so I just kept hacking at the ivy wildly, hoping I'd hit it by accident. The ivy punched me in the stomach, and I hacked off the cage-like limb of green. It twitched at my feet, almost like an actual arm, and I shuddered.

"Please," I begged, "Let us go!"

The ivy didn't respond. I knew it must have heard me if it decided to shut up Sam and Simone, but it must have decided that listening to me wasn't worth it. Rude.

"Give me Sam's sword!" Annalyn yelled, stretching her fingers out. The ivy wrapped around her wrists squeezed hard, and she thrust her elbow out against it. She managed to snap some of the vines, reaching for me.

Without anything else to do, I threw the sword at her. Her fingers closed around it for just a second before the ivy ripped it away. An arm made of the pure stems of the ivy held the sword against me.

Before I could even think, the ivy arm stabbed out.

Chapter Thirteen

I Get to Beat Up Some Ivy

I screamed and thrust out my sword to meet its blow, the metal screeched. I jumped back but the arm stretched out and tried to take my head off. I dove to the ground, flattening myself against the dirt. I rolled to the side, throwing my weight into the blow only to be met with a hit to the face with another arm of ivy.

White hot pain raced through my nose. Spots stained my vision, I shut my eyes tight and threw out my sword blindly. I felt it go through the threats of stems connecting the ivy arm to itself. It fell to the ground, and I braced myself for another attack, but nothing came.

I opened my eyes to see that the ivy was retreating. It gently released Annalyn, threw Simone into a tree, and Sam got the pleasure of being smacked into the mud. The boat grew legs and bounded off into the forest without a glance back. At least, I don't think it glanced back, I don't know what that danged ivy saw with.

Annalyn pushed herself off the ground with shaking arms, marked with lines where the ivy had constricted her. Simone swung down from the branch of her tree and Sam just kind of laid there in the mud.

"All in favor of just flying until the sun sets?" Annalyn raised her hand, as did Sam, from the mud, and me, Simone raised her own hand in agreement and made Sam get the mud off himself in the river before turning us into magpies and taking off into the sky.

My flying was wobbly at first, and with a couple of screeched-out instructions from Annalyn and Simone, I was able to not nearly fall out of the sky every time I had to flap my wings. The wind shaped itself around me, catching my wings and letting me glide. The river snaked around on the ground beneath us.

We followed its path for hours. My arms, or now wings, already hurt but Simone was right, flying could be just as tiring as walking. I would probably be ripped after this quest.

Finally, the sun had lowered itself below the horizon, signaling us to land and rest. Traveling at night would have probably cut the time span of the journey in half, but on the island, the night was *dark*. There wasn't any light pollution or lamps or anything, only the light of the stars and the moon. The sky was beautiful at night, but we all still needed sleep.

We flew for a while until the sun sank well below the horizon, and it was getting too dark to see. Simone gilded downward slowly.

"Come on guys, we need to set up camp," Simone chirped, sounding out of breath, "I have some tarp in my bag, we can make a shelter."

We landed next to a truly massive tree. I could have hollowed it out and made a three-story house out of it. No, seriously, it was about twenty feet wide. The branches were as thick as regular trees, and the leaves were so thick it was like a swath of winter green spread over a hundred square feet. The tree was blanketed in pale lilac flowers with black centers that seemed to crawl from the middle of the flowers like shadows creeping across the ground.

"Why don't we make camp in that tree? I see a branch that would be perfect to sleep on." Annalyn suggested.

Simone looked at the tree, eying it suspiciously. "Where? I don't see any that would work."

"Here, I'll show you," Annalyn grabbed her by the waist, and the grass underneath them launched them up towards the branches of the tree. Annalyn showed her a branch that was shaped in a way that looked flat enough to set up camp on.

It was about nine feet wide and fifteen feet long. The branches coming off that limb added width; the branches above it would protect us from weather, and the tree limb was bent in a way that it would protect us from the wind.

It was pretty much perfect. Annalyn brought Simone back down. Honestly, I could have slept right there on the ground without complaint. I was exhausted, and I was really ready to just collapse.

"I say let's just get it over with as fast as we can so that we can go to sleep. I'm *exhausted*," Sam said.

"Uh-huh," I looked at Simone pleadingly, though I was sure that she would probably agree with Annalyn.

"Alright, I'll get us up there," Simone said. She turned us all into birds and we flew up to the branch that Annalyn was talking about.

Simone turned us back, and as we were setting up our tents, Sam blurted, "You turn us into birds a lot."

Simone thought for a second, "I guess I do."

"Why? Do you like that animal? Or?" Sam pressed.

Simone paused, contemplating his question. "I don't know."

Once we all had our bedrolls set up, we started a fire. The tree had edible mushrooms growing all over it, Simone cooked them with a fish that she and Annalyn had caught earlier.

We ate in silence and I could have sworn that the color of the flowers on the tree had changed. I started sweating with the fire so close and a pit of dread weighed down my stomach.

Oh, Klotho, you must really be tired to be seeing things. I told myself.

Simone pointed directly at me, "Klotho, you're on first watch. Sam, your second."

I groaned, "Do I have to?"

"Yes, I'm sorry, but at least you'll have the rest of the night to sleep instead of getting woken up for the second, third, or fourth watch," Simone told me.

I sighed, "Ok."

As the others lay in their bedrolls, I sat by the glow of the fire. As I sat, I could have sworn that the bark underneath my legs got rougher. I found myself changing positions more often to get comfortable.

While the fire started to die, the only thing I could think about was the Ivy. Why did it attack us like that? Ivy wasn't known to be aggressive, so I guess this must have been some magical variety. But that didn't explain its presence on the boat.

I spaced out and was just staring into the distance. By the time I snapped back to reality, the only light was a thick crescent moon, and the only sounds were the sounds of the forest and the breathing of the others as they slept.

I couldn't see anything. I've never been super scared of the dark, but I definitely don't like it. I wished I had some light and, as I curled up, sitting with my knees to my chest, warmth.

I wish I could start a fire, I thought. But I couldn't leave the tree; I wouldn't be able to find my way back. It was too dark.

I sighed and lay on my back, staring at the stars.

This is so boring. My mind groaned. I started counting the stars to pass the time like an idiot. Why like an idiot? Well, you know the old trick with falling asleep is to count sheep? Yeah, it turns out that works on stars, too, and before I knew it, I was asleep.

I was in the sky again. The same air nymph was in front of me, something felt odd. It was day time, but I felt like the cloud I was sitting on was tilting, and tilting.

"Klotho, wake up. You are all going to die unless you *wake up.*" The nymph looked perfectly calm and stoic. Her voice seemed to double in volume when she told me to wake up. I couldn't understand what she was talking about. I was out of the tunnel; I was safe now.

The cloud kept tilting, and tilting until I fell off as the sky nymph just kept repeating that I needed to wake up.

The sky opened up underneath me, a crack of darkness filled with stars. I fell and fell, screaming and screaming until—

I shot up from my back. Panting. My stomach felt like I had left it back in that dream. The branch of the tree that we were all on was tilting, moving to the trunk of the enormous tree.

I screamed, "WAKE UP! WAKE UP! WAKE UP!" As loud as I could at all the others. Simone shot up first, her hair flew directly into my face as I clambered up to avoid the tree. She turned her ring into a lantern. The tree's bark had gone from dull oak to deep chocolate, the roughness gave me foot and handholds to climb.

Simone swore and smacked Sam's face to wake him up.

"EVERYBODY OFF!" She yelled. She grabbed my arm, turned the lantern back into her ring, grabbed Sam, and jumped out of the tree. She turned us into bats mid-fall, and a fourth bat followed behind us, Annalyn. I hadn't noticed her on the tree since I was a bit too busy freaking out about the fact that IT WAS MOVING.

We landed in, according to my new echolocation, a ruin with no ceiling but a few pillars remaining. Simone turned us back and turned her ring into a lantern. She set it down, the warm glow calmed me.

"What was that?" I whimpered, terrified. This island's plants were a lot more dangerous than I thought. Probably more than some monsters. That tree was trying to kill us, just like the ivy.

"That was a changing tree. They can change form to whatever's most convenient for them; they get a lot of their energy by absorbing the living things that land on them or try to sleep on them," Simone explained.

"Is there any way to tell them apart from regular trees?" Sam asked. Clearly, he was ready to call Simone an idiot for not seeing it if she already knew what it was.

"No, they can grow really large, but so can plenty of other trees on the island; the only people that have ever been able to successfully recognize one are people with plant powers, and even that's rare," Simone told him.

"Well, of course, we just happened to try and sleep in one!" Sam pouted.

"Yeah, that's just our luck, I guess," I sighed. *Why do we always get into trouble?*

"Can we just crash here? I'm exhausted," I practically begged. I had only gotten maybe a half hour of sleep from what I could tell.

"Yeah, Klotho, go to sleep first, I'll watch out for the rest of the night," Simone sighed. I didn't even thank her. I just got into my bedroll and drifted off.

When I woke up, the sun hadn't quite risen yet. It was light enough to see.

Simone leaned against one of the pillars, with her mind clearly elsewhere. I sat up, walked over to her, and snapped my fingers under her chin. She jolted and stared at me for a second, trying to process who I was.

"So how exactly is this going to work when we get to the underworld?" I asked, sitting down next to her.

"Well, I have this notebook," Simone pulled out a spiral bound notebook. On the cover there were all different shades of blue and black flowers with little swirling gold patterns behind them on a deep, cold gray background. The spirals were gold, though probably not real.

"You have a notebook?" I asked.

"I mostly use it for drawing, but I figured it wouldn't hurt to use it to write down what Hades says," Simone explained, "Back to your question, the plan after that is to use the exit room to get back to camp, it's powered by an underworld nymph, we tell her where we want to go, she tells us what we need to do to get her to send us to the next nymph, she kicks us off, etcetera etcetera until we're back at camp."

This made me nervous; so many steps, and she said we would have to go through some sort of test. What if the nymphs were like that other nymph? What if they tried to kill us just for their own entertainment?

"Is there any other way to get out of the underworld?" I asked quietly so that I didn't wake the others.

"Not that I know of," she said. "Don't worry, the Nymphs are pretty kind from what I remember."

"From what you remember?" I asked. I knew she had been to the underworld before, but I would have expected her to know more about the route. Maybe if we'd followed her route when she went, we wouldn't have run into the changing tree or the awful Naiad. Simone did mention avoiding that section of the river.

"It was all a blur, I barely had enough energy to think, so the only thing I can really remember are some of the tasks that they gave me and which nymphs they were," Simone explained.

"Who were they? Also, there are underworld nymphs?" I asked.

"Yup, there are underworld nymphs; they're called the Lampades, the one that greets us in the underworld is named Georgia. She's married to Acheron. I don't exactly remember what the task she gave me was, but I think that she took a while to appear. The second nymph was an Aura; her name was Strata, and her task for me was to find a way to bottle a cloud without ever going up to the sky."

"But that's impossible, why would she give you an impossible task if it's her job to get you back to camp?" I interrupted.

"It's not impossible; clouds are made of water, so I went to the nearest stream and took some water," Simone said, grinning at her own cleverness.

"And she accepted that?" It seemed too easy somehow like the Aura would laugh and tell Simone, 'Nice try.' Maybe that would happen with us, that we try to get something for a nymph using cleverness, and the nymph won't accept.

"Yup, the third that I met was a dryad, her name was Willow, her task was for me to find a way to burn her branches without damaging the tree at all," Simone slid down the pillar, and I sat down across from her. She tapped her foot against the marble, the short bronze heel of her shoe clacked against it.

"Oh, that's an easy one, you'd just have to break it off," with Simone's changing ring, that seemed like a task that could be done in a matter of minutes.

"That would damage the tree. Also, the only thing she gave me to start the fire was a broken piece of glass to accomplish the entire task. I had to find a dried, dead branch, which happened to be really thick because the universe hates me, and cut through that with the broken glass, then I had to actually get it to burn with the glass shard. It took me a *while* to get it done."

"How many nymphs did you have to deal with?" I asked, my eyebrows furrowing.

"Four, the last one was a Naiad; her name was River, and her task for me was to find a way up the river without a boat and without getting on land. She basically just made me go up the half-mile left of the journey back to camp myself," Simone told me casually.

"And you did it? Just swam upriver for half a mile like it was nothing?" Good and awful gods, I had water powers, and that sounded like a plea for death.

"Well, yeah, I can turn into a swimming animal, you know. I just took the form of a salmon and swore if I ran into any bears, I would make Hades wish he didn't run the underworld." She picked a piece of dirt from under her nails.

Chapter Fourteen

I Get The Crap Beaten Out of Me by a Glorified Piece Of Paper

I swallowed hard, these tasks could end up being a problem.

"So, we either do a bunch of tasks that could potentially kill us, or what?" I asked, hoping that there was another option.

"Or we'll take thrice as long-suffering our way back up to camp, the tasks are the fastest and the least likely to get us to die."

"Least likely? The last one was basically just, 'Go up the river without getting on land, don't die. Good freaking luck. If we have to do one of those, I think I've got us covered, but still. It's scary."

"We should get going, I think we're close," Simone informed me, "We need to find the river to follow or a landmark that shows us where exactly on the island we are." She stood up, "ALRIGHT, EVERYBODY UP." Her voice was projected to a volume that made it sound like she was speaking through a microphone.

Sam groaned, he mumbled something about not getting enough sleep, and then got up, rubbing his eyes.

"Ok guys, we really need to hurry up. We don't have forever and we have been out here for way too long, besides, Hades is starting to get antsy," Simone said.

"How do you know?" Annalyn asked, her voice a bit annoyed as if she was really saying, 'Can this girl quit acting like she knows what everyone is thinking?' Instead of her actual question.

"He contacted me through my dreams, he says that the longer we take the harder it will be to find his helmet," She answered, seeming to not notice Annalyn's tone.

"I feel bad for him. If someone broke into my house and stole my stuff, I'd be anxious too," I commented. Though I truly believed this, Hades was a terrifying figure as the lord of the dead. I was afraid that when we came down, he would decide to just keep us there. After all, I was aware that what goes into the underworld should stay in the underworld.

Simone had all of us be quiet and listen to the sound of the river rushing.

"Does anyone hear anything? I'm getting bored," Sam asked.

I strained my ears; all I heard was the rustling of leaves and an oddly sharper rustle. Like something was running through the trees.

Wait, something running through the trees. Knowing this island, that couldn't be good.

"I heard something," I whispered, though I didn't need to.

"Really? Where?" Simone asked, turning in a slow circle, pretending to examine the structure around us.

"In the trees, it sounded like something running," I informed her.

Simone's face went from hopeful to anxious. Her lips pressed together and seemed to strain her ears to try and hear what I'd heard. I heard the noise again, her eyes widened in a that-is-definitely-not-a-good-sign look.

"Do we need to be quieter?" I murmured.

Simone shook her head, "My rule with monsters is, if you can hear it, it can hear you. We should just keep going, but get your weapons out and ready."

"That sounds like the best we can do," Annalyn relented. She walked in front of us and started leading the way. As we walked, the nervousness in my stomach just kept building like air in a balloon.

The forest around me was bustling with life, chirping birds, crickets, and rustling leaves. Sam walked next to me; he was quiet. Without anything else to do, I searched my own memories for entertainment and snickered when I came upon a good one.

"What?" Sam asked, grinning his impish grin.

"Oh, there was a time that Mrs. E chucked a lizard across the classroom," I giggled.

Simone joined the conversation, "Sorry, she what?"

"Yeah, in second grade someone brought a lizard into class in their backpack. It got out and I guess it jumped up on her desk, so she screamed and threw it across the classroom," I explained through laughs.

"That lizard really said I believe I can fly, huh?" Simone commented.

"Oh, but it gets better, it flew out the open window and landed on the windshield of a truck," I continued.

Simone snorted, "Imagine the driver though, 'aww dammit! Stupid lizard flying from an elementary school window! I'm late!"

I laughed so hard I wasn't even making noise. I probably just looked like I was in pain, but Sam was laughing too so I figured that it was probably fine.

"And the other drivers, 'stupid traumatized kids! Ruining the ambiance of the ride!'" Simone added.

I had to lean against a tree for support. When I was finally able to get the laughing under control, I wiped my eyes from laughing so hard and was able to keep going.

"Oh, there was a time at Nikephoros Academy, when someone got tangled in the safety net in the Flameheart dwelling area," Simone recounted.

"What?" I was confused, but I still giggled at the thought.

"Well, in all of the dwelling rooms, there are, like, play areas I guess you would call them. Fleamheart's is a rock wall with a safety net, and some kid got tangled in it." I wheezed at how normal she made it sound. Like this happened every other Friday or something.

The trees started to clear and I was soon walking on a dirt path. Small wooden houses with straw roofs lined the road, they were shabbily made, but pretty sturdy looking. There was one that was bigger than all the others in the middle.

My stomach churned, the last time I was in anything that even remotely resembled this we got kidnapped and attacked. I heard a whooshing sound and everything went black.

I was in a box. It was dark all around me, until the walls of the box lit on fire and it started closing in while filling with water. I screamed as loud as I could. I couldn't escape no matter how hard I pushed on the sides of the wall.

Then I was in liquid, maybe water. It was cool, no cold, no *freezing*. It was so cold my skin hurt. I curled up and shivered but everything around me was so cold. My lungs burned as I tried to breathe. The liquid, which I now knew was definitely not water, filled my throat, burning me with cold. It felt like my insides were freezing. I gagged and nearly threw up, but I couldn't get the cold out of my system. I sank, completely paralyzed and in so much pain. I hit a wall, I didn't even register what it felt like, I just hit it as hard as I could. It broke the wall and all of the liquid disappeared.

I was now in a white room. It started to fill with smoke, it smelled like burning sugar. The sickly scent clogged my nostrils, and blisters started to form on my skin. I coughed and gagged as the room filled with gas, I collapsed as soon as my lungs started to burn.

Then there was a glass box around me. A cloud floated beside me. I was so high up; I could hardly see the ground. It was all just a blur of green and brown. I nearly had a heart attack; I was terrified of heights. I fell over and onto my butt hard. Too hard. The glass shattered and I fell screaming from the sky.

The wind whipped my face and my hair flew up behind me. I was falling feet first so my shirt almost flew right off. I flipped in the air and my eyes watered with fear. I would become a grease spot on the ground wherever I was falling. I would have to get scraped off the ground.

As the ground got closer and closer, a rift opened in the earth. I kept falling into that dark rift. It was starting to look like I would just fall forever when I landed. I was in a dark cave. It was just rocks, all around me. I heard the buzzing of thousands of wings and I was swarmed by mosquitos. I screamed as they started to suck my blood, swatting at them. It seemed that every time I got one off ten more would take its place. I was getting sucked dry and the itchiness was unbearable.

Then, as soon as the nightmare started it was over. I was on the ground, my face in the dirt. I lay there, trying to process what just happened.

"Simone? Annalyn?" Someone said.

I stood up, there was a girl in front of me. She had round, garnet red eyes and chin-length poofy hair, parted on the side. It was dusty brown and curly. Her nose was long and pointy. Her pale skin was *covered* in freckles. She was wearing a wrinkled and ripped sage green t-shirt, dark gray jean shorts, and sneakers that looked like they had been through a bladed ringer and several dust baths. I couldn't even tell what color they were supposed to be. Her arms were outstretched towards us as if she had just been using some of her powers on us.

There was a girl next to her, she had long, straight black hair, parted in the middle with curtain bangs. She had deeply tanned skin, and onyx black monolid eyes that seemed to sparkle with stars. Her face was thin and V-shaped. She wore a tight navy-blue t-shirt, black shorts with white drawstrings, and gray sneakers that weren't nearly as covered in mud as the other girl's but still pretty dirty.

"Who are you two?" I asked, confused.

Simone stood up, "Fiona?" She looked at the girl with black hair, "Ji-Min? What are you two doing here?" She looked almost as confused as I was.

"We came back. We're trying to find our way to camp and we've been hanging out here for a while," The one with black hair, Ji-Min, said. Her voice was slightly jumpy like she was always nervous. But it was also soothing and quiet.

"You guys... came back?" Simone asked. I looked at Annalyn for answers,

"That's one girl that was bullied out of camp," Annalyn whispered pointing at Ji-Min. "And she left for a few years, I don't know why," She pointed at Fiona. My heart sank, no wonder she sounded jumpy.

"Yeah," Fiona said. "I thought we'd give it another shot."

"That's great, I hope it goes better for you guys, how old are you two now?" Simone asked.

"Well, I'm fifteen, and so is Fiona," Ji-Min said, they both seemed to finally notice me.

"Oh, you're new. We used to be campers here, as you know, I'm Fiona, and Ji-Min is my friend," Fiona said.

"That's nice, I'm Klotho, I haven't been here for very long," I told them shyly.

"Nice to meet you." Fiona thrust her hand outward for me to shake. She strangled my hand in her vice-like grip and shook it so hard my arm hurt.

"What are your powers?" She asked. I stared at her for a second. Her freckled cheeks grew red, "Oh sorry! I didn't mean to be rude—I was just curious." She said quickly.

"Oh no, I'm just not used to people asking me yet, I guess. I can control wind and liquids, and I can heal people by singing. Quite the Disney princess power." I listed off, trying for a bit of humor.

"I think it's cool." Ji-Min quietly assured me. They led us to the larger building in the middle. Fiona said that they had a map that they could lend us. However, Simone seemed reluctant to take it.

"We really shouldn't take it; we can just use the river as our map. And you guys need it more anyway," Simone told them.

"We have another one, and we've been meaning to get rid of this, but we figured we would keep it anyway, really take it," Fiona thrust the large rectangular map into Simone's hands. Simone unfolded it and there was a dot on a drawing of the island. There was a compass rose in the right bottom corner and a little map of camp on the northwestern corner of the island. There were a bunch of various temples drawn everywhere. There was even a little drawing of Nikephros Academy. A drawing of Olympus dotted the furthest north piece of the island. Judging by the key, it looked to be a few miles north of the farthest edge of the Nikephros Academy grounds, I hadn't realized that it was north of the camp. There were also a bunch of landmarks that were marked on the island.

The underworld entrance was the *dead* center (hehe, get it?) on the island. There was a glowing blue dot, seemingly where we were. It was only about a fourth of the way to the center of the island. I groaned internally, why did this mission have to feel so long?

"Oh, you need to transfer ownership," Simone said, pointing at the initials on the dot. I hadn't noticed them before.

"Right," Ji-Min took the map, and on the back, there was her name in curly print. Ji-Min Moon. "I need an eraser and a pen,"

Simone handed her both and Ji Min wrote, erased her name and handed the map to Simone. Simone Morena Horova. Simone printed neatly.

Underneath a spot that said, 'Destination', she wrote, 'Underworld'.

"Your last name is Horova?" I asked, "Is that Russian?"

She sighed in frustration, "No, it's Slovakian, I am not Russian, it means mountains or something like that."

"You have a middle name?" Sam looked at the map.

"Yes, let's go," Simone said.

We said goodbye and Simone handed Annalyn the map because she knew how to read it the best. The problem was that Annalyn walked slower than usual when she was looking at the map, and she wouldn't speed up because she didn't want to crash into anything.

We walked east, the dot that showed where we were was only a little bit west of the river, and from there we could follow it directly to the underworld entrance.

I heard rushing water and excitedly we all sped up and broke through the tree line. There was a large fallen tree on the bank.

"Alright, Klotho, go to that end, Annalyn, can you use your plant powers to get that log into the river? We can use it as a boat," Simone assigned. Annalyn and I did as she asked, though the log was really heavy. I was about to get in the front, but Simone stopped me. "You'll be our rudder; you should sit in the back so that it's easier."

I obliged, but I wasn't all too happy about it. Simone handed me the map and got on right in front of me. The river current pushed us forward and I held onto the trunk of the tree with the map face down on the log. I was too scared to fall off to let go with even one hand.

We came to a fork in the river, I turned the log onto the path that I guessed was correct. The map shook out of my grip. I thought it was going to blow away in the wind and gripped tighter. The map wiggled its way out of my hand and floated next to me, it rolled itself up and started smacking me in the head.

I yelped and let go of the log to try and see it away, but that piece of paper was more stubborn than most of my classmates. It hit my head so hard that it knocked me right off of the log. Simone yelled out in alarm. She grabbed my arm and yanked me up as best she could. I was able to get back onto the log, but the map kept smacking me.

"Klotho, turn us back down the other part of the river! The map is trying to tell you that we went the wrong way!" Simone told me, snatching the rolled-up map out of the air as it shook. I did as she told me as quickly as I could, my temples throbbing with effort, to avoid the wrath of that surprisingly spirited old map.

We floated down the river until it got too rocky to keep going on the log. I had the current push us ashore and we decided to walk until we found something to eat. Whenever we tried to get through the tree line, the map would beat us back. We were forced to walk in a single-file line right on the edge of the river.

I saw a brightly colored fish jump out of the water. Simone wasted no time, turning into a bird to catch it. We fought the map, yes, you did read that right, I fought a map, to get to a spot in the trees. Simone grabbed hold of the map and shoved it into her bag, closing it as the map shook violently.

"We aren't pieces of parchment, we need to eat you know," Simone muttered to the map.

I am never going to get over being bossed around by an old piece of paper. I thought to myself as Simone cooked the fish over a fire that Sam made. We didn't have anything else to eat it with, but it tasted really good. We had eaten fish for petty mush every meal of the entire mission, but I hadn't gotten sick of it quite yet.

As we ate, the map managed to get itself out of Simone's bag and hit her so hard she yelped in pain. It flew over to me and smacked me too. When it gave all of us the same treatment, I heard a shriek, like a chicken.

A woman who looked half chicken flew into view and I screamed, realizing what the map was trying to tell me. The chicken lady, a harpy, flew after Annalyn. Simone jumped at it, dagger in hand and stabbed it. I pulled Sam, who was sitting, frozen, off of the ground and the map beat us back to the river bank.

Fear bloomed deep in my gut, accompanied by that familiar sensation of my heart pounding in my ears. The current roared behind me while that chunk of palaver smacked me in the nose.

I heard a scream; I didn't know whether it was Simone or the harpy. Surprisingly, Sam tried to get past it. Annalyn stayed back. The map hit his face several times. He kept fighting until it unrolled to attack him with papercuts.

"Someone needs to go help her!" Annalyn yelled.

"Why can't you do it?" Sam retorted, rubbing his cheek where the map had cut him.

"I'm not fighting that map. I mean, look what it did to you," She replied, shifting on the balls of her feet anxiously.

"I can try," I crouched and ran around a tree to get past the map, but it was smart enough to see (can it even, see?) me coming. I engaged in battle with what was probably the most tenacious map known to man, woman, toddler, or beluga whale.

The map hit my stomach, the paper bending on impact. I smacked it back with my palm and tried to step forward. It flew right at me and hit me on the top of my head. I ducked underneath but it hit my chest and pain spiked the area. The map was unrolled and wrapped around my head to blind me. I was able to pull it off without ripping it, but I got dangerously close.

The map rolled itself up as tight as it could, wound up, (which looked very odd since it was just floating and didn't really need to wind up), and started battering me right in the face.

I grabbed the rolled-up map, threw it aside as hard as I could, and ran into the trees. Simone was tussling with the harpy, which had been stabbed several times but she was still going strong. Simone was scratched up and bruised, she turned into a bird to slip out of the harpy's grasp.

I ran to help her, swinging my sword at the harpy. But my arm was intercepted by the map. It hit me in the stomach so hard that I fell back, which was a surprisingly good thing since the way I swung, my sword was on track to decapitate Simone.

Simone got behind the harpy and stabbed her in the back of the neck. The harpy choked, blood slipping through her opened skin. After a few seconds, she fell, dead. Her crimson blood tainted the grass.

The map continued to swat me like I was a fly. I covered my face and rolled onto my side, curling up to keep it from hitting me in the stomach again.

Seriously, what did I do for this thing to hate me so much? I wondered. The map stopped suddenly. I opened my eyes,

Simone had grabbed the map, "This thing is really getting on my nerves."

Chapter Fifteen

Turns out Blue-Leaf Field Has a Much Darker Meaning

"**Is** it going to keep attacking us if we go the wrong way?" I asked. Simone had done some sort of spell on it; I think she de-cursed it or something.

"Now it'll just shake and roll up to point to where you're supposed to go," Simone told all of us as we made our way down the river bank. "I think that the spell was probably done as a prank and no one bothered to fix it."

"Well, it's a good thing that you got it back to normal, stupid thing almost busted my lip," Sam said, his bottom lip was purple and swollen.

"Yeah, why did it do that?" Simone asked, "I thought it only attacked when someone tried to get past it."

"He did," I blurted.

"What?" Simone turned around on her face with a look of shock with a hint of skepticism. She walked up and examined him, poking at his bruises. "I'm surprised you're still alive, Sam. That chunk of paper has a lot of anger."

Annalyn snorted with laughter.

After a long time walking on the bank of the river, Simone took over map duty because we were making the progress of a snail at the pace Annalyn had us on. No shade to her, just that we needed to go faster than that if we wanted to actually get anywhere.

The trees cleared suddenly. Usually, I couldn't see super far forward because of the trees and bushes of the forest, but now I could see how the river sliced through a rolling carpet of warm and cool greens, some spots looking almost blue. It babbled quietly as it flowed. But the field wasn't all grass. There were shamrocks too, hundreds of thousands.

It was a pretty large stretch of field; I couldn't really see where the trees started again. It seemed that all plants other than grass and some flowers had collectively decided to not grow in this particular area.

"What's this place called?" I asked,

"Blue-leaf field," Simone answered, staring intently at the map. It was a pretty fitting name, considering that the leaves were all a very cool shade of green, some of them light and frosty, some of them deeper.

"Fitting name," Sam pointed out, gesturing to a forget-me-not at his feet.

"Yeah, I guess it is," Simone agreed. "It'll take us a while to get through it, it's 3 miles across."

"We'd better get going then," Annalyn sighed. As we walked the shamrocks always seemed to be covered in morning dew, even though it was now afternoon. My shoes got soaked in it, and the grass had turned my previously dirty and mud-stained white shoes, to grass-stain-green.

We walked over the rolling hills for so long I was starting to wonder if this dang field would ever end. We would stop for ten minute breaks every hour to drink water, and rest our legs and our shoes. Seriously though, even in the first six days of this mission, my shoes had gone through it. They were still in one piece but I felt like I could run a few paces and they would just give up on me.

We stopped a few times because Annalyn kept getting rocks in her shoes.

By the tenth time, she said, 'Give me a second, I have a rock in my shoe,' I could tell that the others were getting frustrated with her too.

Seriously? Why does this girl keep getting rocks in her shoe, when I haven't gotten any? I wondered.

It seemed that every ten or twenty minutes she would have to get a new rock out of her shoe. The rocks seemed to be really small since she usually got them out without even taking her shoe off, but it took her five minutes each time.

Sam was grumbling incoherently when she had to stop for the *seventeenth time*. And Simone was visibly aggravated, but she kept her mouth shut anyway.

Once she was finally done, the sun was setting. According to the map, we had walked about 5. Good, considering we had only been there for two hours.

We had lost our tents but Simone had an entire tarp in that bag she always carried. I was seriously starting to wonder how much she could fit in the thing.

"So, we just lay the tarp over ourselves?" I asked. It didn't sound comfortable since the tarp was just that, a tarp.

"Yes Klotho, just lay this giant black tarp over yourself and three other people, like you're at a sleepover. No, I can turn my ring into a frame for it." Simone said, flashing her silver ring.

"Why didn't you do that all of the other times that we got stuck without tents?" Sam questioned.

"We had some form of shelter all of those times, I didn't need to," She shrugged.

"Well, it would have sure been helpful, wouldn't it?" Sam crossed his arms. I sat down next to Annalyn to watch the argument unfold.

"Oh, so if we get attacked at night what do you expect me to do? Turn into a fire dragon, torch the monster and light up the whole forest? Or an ice dragon and freeze everything within fifteen feet?" Simone asked sarcastically.

Sam grumbled something about a waste of powers, as Simone stabbed the wooden frame into the ground. It was a six by seven-foot box and Simone tied the tarp over it so that the two longer sides were left open and it was about three feet tall.

"This should be good." Simone tied the last part of the tarp onto the frame. She tried to shake it but thankfully she had shoved it into the ground hard enough for it to not move. She smiled with satisfaction and sent Sam to get dried grass by the river for kindling and Annalyn to go find or grow some mushrooms or fruit.

Annalyn came back with Galaxy Buds. She said that she couldn't find any mushrooms and that it was the only plant that would grow in the soil around the field.

Odd, I thought. I knew about different limitations when it came to growing things, but I had never heard of something like that happening. I didn't care much though. We didn't need the fire for cooking much so we just huddled around it, stuffing our faces with galaxy buds and shamrocks, which Simone told us were edible. Sam didn't take any, I guess it was too weird for him.

I lay under the tarp tied over their wooden frame that night and felt a sense of dread. I couldn't place my finger on it but I just felt like something was a bit wrong. I ignored it, even though that hadn't ended very well for me in the past. I figured it was just the sound of people breathing next to me and I fell asleep.

I was shrouded in a calm darkness, it kept getting tighter, especially around my chest, but it wasn't painful, just a little uncomfortable. I heard whispering around me, disembodied voices coming from the endless darkness, until...

It wasn't dark anymore. I was in a pine forest, except, everything had a sort of blue cast over it. It was silent except for the sound of crickets. I heard a rustling in a wild blueberry bush in front of me. For some reason, I walked over and pulled back the bush. A twitching demonic fairy bunny lay on its side. Its jaw had been extended and so had its legs, the way that they had when one attacked me.

It looked sick, or hurt, whatever I felt bad for it but I was too scared to touch it. What if it was faking? What if it would attack me if I got any closer?

"Go on, help the little thing." A deep voice said it seemed to be coming from all around me. *"Don't you want to help it? Go on, get closer, it needs your help."* It continued.

I wanted to, I wanted to so badly, but I sensed that this voice did not want anything good.

Besides, I was too scared to help it, even without the voice telling me to anyway.

"Why won't you go help it? It'll be too late soon; YOU NEED TO HELP IT NOW." It said insistently. The voice sounded almost doubled now. As if two or three people were speaking at once.

"It'll hurt me!" I retorted stupidly.

"You selfish girl, you won't risk injury to help a poor creature in need. Shame on your family." I was getting shamed by something that, for all I know, wanted the absolute worst for me. But I felt awful. The creature looked like it was in so much pain. I wanted to lean down to try and use my powers to heal it, but I was too scared, the tightness in my chest had risen since the forest appeared. It was painful now.

The voice seemed to be reading my mind.

"Go on, help it, go on." As I was about to kneel down, I was shaken awake by Simone. The tarp was gone, and so was the frame. Simone's ring was back on her finger.

For a second, I thought that it was morning, but the sky was dark, the only light was the glow of the hundreds of shamrocks. My mouth hung open. A blue fog seemed to have settled over the fields, but it smelled like leaves and smoke, and it was thick.

Air was coming into my nose but I felt like I was being suffocated.

"Klotho, we need to—" Simone coughed like a dying horse, "go, this isn't normal." She coughed again. Annalyn was trying to stop whatever the plants were doing, but she had no luck.

"We can't possibly get out of the field in time!" I fretted.

"No, we can't. I can't get us into the air on my—" She coughed so hard it sounded like it hurt, I coughed too, "—own, you'll need to help me." She finished.

"I can try," I said, coughing right afterward because of the fog. Simone ran into the field and turned into a pale blue dragon. It was big, big enough for Sam, Annalyn, and I to get on. Thankfully they took the hint without needing any orders. As the dragon Simone had turned into, flapped her wings and caught air I had the wind push us all up, though I don't know how much it actually helped.

We stayed there for a long time. How long? It must have been at least thirty minutes. As the sun rose over the horizon, the shamrocks stopped glowing, and the fog vanished. Simone landed and turned back, getting crushed underneath us. She yelped and wheezed when we got off.

She lay face down on the ground.

"What happened?" I asked.

"I think that these are some magical versions of a shamrock, at night when they cool down, they secrete a blue fog that makes it hard to breathe. It's not called blue-leaf-field because the shamrocks look blue, it's because sleeping in it will turn you blue since you'll essentially suffocate to death," Annalyn put together.

"But that's only supposed to happen in fall and winter," Simone grumbled.

I swallowed hard. *Of course, we ended up in a deadly field, and we won't be able to get out until at least a few hours from now.*

Simone stood back up, clearly winded. It must have been hard to carry three people on your back while you can barely breathe, even if you do get help. My head throbbed from the power use, but noticeably less than when I'd first tried to use the wind.

"We need to get out of here as fast as we can, we got lucky once but I'm not sure we'll get lucky a second time." Simone stood back up.

I nodded. Ten minutes into walking I stepped straight into a hole, my leg fell in, my leg sunk into the hole all the way to my thigh and I shrieked in surprise before my foot hit something at the bottom. It wasn't more dirt, and it felt... fluffy. Soft too.

"Klotho, you good?" Simone turned around from being so far in front of me. I heard a growl and something clamped its sharp teeth around my foot.

I screamed in terror and tried to yank my leg out but I was only able to get a few inches out before I was dragged back down. It felt like my foot was being ripped off. Pain ripped through my ankle and blood roared in my ears.

Simone and Annalyn grabbed me under the arms and pulled me up. Sam had his sword out and was waiting to kill the thing that bit me. The thing pulled down again and I tried to use my other leg to push myself up. I felt the teeth of the monster digging into my skin and my eyes filled with tears and I yelped and kicked. I felt like I was being pulled apart, with the monster in the hole pulling me down and Simone and Annalyn pulling me up.

I bent my free leg and pushed up as hard as I could, ripping my leg out of the hole and causing a flashing pain in my ankle. I looked down at my foot and saw the demonic fairy bunny with its extended jaw clamped around my ankle. Blood covered my shoe and I shrieked, kicking the monster as many times as I could. It jumped off and growled at me, its long ears stood straight up.

I turned my ring into my sword and stepped back, limping on my injured leg.

The thing raised its horrifyingly stretched jaw and opened its mouth, showing at least thirty teeth covered in my bright blood. It made a noise like a growling squeak, and hundreds more of its kind emerged from burrows in the ground all around the field.

"What are those things?" My voice shook with the question.

"Those are trick bunnies, they bend their legs and retract their jaws to look like cute little bunnies to attract their prey, and then they reveal their true form," Simone whispered, standing still as a statue.

Nothing in the field moved for what seemed like hours and then every single trick-bunny in the field lunged towards us.

CHAPTER SIXTEEN

RETURN OF THE DEMONIC FAIRY-BUNNIES

I slashed at the one closest to me as my heart beat rapidly. I slashed the one that had bet me across the leg, I blocked another from jumping onto me. Three lunged at me all at once and I swung my sword across their necks. Bright red blood sprayed over my shirt and shoes.

"We can't fight them all!" Sam yelled as he backed up, bumping into me as I threw away one of the trick bunnies. The claws of another dug into my leg and I yelped in pain. I kicked the creature away the best that I could.

"We might not have to! Get close!" Simone called out, moving with Annoying towards Sam and me. She turned into a massive ice dragon, and I do mean massive, at least 25 feet long, and roared. The screeching, low noise

The trick bunnies froze and looked up at Simone's new dragon-ny makeover. She breathed in, and I hit the deck with Sam and Annalyn. I felt an ice-cold blast of air over my head and the high-pitched wails of the trick bunnies. I heard their feet sliding Ariadne in the grass in an attempt to get away, but they had no such luck.

When I looked back up from the grass, half of the trick bunnies were frozen solid. Ice clung to their fur, and their eyes were stuck in their sockets, staring at Simone. The remaining horde of trick bunnies ran at her, I shot up with Sam and engaged in battle with the furry creatures. Annalyn grew out the shamrocks and started strangling the trick bunnies like a morbid St. Patrick's Day celebration.

I swung my sword, two-handed since my hands were shaking too hard to hold it with just one. I managed to smack two trick bunnies to the side and lob off the head of one more. Pale bone showed through the cut, and the crunch made the color drain from my face.

Simone breathed out again, frosting over my hair and freezing ten trick bunnies solid in front of me. Sam reached out his hand and the eyes of a good half of the remaining trick bunnies went cloudy, they whimpered and whined, shaking their heads around for sight. While they were distracted, Annalyn Sam and I clambered onto Simone's back and she took off.

I clung to Annalyn's shoulders, shivering and trying to rub the frost off of my hair. We landed on the other side of the field and basically ran into the forest.

"Well, that was a disaster." Simone hit a branch in her way hard with her dagger. "Lesson learned: never sleep in a Blue-Leaf field as long as you like breathing."

"Yup, but feel free if you like giant trick bunnies," I giggled as my fear faded.

I started getting nervous again when the sound of Simone and Annalyn's incoherent chatting faded.

"What's wrong?" I asked, they stopped in front of a massive fallen tree. The leaves were shifting in shape, its bark changing in texture and color. It was a changing tree, but it was completely uprooted and on its side. Some of its branches were burnt to a crisp, others still sported small flames.

Annalyn's face was ashen.

"What happened?" I stepped up to the tree and stared in awe. What could possibly have done this to such a massive tree?

182

What did this? I asked myself, sifting through all the fire-breathing monsters that I could think of.

"I don't know, but I'd rather not stick around to find out," Simone said.

"Oh please, it was probably just lightning," Sam brushed it off.

"Ah yes, because there was *totally*, a storm that we couldn't see or hear last night that knocked down a changing tree and nothing else. Because that's a reasonable explanation Sam, high five, gold star." Simone rolled her eyes, "No. Changing trees like this don't just get knocked down by lightning. Something else did this, I can't think of a lot of monsters that can."

I gulped, the last changing tree that we ran into had nearly killed us. It tried to absorb us and take our lives to make itself stronger. This one was smaller by comparison, but it still would have towered over the other trees in the area.

"We should just go around it, and be extra quiet," Annalyn told us. No one argued, but as I walked underneath the exposed roots of the tree, I felt like something was just wrong. An all-encompassing feeling of pure dread. Something bad was going to happen, and soon.

The question struck me again, *what did this?* I couldn't figure out an explanation, and neither did Simone or Annalyn and they had been here for a lot longer than Sam and I.

The creatures on this island were terrifying enough. Anything that could tear down a massive, life-sucking, tree, wasn't exactly something that I would like to see. I rubbed the goosebumps on my arms.

I walked faster to catch up with Sam, "What do you think it was?" I asked, slowing down to match his pace after I had sped up to catch up to him.

"I don't know, my best guess is a dragon, but for all I know they can't tear up changing trees no matter how big they are," Sam replied, speaking quietly to avoid attracting unwanted attention.

"Maybe it was a dragon and something else?" I suggested. It sounded odd coming out of my mouth but it was better than nothing.

"I mean I guess it's possible, but dragons aren't known to work with other monsters and the only thing that I can think of that could have pulled that tree out of the ground is a cyclops or a Hecatoncheires, but they don't have any sort of fire abilities. It might have been some sort of island monster that I haven't learned about yet, but I just hope that this mess isn't going to come back to bite us." Sam shivered.

I understood what he meant. We'd dealt with enough on this cursed mission and I had just about had it with our horrible luck. I was sick and tired of being somewhere and the universe just going, 'Oh, you wanted peace? Well, good flipping luck! Here's a monster, or some other thing that tries to kill you'.

Thankfully, nothing jumped out of the bushes to attack us, stomped through the trees, or really anything. We just went on our way as normal until I felt like my legs were going to fall off of my torso, you know, the usual.

We stopped to take a break. Simone handed us each some dried apple slices from that danged bag. I wouldn't be surprised if she had an entire queen-sized bed in there.

"What do you *not* have in there?" I asked as I nibbled on my apple slices.

Simone grinned, "You mean other than buildings and wildlife?"

"Ok, better question: how much can that darned bag fit in it?" Sam corrected, grinning.

"Basically, anything within reason, if it can fit through the opening, it'll fit in the bag," Simone explained.

"So, you do have everything physically possible in that bag," I translated.

Simone snickered, so did Annalyn.

"Yeah, I guess."

Lunch was quick because of our small amount of food. None of us felt like trying to roam the forest for more.

As we walked, I kept hearing a rustling in the trees and bushes. I tried to convince myself that it was just the wind, but I could feel eyes on me for seemingly no reason. It was nothing, it was probably nothing. So why couldn't I shake this feeling?

The trees seemed to whisper to me. As if asking who killed the changing tree. Wondering if the same would happen to them. I couldn't help but wonder the same.

The rustling kept getting closer and closer until I just couldn't take it anymore.

"Sam? I hear something," I was terrified, Sam stopped, silently listening for whatever it was that I'd heard.

Wind blasted us from all directions, then pushed and pulled us all until we were holding onto trees trying to stay on the ground.

"What is going on?" I yelled over the howling wind, my eyes watered from the wind.

"I don't know!" Sam yelled back. Suddenly, the wind stopped. I fell from a meter in the air nearly into my face. I was able to catch myself with my hands and a blast of my own wind, but my knees hit the ground so hard I yelped in pain.

"We need to find a temple right now," Simone said, her voice filled with barely disguised panic.

"What? Why?" Annalyn asked. Her hands were trembling slightly.

"I'll walk and talk." While she rushed us Simone explained that we had most likely been attacked by some form of ghost or wind spirit and that we should perform a seance to figure out what we did to upset them, or just to get them to leave us alone.

She told us that temples were a dime a dozen on the island as she looked for the nearest one on the map. It was thankfully only a fifteen-minute walk away.

When we reached the ruins of what was once a building Simone practically ran under the barely supported part of the roof that was still intact. Vines and moss had overtaken the marble columns and cracked floor.

Simone ruffled through her bag roughly,

"What are you looking for?" I asked, hoping that I could help.

"Candles, or crayons, they burn and I can set them up, I have matches already," Simone pulled out seven and a half beaten-up crayons that seemed to not be there for any particular reason. She carefully set them up in a circle around her and lit them each, the half one she lit extra carefully.

"What are you doing?" I asked.

"I'm summoning the spirits that keep bothering us," Simone told me bluntly.

"What?" I asked.

"Shhhhh," Sam shushed me.

She lifted her hands and whispered, a voice so soft and indistinct she sounded almost like a ghost herself. The wind picked up; the orange flames of the candles grew brighter. Still whispering, Simone pulled out a spare piece of paper.

I didn't understand her but I felt like she had asked a question. Then she stopped and waited, Sam and Annalyn were ready to fight while I cowered behind a pillar. I had been taught to never mess with the paranormal, and I wasn't about to test the theories today.

The paper swirled and lifted in the wind. It flipped over and flew around in the air for a second. The candles were blown out. The paper landed in front of her.

Simone picked up the piece of paper, she mumbled what sounded like a goodbye. When she read the note, she looked back at us furiously, standing up and holding out the piece of paper. To my surprise, it was written in English.

We have been summoned by one who called you their friend,

We torment to warn you to see who it is,

But if you wish, we shall leave you all be,

Until we are summoned again to run free.

"Which one of you did this? Why would any of you summon spirits of some kind? Was it an accident?" She looked utterly furious.

"Simone! Calm down, none of us summoned a ghost, I don't think any of us even *know* how to summon ghosts," Annalyn argued. She seemed nervous, which made sense since we could have been haunted for only the gods know how long.

Simone didn't falter. "Well, anyone at camp who does is getting interrogated as soon as we get back, and I swear to every god I will skin them alive when I find out who did it." She crumpled the piece of paper and aggressively shoved the melting and burned crayons back into her bag.

"I didn't know that crayons burned," I commented, desperate to get Simone to quit glaring at everything.

"They can burn for up to fourteen minutes," Simone said, she kept moving at her ridiculously fast pace, seriously though, she walked at my jogging speed. I had to run to catch up to her every few minutes.

"Why did you take us straight to the temple to communicate with the spirits?" I asked.

"I don't know, Klotho, maybe because we were lifted off of the ground for no reason on an otherwise non-windy day," Simone grumbled.

"Didn't the note say that someone who called you a friend sent them?" I asked. She seemed so certain that it was someone she knew one second.

"That could mean anyone, I asked for all of us, not just me." Simone hit a branch out of the way, but it snapped back and hit her face so hard she yelled out in pain in another language.

"Hey!" A nymph appeared right next to her and in front of me. We both shrieked in surprise. "No swearing! There are young nymphs here!" She whispered the last part.

"Oh, sorry. I didn't mean to uhh... well I didn't mean to swear," Simone stammered and pushed past the nymph.

"What language was that?" I asked, she mentioned having a Slovakian surname.

"No, that was Slovakian, it essentially means 'aww crap'," Simone said.

"I wonder what crap is going to happen to us next," Sam said to me as we walked, I had finally slowed down to my regular pace.

"Yeah, at least we know what caused it this time," I responded.

"True, I'm pretty sure that we're going to get to the mountains soon," Sam said.

"Excuse me, what?" I asked.

"There are two mountain ranges on the island, you might not have noticed them on the map. There's one north of Nikephros Academy and one near the center of the island." Sam said.

"Do they have names?" I asked.

"Well, the northern range is called the Hollow Hall, and the southern range is called the Shimmering Slopes." Sam explained, "It would take forever to go around them so we're following the river through them instead. Get ready to suffer uphill for hours."

I groaned. I'd never climbed a mountain before but I figured that after the first few steps uphill I would hate it. We had mostly traveled along a pretty flat plain, and I lived in, let me just check the US map really quick, mountain-less Minnesota, so I was not used to uphill slopes.

As we walked, I could start to see the mountains clearer through the trees. We were coming up in a valley between two mountains and the river went up, up into the rocks of the two mountains and into a lake, it went over that and the river seemed to have fallen away.

The 'valley' was really just like a relatively small V-shaped chunk had been taken out of a single mountain and smoothed down, making the mountain look like it was scooping towards us. It was a *very* steep slope, with large rocks and boulders along with many groups of trees.

"We have to climb that?" I asked, gesturing to the mountain as we got to the clearing at the base of it.

"Yeah, there is no way we're going all the way up there on foot. I'll turn us into birds, we can fly over," Simone shoved the map in her bag and we all shape-shifted into ravens. Simone launched off the ground first, the rest of us following closely behind.

We soared over the mountains that the river cut through and slipped over. We had almost gotten through the valley in which the river flowed into a lake and I spotted something. It was a flash of pale pink.

"Hey! I see something!" I chirped loudly over the wind.

"What?" Simone chirped back, her little black head turning and her beady black eyes searched for what I was talking about. I had turned to fly closer to the pink spot. It started to become easier to see, and, wait, "Is that a kid?" I asked, startled.

"Hold on, it could be a monster, you all stay up here, I'll take a closer look." Simone swooped down and I saw her stop and turn back into a human. I couldn't tell exactly what she was doing but she seemed to say something to the kid and flew up to us back as a bird.

"It's a kid, a young one, we should go down and help her out," Simone told us.

"Who leaves a kid on a mountain?" Sam wondered as we glided down towards the small spot of pink in the rocks.

Chapter Seventeen

A Small Child is Not a Great Thing to Bring on a Hike

SIMONE turned us back and I got a better look at the girl.

She was small, probably only six or seven. She had, curling golden hair, a pale face with pink-tinged cheeks, and bright green eyes like mine. They had a cooler tone and as I looked closer, I realized that there were bits of blue and yellow floating around inside. She was wearing a pale pink dress with a white Peter Pan collar and short sleeves with a white skirt hem and white waistband. Her shoes were little white tennis shoes with pink Velcro straps. The dress was stained with mud and had tears from sticks. She was a very cute child, though her eyes were puffy and red like she had been crying.

Poor kid, she's probably terrified. I thought. I knew I was terrified when I first came to the island. She was at most seven.

Simone knelt down to the girl and said, "Hello there, I'm Simone, what's your name?" Her voice was gentle.

"I'm Elanor," The girl said, her large eyes looking around the group. She gasped, "Your hair is like a carrot!" She pointed at me.

I blushed and giggled, "Uh, yeah it is."

"And yours is also puffy!" She patted Simone's hair, she had washed it in the river when she was on watch the night before, and that morning when she brushed it, it poofed up like crazy, she had taken it out when we started to fly over the mountains so as to not lose the hair tie.

"Yeah, it really is. How did you get here?" Simone questioned.

"My sissy dropped me off." She answered simply.

"And what is your sissy's name?' Simone asked. She offered the girl her hand. The little girl took Simone's long fingers in her small ones and started walking. I guess she figured that making the girl fly the rest of the way wasn't a good idea.

"Fiona. She said that if I walk far enough, I get to see a dragon! And a magic school!" She sounded in awe. My heart ached for her; Fiona had seemed so nice when I met her. Why would she leave her sister like this?"

"Did she?" Simone said, her voice was a calm whisper. A deadly wind waiting to howl at its victim. I didn't know as much about Simone as I wanted to, but I knew enough. She would not go lightly on Fiona when she got back to camp.

When. The choice of words in my thoughts reassured me. Subconsciously, I was sure that I would be fine, so why couldn't I think that consciously?

"Well, has she told you about Camp Myth?" Simone asked. She gripped the hem of her shirt tightly with her free hand. She was angry, but she wasn't showing Elenor.

"A little," the girl made a gesture with her small fingers to show a small space between them.

"Well, she was telling the truth about the dragons, and the school. But walking on the island without a weapon is dangerous. There are monsters, and if they can find you, they'll eat you," Simona said lightly, like she was only telling a story, but I knew better. She squeezed the girl's hand.

"Why would she leave me then? She has a pointy thing. I don't. Where do I get one?" Her mind seemed to be going in all different places at once.

"At Camp Myth, how long have you been alone out here?" Simone asked.

"It's been like a week, I think. The sun has gone over my head three times already. And I slept in the trees when it got dark. I drank from the river. The water is really cold," The girl went on. Simone smiled and acted interested, but I could nearly feel her anger.

The kid was only six. Who leaves their six-year-old sister out on her own, on the island of all places? I clenched my fists. There was no way I'd be brave enough to stand up to Fiona, in that case, I would also be standing up to Ji-Min. They could definitely beat me in a fight.

"I'm tired. Can you carry me?" The girl asked after a long silence. It had been over a half hour since we started walking, at least, that's what my notoriously accurate internal clock told me.

Simone knelt down in front of the girl with her arms out, ready to let Elenor onto her back. She clambered up and Simone stood.

"Woah, this is what it feels like to be tall," Elenor's large eyes are glinting with happiness. It made me smile. This girl was so untouched by her sister's negligence, such an innocent little kid. I hoped that the island wouldn't ruin that too badly.

Elenor continued to chatter everyone's ears off. I normally didn't mind talkative kids, but jeez, she talked a *lot*.

Simone started slowing down, the weight of the child on her back was affecting her. Annalyn had been very quiet this entire time. Normally she would chat quietly with Simone when we walked, but she had been getting quieter.

Eventually, the girl fell quiet, resting her head on Simone's shoulder. I sped up to catch up with her, I had questions. Despite her having, you know, a literal child on her back, she was still faster than me.

"Where are we taking her? Is she just going to come with us?" I whispered. I wasn't quite sure if Elenor was asleep or not, but there was no way of really knowing when she had gotten up and started walking.

"Goodness no. We can't take a six-year-old to the underworld with us. We're heading to one of the teleportation temples. They're scattered over the island, I'm not exactly sure how old they are, but they only go to one of two places. Nikephros Academy, and Camp Myth. If it goes to Nikephros Academy, Medea will find her, same for if she gets to camp." Simone then said in a low voice, "I'm going to skin her alive."

"I'll clean the mess afterward," Sam said, nodding. "Who would just... just leave Elenor like that? Why would she?"

"It attracts more attention, having a chattering little kid with you," Simone explained, though she clenched her jaw.

"That doesn't make it right," Sam crossed his arms. I nodded in agreement, I was pretty cowardly myself, but I hoped that I would never leave a kid on their own because of my fear.

It had been a long time since we found Elanor. Hours. My legs ached, and the rocks under the souls of my shoes made my feet feel like they had been tenderized. Elenor had woken up after a while of being carried, and she volunteered to walk on her own. She was able to for a solid 30 minutes before she asked to be carried again. That time Annalyn had volunteered and she carried Elenor down until she slipped on a rock and nearly crushed the poor kid beneath her. Sam took her for the fifteen minutes that it took us to get the rest of the way down.

We were in a valley now. Filled with grass, bushes, and flowers. The ground was still rocky, but it was clear of most trees. I saw a marble building, well, it wasn't as much a building as an open-air pavilion. It had six pillars on a circular base. It looked new, it wasn't cracked or overtaken by vines, like the other temples I had seen.

We practically ran to it. The jostling made Elenor yelp.

"What's going on? Are you going to leave me here?" Elenor asked. Her voice was nervous.

"No, this will take you to the camp, or the magic school. A lady named Medea will help you then," Simone told the girl to step onto the platform. Elenor stood in the center of it and Simone inserted her crystal into a hole in one of the pillars. I hadn't noticed it before.

Elenor waved goodbye before beams of shadow burst from the pillars and whisked her away. I desperately wanted to do the same.

"Couldn't we have used one of these to get here? Or to leave?" I asked. I was seriously frustrated with this damned mission.

"No. The way these work is a one-way system. The shadows just kind of toss you into camp at random. There aren't any of these that lead out of camp or school, and there aren't any working ones further south than this."

"Well, then why do we need them? Is finding random kids while out on missions such a common occurrence that these are a necessity?" I questioned further.

"No. But it is important to be able to get back to camp really quickly in a life-or-death situation," Sam explained to me. "Believe me, I also wish that we could have just taken one of these to save ourselves the headache." He rubbed his back groaning. Clearly carrying Elenor had done a number on it.

"Hurts?" I asked, stupidly.

"Yeah," Sam bent backward to stretch his back again.

"Are we going to sleep here?" I asked. The sun was low in the sky. Not setting yet, but close.

"I think we should try to travel through the night," Annalyn told us and was immediately met with Sam's protests. "Think about it, we've been walking for days and we've barely made any significant progress. We keep getting attacked in the middle of the night because we're not moving."

I resisted a groan. It was perfectly logical. Oh, why did it have to be perfectly logical?

"Sounds alright with me," Simone said nonchalantly.

"But we have to sleep!" I argued. It wasn't that I didn't want to make progress, but I was tired and I did *not* like the idea of traveling at night. Walking through deadly forests with basically no knowledge of where we were going was scary enough but at night? That was a new level.

"We can sleep tomorrow night," Annalyn clearly wasn't backing down, Simone didn't seem to care, and Sam just shook his head, knowing we'd lost. I sighed. My sword sprang into form in my hand.

"Are we going now?" I asked.

"Yup," Annalyn and Simone said in unison.

With that, we started walking. We followed the river as it cut through the mountains. As I walked, I noticed that the ledge of the cliff we were walking on was getting narrower and narrower. I did my best to just press myself against the cliff face and keep walking. We would be fine. My shoulder scraped against the rough gray rock.

My hair caught on the little bits of stone that jutted out. I didn't dare to tilt my head to free it. My heart was racing as fast as my thoughts. I didn't like heights. Especially not when standing over a roaring river filled with rocks that could shred me if I fell in. We were ten feet off the ground and above the river.

The ledges that we were walking on dipped and I had to jump down. Sam was behind me. I pressed myself against the wall. It was such a dip that the water from the river glazed it with water. Both Simone and Annalyn had made the jump before me. But Simone had turned into a bird, and Annalyn had used some weeds from the river as stairs. I could try to use the after, but that gave me the risk of slipping. I could try to use the wind, but what good would that do? Make me float and fall into the river? I would just have to jump.

I took a deep breath, bent my legs and... fell. I had tried to stop myself from jumping at the last second and I had lost my balance. I shrieked and grabbed at the first thing that I could. A rock sticking out of the cliff face. I hung two inches over the dip in the ledge.

I let go of the rock, landing on the ledge. My face was red with embarrassment.

"Klotho, move, I'm about to jump," Sam warned. His feet left the ledge and when he landed behind me his leg slipped. There was a flash and I heard him scream. He grabbed the first thing he could: me.

I shrieked and grabbed a rock on the cliff face. Using it as an anchor to keep Sam from pulling me into the river. Everything looked white and bright.

"What's going on?" I asked. I clutched the wall. I couldn't see, the light hurt my eyes.

"Oh no," Sam muttered. I couldn't see him, but I heard him step away.

"What?" Annalyn asked.

"I accidentally used my powers on all of you. You guys won't be able to see for a good hour," Sam told us.

"WHAT?!" Annalyn, Simone, and I, all yelled. I don't think there could have been a much worse place to be blinded than on the side of a cliff, and of course, that was where we were.

"What are we going to do?" I asked, trying to keep the shaking out of my voice. "Can you turn it off?"

"Nope, I guess we'll have to keep walking until we get to solid land," Sam murmured. Easy for him to say, at least he could see.

"We won't get to solid land in an hour," Annalyn grumbles. She was probably shaking her head, I couldn't tell, I was blind as a mole.

"Well, what can we do? It's not like Sam has enough hands to guide us all." Simone said sarcastically. She was clearly trying to keep the atmosphere lighter, to keep us from panicking. It didn't work. I was trying to hold back my tears of panic. Being blind was scary. I had relied on my sight so much throughout my life, that I was completely defenseless without it.

"Could you turn us into an animal to like, reset our vision?" Annalyn asked.

"That won't work," Sam interjected before Simone could answer.

"Then maybe turn us into something like an axolotl or a bat, something that doesn't necessarily *need* to see," Annalyn suggested.

That was a valid point, and an axolotl could swim, so we would not have to walk, a bat could use echolocation and we could fly.

"I think I could try the axolotl, we would need somewhere better to fall into flight for bats," Simone replied.

"Wait, bats need to fall into flight?" I asked. I had always found it strange that they hung upside down in caves, but I didn't know that that was for any particular purpose.

"Yup," Simone answered, before explaining: "Their wings aren't strong enough to take off like birds so they have to fall into flight."

"So, are you going to transform us, or not?" Sam asked.

"Oh, yeah."

I was suddenly smaller. My body was almost entirely covered by the thin layer of water that had wetted my shoes and socks previously. I started swimming when Simone made a noise. The current of the river pulled me along and all I needed to do was avoid the rocks.

It was a bit difficult since I *really* couldn't see, but I didn't get crushed up like mashed potatoes so I'd say it was a success. I could feel little weeds tickle my underbelly. The cool water of the river smoothed past me. Even blinded, I felt calm. I was really in my element here; it was almost like I was flying.

It seemed like only an instant had passed but my eyesight was slowly fading back into focus. Being blinded by Sam's powers meant that, like I've said before, everything was bright white. Now, as my vision fizzled back, it was darker. I was surprised to find that I liked it better that way. The dark is one of my fears, I don't like being in the dark, but eternal light is just as bad. Darkness is more calming. I can't sleep unless it's at least a little dark. But light is what allows me to see, at least most of the time. I hadn't ever realized what a gift that was until the roles flipped.

The trickle of the river got faster, and I could see more shapes that looked like rocks. The other three axolotls in my limited view seemed to notice it too. One of them, Simone, started to veer off to the bank of the river. My eyesight was still bad, considering I was an axolotl, but I could still see a tree shape above the water where I was.

Simone and Sam had surfaced there. I saw the shapes of their small forms turn back to their regular, human forms. They looked huge to me because I was so small. I veered off to the bank, I was excited to get back to my human form just as much as I loved swimming in the river without nearly dying.

Have I ever swum in the river before without nearly dying? I asked myself. I thought for a second, going through my memories of the mission so far. *I don't think so. Wow, I am missing out.* I crawled onto the bank of the river and I grew back to my normal size. I was on all fours on the river bank, the mud squishing under my hands.

"Well, I can see properly now," I said. My eyes adjust to seeing more than blurry shapes. We were now on what seemed to be a large flat rock on the side of the mountain, it was about ten-by-ten feet and shaped more like a triangle than anything else. It felt like a tiny island in the sea of rocks and single trees sprouting up out of the gaps.

A single tree grew out of a crack in it. Or at least, I had thought it was a tree when I was in the river, it was really more of a shrub. The leaves were pale green like they were frosted over. The stems were pale lavender. It was a strange combination, no doubt, but it was pretty. It looked too dainty to live in such a sharp-edged place.

I found myself wondering where Annalyn had gotten those scars, Simone said she'd gone to the underworld before, had Annalyn gone with her? And Sam? What made him decide that almost getting me killed while taking me to the island and suffering the wrath of a pre-teen assistant director was worth it? I glanced down at my hand, the nail of my pointer finger was slowly starting to grow back, and the dent in my arm, while still throbbing, was closed and all that was left of the wound was a bruise. The cuts at my throat had healed, though the ones on my side had stubbornly refused to fully heal as of now.

It was getting dark. I could see the setting sun; it was barely visible. The sky was beautiful. The clouds looked blue on the top, but they were lit a pink-orange on the bottom, the sun a spot of lava, slowly sinking out of sight behind the peaks of the mountains. The sky was deeper blue.

"Yeah, thanks for that, *Sam*," Simone said sarcastically, glaring at him.

"It was an accident!" He snapped, his tanned skin turning red. Then he added quietly: "Sorry."

"It's ok, at least it gave us an excuse to move faster," Annalyn told him.

"We could have died; axolotls are nocturnal and the river is not their natural habitat. We're lucky to be alive. And no, a fish would not have been any better, or a salamander, or really anything else," Simone snipped back.

I had never really seen her argue with Annalyn before, she seemed to just go along with whatever the girl had to say. I guess it was fair. Though his powers malfunctioning had been an accident, brought on by the startling experience of nearly falling into the river. I was also a bit annoyed; I realized I was a bit annoyed with *all* of them.

Wow, it's only been a week and I'm sick of being on the road, or trail, I guess. I hadn't had much interaction with any humans other than them for a *while.* I was tired, and I wanted a break. I sighed, this wouldn't help me at all. What would help me was getting to the underworld faster so that I could just get this danged quest over with.

I heard rustling in the bushes. I froze. Rustling meant monsters, which meant fighting, which I had had *enough of.* The sun had gone down completely. The sky was deeper blue now, I could still see, but I wouldn't be able to in a little while.

"Let's go," Sam said, getting to walk.

We slowly started making our way down the side of the mountain, this one was very, *very,* Rockey. It wasn't a sheer drop, but one wrong step would still probably send your tenderized corpse to the underworld. Because of this, I focused on nothing other than where I was stepping.

No one said a word, probably to keep from falling and getting themselves crushed to death by rocks, so you can imagine my surprise when the silence was broken by an ear-piercing shriek.

Chapter Eighteen

The Flock of Glorified Pidgins

I looked back at the sky in pure horror. A massive flock of black shapes was flying straight toward us. Birds. Normally, I wouldn't have batted an eyelash, but normally, I was not on a crazy island on my way to the underworld. Normally, I did not have to fight a monster or almost die basically every day. Normally, I would not be phased by a flock of what looked like pigeons.

But this was not a normal situation. These were most likely some crazy monsters either from Greek mythology, or something pulled right out of hell. Whatever it was, it wasn't good.

"That's not good," Sam whimpered.

"Stymphalian birds. They look kinda like pigeons but their beaks and claws are metal," Simone explained for my benefit, then added: "They're probably going to tear us to shreds."

She sped up and gestured for us to speed up too.

"Oh well, that's wonderful. Anything you can turn us into to save ourselves?" Sam asked, twisting his sword in his hand.

"Well, I could turn us into birds and we could fly for our lives, but I doubt that that would do us much good," Simone said. "Sam, maybe your singing can scare them away."

"Oh, come on," Sam rolled his eyes. "Now is not the time for jokes."

"No, I'm serious, your voice crack nearly shattered a glass pane and made Anastasia's ears bleed, Heracles defeated the first round of the things by scaring them into the air and killing them that way," Simone said.

Oh ouch. I thought to myself. We were basically running down the mountain now, at least, as close to running as we could get, while Simone was roasting Sam with strategy.

"Who's Anastasia?" I asked, trying to distract myself from the sounds of screeching birds growing closer.

"She's a camper and a student. One of her powers is enhanced hearing, and she can turn it off when she needs to. She was dared not to turn her powers off that night, and, well..." Annalyn explained. She trailed off. The birds had swooped down and were now diving straight towards us, and the formerly very small shapes were quickly getting bigger.

"Screw Sam's singing torture! Run!" I screamed and just booked it as fast as I could down the rocks. I was stumbling with every other step, but I didn't dare slow down. Blood rushed in my ears and my heart pounded in my chest so hard it almost hurt. My throat felt like it was bleeding, the way it felt after the pacer test.

I could hear the others running down the mountain behind me. It felt strange to be in the front for once, or at least, it would have *if I wasn't being chased down a mountain by a bunch of murderous pigeons.* Where were we? Oh yeah.

I put my foot and all of my weight onto a large flat rock that was shaped like a massive dinner plate, and just by luck, the rock moved and started sliding down the side of the mountain. I was screaming as I balanced for dear life on that rock. I hurdled down the rocky side of the mountain like I was on a sled. The rock conveniently avoided any others for a good, well, I wasn't exactly sure how long, I was too busy being scared out of my wits, but my point is that the rushing wind that passed around the rock soon stopped. At least from what the rock knew.

The stone slammed directly into another, much more stable rock, sending a shock through my body as I was thrown forward. The sound echoed over the mountainside.

I flew through the air like a bird myself, except I didn't have wings to slow my fall. I screamed as loud as physically possible, not caring what was behind me, only caring about what was below.

I am going to die. I am going to die. I am going to die. I am going to get crushed to death by rocks! My panicked mind screamed. I begged for the wind to grow stronger, to allow me at least a few seconds to land on my feet instead of my face. The wind grew behind me, slipping under my body and around me. I threw my arms up, hoping that I would float up like that time when we got thrown around by that water nymph. I remembered the pain in my shoulder from the bird and it ached. The wound still hadn't fully healed.

The wind picked up, picked *me* up. And suddenly I was floating. The birds were all around me. Flying in a circle. I could see three other groups all surrounding the others. The pigeon-like birds dove at me. I shrieked as the birds attacked. Little bronze beaks pecking my arms, their claws scraping at my legs and hair. I screamed in pure terror and threw my arms up to shield my face, forgetting that I was controlling the wind with my arms.

I was thrust upwards and the birds scattered for a second. Not because of my sudden movement, I realized, it was because of my shriek. They hadn't attacked me when I was hurdling down the side of the mountain because I had been screaming the whole time.

"Sam, start singing!" I screamed, he would be able to scare them away on his own. I made the wind lower me to the ground as quickly as I could without breaking my legs. "Annalyn! Simone! Start screaming!"

Sam and Annalyn stared at me for a second. Then Simone yelled, "YOU GUYS HEARD HER! SAM, TIME TO SHOW THESE GLORIFIED PIGEONS YOUR KARAOKE SKILLS!"

I was now standing on a large rock that stuck out of the mountainside. I jumped down from it and hid under the space. I covered my ears as I heard the others start to follow my orders. I started screaming too. Through my own screaming and with my hands over my ears, I could hear Sam belting out the lyrics to 'You Belong With Me' by Taylor Swift.

Simone was right, I could definitely see how his voice cracks could make somebody's ears bleed. The beating of wings started growing further away, I knew that the birds wouldn't completely give up just because of some badly sung Taylor Swift, and some screaming. What else could we do? What else could I do?

My voice was getting hoarse, screaming is tiring especially when you've been screaming as much as I have. I heard the roar of a dragon and peeked my head out from underneath the rock. Sam's singing quickly turned to screaming, and I saw that this dragon was *not* the work of Simone's shapeshifting.

It was large, and its wings were spread out. The snout was more stout than the other dragons I had seen, at least from what I could tell from its silhouette. It looked stronger, and the legs and tail were also thicker. They looked like they were made for breaking rocks, the tail was long and thick, it had barbs in the end, and it looked as though it could knock anything over.

I couldn't quite tell whether it was a female or male dragon. I had never seen one that looked like this. It growled such a low sound that I could feel it in my stomach. I nearly wet myself.

This dragon was built like a tank, its wings were the smallest I had seen, but they had spikes on the shoulders and the joint in the middle of the wing. The skin in between the bones was thick and tough. They wouldn't be the best for flying, but they were still weapons.

I tucked myself back under the rock. The deadly pigeons swarmed the dragon and it roared again, my ears rang from the sound. The pigeons screeched and grew louder, but there were fewer of them. I looked back at the dragon.

It's not after us. I realized. A smile spread across my face. I searched the rocks for the others. Sam and Annalyn were underneath a large rock that jutted out from the side of the mountain like me. They were further up and closer to the dragon. Simone was underneath her own rock, and she was closer to me. She was on my right, and Sam and Annalyn were on my left.

Annalyn held Sam's mouth shut. Simone knelt underneath the rock with her dagger ready, her head peeking out from behind the rock. They had all gotten the idea to hide, *we* had all gotten the idea to hide. The dragon clearly wasn't interested in us, though. It was only going for the stymphalian birds.

I caught Simone's eyes and she mouthed something that looked like 'keep quiet and wait' but I wasn't exactly sure. I just knew for sure that the 'keep quiet' part was important, so that's what I did. I held my hand over my mouth and shut my eyes, focusing on the sounds around me. I heard a growl, a roar, the shrieks of birds as they were devoured.

I was shaking, I couldn't listen to that anymore. But I needed to know what was going on, didn't I? *The others will tell me when it's safe to come out.* I told myself. I covered my arms and screwed my eyes shut tight.

For a long time, all I could hear were the muffled sounds of the dragon roaring and growling, and eating the stymphalian birds. That perfectly timed trauma had me pressing the heels of my palms against my ears. I tried to tune out the sounds, but I found that pretty impossible since I had nothing else to focus on other than the pain in my ankles and calves.

I opened my eyes, I couldn't tilt my head to look at the sky with the way I was sitting, and my ankles hurt so bad it felt like they were breaking, so I took my hands off of my ears and set them down beside me. The small rocks and chunks of dirt moved under my palms. I slid my feet carefully out from under me and sat down. A roar echoed from the dragon, and I gritted my teeth. I heard the flapping of large wings, beating against the air like it was battling the sky, and I didn't dare move until I couldn't hear it anymore.

I slowly peeked my head out from underneath the rock. The sky was littered with stars, the half-moon glowed from in between two clouds. I saw Simone's silhouette emerge from underneath her rock and stand on another one. Sam and Annalyn came out shortly after. I slowly crawled out from under the rock.

"Guys?" I asked. My voice was quiet, and horse. I realized that they couldn't hear me. "GUYS!" I yelled, more sure of myself.

I saw Simone's shoulders turn. "Klotho?" Her voice projected down the mountainside. Her glowing eyes shone down at me.

I stepped carefully up to the spot where the others had converged. "So... what do we do now?" I wondered. It was really, *really*, dark.

"We walk, but we have to stay together more, so pick up the pace." Simone's ring turned into a small lantern that emitted a calm blue light. The pale blue glow made her look like a ghost, combined with Annalyn's doll-like features, and Sam's messy hair and tear-stained face, they could have been a group in a horror movie.

Wait, I thought. *Was Sam crying?* Huh, I guess I'd thought that I was only me.

"We all ready to go?" Simone asked. I nodded, and so did Sam and Annalyn.

Simone went first, the blue light of her lantern spilling over the rocks ahead of us. I looked directly at the ground, only focusing on where I was stepping. Annalyn bumped into me and I stumbled forward. I yelped. The smaller rocks slipped from under my feet and I fell over. I fell directly into Sam, and he yelled out.

"Klotho! Be careful!" He warned when she stopped and I pulled myself up by his shoulders.

"It wasn't my fault! Annalyn tripped and she fell into me!" I told him. "Sorry, Annalyn."

"It's alright, I should also be more careful, to avoid becoming gifted-one-dominos," She replied.

"Guys hurry up!" Simone yelled back at us. We had fallen behind by a good few yards, and it was hard to see where we were going without Simone's lantern lighting our path closely. Sam jogged down to her, but I just did my best to speed up my walking. I had felt what it was like to hurl down a mountain unintentionally, and I figured falling after running wouldn't be too different from that awful experience.

"Coming!" Annalyn yelled back, pushing me to the side and hurting in front of me. Normally I wouldn't have minded, but I was in the dark after getting attacked by a bunch of glorified pigeons. Plus, listening to them get eaten by a dragon. I was still shaken up; I could still hear the horrible sounds of the birds getting eaten. I tried to push the sounds out of my mind.

I walked even faster; I tried to make my strides larger to compensate for my careful steps. The speed would make it easier to slip. The darkness would add to that even more, and since I was slower than the others already, there was a good chance that not being able to see anything would become a very real problem for me, very soon, if I didn't speed up.

I started jumping from rock to rock, my eyelids were starting to get heavy. I smacked myself in the face. *Come on, Klotho, you need to stay awake.* The adrenaline from the stymphalian bird attack had faded. I was tired. I blinked hard and opened my eyes wide. Ugh, I wished I had water to splash into my face to wake myself up. I jumped to the next rock; my foot went hard straight onto the thin end. I swayed from side to side, yelping.

I threw my arms out to catch myself and stepped forward. It was only light enough for me to see that I did *not* step in the right place. I fell four feet into a bunch of gravel. I screamed when I flunked below my waist, and my feet stuck out into some fort of underground space that I couldn't see.

"Help!" I screamed. My voice bounced over the rocks and Simone's glowing eyes, now far away, turned to me. The light of the lantern followed her turn and she, Sam and Annalyn started all running towards me. I was grabbing rock around me trying to pull myself back up, but I'd never really had that much arm strength. My skin still stung from the bird's beaks.

"Sam, hold the lantern," Simone ordered, shoving the iron handle into his hands.

She walked over to me, careful to not step on the section of gravel that had me waist-deep and unable to move. She grabbed my hands and pulled me upwards. I couldn't really help her with my legs, since they were, you know, buried in tiny rocks, but I did my best to pull myself up and only really use her as an anchor.

When my legs came out so that my thighs were free, I pulled my right leg out, the gravel sticking to my knee as I pushed myself up, freeing my other leg. I breathed heavily, my hands were sweaty and felt like they had been crushed by Simone's grip.

"Thanks," I panted. I looked down at the hole I had created, the gravel falling in on itself and disappearing. I heard a splash.

"What's in the hole?" Sam asked.

"Well, I don't know Sam, clearly the splash gives *nothing* away so it's just going to be a mystery," Simone responded, her voice drenched in sarcasm.

"It could be something other than water you know," Sam retorted. I would have probably seen his face go red if it wasn't so dark, and the blue light didn't make everyone look like they were in grayscale.

"That's true," Annalyn agreed, "Klotho, why don't you get a bit of it to float up here so that we can see?"

"Um, I can try." I held my hand above the hole.

"We don't need to, though, what we need is to keep moving," Simone argued.

"Wouldn't it be better to know though? Like, in case there's a sinkhole and we all fall into the liquid down there," Annalyn brought up a good point.

Simone sighed, "Fine." She lifted the lantern so that I could see inside the hole better. "But only five minutes, at *most*."

I focused on the liquid at the bottom of the hole, imagining it stretching towards the sky, towards my hand, and breaking apart from the rest of the liquid in the hole. The little blob of liquid that I had summoned floated out of the hole. It was, to no one's surprise: water. The blue light of the lantern glistened on the clear liquid.

"See? Just water. Now let's go." Simone turned away.

"Wait, there's something different about it," I called. I didn't know what it was that I felt, but whatever it was probably wasn't any good, at least, considering the other stuff on the island. I kept feeling the need to play around with it, to figure out what was so different.

"What?" Simone asked, a little irritably.

"I'm not sure, it's probably nothing," I dropped the blob into the water. The *sploosh* that followed sounded just like normal water.

It could be a good thing. Some tiny little hopeful corner of my mind said. *There is beauty on the island.* My mind flashed to the midnight jewels, their rough and star-like surface. The shine of the dragon's scales, even though they were dangerous, the flowers and trees. All of that beauty, forgotten because of the ugliness of the monsters. I scolded myself for ignoring it.

The walk down the mountain went better when I didn't pay so much attention to the floor, and paid more attention to actually staying with the group. I found myself used to the ache in my legs and back, after a good too long walking this much every day.

"What type of dragon was that?" I asked, feeling the need to break the silence.

"That was a stone dragon, they aren't as vicious as fire dragons, but they're the strongest type," Simone explained as she jumped down from a large rock. "The problem with them is that they can't fly very well."

"Why not?" I asked.

"Well, you saw the size of his wings, they just can't lift them off of the ground properly," Simone replied. I jumped down from a large rock and my leg slipped. I yelled out as my ankle twisted beneath me. I bit my lip as my ankle throbbed. I held it for a minute, allowing myself to stop for a second to recover.

"Klotho? Are you ok?" Annalyn jumped down next to me.

"Yeah, I just landed badly," I accepted her hand as she pulled me up, her palms were sweaty. My eyes were wide open now. The pain had woken me up. When I continued walking my ankle throbbed.

The light of the moon was starting to get replaced by the sun, which was still well under the horizon. Simone's lantern soon became useless, and unnecessary. The sky was now a mid-tone blue, with fluffy white clouds, and a cool breeze. I imagined the nymph that had contacted me in my dreams. I wondered how she knew me. She hadn't contacted me in a while. Was she up there somewhere? Hiding in the clouds?

Chapter Nineteen

Ashes, Ashes, We All Fall—Oh Not Again

*Y*UP, *walking through mountains sucks*. I decided. It was about four hours into the walk that day. The rocks made my feet bleed in multiple places because of blisters. The river cut through the mountains so cleanly that a lot of the time we were walking on about a foot of the river bank and had to all walk in a line with no way to switch who went first. Normally, I was placed in the back since I was slow, and Simone, who was too fast of a walker for her own good, was in the front.

I jumped when I saw a little lizard scurry between my feet, yelping. I caught myself before falling into the river and my face went red with embarrassment. I lowered my head and kept walking. The river had been getting louder and louder, I figured it was just rapids since it was getting pretty rocky here. The water rushed over the rocks, clear as crystal. A school of fish passed in between some rocks, their scales flashing blue and purple.

I bumped into Sam.

"Hey!" He yelped, bumping into Annalyn, she also helped and she fell over since Simone was too far ahead for her to bump into.

"Klotho watch it!" She scolded.

I shrank behind Sam, away from her glare, her knees covered in gravel.

"Sorry, I wasn't paying attention," I replied, glancing at Simone who had stopped, looking back at us.

"Well be more careful, I don't want to fall again," Annalyn warned, shaking her finger at me. She continued walking, dusting off her knees and hands. Simone didn't move, her head turned to the path. She was probably waiting for us.

As I walked, the River only seemed to get higher and higher, and louder. Roaring like a dragon. I had to walk with my back to the wall of rock that trapped us next to the river. The river grew too high to continue walking, where Simone had stopped.

"We're going to have to jump onto rocks, to get through, be careful," Sam assessed, his eyes skimming the river.

"Yeah, I'll go first, try to jump where I do," Simone agreed, she leaped like a deer onto a small, slanted rock that was mostly dry, then onto a soaked log. Annalyn followed, wobbling a bit on the rock before Simone jumped onto another rock that I couldn't quite see. Sam jumped, very nearly falling off of the rock, before jumping to another rock instead of the log so as to not fall into the river.

I braced myself, bending my legs and jumping onto the rock. I caught myself surprisingly well, though the roar of the rushing water was quick to wash away any sense of victory. I did my best to jump onto the log, but I bent my legs too much and put too much power into the jump. I landed too hard and on the back of my heel.

I screamed and grabbed the first thing within reach, Sam. He yelled out a curse and screamed as we plummeted like stones into the water. The shock of the river was instant, I'd thought that the water was cold before, but up in the mountains, it was practically ice.

Sam's arm reached out and wrenched Annalyn from the rock that she was on in an attempt to save himself. I heard her high-pitched shriek as she tumbled after us, she wasn't strong enough and she wasn't balanced enough either. I saw a flash of brown hair above the water, holding out a hand, and I reached out to grab it. I didn't grab a hand, in fact, I had grabbed Simone's ankle, because I'm just that amazing. She screamed like a dying bird as she was pulled into the water with us.

The river dragged us around like bits of driftwood, I dove around rocks and fallen trees. I did not want to repeat the whole slam-my-head-into-a-rock-and-split -it-open experience again. I was so focused on the rocks, that I didn't even notice the water roaring louder as it dropped off into many waterfalls.

I screamed as a large chunk of wood appeared in my bubble-filled vision. I let out a bubbly scream as I smacked into the wood. I almost felt my brain rattling in my skull. I didn't have the strength to move through the pain as my body was pushed under the log and over the edge of the first fall.

I didn't have the energy to do anything, I just plummeted towards the rocks at the bottom of the fall, my stomach dropping. My head felt like it had been stuffed with cotton balls. I vaguely heard the screams of the others as they were also pushed over.

I felt the wind around me get stronger, it spun around me, stronger and faster than me. I felt like I should have shattered against its force. I was pulled around, spinning. I forced my eyes open, trying to ignore the pain that made tears roll down my face.

I gasped, very nearly forgetting the pain altogether. The wind around me was filled with forest debris, sticks and leaves and dirt, even whole small tree trunks that had been torn out of the ground. The wind was so loud I was worried that I was going to go deaf. My mind wandered for a second, past the panic of being, well, yanked around like an unwilling child on a windy carousel of death. How did tornados even happen on the island? Wouldn't the place not be suitable for the weather needed to create a tornado anyway?

Oh, please, I'm about to die and I start thinking about the climate of all things. I scolded myself. I tried to stop the wind, or at least slow it down. My head felt like it was being pounded. I saw Annalyn's mouth open, but she shut it quickly. The wind was too loud to hear anything anyway. I imagined the tornado like a whirling piece of cloth. I imagined placing a hand over it to stifle it.

I felt the wind slow down, and my body plummeted. I screamed, but I couldn't hear myself. I didn't have the strength to stop my fall, I didn't have the strength to stop any of us. I stopped falling suddenly, caught by a pair of arms. Thin arms.

I looked up. It was the face of the wind nymph in my dreams. The wind nymph that had already saved me twice. "Hello, Klotho." She said, smiling, even though my ears rang from the sound of the tornado's wind, I smiled at the words. She had saved me yet again.

"How did you know?" I asked.

"Who do you think sent the tornado?" She replied. "Lady Artemis sent me."

My mind flashed to the others. I imagined them falling to their deaths, their broken bodies on the ground. Then I saw myself if I had to complete the mission without them. Torn apart by monsters.

"Wait! What about—"

"My friends have caught your companions," She replied, cutting me off. "We'll bring you back to the ground in a safer place."

I nodded. She started flying so fast it felt like we had been turned into wind ourselves. The next thing I knew, we were on the ground, in a large valley. Soft, green grass filled it, along with sparse groups of small yellow flowers.

There was a group of deer, strange, at least to me. I had never seen a deer before; I had always been taught that they were skittish and shy. These deer were deep black. One of the doe's was white as fresh snow, not the stuff that you see piled up by stores at the end of winter, the kind that you see outside your window the day of the first snow.

I saw a flash of silver in the group. The few male deer in the group had *silver antlers*. And I noticed that they also had silver in the undersides of their stomachs, and tails. The small fawns had silver spots.

"What are they?" I gasped.

"Star-flecked deer," Simone answered. "Some say that at night they can fly through the sky, sending calming dreams to anyone who their hooves line up with as they bound across the sky."

Sam scoffed, "What is it with these children's stories? 'Deer that can fly and send people dreams' please."

"There's some truth to it; they have been spotted flying around. The dream thing is mostly speculation," Annalyn said, smoothing her shirt.

"Thank you, guys, you saved our lives," I said to the nymphs.

"You are very welcome, we must go now," The nymph that caught me said, her voice tighter. She was eager to leave. That sent off alarm bells, what if there was some sort of monster she was trying to get away from? Then it occurred to me that she was just in her opposite element, she was probably eager to go back to her sky, to where she belonged.

I nodded to her.

"Good luck with your mission," One of the nymphs told us. She had a deeper skin tone, though it was still gray like a storm cloud. Her hair was white, frizzy and puffy.

"Thank you," We all said at once. The nymphs whooshed away in a gust of wind.

"They're nice," Sam remarked.

"Yeah, saving our sorry butts is a pretty nice favor," Simone said snarkily. "Now, let's see where in this Hades-forsaken Mountain range we are." Simone slung her bag off of her shoulder and onto the ground, she yanked the map out and unrolled it. The paper crinkled in her hands.

"Remember when that map tried to kill us?" Sam asked, he sounded as if he were remembering a funny story, rather than a near-death experience.

"Yeah, when I find the person who cursed it, they're going to have one hell of a time," Simone's grip on the paper tightened. "Right now, we're at the edge of the range, we'll only have to go for maybe another day before we get to some grassland. The entrance to the underworld is a flower field. I don't remember exactly what we have to do to get down there, but we'll figure it out."

She started walking along the edge of the river before anyone could respond. The trek was rather peaceful, though something that struck me as odd was that the herd of deer seemed to follow us. Whenever we got to a new clearing in the trees and rocks, they would be there, grazing, nuzzling each other. The deer were beautiful, and from what I had gathered over the course of the mission, among the few types of magical creatures on the island that weren't out to kill me.

Soon enough, the mountains started to get smaller, and the rocks sparser. At the top of a large hill that we had been forced to climb in order to follow the river without swimming, I could see the grassland that Simona had mentioned.

Ahead were just open fields of tall grass that rippled like water in the wind. Tick heaven. I grimaced at the thought. I had never seen a tick before, but I remembered learning about them vividly. All of the diseases that they carried seemed terrifying, along with the fact that you could go hours without noticing them and that they wouldn't stop sucking blood until they literally couldn't.

So saw types of wildflowers bursting from the ground in seemingly very random places, poppies and daisies. This clearly wasn't the flower field that led to the underworld, considering that it was utterly massive and the flowers were sparse, split by blades of soft, green grass.

The river appeared to have grown wider, without any rocks to stifle its width. It flowed slower because of its new width, and smoother. The bank of the river was easier to follow because it was always visible and the ground, though rolling with small hills, didn't have any visible obstacles.

There were still rocks on the ground where we were, and there were only small spurts of grass and moss emerging from the gaps. The sun had risen to high noon, it baked the top of my head and my back more so than it had in the forest when we had been surrounded by trees.

Even though the fear of getting my head ripped off and swallowed whole by a monster, I missed it. The forest was so beautiful, and, more importantly, it shaded us from the sun. The rocks only really did that if they were taller than me, and facing the right direction, and that was rare to have.

I felt my pale skin burning, red-head genetics meant that I burnt like a pancake in the sun, but never got tan. It hadn't been a massive problem before, due to the trees and the shade, but now I was sure that I would burn up.

"Hey, Simone," I called out.

"Yeah?" She asked, looking back at me.

"Do you have any sunscreen?" I questioned.

"Hold on, I'll check." Simone started rifling through her bag while walking, she slowed down a significant amount, about to my pace, which was like a sea turtle out of water. She handed me a bottle of sunscreen and it squirted oil at me when I tried to squeeze some out, clearly, the contents had separated. I stopped to shake the bottle hard and when I tried again, I got an oily blob of sunscreen. Still awful but it would have to do.

I rubbed it onto my face, arms, and legs, and handed the bottle back to Simone. Or at least, I would have, if she wasn't twenty feet in front of me. I groaned and jogged to catch up with her. I wished that she would wait for me, but I figured it was too late to ask.

"Thanks for the sunscreen." I handed her the bottle.

She nodded and slipped it back into the bag. I spotted a house in the distance.

"People live out here?" I asked, pointing to it. The open fields were otherwise very empty, so the house stuck out like a sore thumb.

"Yup, most likely that's a former camper that didn't want to stay at camp through their adult years and moved out onto another part of the island. It could also be someone who got kicked out of camp or school for some sort of serious crime," Simone explained.

"What's the chance that it's the second one?" I asked gulping. This could either end with being able to sleep in a bed for the first time since the mission started or a fight against a much more experienced fighter.

"Pretty low. From what Medea told me there haven't been any since thirty-six years ago, and she would be 55 now," Simone replied. "Most likely she's been dead for a while."

"Huh?" What did she mean? Did somebody find a body that they thought was hers?

"When you get kicked out of camp, you get kicked out without anything other than the clothes on your back and your weapon. It's really rare to survive for long enough to build a house and find a source of clean water and food before getting picked off by island monsters. Those that do are always found by someone, and wherever they've decided to house themselves become well-known places to avoid," Simone told me as I struggled to keep up with her. I massaged a stitch in my side.

"What would they have to do to get kicked out?" I asked.

"Committing an unjustified murder, or assault," Simone said, her expression growing darker.

"How do you justify killing someone?" I asked quietly.

"If they hurt you badly, you have to have proof of it though, and a really strong argument," Simone said, which comforted me a bit, at least they wouldn't just take someone's word for it if someone got hurt.

"What about the two that tried to strangle that boy?" I asked.

Simone grimaced, "There wasn't enough proof that they did it to kick them out. He was attacked at night, and he didn't see who did it. The Allen's had an alibi, that was proven by their friend, but no one really believes them. I told the kid who got attacked to just tell everyone that they did it, the Allen's have had a bad reputation ever since."

"What if they're innocent?" I asked, "There are monsters everywhere, what if one of them was able to get into camp?"

"Monsters can't get into camp, and even if they did, they don't look like humans, much less teenagers," Simone replied.

The house was only about 100 feet away now.

"Do you think that the person who lives there would take us in for the night? Or feed us? I know we need to keep moving, but I really want to sleep with a proper roof over my head for once," Annalyn suggested.

Simone thought for a moment, "Alright, but if even one of us gets a creepy vibe, we're leaving," She decided.

I looked at Sam and Annalyn and they nodded. The condition seemed reasonable, considering the possibility of the person living there being a murderer. We nodded in agreement and walked over to the house. It was made of brown wood, thick logs that I had no idea where they could have been hauled out of, and yellow flowers perched on the windows beside the door. The wood of the porch steps creaked under my feet.

Simone cleared her throat and knocked three times on the door. She winced at the hardwood and stretched her fingers.

A middle-aged woman, quite bony in figure and clad in worn jeans and a loose yellow shirt. Her skin was suntanned and she had wrinkles around her eyes. Her eyes were brown, they were unusual in that they looked quite flat. No color variation, no flecks of another color, no glowing, not even much shine.

She cocked her head to the side when she saw us.

"Children? What errand have you been sent on?" She asked. Her voice was scratched up, but not unkind. She didn't seem particularly welcoming, but no creep alarms were going off yet.

"We need to get to the underworld; we were wondering if you would take us in for the night?" Annalyn asked before anyone else could say different.

She stared at us for a moment. "What are all of your powers?" She asked suspiciously. I gulped, if she turned us away, we would have to spend yet another night out in the open. I couldn't really blame her, we were a bunch of strange dirty children at her doorstep, all armed and likely to have the ability to beat her in a fight. At least, Sam, Annalyn, and Simone could if they worked together.

"I can shapeshift, turn invisible, and see people's imaginations," Simone listed off.

"I can control plants, create light, and shrink in size," Annalyn told the woman.

"I can blind people temporarily, change personalities temporarily, and see in the dark," Sam explained.

"I can control winds and liquids, and I can heal people by singing or humming," I said nervously.

"The redhead is new?" The woman asked, raising a dark brown eyebrow.

Annalyn and Sam nodded. The woman grinned with slightly yellowed teeth. A genuine smile, that reached her eyes. "I see, come in, I've made some soup, you can take some from the pot. I'll prepare a room for all of you.

The woman opened the door wide enough to see inside. The walls were painted white, and made of thinner boards. The floor was still hard and wooden. There was a couch pushed against the back of the room, it was small, with a coffee table in front of it that had liquid stains, and a small shelf with at least twenty books on it.

The room opened to a small kitchen, a table made for only one person and a large black pot on the stove. The lid of the pot was askew with the handle of a ladle sticking out of it. She pulled down four bowls and handed them to us before walking out of the room, leaving us to our own devices.

Chapter Twenty

Murderer, or Not a Murderer?

I sat down on the floor with the others, a still-warm bowl of vegetable soup in my hands. It was also too salty, and I wasn't a fan of the peas, but I didn't complain. Simona was in a corner, which was an odd choice in my opinion. The open wall offered a better backrest.

"Why the corner?" I asked.

"I like corners," She answered.

My spoon was carved out of wood, and we had found it in a drawer. It was roughly carved and I had to be careful so that it didn't give me a splinter.

"Anybody getting any 'run as fast and far as you can' vibes yet?" Simona asked, having finished her soup in record time. She set her metal bowl on the small table, the spoon inside.

"Nope," I replied. The others seemed to agree.

"Do you think she'll let us shower? My hair is super greasy," Sam wondered, running his fingers through his admittedly gross hair. My own hair needed some serious maintenance, it was dirtied, not to the point that you couldn't see its fiery tone, but enough to make it duller with dirt and mud.

That wasn't even mentioning the state of my clothes, my shoes had been white when I got to the island, and now they looked like a mix of green and brown. My shirt had a hole in it, and my jean shorts were muddy and now genuinely distressed. I looked like I had been shoved through a dirty spiked wringer.

The woman stepped into the room, and to my surprise, and joy, she had two towels and several articles of clothing in her hands. Three pairs of girls' shirts, and nothing for Sam. He would have to keep his shorts from before, which were in a better condition than anyone else's. She had brought us black shirts made of thin cotton, along with soap, conditioner, and shampoo. She told us that there was a well with a curtain set up over it outside so that we could take showers properly, or, as properly as we could all the way out here.

"I know very well what it's like to be on your own out there. You four deserve it." Her trust made me nervous. This woman had cleared us of any danger that she may have sensed, which was good, but it could also mean that she was planning to hurt us.

Oh, come on, look at yourself, she shouldn't be scared of you. I told myself.

Simone called going first, running to the woman's side and snatching a towel, a set of clothes, and the bath products. The woman had Sam, Annalyn and I sit in her living room while we waited for Simone.

"Why are you kids heading to the underworld?" The woman asked us. She set herself down on a chair she had pulled from the table in the kitchen. The three of us that were in the house squished together on the small couch. I tried to sit away from the cushions, I didn't want to get the couch too dirty.

"Hades's helmet is gone, we're going to get more details about the disappearance," Sam said casually.

"Couldn't he have just come to you?" The woman asked a question that I hadn't thought of but probably should have.

I cocked my head to the side and turned to Sam and Annalyn.

"Could he?" If he could, then why not do that rather than sending us all the way through the island? Why put us through all of this if there was an easier way?

"No, not if we wanted to get any meaningful detail out of it. Unlike a lot of the other gods, Hades has a full-time job. He runs the land of the freaking dead. Do you know how many people have died in human history? A lot. He has enough work to do without taking interviews," Annalyn explained, I heard a sense of bitterness in her voice.

"What does Simone think of him?" She seemed to have such strong opinions about the other gods, I wondered what kind of train she would be crashing into his ego when we finally got down to the underworld.

"She actually respects him, which is a massive surprise, I know, but he's one of the nicer gods. Other than the whole 'kidnapping his own wife' thing he's a pretty stand-up guy. Ethan, and everyone else in the Hades dwelling, is in good hands," Sam replied.

The woman nodded. "Hades is among the more trustworthy, but immortals are not to be trifled with. They are like ghosts, they have only their own motivations in mind. Some may truly care for you, but the ones that don't feel any responsibility over your life will be different."

"Who was your guide?" I wondered. I wasn't quite sure whether it would be appropriate to ask about her powers, though, most gifted ones that I had met so far had asked me about mine.

"Mine was Ares. As was my sister's, I never listened to his advice. It was always close to violence, but he claimed first, so I was stuck with him," She sighed. "I'm still stuck with him, guides can change very, very, *very*, rarely, but that didn't happen to me."

I thought of Poseidon; he hadn't given me much advice at all. But he seemed alright, at least, I hoped he would be if I ended up needing him.

"You have a sister?" Annalyn asked. Her black eyebrow raised, making her large eyes look even bigger.

"Yes, a twin, she has done some bad things, but she won't hurt you. She lives further south, and she hasn't made plans to meet me today, so you don't have to worry about her," she said.

Now *that* sent a chill down my spine. Her sister might have hurt people, or maybe she stole stuff. Since the sister wasn't coming, I wasn't super worried. But I made a mental note to sleep with one eye open. Just in case.

Simone stepped back through the door, looking majorly grateful. Her usually very puffy hair was looking almost flat, and nearly black due to the water darkening it. She set to brushing her hair, which sent splashes of water flying from her hair, and sounds that you would think belonged to someone brushing a carpet.

Once she was done, she shoved the hairbrush in her bag and shook her head around, sending more cold water flying.

The black shirt that the woman had given her was so long it almost covered her shorts, though they somehow fit her just fine. Still, she and the woman were very different sizes.

"Where did you get these?" Simone asked handing her towel to the woman who used one of her powers to dry it and gave a fresh towel to Annalyn.

"Oh, they were mine when I was your age, dear. It's a wonder they fit you so well, I hope that they will fit you two alright," The woman said to me and Annalyn, who was halfway out the door. Annalyn nodded to her before shutting the door.

"Thank you for your hospitality miss, what's your name?" Simone asked.

"Oh, you're welcome, I'm Alona," The woman informed us, her smile brightening her matte brown eyes. Simone transformed into a raven and perched on the corner of the couch behind me. "I heard that you were looking for the underworld entrance, good luck to you children. When I had to go, I wasn't able to get through." The woman's expression darkened.

"I've gone through once before, I'd better be able to do it again," Simona said, briefly turning back into her human form. Her knee hit my head and I winced.

"Sorry." She turned back into a raven.

"Impressive, but you are all too young to be out on your own as it is. None of you mentioned time travel as a power of yours, so you must have been younger," Alona shook her head.

"There are campers with time travel?" I asked, turning to Sam.

"No, but I've heard stories about one, he died a few years before I came to camp," Sam replied. "His power was limited though, he could only travel back in time, and he wasn't allowed to change anything when he went."

"I knew him, his name was Amir, he was one of Zeus's, unfortunately," Annalyn added, her tone truly bitter.

"What did Zeus tell him?" I asked. Simone had mentioned Zeus's gifted ones never lasting long, but I'd thought it must have been hyperbole.

"He asked for help with a quest and Zeus told him that the river would carry him to his destination. He ended up getting chucked over a waterfall because he couldn't get out of the boat in time. He was 14, and his quest partner, Dani, died with him," Annalyn told the story darkly, looking at the floor. Suddenly I could see her sitting in the Demeter dwelling, crying over the death of a child she knew.

"Just another reminder that Zeus ruins anything he touches," Simone added, now standing beside the couch. I jumped. Seriously, she needed to start sounding a signal that she'd turned back. She once again transformed into a raven. Her feathers reflected a rainbow in the light, blues purples and greens that didn't match the now heavy mood.

"The other gods aren't so bad though, many care very much about their gifted ones," Alona added, "I'm going to prepare some tea. What kinds do you like?" She said standing up, I heard her joints crack ever so slightly, reminding me that this woman was relatively old. Somehow, it struck me as strange. We had been barely surviving, and I hadn't seen any gifted one over the age of sixteen or seventeen at camp. But this woman was proof that we could survive to adulthood, what had told me that we couldn't was unknown though. Why hadn't I thought that we could survive?

"I like green," Sam interrupted my train of thought.

"So do I," Simone agreed. I nodded, though I wasn't a big fan of tea at all. I figured since Alona was making it, I might as well take some.

Alona nodded and headed to the kitchen. While she was gone, Annalyn came back, I took the towel that Simone had used, as it was now dry, and hopefully cleaned with Alona's power, along with the shirt and shorts. I went behind the house to see a large canvas curtain, it was white, but I could see it was wet and it had dirt on the edges.

I opened it and found a spigot coming out of the ground. The grass was wet under my bare feet. I set the shampoo and soap bottles down on the ground and started the spigot. The water was uncomfortably cold, but I sucked it up and soaked my hair and body with it. I rubbed shampoo into my hair, and used my fingers to detangle my hair after slathering it with conditioner.

I got all soaped up and turned on the icy cold water. After I was done drying myself off with the surprisingly warm towel, I had my undergarments, and shirt on when I heard a scream. Glass shattered and I saw a transformed

Simone crashing through the window. She was a turtle before she turned into a small bird. Trying to get away from a woman who looked remarkably like Alona. But this woman's eyes were the opposite of her sisters, shining like copper wheels. I didn't doubt that, if I wanted to, I would be able to see my reflection in her irises. I didn't bother even putting on my shoes, I got my sword ready as I watched Simone fly with what looked like an injured wing away from the woman.

This woman was also wearing different clothes than her sister, ragged leggings and a white shirt. She was also thinner, almost unhealthily. She was holding a bat.

"What's happening?" I screamed, "Why are you attacking us?"

"The camp sent me into the woods with NOTHING, they were going to leave me to die all because I sent one worthless girl into the underworld. She would do the same to you!" The woman snarled at me. Pointing frantically, but Simone was nowhere to be seen.

"What did you do to her?" I asked, stepping back.

She would be 55 now. Simone had told me. This woman had killed someone at camp. This woman appeared to still be in fighting form. This woman was going to kill Simone, or maybe me too.

I was going to have to defend myself without pants or shoes. This would have been funny, this would have been so, so funny to all of my friends back home in Minnesota, but it was not funny to me at the moment.

Simone appeared behind the woman and kicked the back of her knee. I saw a bruise on her arm that looked really bad before she vanished again.

"Fine then, if we're playing dirty," She lunged at me and swung her bat. I leaped out of the way, and the wood grazed my shoulder. I lost my balance and fell; I scrambled up the best I could and ran around the house to the door.

Alona rushed out, nearly plowing right into me.

"ARIEL! STOP THIS!" She screamed. The woman sprinted over to me and swung next to me, clearly assuming that Simone would be there. I screamed and dodged it, though she wasn't aiming at me. I slammed into the house, and Alona pushed me inside, she didn't say anything but the message was clear.

Hide.

I sprinted inside, I was not about to fight a crazy lady with a bat today, especially while I wasn't wearing pants or shoes. The floor was rough under my bare feet, and I was sure I would get a splinter but I didn't care.

My heart hammered in my chest.

I threw open one door, that was just a bunch of shelves with blankets, old clothes, and a space where the towels the woman had given us had probably been. I shut that door and ran into the kitchen. The cupboards near the ground were too small, and the ones above the stove would be too hard to get into.

I ran through another door; it was a large room with a bed. The frame was wooden and simple, the blanket was dusty blue with a white pillow and white sheets. I shut the door behind me and locked it. There was a large wardrobe. I threw the doors open and found that I could fit. I shoved myself between the pants and shirts and a single plain dress, and closed the door, leaving it open just enough to see.

I sat there in the smell of cotton, in the dark for a while. It felt like hours. But it was only a few minutes. I heard a scream that was so loud, I flinched. I heard another *crash*; this was accompanied by the sound of splintering wood.

I saw a chunk of broken wood fly from the door of the room.

"ARIEL!" I heard Alona scream. "She's not in there, and don't hurt her! She didn't kick you out!" Alona ran in after Ariel and grabbed her arm. Trying to stop her sister from doing more damage to her house.

"But she would! She would do it!" Ariel yelled back, furious.

"That's because she knows it's wrong, you made a mistake, and they were cruel to send you alone, with nothing, but that girl was worth something to someone! Why don't you understand? She didn't deserve it!" Alona replied. I had a sense that Ariel might refrain from hurting her sister, but I had no idea what that woman was capable of.

She had killed a girl after all.

I heard the buzzing of wings, a fly. I would swat it normally, but I didn't want to make a noise that Ariel would notice. The fly landed on my knee, which was curled to my chest.

"You don't understand! I had to! Ares told me I had to!" Ariel argued.

"Ares can be wrong!" Alona retorted. "Now you must leave these children alone!" She tried to pull her sister out of the room, but Ariel twisted Alona's arm. Alona yelped in pain and fell. Ariel had her pinned.

"You've held me back from my revenge for too long." Ariel kicked her sister in the ribs and smashed her bat into the wardrobe. I couldn't keep myself from screaming as the door on my right side got smashed in. I jumped up, hitting my head on the ceiling of the wardrobe and realized that I was cornered.

I couldn't run anywhere, and I was not as strong as this woman. I pulled out my sword and cowered, hoping that Ariel would decide I wasn't worth killing and move on in her attempt to bash Simone's head in.

"Ok, little redhead, where's your friend?" Ariel asked, her voice playfully kind, as though she was trying on a mask.

I shook like a chihuahua. "I—I—don't—"

"YES, YOU DO! YOU'RE PROTECTING HER! She would betray you if she thought it was right! She would!" Ariel screamed.

"That's a good thing!" Sam screamed from the other side of the room. "It means she wouldn't help us hurt anyone!"

I rolled out of the wardrobe, still shaking beyond reason.

On my feet, I thought. I pushed myself up against the wall. I couldn't fight her all alone, not when she had that bat, but Sam being here would heighten my chances, at least a bit. At least I would have an opportunity to say goodbye before my head got bashed.

My legs were shaking to the point where standing was its own battle. But I stayed up. The room had one window, if things got too bad, I could break it and jump out. Ariel seemed only more angered by Sam's comment.

She leaped at him like a charging bull, her bat flying at his head. He thrust his arm out and booked it to the other side of the room from where he was standing. Ariel screamed, I saw her eyes, rolled back inside of her head. Sam had blinded her. He had saved us from her wrath.

At least, for a little while.

She swung her bat around in a circle, knocking an oil lamp off a nightstand, and shattering it. The other side of her swing put a hole in a wall. Sam was hiding in a corner. Annalyn came rushing through the door. She was nearly clubbed over the head with a strike.

She screamed and ducked just in time and then she rolled forward, under a spinning strike that sent the top half of the door into splinters. Her mace was in her hands, but the reach wouldn't be enough to get Ariel to stop.

Alona was on the ground groaning; she pushed herself up with one of her bedposts. She was holding her rib cage. She yelped in pain as she pushed herself up further, all the way to her feet. My hands were sweating profusely and the grip on my sword was weakening.

234

I was frozen in my spot. Fear blooming in my limbs.

She needs to calm down. How can I get her to calm down? I wondered.

I thought of the green tea that the woman had been brewing, the smell was all throughout the house. Green tea, as if that was going to work. What was I going to do? Shove it down her throat? No, I needed something else to get her to shut up and stop.

I inched towards Sam. Then I couldn't hold it and ran to him. Ariel swung and managed to hit my leg. I screamed and dove away, tears welling in my eyes.

"How long will it last?" I asked Sam.

"The blindness? Or the pain of having your leg slammed into?" Sam grabbed me under the arms and hauled me up and away from Ariel. I nearly yelped when my leg smacked into the bed frame as he pulled me over it. I was just able to hold it in, biting my lip so hard that I tasted blood.

"I will kill all of you then!" Ariel screamed. She flung her bat around the room. I saw her copper-wheel eyes, clouded with white. She had at least a bit of vision.

"No, you won't," Simone appeared right next to Ariel and yanked the bat out of her hand. She threw it out the door. Next thing I knew, she had her dagger in her hand. She pressed it to Ariel's throat.

"You're right about one thing, I will hurt anyone if I need to," Simone spoke with deadly calm, and suddenly, I could see her stabbing Ariel for threatening us.

"Then that makes us the same," Ariel said, smiling cruelly. I saw Simone flinch.

"No, we're not the same, you hurt people, even when you don't have to," Simone retorted. "Now, you will leave this house, and get as far away from it as you can."

"Or what?" Ariel seems to have forgotten that Simone was the one with the knife here.

"Or, it will be off with your head," Simone warned.

Chapter Twenty-One

We Get a Ride From Some Fancy Deer

AFTER Ariel hightailed it away from Alona's house, I put my pants and shoes on. The shorts were a little big on me, but I decided not to complain. We helped Alona cover her windows, and it turned out that one of her powers was mending things, so all we had to do was put together the pieces of glass. The door that Ariel had partially smashed would have to be remade, but getting a door was less important than fixing windows, Alona had said.

Simone had a gnarly bruise on one of her arms due to Ariel hitting her, though, when Alona tested it, her arm wasn't broken. I had a bruise on my leg from Ariel's tantrum as well, though mine wasn't super bad, it would hurt for a good while. I was given some tea, that Alona aided her powers to heat up.

I saw Simone looking at our map, her eyes following something. She was on the couch, Sam, Alona and Annalyn were playing with a deck of cards. I sat down next to Simone and peeked over her shoulder. A red dot was on the map. She had a pen in her hand.

"Whatcha doin'?" I asked, sipping my tea. I had added a decent amount of honey to it.

"Waiting until she reaches her place of living. I'll give the campers the location so that they can avoid it." Simone said the red dot stopped on the map.

"How did you get that to work?" I asked. Simone grinned.

"When I was a fly, I was able to get a little bit of star bloom pollen on her clothes. If you rub the pollen onto someone, and then onto a map then it will show you where the person you rubbed it on is." Simone explained.

"That's cool, how does it work?" I asked.

"Well, maps made on the island are usually made partially with star bloom pollen, the magic of the plant is what makes it good for navigation. It makes the paper brighter, as it glows slightly. The pollen can make a connection with more pollen, and translate that into a bright spot on a map, that bright spot is where the person is on that map." She told me.

"Huh, nice." I realized that I should probably take care of my hair, so I took the brush and set to work.

Afterward, we just kinda hung out at Alona's house until the night. She gave us dinner and led us to a larger room. She had set up several mats for us, all with a pillow and a blanket. She said that she only had a room big enough for two of us to be right next to each other. We assured her that we would be fine and that having a roof over our heads was a blessing as it was.

"So, who's getting sacrificed to sleep next to Sam?" Simone asked.

"Hey!" Sam yelped back.

"I can," Annalyn offered.

"Thank you! And to warn you, I'm a restless sleeper." Sam glared at Simone.

"If you kick me, I'll bash you over the head with my mace," Annalyn replied. Sam gulped nervously. Simone gave me a look, seeming to ask me how prepared she should be to take a page out of Annalyn's book and skin me alive or something.

"You should worry about me, I'm mostly still," I said, raising my hands as a show of peace.

"You'd better be, the one night I don't have to watch, I'm sleeping. If anyone wakes me up before the sun rises, I will have your head." Simone responded.

I went over to a mat and laid down. It didn't do much to cushion my back from the floor. The pillow was nice though. I pulled the blanket over myself. Simone lay down on the mat right next to me. Someone flicked the lights off and I heard the person whose head would be behind mine lay down.

I closed my eyes and drifted off to sleep.

I woke up and sat up on the mat. The sun was shining through the window in the room, through the curtains that had been pulled shut the night before. But... something was different. The light was more brown than yellow, like pale wheat. I looked around, the pillows on the mats were askew and the blankets bunched up and thrown to the side.

They must have woken up without me. I thought. I got up, my shoulder was eerily quiet. I opened the door to the living room.

I saw Alona lying on the couch. I went over to her and turned her over.

"Alona? Where are-" I screamed. Her head fell off her body, thudding to the ground horrifically. I booked it out the door. I crashed onto the porch and leaned on the house, closing my eyes and silently panicking.

What killed her? Is it here? Do I need to fight? My thoughts raced. I tried to turn my bracelet into my sword, but it was gone. Sadness crashed into me, maybe if I had been awake to stop it, then Alona wouldn't be dead. The sky was the color of wheat when I looked up, the grass looking dingy, I saw the edge of something black peeking under the porch.

I leaned over it against my better judgment, to take a look. It was Sam, or rather, half of his face and part of the black shirt he had been given. I screamed and gagged. I looked away as fast as I could and ran to the back of the house.

It was a massacre. Chunks of bodies, a hand, a foot, even a nose, locks of hair, still attached to a piece of scalp, and the blood. Oh, the blood. There were puddles of it. The sky grew orange, then red to match the blood.

The harsh colors made my fear skyrocket, though, seeing severed limbs and the bodies of two people was unnerving enough. I actually puked this time. I faced the wall of the house, not wanting to see anymore. I was crushing now.

My legs crumbled under me. The bruise on my leg throbbed, but I didn't care. *What did it do? What killed them?* I wondered.

"See what could happen now, child? You can stop it. If only you prove yourself when you have the chance." A deep, cruel, voice echoed from below me. A god of some kind for sure, but why would one show me this? To scare me into succeeding? That wouldn't work. I would panic and mess up.

The ground cracked under me, dry and dead. It was like a glass plate that got stabbed. The ground was soaked for a second, soaked with blood, the blood of my friends, it dried again, stained brown now. It cracked more, the black of the cracks taking over my sight. I was falling.

I fell and fell, and sat up on the mat, sweat condensing on my brow. I breathed heavily the dropped feeling in my stomach fading slowly. I felt my heart beating in my head. I sucked in a panicked breath, looking to my left side to see if the others were there.

Yup, I could see Simone's silhouette, sleeping on her side, her eyes must have been shut, because I couldn't see their glow. Annalyn was across from Simone, her black hair spread out like spider legs around her head on her pillow. She was on her back. Sam was next to her, his head thankfully all in one piece.

It was a dream. I realized. *Thank the gods.* I laid back down, letting out a breath.

Simone sat up next to me. Her eyes opened, and their glow put spots in my vision, as the room was otherwise very dark. Normally I found the glow slightly comforting, a sign that she was still ok, and ready to set a monster's ego on fire, but now I found them haunting. A sign that she can be taken just like I can.

I remembered Annalyn's eyes, their bright brown, the churn of the earth that can be dulled so fast. Sam's copper is somehow still able to rust. Their eyes showed their power, but they also showed their weakness. Light can be snuffed out, soil dries up, and brightness goes dull with sun- exposure.

"What's up with you?" She whispered so softly I could hardly hear her.

"Just a nightmare, I'm fine," I whispered back.

"If you fall asleep again you won't have another nightmare." She said, but it wasn't her voice I heard. It was Vega. Vega, the girl who I thought was crazy, but now Simone was speaking just like her.

"Huh?" I muttered.

"The deer, they're nearby, one of them will fly over you and you'll have a good dream, or no dream at all," Simone told me.

"How can you tell?' I asked.

"You don't feel it? The calmness, the safety? The island creatures aren't all malevolent, but enough are for it to not feel safe like this when we're

241

away from camp and school. You can feel when something nice is near you, I can feel it, Vega can feel it. Maybe you haven't been here long enough to notice, but you must feel it too." Simone said, her eyes closing calmly. She opened them again and scrutinized my expression.

I looked away, breathed and just tried to feel what was around me. Normally it was dangerous, a slight panic as I knew I could die at any moment, but now it was... tranquil. Like I could lie back and just sleep peacefully.

I laid back onto my pillow, with the sudden urge to sink into the calmness. I heard Simone lie back down too. "You'll sleep better this time." She said with confidence.

I closed my eyes and saw stars dotting a black sky. A black shape with little stars dotting its hindquarters galloped above me, followed by more. The star-flecked deer. One flew down to me and tapped her nose to my chest. She was a fawn, and she only came up to my chest in height.

I'm about 5 feet tall, so she was small. She circled me once and then launched back into the sky. It was wonderful, watching them fly above me, standing in the open field under the glow of all those stars.

I felt a nudge at my side and a warm breath on my face. I opened my eyes to see a star-flecked deer standing above me, a doe. I gasped and pushed myself back. I accidentally put my hand on the side of Annalyn's face. There were two Doe's, a deer, and a young doe, not quite old enough to lose her spots, but old enough to be almost the same size as the adults.

Annalyn cried out and smacked my arm, getting up and freezing in shock at the sight of the deer. Sam groggily groaned and he too froze. Simone was staring at them, clearly, I had awakened her, or she had woken up on her own. I didn't really care. I had never been so close to a deer before, magical or not.

"What? How did they get in?" I whispered. We were all sitting, gawking at the majestic animals. Simone stood up and stepped over my legs. Her feet were bare, I worried that one of the deer would step on her toes.

She reached out her hand to the doe with the coat that shone in the minimal light, blue and purple, like a raven's feathers. Her eyes were pale silvery blue like a lake in moonlight or the brightest day. No, her eyes were blue fire, the fawn's eyes were hot yellow, bright and innocent. It was the one that had leaned over me. The male deer had pale lavender eyes, and the other doe had eyes that leaned a bit more to purple as well.

She touched the beautiful creature's snout. The doe leaned into it.

"They came to give us a ride." Annalyn realized before seemingly anyone else.

"How did they get in here?" I asked.

"What's wrong? Are you three—" Alona froze at the door at the sight of the

deer?

"They came to get us, we should go," Simone explained.

Alona nodded. "Of course, good luck on your mission." Alona backed away.

Simone left the room, and the doe she petted followed her. I left and the fawn followed me outside after Simone. Ananlyn came out with the deer, the silver antlers having to duck under the door. Sam came out with the indigo-eyed doe.

Alona stood on the porch watching us in awe. The fawn next to me knelt down and I gently put my leg over her neck. I held her by the neck. The fawn stood, her spine digging into my crotch. Simone and Annalyn sat gracefully on their steeds, and Sam had to take a couple of tries to get onto his.

Simone's doe took off in a run, then all our others. I yelped as the deer bumped across the flat fields, I yelled on tight, my stomach dropping as my fawn jumped into the black night sky. Sam whooped in excitement; I was trembling with my eyes shut. Knowing me, I would get shaken off and fall to my death.

"Klotho you need to see this view!" Sam yelled over the wind.

I forced my eyes open and gasped. The stars were high above us and the ground was below us, the river glowed like flowing glitter and the scales of fish reflected in the starlight and moonlight. The clouds were nonexistent, and the only wind was because of the deer.

I looked beneath my fawn hooves and my mouth only dropped open further. Glowing white and silvery glitter trailed from the hooves every time they struck the air in the graceful bounds that my deer took. All of the deer had that. How had I not noticed in my dream?

I heard a strange sound; it was an animal that I hadn't heard before and I came from behind me. I looked back as much as holding on would allow and saw tens more star-flecked deer. They caught up to us. I turned back forward and, since my mouth was open, a bug flew into my mouth, I coughed and reached and spat.

"You, ok?" Simone yelled, her voice carrying easily over the wind.

"Yeah, I just swallowed a bug!" I yelled back. Sam backed out a laugh that was swallowed by the wind.

I saw a herd of something on the ground. I didn't particularly care what they were, they couldn't get us all the way up here anyway. I closed my eyes and just let the fawn do the work for me. Up and down and up and down, her soft fur was warm against my skin.

"Have you ever ridden like this before?!" I yelled, mostly at Simone, but I was also curious about the others.

"No!" They all yelled back.

I saw something soaring beneath us. My fawn jumped up next to Sam, the thing only came closer.

"Hey, what's that?" I asked.

"I don't know, it looks kinda like a dragon." Sam squinted, or at least that's what he probably did, I couldn't see him very well.

I saw the flame of silver on curling horns. "A moon dragon!" I realized.

The fawn I rode on jumped up, behind another larger deer, seemingly afraid. I wasn't quite sure whether I should be or not. I had met two dragons that weren't actively trying to murder us, well, that fire dragon tried to kill us at first... so I'm not sure it counts, but whatever.

Moon dragons seemed a bit tamer from what I'd seen and Simone had told me, but those horns were pretty sharp, and they did still have teeth... and claws.

"Should I be worried?" I yelled, mostly in Simone's direction, as she seemed to know the most about dragons.

"I don't think so..." Simone said, partially straightening her back and turning to look at the dragon. "He doesn't look like he's trying to eat us." The deer slowed, some surrounding the dragon. The fawns cowered behind their mothers. The dragon looked around, blue eyes glowing and the scale in between his eyes was fully black like the new moon.

It looked serene, and then it shifted to look towards my right, as my fawn had stopped mid-air. The dragon spotted Annalyn and Simone and freaked. Out.

It roared and reared up, sending a burst of light at Annalyn. She screamed and her deer jumped away just in time for her not to get singed. It opened its mouth again, and this time shadows jumped out, nearly blasting Annalyn and Simone right off their deer.

I screamed and flinched away, forgetting that I was high above the ground. I nearly fell off the fawn and had to grab her neck to steady myself. The dragon flew at Annalyn, claws outstretched. She steered her deer by its horns away and the deer made a deep sound, and jumped away. The dragon caught itself on black wings, white teeth showing.

I opened its wings and seemed to spread out its whole body, suddenly, everything went totally black, as the world had flooded with darkness. I couldn't even see the stars. I heard screams and that deep sound that had exited Annalyn's deer. I screamed too, and suddenly, the darkness receded. The dragon blasted its white light at Annalyn again, but without my knowledge, she was nearly right next to me.

I screamed as my fawn leaped out of the way. The light left spots in my vision. I looked at Simone for guidance, I could only kind of fight on the ground, in the air on a fawn. I would be dead in seconds if I tried.

The dragon spread its wings and glowed, kind of like Simone had when she'd turned into one. I closed my eyes and covered my eyes. It heated my arms and legs, and when it cooled down, I knew it was over.

The shadows seemed more merciful than the bursts of light that the dragon was spitting out. Light meant heat, heat meant burns, and bright light for too long meant blindness. Sure, shadows were temporary blindness, but light could cause permanent damage.

I opened my eyes to see the dragon flying right at me. I screamed and the fawn thankfully chucked herself to my right. Annalyn's deer took her to my left, separating us. The dragon circled her, trapping her and her deer effectively.

Another moon dragon soared towards it. I looked around, but only Sam was on a deer, it must have been Simone. She growled at the moon dragon currently circling Annalyn. The dragon growled back. She spread her wings and straightened up her long tail lashing. She roared at the dragon in what must have been a threatening way.

The dragon growled back, and gilded to the ground. Simone turned into a bird and went back to her doe, when she turned back the doe seemed startled but got going again. My fawn had to get pushed by another doe, its mother I assumed, to make her keep going.

"Why did the dragon go for Annalyn like that?" I asked when my fawn caught up with Simone's.

"I'm not entirely sure, he basically told me that she would hurt us, I told him that she wouldn't and to leave her alone." She told me, quite an odd thing to come out of a dragon. It gave me an odd feeling, Annalyn seemed very quiet, and she was pretty nice from what I knew. She would never hurt us, I knew that, so why did I feel like the food in my stomach had gone sour?

It was the height most likely; heights had freaked me out before, I just hadn't noticed it until we got attacked by something on our wings. Now I was spooked, great. Dragons were beautiful, along with almost anything on the island, but they had proven to me time and time again that they were not to be messed with. A chill went down my spine.

I could see the hints of morning sun rising in the east, the deer started to lower themselves to the ground.

"Why are they doing that?" I yelled over the wind. Sam seemed to snap out of his trance, clearly, he had spaced out.

"Oh, they can't fly during the day, if the sun is up, then they'll fall right out of the sky," Sam explained.

I winced. The sun hadn't risen yet, but it would soon, and I had fallen out of the sky enough already, thank you. My fawn leaped downwards in such a steep arc I screamed and grabbed her by the ears, closing my eyes. This only made it more terrifying because *not* being able to see where you're going is way worse than seeing where you're going and not liking it.

The next thing I knew, I landed hard on my back in the soft grass. I hit my head on the ground so hard it forced tears to my eyes. I sat up and held my head, it hurt badly enough to get some tears out of my eyes.

"You ok?" Simone asked, kneeling in front of me.

"Yeah." I sniffled. I was perfectly safe for what felt like the first time in years, but for some reason, the tears didn't stop. It seemed that all of the stress and fear that had accumulated had found a way out when I was perfectly fine for once. I felt like a little kid again, crying over a scraped knee.

"Stress?" Sam asked, I heard him plop down next to me.

"I guess," I replied. "Sorry, I shouldn't be crying right now. We're all fine." I wiped my eyes with my hands.

"Don't be sorry, you're allowed to let out your stress, now might be the best time in the mission to cry. Tears are really inconvenient because they cloud your vision, the best time to cry is when you don't need to see." Simone explained. "Get it all out before we get attacked for your own sake."

That made me giggle, my eyes stopped burning, and the flow of tears slowed down.

"Only you would call crying inconvenient," Sam said with a smile.

Annalyn laughed. It was a high-pitched, clear sound. My vision cleared as the last of my tears disappeared, I realized we were in a small clearing of green grass, surrounded by flowery bushes. The deer had moved out of sight, likely running off to go graze or something. The bushes had left the color of blue spruce, with ice blue flowers that looked fuzzy and glittered in the rising sun as though covered in frost. The flowers were shaped like lilies, but their petals were more angular, and those pollen string things had what looked like little ice crystals on the ends.

"What are these?" I asked, reaching my hand out to touch them. As I leaned closer, I felt the air grow cold, and the ears still on my face froze over. Simone stopped my hand.

"Ice lilies. Touching them can give you ice burns because they're so cold." She explained. I squished my cheeks to break the frozen tears off my face and brushed frost off of the front of my shirt.

I turned in a circle. There was a narrow path out of the field of Ice lilies surrounding us. When I say field, I do mean a field, the ice lilies stretched far enough that I could hardly see where they ended.

CHAPTER TWENTY-TWO

FREEZING FLOWERS MESS UP OUR POWERS

"**HOW** are we going to walk through that path without touching them?" Annalyn asked.

"We're not, Simone can just turn us into birds and we'll fly out of here," Sam said confidently.

"Uhh, about that, I can't," Simone replied. "Unless you want to stay a bird forever, no one is getting transformed."

I felt like someone had just stabbed me in the stomach. I looked at Simone like she had just grown a third ear in her forehead. She turned into birds all the time, and it had done us a lot of good so far. Why couldn't she now, when we needed it the most?

"What? Why not?" Sam questioned.

"For thousands of years, ice was used to preserve things, sort of stopping time. Lakes freeze in winter, animals hibernate, and any transformation that starts in fall stops. If you change your form around an ice lily, you will keep that form for the rest of your life, or until you can find a god to turn your back," Simone explained.

"Yeah, and they only sprout in winter. They reach their full size in about a week, and then never grow any bigger after that, the only thing that changes are how much pollen they have floating around them," Annalyn added.

"How do we get out? That path is way too small to get out of here in any reasonable amount of time," Sam kicked the dirt.

"Guess we'll just have to go through the path and hope for the best." Annalyn shrugged and gestured for one of us to go first. I automatically looked at Simone. So, did Sam.

"What?" She demanded.

"You walk the fastest," Sam pointed out.

She grumbled under her breath and started slowly making her way up the path. Well, slowly for her, she was actually going at a reasonable walking pace for once. Though I wouldn't call it 'slow' for walking through a bunch of flowers that could easily put both of her legs out of commission.

Annalyn went next, then Sam, and finally, me.

I held my arms out to my sides for balance as I walked at a snail's pace through the thin path. I could feel the flowers freezing the hairs on my legs and it set an uncomfortable chill on my feet.

Stupid flowers.

I shivered but made myself keep going, slow and steady. I spaced out, my movements were so mechanical that it was hard to focus and to be honest, for now, I didn't really need to. The path was straight, and the flowers weren't trying to grab me or anyth--nope, stop right there, with my luck that would trigger the flowers to expand like yeast and kill us all.

I silently cursed myself and banished the thought as best I could. I turned my gaze to the ground and focused on not slipping on the loose, dry dirt. The trail started to become an upward slope, it became such a steep angle that I had to stop and take a break every five steps. I was not built for this. I was basically a twig on my legs, and I was just as weak as I looked. Any muscle that I got from this mission so far was proving to be basically useless.

After only fifteen minutes I was panting like a wild dog and holding myself up on my knees. For a moment all I did was breathe, I wished I could sit down, but the path was too tight for that. Sam stopped ahead of me.

"You, ok?" Sam asked, sounding a little breathy on his own.

"I... I can't... give me a break..." I said between heaves of air that made my nose and throat go cold.

"Klotho, you can absolutely do it, come on," Sam told me.

"No Sam! I can't! I'm not built for this! I'm practically a twig, I've survived out of sheer luck, I have no idea what got me up that other mountain, but whatever it is ran out," I snapped.

Sam held out his hand to me.

"We are strong kids, you aren't built for this now, but you will be. Come on," Sam ordered. I stared at his hand, not entirely sure what to do with it. I grasped it, and Sam practically pulled me up the hill, panting more than I was from the extra effort of dragging me. But I didn't let go of his hand, not even after mine started to sweat.

Throughout the climb I kept repeating the words to myself, *we are strong, we are strong.*

When we reached the summit of the hill, we were treated to a sheer drop directly into a massive pit of ice lilies. Thankfully, none of us fell in, but Simone was close. Literally, she was about an inch away from the edge of the drop.

The path was just too narrow to turn around, so if we wanted to back up, I would be leading, walking backward. Oh boy, now I could see myself slipping and getting flash-frozen like a chicken nugget. I shivered.

"What are we going to do about that?" I asked shakily.

"Annalyn?" Sam glanced at her.

She shook her head. "The flowers won't let us change; I can't change them."

"I don't have the coordination to back all the way down," I chimed in before anyone could suggest it.

"No, you don't," Simona muttered, which was rude even though I agreed with her. "Do you think you would be able to catch us though?"

"Catch us?" My mind spun, catching me at jumping, which meant that Simone had just suggested that we *jump from the cliff,* and risk getting turned into ice statues.

"Probably not without creating a tornado like the last time," I replied, terrified that Simone would go 'Oh well,' and punt us off of the cliff anyway.

Oh, quit it, no one is going to hurl you into a bunch of Frosty the Snowman's flowery friends like a dodgeball. Pull. Yourself. Together. I told—oh heck—*demanded* myself.

"Never mind, plan B: it is," Simone said.

"What's plan B?" Sam and I asked. Annalyn raised an eyebrow.

"Calling a god to assist." Simone dug through her bag, seriously, how many times had that thing saved us already?

"What do you need?" I asked, curious.

"Something to pick up the flowers with, I'm going to offer them to Khione as an offering, see if she'll help us out," Simone replied, coming up with a couple of cloth handkerchiefs.

"And if she doesn't?" I wondered.

"We accept our fates," Simone replied, kneeling down to the flowers and ripping them out of the ground with the disrespect you give someone who insulted your mother. Normally, I would feel bad for the flowers, but since they could turn me into a monster's mid-summer popsicle, I didn't care.

"Oh, well that's a cheerful thought Simone, you know, if you want to freak us out you can just tell us that," Sam spats back, rubbing his arms against the cold that the flowers gave off. Simone ignored him, twisting the flowers into each other until they wrapped around into a flower crown.

"Lady Khione, accept my offering, and help us out of this field of gods forsaken frost-flowers." Simone held out the crown over the edge of the cliff. The crown glowed icy blue and vanished out of her hands, vanishing in a burst of snow. I felt a cold wind blow, as if straight through me.

"Did she accept it?" I asked, unsure if the vanishing meant 'What the heck is this' or 'Sure, I don't want you to die here either'. I really, *really* hoped that it was the latter.

"Yes, but I'm not sure if she's going to help us or not," Annalyn replied, staring intently at a flower. The flower shivered slightly under her gaze, but she let out a breath and it stopped. She noticed me staring and said: "Just making sure there's nothing I can do about it."

"Ah," I nodded. I heard something in the distance. An icy roar. I spun around, nearly falling into the flowers, to see a dragon flying towards us. It had icy white scales that looked like they were covered in frost, and sharp features, the horns like icicles.

"What type of dragon is that?" I wondered.

"An ice dragon, normally they only migrate here in the winter, Khione must have heard us," Simone practically yelled, she waved her arms in the sky to signal to the dragon where we were. The skin on its wings sparkled like freshly fallen snow.

"Are ice dragons friendly?" I asked.

"Oh, no, not in the slightest. They don't go after gifted ones per se, but they aren't very forgiving," Simone replied.

"Well, that's comforting," Sam murmured.

Honestly, I didn't care anymore. All I wanted was to be out of these flowers.

The ice dragon swooped down beside us, hovering a few feet away from the cliff. To get on, we would have to take a chance and jump. Great. The last time I had to jump off something, I chickened out and Simone had to push me. That would work here. I had to actually bend my legs and do it. The thought made me shiver, though, maybe that was partly the flowers' fault.

"Alright, Klotho, you go first," Annalyn ordered.

"WHAT?!" I shrieked.

"It's the safest for you to jump on while there aren't any obstacles. Sam goes next, then me, and finally Simone," She explained, "So, just—" She pushed me in front of her, so close to the edge of the cliff that a little pebble cascaded down the sheer drop. "—don't think about it."

I felt like I was going to be sick.

Ok, breathe. I told myself. *Just bend the legs, and jump onto the semi-aggressive dragon. Easy.* I breathed in, and the inside of my nose went cold from the flowers. I looked at the point where I would want to land and jumped with a shriek.

I flew through the air and landed hard on the dragon. My feet slipping, in my panic for something to grab onto I hooked my arm around the dragon's neck. Both of my feet dangled off the dragon, and I scrambled to put one leg on the other side of its torso.

I was practically strangling it by the time I got myself into position.

"Settled?" Annalyn yelled.

"Yup!" I held a shaky thumb-up to them. I was trembling so hard you would have thought it was negative 40 degrees.

The dragon snorted, and a puff of cold smoke floated into the air. I saw Sam jump, but the way he did it he kind of did it on one foot, so he flew sideways at the dragon, instead of right at it. Now, that doesn't sound quite so bad assuming that he doesn't mind landing in a very uncomfortable way, and gets enough height.

One small problem: he didn't get enough height.

San shrieked like he was getting tortured to death, and he reached out, grabbing the foot of the dragon and dangling it like laundry. The dragon didn't seem very happy about this arrangement, and it waved its front leg around and scratched at Sam with its back leg in an attempt to either push him off to his death or get him up onto the dragon's back. I couldn't tell which.

Either way, I wasn't about to let the dragon turn Sam into child-flavored ice. I took in a breath, and reached down, hoping to pull Sam up, or at least give him something to hold on to so that he could pull himself up. Sam pulled himself a bit higher and reached up. I saw his arm shaking with the effort.

All I got were his fingers. I loosened my arm around the dragon's neck, just so that I could lean lower. Sam relaxed for a fraction of a second, then shifted his grasp to a very firm hold on my hand. It strangled my fingers and cut off my circulation, but I had bigger problems. I did my best to pull him up, and towards me, but I wasn't very strong. I tightened my arm around the dragon's neck and used it as leverage to get Sam to a point where he could get up on his own.

Sam swung his leg over and hung on to my waist so tight I could hardly breathe. I would have told him to stop, but I was basically doing the same thing to the dragon, so I didn't complain. The dragon's wings flapped much harder than they had been going. For a second, I was confused as to why, but when we started sailing through the air, I freaked out.

I heard Annalyn and Simone screaming for us to stop it, but I was in the front and I didn't know what to do other than just yelling at it to stop. So, that's what I did. Sam and I were screaming at it, but it didn't seem to hear us. If it did, it didn't care what we were saying. My arms were wrapped around the dragon's neck, the cold scales rubbing against me. *I could pull it by the neck. I thought, but what if I strangle it by accident?*

Which would I hate more, falling with a possibly dead or very angry ice dragon, or getting separated from the group with no guarantee that the dragon would go back for them? Decisions are hard sometimes, if we fell, I could just make a tornado. But that would then proceed to rip up the flowers and risk us touching them even more. I hadn't been able to get a strong enough wind to save us without creating a tornado before, so that was basically out of the question. The river? Water wouldn't be fun either, and if the flowers were anywhere near it, the water was sure to be freezing. Sam could blind the dragon, but that would most likely end with us crashing, and certainly with a very angry dragon. I didn't see how changing its personality could help.

We were effectively trapped on the back of a ten-foot-long killing machine. With no way to get off without tumbling to our deaths. No possibility of turning the thing around. We were officially screwed. If I had a piece of paper, or just Simone's bag since the thing must have had paper in it somewhere, I would have written my will.

The dragon swooped to the ground and reared back, throwing both Sam and me off. I screamed, twisting in the air to try and avoid landing flat on my back. I ended up slamming into the ground on my side instead, which sent sharp stabs of pain through my arm, hip, and ribs. Sam was lucky enough to have landed in a bush. Or at least, I thought he had been lucky, which was quickly corrected by his screams of agony.

The dragon took off into the sky and I shoved myself up, running over to Sam despite my hip feeling like a paper straw that someone's been drinking out of. Upon closer inspection, the bush was a thorn bush, and Sam had been slapped into its full force by good old gravity.

"Sam? Oh no, here let me help," I grabbed his forearms and pulled him up out of the bush. It was easy enough with his help, though he had to grit his teeth and the bush stuck to him like they didn't want to let him go.

He crashed onto his butt on the grass, yelping in pain as he must have had at least a few thorns stuck in his rear. The back of his shirt looked like a pincushion. Black little thorns pricked the fabric all over, along with his upper arms, it wasn't wet with blood yet, but that had to hurt.

"Oh boy," I muttered.

"How bad is it?" Sam forced out.

"You tell me, it looks like you got half-transformed into a pin cushion," I lifted my hand and touched one of the little thorns, Sam flicked and I pulled back. "You're going to have to hold still if you want this to go fast."

Sam groaned.

"Okay, three, two, one," I pulled out one of the little thorns and heard a sharp intake of breath. "Okay, one down, hold on a second let me count, one, two, three...oh boy," At least several hundred more to go. I did not envy Sam at that moment, and if that bush was poisonous? Screw it, I would have started digging Sam's grave right at that moment.

"This is going to take a while, isn't it?" Sam asked.

"Yup, get ready," I plucked a thorn. Sam yelped. "Sorry."

More thorns pulled, more of me apologizing after everyone. Eventually, the yelping from Sam stopped, and he just winced every time. I was able to get about half of his back down before I heard wings flapping. I turned around, Sam following suit with a gasp of pain. Several thorns popped out of his back on their own with the turn. The ice dragon was flying back with

Annalyn's no Simone on its back, I couldn't control the massive grin that spread across my face. Of course! It was just taking two trips. This was great!

It flapped its wings through the air, I saw Annalyn gripping its neck. I was so distracted by the thought that we wouldn't get separated after all, that I failed to notice the spear flying right at the dragon's heart.

A shriek sounded, I wasn't sure whether it was me or Sam. It didn't matter, the spear pierced the dragon's chest, and down it went like a sack of bricks. I heard Simone screaming since she was so loud, and the next thing I knew I was sprinting towards them, forgetting Sam in my panic. They had fallen from a lovely ten-ish feet in the air, over the river.

Instinctively, my hand shot out, sending a blanket of river water to catch them, ending up with actually enough water. Right as I did it, I knew something was wrong. Annalyn and Simone slammed into it, and the give was enough to make sure that they didn't fall through completely while getting submerged in it, though my temples throbbed. The bottom of the bubble began to freeze. I got startled and dropped the water right away, which sent Annayln and Simone tumbling out of the sky.

I was screaming, Sam was screaming, and I could hear both Annalyn and Simone screaming. I sprinted towards them like my life depended on it, the dragon had already crashed into the river bank, its blood pouring into the river and blooming like a flower of death inside as it washed away. I saw a little sheet of ice forming around where the dragon's scales touched, and then it would get washed away by the current.

Simone was half-buried in a bush like Sam, and Annalyn was on the bank of the river partly submerged in the soft mud.

"Aaaah!" Simone sucked in a painful breath through her teeth. Clearly, the bush had been a thorn bush just like Sam's. I went to help her while Sam fished Annalyn out of the mud.

Annalyn groaned, "Of course, someone kills the thing while we're on it." She wiped mud out of her hair to the best of her ability, but her clothing looked less than ideal, and she would need to get blasted with water for it all to come out.

I pulled Simone out of the bush with a yell of pain.

"It's ok, it happened to Sam too and he doesn't look like he's dying of poisoning," I assured her.

"You got them out of him?" She asked.

"Not all of them, but I'm kind of close," I looked back at Sam, his entire lower back was loaded with thorns. I sighed, resolving to get Sam done first before switching to Simone. Thankfully, Sam sat still while I did it. Annalyn and Simone checked each other and themselves for breaks in case they had taken out a bone or two from the fall. They found nothing super bad, just bruises, and they were shivering like maniacs.

"What the heck was wrong with that water, Klotho?" Simone questioned; her teeth chattered as she spoke.

"I don't know, I was trying to help but the water just froze," I replied.

"It was those darned flowers, they must have messed up Klotho's powers," Annalyn added.

Annalyn had dipped herself all the way in the river in an attempt to get all of the mud off. It mostly worked, but bits of mud still stuck in her hair and on her clothes. Not much she could really do about that.

Annalyn began the process of getting the thorns out of Simone, who cried out after nearly each one at first. But like Sam, eventually, she seemed to get used to it, and as the hours stretched with us working on Sam and Simone in order to get them dethroned, the sun rose to its midday spot. My stomach gurgled with hunger, and the surface of my skin was hot and probably in the process of burning.

"My back hurts, when I sit up straight again it's going to crackle like a bendy straw," Simone complained. I snorted a laugh.

Blood coated my fingers from wiping it off Sam's back. All of the thorns had collected only on his back, unfortunately, I couldn't say the same for Simone, who was pulling thorns off of the back of her thighs and calves while Annalyn took them out of her back and attempted to comb them out of her hair with her fingers.

"What if I just lift your shirt away? It's hurt like crap but at least you'll have the thorns out of you." Annalyn suggested. Simone's face said something like 'I know what I have to do, but I don't know if I have the strength to do it'. Sam blanched.

"Sounds alright, but how will you get the thorns out of my shirt?" Simone responded.

"I'll knock them off." Annalyn hadn't dropped the idea, so Simone nodded forcefully and yelled out a string of curses as the thorns were pulled out. Annalyn brushed the thorns off it.

I heard a branch snap and whipped my head around.

Chapter Twenty-Three

An Old Lady Traumatizes Us

A GIRL was standing behind a bush. She had straight, deep auburn hair braided down her shoulder all the way to her waist. Her nose was long and pointy, and her eyes were large, framed by long lashes, with irises as red as blood. Most of her skin was covered with what appeared to be thin cotton, likely as a shield from the sun. Her shirt, dusty blue and fastened with small buttons, had long sleeves ending in cuffs at her wrists. The shirt was tucked into her pants, perhaps to avoid exposing her stomach to the sun. Her pants were a dull white and fairly loose, while her worn tennis shoes, held together with multicolored threads, had laces that seemed ready to snap.

She was tall and lanky, but the way her sleeves fluttered in the wind made her appear somewhat muscular. Her braid looked frizzy, probably from rubbing against the fabric all day. Her face bore a long scar starting beneath her eyebrow, cutting through the middle of her lips, and ending on her chin. Her nose, peeling with sunburn, was as red as mine.

Frozen, she stared at us with sparkling red eyes. I was too stunned to move. The others seemed equally rooted in place. The girl moved first, walking sideways toward the dragon, her eyes fixed on us as she pulled the spear from its chest.

"You killed the dragon?" I blurted before I could stop myself.

262

The girl flushed with embarrassment. "Yes, I… thought you were here to hurt me." Her blood-red eyes flicked to Simone and widened. "Simone? Is that you?"

Simone stood; her own eyes wide with surprise. "Calantha."

"You have thorns in your hair," Calantha noted. Simone grabbed her hair, violently picking out thorns and flinging them to the ground while muttering something about "freaking bushes" under her breath.

"Thanks to that," Sam gestured at the blood-covered spear, his tone laced with annoyance. Calantha blushed again and mumbled an apology, tapping the shaft of the spear nervously. I lifted the back of Sam's shirt to remove the remaining thorns. He yelped in pain as I brushed them off and let the shirt fall.

"Sorry," I said.

"It's okay. Better out than in. Just give me a warning next time," Sam groaned, wincing as he touched his back, only to flinch immediately.

"I can help with the thorns. The pain won't go away, but I can make the blood stop," Calantha offered. Her voice sounded eager to assist, and without waiting for permission, she hopped across the rocks to our side of the river, holding her hands over Simone. I watched the bright red blood dry into small scabs.

"Do Sam too!" I shot to my feet, pointing at Sam, who still sat on the ground. Without hesitation, Calantha repeated the process for him. Controlling blood—what a cool power. Annalyn had mentioned someone with such an ability before. Sam seemed uneasy, though he thanked her regardless. Bullied out of camp? No, it had to be someone else. Calantha seemed too sweet to bully anyone, much less to be bullied herself.

"How's it going out here for you?" Simone asked, a hint of sadness in her voice. Were Simone and Calantha friends before she left?

"Really good, actually. I found an abandoned house. It was a little run-down, but a nearby lady helped me fix it up. I hunt most of my food, but I have vegetables and berries growing in the backyard and a few chickens," Calantha replied, her happiness evident. The mention of the "lady" made me uneasy. Could it be the crazy one who had tried to kill us?

My stomach growled loudly, interrupting my thoughts and drawing everyone's attention. My cheeks burned for no reason. Calantha's eyes lit up.

"Have you guys eaten in the past few hours?" she asked.

"Well, no—"

"I have food. You can eat with me," she offered, more like ordered.

"Oh, we wouldn't want to intrude—"

"You won't be. I have plenty to share. It's the least I can do after crashing into you," Calantha said firmly. She wasn't budging, and I saw no harm in accepting. What was she going to do, poison us? While possible, I doubted it—she had no reason to hurt us.

She leapt back over the river, clearly expecting us to follow. Sam held me back as I moved to follow Simone.

"What is it?" I asked.

"Don't you think her power is a little sinister?" he whispered.

"No, why?"

"She can control blood. She could hurt us really badly if she wanted to." His reasoning confused me.

"Well, you can blind people. Does that mean you'll blind anyone who comes near you?" I retorted, hopping onto a rock to catch up with Annalyn, Simone, and Calantha. Sam didn't respond.

We followed Calantha to her house, a small, single-story building that was wide but not very tall. The original dark wood had lighter caramel-toned repairs. The tightly shuttered windows seemed designed to keep bugs out. I couldn't tell how light would reach the interior. The chimney in the middle was inactive, with no smoke rising.

Through the trees, I saw another house of similar style. Calantha opened her door and let us in. The house was pitch dark until Simone's glowing irises lit up like faint beacons, giving her an eerie, otherworldly appearance. Calantha's red eyes didn't glow but were faintly visible in the dim light.

She slid a panel in the ceiling, flooding the room with sunlight filtered through a finely woven net, likely to keep out insects. The room had a wooden floor, beanbag-like sacks scattered around a table, and an open doorway leading to the kitchen. Glass windows brightened the kitchen, where a fire on a grated hearth suggested the chimney above it.

Calantha disappeared into the kitchen and returned with a basket of fruits. Annalyn took them without hesitation, so I assumed they were safe. I picked a small yellow fruit with a pink leaf. It was the size of my eyeball and squirted sour juice when I bit into it. It wasn't great, but it was better than nothing, so I swallowed it quickly.

"I have more stored. Could one of you start the fire?" Calantha asked. Simone and Annalyn set to work immediately, placing sticks and layering them with what looked like cattail fluff and cotton from a metal box. Annalyn struck a match, igniting the fluff into an instant blaze.

I sat back, grateful for the shade. My skin felt seared despite layers of sunscreen. At least my back was covered. Sam sat beside me, tense.

"You okay?" I asked.

Sam looked up. "Oh, no, I'm fine. Just tired." Fair enough. We had just trekked across an island.

Calantha returned with a pot and basket, placing the pot of water and wild rice on the grate. She seasoned vegetables—potatoes, peas, and carrots—and began steaming them in another pot.

"While we wait, what are you all here for?" Calantha asked, sitting by the fire.

"Hades lost his helmet. He's too busy to come to us, so we have to go to him and find out what happened," Simone explained. "What about you? How did you end up here?"

"I hung around for a while, moving between temples or houses that weren't overrun by monsters or bugs. I couldn't build anything myself. Then I met Ada—she brought me here," Calantha said.

"Ada?" Sam asked, glancing over at me with a concerned expression. I returned the gaze, a flicker of worry in my eyes. What if it was Ariel calling herself by another name?

"Yeah, she's this really sweet old lady. She can't fight anymore, but she helps me gather food and water," Calantha explained. Just as she finished speaking, a knock echoed from the door. I turned to see Calantha rush over, swinging the door open with a creak to reveal an elderly woman holding a basket of bread.

Her hair was white, neatly braided down her back, and her face, like a map of time, was etched with wrinkles. Her eyes, dark as night, seemed to consume everything no discernible iris, only an intensely dark center that might've been the iris. The rest of her eye had an uncanny blackness to it. Her tawny skin, dotted with age spots, likely bore the imprint of many years spent under the sun. Her worn dress, a faded blend of light blue and white, hung loosely on her thin frame, and her leather sandals, imperfectly stitched, completed the modest look. The circles of light in her eyes shifted toward us as she smiled kindly.

"Who are these children, Calantha? Have they left Camp Myth like you?" she inquired, her voice carrying a small but distinct accent I couldn't quite place.

"Oh, no, ma'am, we're just on a mission," Annalyn answered.
The woman—likely Ada—nodded thoughtfully. "Where are you children headed?"

"The Underworld," Simone replied. "Hades lost his helmet, and since he can't leave to tell us what happened, we're going to him."

"Well, I hope he recovers it soon." Ada's tone was tinged with concern. "How did Calantha come across you?"

Calantha let her inside and led her toward the kitchen.

"She kind of shot down a dragon from a field of ice lilies where Annalyn and Simone were," I explained.

"Ice lilies?" Ada's eyebrows knit together. "How did you manage to get a dragon near them?"

"We asked Khione for help. She sent an ice dragon to pick us up," Sam explained. Ada's expression tightened.

"Ice dragons aren't particularly friendly," she said, her voice tinged with nervousness.
"It's fine," Simone reassured her, waving off her concern. "He didn't care much. He thought we were too small to bother with anyway."

"You can read minds, dear?" Ada asked, her gaze shifting to Calantha with sudden apprehension. That struck a chord in me. It reminded me of something I had been told—an elusive memory that I couldn't fully grasp, no clear face, no distinct words, just the lingering impression of a forgotten idea.

Simone shook her head. "No, I just see the imaginations of those around me."

"That's fascinating. How was that received?" Ada asked, her curiosity piqued.

The question took on new meaning. I remembered the story Annalyn had told me—the one about the girl who could control blood and had been shunned from camp. Calantha's presence suddenly made more sense to me, and I began to connect the dots.

Simone hesitated, glancing at me, and then replied, "It was received okay. Not nearly as badly as it could have been... not nearly as badly as Calantha's."

"That's good to hear," Ada responded with a smile, patting Simone on the back affectionately. I found myself wondering if Ada had ever had children of her own or perhaps a partner. Had she been living out here alone? I dismissed the thought—for as much as she may have lived in solitude, she clearly had Calantha.

"How long have you been living out here?" I asked, my curiosity getting the better of me. "Wait, how old are you?"

"Two years," Calantha answered, "and I'm fourteen."

"You know," Ada mused, "I was her age when I left camp. No one could quite see past my eyes."

Her words carried no trace of anger or resentment—just the wisdom of someone who had seen too much. I felt a twinge of unease, realizing that a child could be ostracized so easily for something as arbitrary as eye color. It struck me: What if that was something I'd face one day?

My thoughts were abruptly interrupted when the wall behind Ada exploded.

I screamed without thinking and, before I could even consider the others, ran toward the front of the house. I yanked the door open, and the pungent sting of smoke immediately assaulted my eyes. A familiar dragon's roar echoed from behind me.

I spun around, my sword magically appearing in my hands as though my body had instinctively called for it. But my hands trembled too much to properly wield it.

The others dashed out after me, Calantha leading the charge. When Ada emerged, Annalyn and Simone trailing her, she looked terrified. My stomach plummeted as I recognized her fear. She had been on this island for decades—what could this dragon possibly do that could scare her?

"Why is it here?" My whisper shook, but it didn't matter. The dragon could certainly hear me, though I didn't want it to. My mind longed to swap my wretched singing power for something more practical—like invisibility—especially when facing a dragon capable of incinerating everything in its path.

"I'm not sure," Ada responded hurriedly. "I knew there was a fire dragon nest nearby, but—"

Her explanation was cut off by a deafening screech as the dragon flew overhead, flames blasting into the air. It looked down at us with piercing eyes.

"Explanations later, scatter!" Calantha shouted, grabbing Ada by the arm and pulling her away from the dragon.

I followed, diving into the underbrush. But it quickly became apparent that my strategy wasn't the best choice when the dragon unleashed another blast of fire toward the bush I was hiding behind. I barely managed to avoid being burned alive, but I couldn't escape unscathed—the fire singed my arm and half of my right leg. The pain was unbearable, and I screamed, despite desperately trying to keep it in.

A second later, the dragon's massive tail swung, crashing into me like a battering ram.

I slammed into a tree, and agony exploded across my stomach and back. I crumpled to the ground, conscious but barely able to move, my body wracked with pain. Tears, whether from pain or fear, streamed down my face.

I could barely keep track of what happened next. The dragon hissed as it tried to swipe a large bird away with its foreleg, but the bird narrowly dodged, shifting back into her human form. Simone flew at the dragon, her dagger raised—but when she landed on its back, the blade merely slid across its scales, and she was flung back.

Grass wrapped around the dragon's front legs, trying to hold it down—but it wasn't interested in being restrained. It reared back, swiping its tail. Simone quickly turned into a bird again, darting to the dragon's rear, her eyes flashing in my direction.

Her eyes widened in surprise, but that brief moment of distraction was enough. The dragon's tail swung out like a powerful battering ram, hitting Simone's midsection with brutal force. She was sent hurtling into a tree and disappeared behind a bush.

Without hesitation, Calantha lunged from behind a rock, her arms extended toward the dragon, her eyes alight with fierce focus. The dragon screeched as she manipulated its blood, making it thrash violently as if it could sense something was wrong.

Calantha seemed to put everything into her attack—her concentration so absolute that it drained her strength entirely. After roughly three minutes, she collapsed, panting heavily.

My chest barely rose with each ragged breath. My body screamed in agony, and every effort to move sent pulses of sharp pain coursing through me. This was far from over.

The dragon swung its foreleg, but she was not the one to be struck. It was Ada who bore the brunt of the blow. She was sent hurtling to the ground, arms flailing in the air, creating a suffocating blanket of smoke that hovered at her feet.

"RUN!" she screamed. Sam immediately sprang into action, darting beside me and gripping my shoulders. I did my best to assist him with my weight, but my chest and back blazed with agony, and every slightest brush against my burned flesh sent waves of excruciating pain through my body, causing me to gasp.

"No," I barely managed to whisper. Ada couldn't fight. Calantha had warned us of this.

"Klotho, we have to!" Sam insisted, dragging me toward my feet. "ANNALYN! GET SIMONE! CALANTHA!" His commands were a shout over the chaos, desperate. The dragon slowly advanced toward Ada, who had somehow regained her footing. It paused—poised and menacing, as though preparing to strike once more. Ada remained perfectly still; an enigmatic calm etched onto her expression. How she wasn't trembling in fear, how she wasn't broken by terror—was beyond me.

Annalyn appeared beside us, half-dragging Simone, her face strained, panic flashing in her eyes. Calantha stood a mere ten feet behind Ada, tears glistening in her eyes, her legs shaking with fear. The air was thick with tension, no one daring to speak.

Then, a flash of motion—a high-pitched, bloodcurdling scream erupted from Ada. The dragon's maw opened wide, and blood began to drip from its terrible fangs as it began to tear into her.

"Go!" Ada managed to scream; her voice ragged with agony.

The sound of gnawing and gnashing, of bones splintering under force, filled my ears—loud, horrific, unrelenting. The horrific crunch of bone, the squelch of torn flesh as the dragon's sharp, blackened teeth shredded through Ada's body—it was a vision seared into my mind. I couldn't force myself to turn away from it, as if witnessing the nightmare were punishment for some unknowable crime. Calantha's scream pierced the air, her whole body trembling as she stepped back, helpless. Sam struggled with all his might to drag me forward.

"CALANTHA, COME ON!" he shouted urgently.

Gathering her strength, Calantha, despite her fear, managed to tear her gaze away from the horror, sprinting toward us. Her face was streaked with tears, but in that moment, I don't think she even noticed. My desire to flee was intense and selfish—I could feel my panic surge, but I knew in my heart that Sam and Annalyn were more likely to fall if they continued dragging both Simone and me along with them.

Calantha managed to get to Simone, taking her under the arm to help Annalyn carry her. It seemed Simone was heavier than I had been.

I glanced back, expecting to see the dragon tearing through the trees, hurling itself toward us in a deadly pursuit, but—no. The beast soared upward, its massive wings cutting through the air, leaving us behind. Ada's blood dripped steadily from its jaws, staining the sky in its wake.

Chapter Twenty-Four

Grass is a Lot Sturdier Than I Remember

WE reached a field of tall, yellow grass before Calantha collapsed, sobbing. Sam and Annalyn, releasing Simone and me from their grasp, sank to the ground themselves. Annalyn, her countenance etched with genuine shock, immediately attended to my burns. Applying an emollient salve, she assuaged the fiery sensation. Her fingers, traversing my ribs, confirmed the absence of any fractures. She repeated the examination with Simone, likewise discovering no signs of broken bones.

Yet, I felt profoundly broken. This mission had exposed me to a litany of horrors, both witnessed and endured, but nothing could compare to the visceral spectacle of the dragon devouring Ada, her voice echoing with the chilling command to flee. I squeezed my eyelids shut, attempting to banish the gruesome image, only to find it amplified in the recesses of my mind.

Curling into a fetal position, I wept, the rustling of the parched grass mirroring my own internal lamentations. Exhaustion, however, soon overtook me, and I succumbed to slumber. My dreams, a macabre tapestry, were haunted by the specter of Ada's demise and the chilling premonition of others meeting a similar fate within the dragon's maw. I awoke sometime later, disoriented.

Simone, Sam, and Annalyn remained seated amidst the desiccated foliage. Simone, absorbed in artistic endeavors, was sketching, while Annalyn, with a whimsical gesture, was causing the grass to elongate and then contract. Sam, meanwhile, was engaged in the intricate art of braiding the withered blades.

Tears had dried, leaving behind a crusty residue on my cheeks. The burns, miraculously, had vanished, leaving only a tingling sensation and a disconcerting pallor to the affected skin. I sat upright, wincing as the jarring pain of the dragon's tail strikes reverberated through my abdomen and back. Lifting my shirt, I grimaced at the burgeoning bruise, an inky tapestry of purple and blue that extended from my lower ribs to my navel. Calantha, curled into a protective ball a foot away, continued to weep inconsolably. Sam and Annalyn, though visibly distressed, maintained a stoic facade, while Simone, her gaze unusually glazed, remained engrossed in her drawing.

The anomaly, though fleeting, unsettled me. I acknowledged that individuals process grief in diverse ways, yet the profound detachment in Simone's demeanor was disconcerting. The tall grass, swaying rhythmically, resembled a sea of undulating water, its color a peculiar, muted blend of yellow and brown, as if parched by the relentless sun. Standing at a height of approximately three feet, the grass obscured our vision, creating an unsettling sense of isolation. My heart, for a fleeting moment, pounded with a primal fear. What if a monstrous predator lurked within this seemingly innocuous expanse? I chided myself, urging myself to savor the fleeting tranquility. However, the vivid memory of Ada's brutal demise had irrevocably shattered my composure.

The tops of the trees, towering above us like emerald sentinels, appeared deceptively close, a mere ten feet away, a stark reminder of the encroaching forest and its inhabitants. We were not safe. A sudden rustle in the grass caused me to whip my head around, my gaze fixed on the narrow, animal-worn trail behind us. A creature, diminutive in stature, no taller than two feet, was perched on the trail, its gaze unwavering, its eyes the color of rich, dark earth. Crouched in a defensive posture, its torso facing away from us, it was shrouded by a curtain of fallen grass, revealing only its face. Its skin, the color of dried earth, was intricately patterned with cracks. Two slender, branching horns, reminiscent of grass roots, protruded from its head.

"What—" Simone, crawling towards me, froze mid-movement. Calantha, momentarily ceasing her weeping, rose to her feet to observe the creature. Sam and Annalyn, mirroring Simone's cautious movements, also approached, their progress halting abruptly.

Simone, gently touching my arm with her index finger, transmitted a peculiar sensation. It was a unique phenomenon – I could still perceive the physical reality before me, yet another, more profound, image dominated my consciousness. This was not a mere visual impression, but a direct, telepathic message.

Field Folk. They are not inherently malevolent, but their actions can be both beneficial and detrimental. Refrain from speaking, moving, or even breathing.

Simone, with deliberate slowness, withdrew her finger, and the ethereal image dissipated. The Field Folk, its large, expressive eyes blinking slowly, remained motionless, its long eyelashes resembling delicate strands of grass. Then, with a sudden, fluid motion, it vanished into the dense grass, leaving behind only a faint swishing sound. A collective sigh of relief escaped our lips.

"Did that interaction transpire successfully, or did we inadvertently antagonize it?" I inquired, anxious about a potential attack. Despite the creature's small stature, I had learned the hard way never to underestimate the inhabitants of this mysterious island, especially when their numbers might be greater than I thought.

"Their temperament is notoriously unpredictable," Simone replied, her voice laced with uncertainty. "They could have chosen to leave us undisturbed, or they could have retreated to summon reinforcements for violence. Field Folk often serve as guides for Gifted Ones, leading them through treacherous terrain. However, if they see a lack of respect for their domain—" Simone abruptly halted her explanation, seemingly hesitant to elaborate further.

"Can't you, I mean, figure out their intentions?" Sam inquired; his voice tinged with curiosity.

"All I saw were the faces of other Field Folk," Simone confessed, her brow furrowed. "But I don't know what that means."

Annalyn, her gaze fixed on the rapidly darkening sky, observed, "It looks like rain is coming."

Simone, sniffing the air, confirming Annalyn's suspicion, "We should seek shelter."

As if in response to Simone's words, a small group of Field Folk, four in total, emerged from the grass, their appearance remarkably similar to the first one, with subtle variations in color and size.

I held my breath, thinking they would attack. But, after a brief, intense stare, the creatures turned and proceeded along the animal trail.

"They say we should follow them," Simone whispered, rising to her feet and cautiously going after them. Sam and Annalyn followed suit, while I stayed back, my gaze fixed on Calantha. Before I could ask her to come with us, she shook her head, turned, and disappeared into the dense undergrowth of the forest.

The tall grass, brushing against my legs, whispered against my clothing, bringing up a surprising sense of calmness. It brought back memories of a field behind my school, where Samantha and I would occasionally go.

There was another field like that behind my grandparents' house, a place my grandfather hated, fearing mice. He would enlist my help in setting traps, determined to keep the rodents at bay. My grandmother would meticulously inspect me for ticks after each trip. I wondered if ticks even existed on the island.

The Field Folk occasionally glanced back to ensure we were following. The distant rumble of thunder echoed across the horizon, and in response, the creatures picked up their pace, forcing us to jog to keep up. Soon, the initial sprinkle transformed into a torrential downpour, soaking us to the bone.

The creatures, now moving at a full run, urged us forward. The ground beneath our feet became increasingly muddy, and splashes of mud clung to our ankles. Suddenly, the leading creature plunged into a hole, and Simone, halting abruptly, signaled for us to catch up.

"Klotho, you first," Simone commanded, gesturing towards the narrow entrance.

"What? Why me?" I questioned, my enthusiasm for entering a dark, muddy burrow was nonexistent.

"You're the smallest of us," Annalyn explained, gently nudging me. "If the burrow turns out dangerous, you'll be able to get yourself out more easily."

With a mixture of fear and resignation, I crawled headfirst into the burrow. Dirt rained down on me as I pushed through the narrow passage, a small, sharp rock dug into my forearm. I continued to crawl, my head lowered, until the tunnel abruptly ended. I fell with a thud into a large, cavernous space.

I yelped as I landed, instinctively reaching out to break my fall. My hands and feet made contact with the packed dirt floor. I cautiously explored my surroundings, my hands searching for any other solid objects. I found a wall, its surface veined with grass roots, and leaned against it for support.

Shaking off the shock from the fall, I stood up, my movements tentative. I reached towards the entrance, locating the hole through which I had entered.

"It's safe!" I announced, my voice echoing through the cavern. "But be careful with the drop!"

A few minutes later, Simone crawled in, yelling a curse as she fell. She hit the ground with a thud. A lantern flickered to life in her hand, and I gasped. The room was massive. We stood on stairs of packed dirt surrounding the massive chamber. Holes in the walls stood out all around, randomly placed. The field folk skittered around this chamber, jumping from one hole into another. The one that had led us there sat in front of us, seemingly waiting.

Annalyn popped in next and managed to fall directly on top of me, which was fun. After she got her leg off my back and her stomach off my head, we wisely decided to clear the fall-zone of the hole. Sam managed to land more gracefully than the rest of us, rolling back onto his feet when he dropped.

"Showoff," Annalyn muttered.

"You're just jealous that you fell right in the ground," Sam retorted, sticking his tongue out at her.

"She didn't fall on the ground, she fell onto me," I corrected, but my face went red with embarrassment right as the words left me. Sam snorted and covered his mouth to half-heartedly hide his laugh.

"Maybe you should be a showoff too, at least I didn't fall onto Klotho," Sam said, grinning.

Simone cleared her throat, then let out a cough that I can only describe as the sound a zombie from the eleventh century might make when it awakens from the dead.

"We should probably get out of the way of traffic, and the field folk looks like it wants us to follow it," she pointed out. We turned to the field folk, waiting, and it took off into another hole. Simone ushered me in first, and this time I decided not to complain. The dirt crumbled around me as I crawled on my elbows through the tunnel, shifting my feet to slither through like a snake. A poor imitation, but it would have to do. I could hear the others behind me.

I crawled onto the ground of a circular room. It was fairly small, about four feet high and maybe six and a half feet wide all around. There was a table in the center, with a pot of tea sitting on it and five cushions of woven grass around it. There was a grate with a fire smoldering in its pit and a filter of grass roots blocking a hole in the ceiling. The tea was still steaming. The field folk sat behind the table, looking very proud of itself.

"Nice place," I commented, dragging myself out of the hole. I managed to crawl to one of the cushions and arranged my limbs to sit on it. Annalyn pulled herself through next and sat next to me. Sam and Simona sat across from me, and the field folk sat at the head of the table. It went around pouring us all tea. It smelled earthy, and vaguely grassy. I sipped it from the clay cup, and was met with a taste just like the smell. I'd never had tea like this before, but I decided not to question it.

"Can they speak?" I whispered to Annalyn.

"No, not any human language anyway," she replied in normal volume.

We drank our tea, and the creature pointed with a thin finger to another hole. Again, we crawled through, and found ourselves in a room only slightly bigger than what must have been the creature's dining room. The creature set out woven grass blankets, pillows, and mats for us and disappeared into another hole. We managed to arrange the mats with some fiddling that included me getting tangled up in them. Sam had to fish me out and finally put them down the right way. The entire floor had now vanished under the four large mats provided.

"Okay," Annalyn wiped some sweat from her forehead. Stupid? Maybe, but yanking stuff like this around in a cramped space where you can't even stand is difficult.

"I'll go over here." Simone set her pillow and blanket so she would be against the wall. "But do we even have to worry about this right now? It's like five PM at the latest."

"Hey, that field creature gave us bedding, I'm assuming it wants us to use it," Annalyn shrugged. She set her stuff down against another wall, so her head would be at Simone's feet. I set my stuff down so that my head was at Annalyn's feet, and Sam set his stuff so that his head was at my feet. Was I excited about spending the night next to the feet of my friends? No, definitely not. Especially since they haven't showered in a while, but there weren't a lot of better options.

I lay down, and fell asleep faster than I expected.

"Explanations later, scatter!" Calantha yelled, grabbing Ada by the arm and booking it away from the dragon. I followed her lead, diving into the underbrush. I quickly realized that this was a bad idea, when the dragon blasted fire at the bush, I was next to and I was just barely able to avoid getting air-fried. Unfortunately, I could not avoid all the fire, and searing heat encompassed part of my arm and half my right leg. It crawled up my limbs, burning the rest of me. Setting me ablaze like a wooden doll.

I slammed into a tree, pain exploded through my stomach and my back. I crumpled to the ground, conscious but barely able to move. Tears of pain stained my cheeks. I watched as the dragon reared back and attempted to smack a large bird away with its foreleg. The bird exploded into ash and dust.

Grass wrapped around its front legs, trying to hold it down. The dragon was unimpressed by this effort, and reared back. Simone turned into a bird again, hovering behind the dragon. The dragon's eyes clouded, and it screamed. Sam had blinded it, though, I couldn't see him from my vantage point, lying helpless in the grass.

Ada and Calantha were hiding behind a rock, Calantha closing her eyes in concentration. Simone landed behind the dragon, she backed up, appearing to be getting a start. Her eyes flashed to me, her eyes widened, and her distraction was just enough for the dragon to slam its tail into her stomach the way it did to me. She crashed into a tree and vanished behind a bush when she fell to the ground.

Calantha jumped out from behind the rock with her arms outstretched, the dragon screamed as she twisted her hands, moving its blood. The dragon shook like a wet dog, as though it felt like something was on it, and Calantha collapsed after roughly three minutes, panting heavily. I wanted to scream, but my chest barely rose when I tried to breathe as it was.

The dragon swung its foreleg at her, but she wasn't the one to get struck. Ada was. She crashed to the ground at the blow, throwing her arms into the air and creating a blanket of smoke on the ground.

"Klotho, we have to. ANNALYN! GET SIMONE! CALANTHA!" Sam called, dragging me to my feet. The dragon walked to Ada, who was now standing. It stood still for a second, in a position like it was poised to strike. Ada stood completely still, an expression of calm on her face. How she wasn't crying in terror, I had no clue.

Annalyn appeared next to us, half-dragging Simone with her. Calantha was standing ten feet behind Ada, tears welling in her eyes. Her legs trembled. No one dared to speak. There was a sudden movement, and a shrill scream. Then blood dripped from the dragon's mouth as it chewed Ada.

"Go!" Ada was able to scream through her pain.

It was the most horrible sound and sight I had ever heard in my life. It seared itself into my mind, never to be forgotten, and I couldn't make myself turn away. Calantha screamed, backing away. Sam started to drag me to the best of his ability,

"CALANTHA COME ON!"

"COME ON! COME ON!" A strange voice echoed in my head. It screamed, and I felt my stomach drop like I was falling.

My eyes snapped open, and I shrieked. Wind rushed past me as I tumbled into a dark hole with the others. I reached out blindly and my hand caught something like several thin ropes. I clung to them, reaching my tiger hand up and grabbing the wall the same way again. A light bloomed in the darkness of the hole. I looked back behind me to see Annalyn hanging from the wall in much the same way I was, Sam a bit further up, and Simone in raven form holding a lantern in one of her feet.

"What's going on?" My voice trembled. I tried, and failed, to not look down. I immediately regretted it. Whatever hole had opened up beneath us as we slept was bottomless, or, it looked that way. My vision spun, and I forced myself to look back at the wall instead. I had grabbed the grass roots hanging out of the walls, and was now holding on to them for dear life.

"I don't know, we were just sleeping and the next thing I knew we were falling!" Sam called back. Simone screeched indignantly. My wrists and fingers trembled hard. I'd never had very good grip strength, and I wasn't sure how much longer I could hold on.

"I—AAAHHH!" I screeched as one of the roots I was holding snapped. I scrambled to grab another. "—Can't hold on much longer!"

Simone cawed, and I transformed into a raven. I frantically flapped my wings until I was stable, and I saw that Annalyn and Sam had been turned into ravens too.

We flew up to the ceiling of the room we had been staying in, and out the hole.

"Are we going to fight them?" I chirped nervously.

"Absolutely not, we're getting out of here," Sam cawed back. With that decided, we flew as fast as the tunnels allowed, and soon enough, we were back in that massively large chamber with all the different holes. It was empty, thank the gods.

"Okay, which one did we come from?" Simone brought up a good point. The tunnels were dang near identical, and it was practically pitch black, even with her lantern lighting the place up.

"That one, the roots are the same as the one we came from." Annalyn swooped into one of the holes, and the rest of us scrambled to follow her. The light shook violently as we flew, and when we finally burst into the cold night air of the field and turned back into humans, I fell to my knees and panted like a dog. Simone was right, flying really did take a toll, especially done at high speed in utter panic.

The others were breathing heavily too, but their breaths caught in their throats, leaving them silent. I straightened myself to one knee and froze. We weren't alone like I had thought. We were completely and utterly surrounded by field folk. Sharp teeth gleaming, black eyes glittering. The stalks of grass swayed with movement further out around us.

"What is the meaning of this?" Simone demanded. How she managed to keep her wits, I don't know. A hard lump of fear clogged my throat, and my hands shook. I felt my sword appear in my hands, and I had to grip it with both hands. I'd fought monsters before, but never this many. What were the words Simone had shown me?

They aren't known to be violent, but they can hurt as much as they help. Don't speak, don't move, don't even breathe. They weren't known to be violent? I found that very hard to believe, but with the look they were giving us, they were about to be.

One of the field folk stepped forward and scratched writing into the dirt with its claw.

One is here to hurt.

The writing made no sense to me. If they could sense emotions like dragons, then why couldn't they tell that we were harmless?

"Who?" Simone asked, though she clearly didn't believe them. The creatures wiped the dirt away and scratched in a new message.

Don't know. It must not continue.

With that, they lunged.

I screamed and smacked one away with my sword. Another took its place, and I was swarmed. Rough skin on small hands grabbed me, claws dug against my skin, teeth sunk into my leg. I screamed and tried to shake them off, but it didn't do anything. I swiped my sword blindly, I felt it make contact and go through flesh and bone. An unearthly screech echoed in the night.

I opened my eyes and saw that my blade had connected with one of the field folks. It was split in half at the waist and bleeding green.

"What do we do?" I heard Sam scream. I summoned the wind to blast a field folk creature off of me, but it didn't work, and I had to cut the thing open. Swing, slash, cut, kick, I did everything I could, but more just kept coming. To my horror, I watched the bodies of the ones I had cut weave back together as though nothing had happened.

"We need to get out of here!" Simone screamed back, "But if we turn into birds, they'll still catch us."

"Burn the field!" Annalyn cried out. I felt a blast of heat at my back and turned to see Simone holding a flamethrower and Annalyn with one just like it.

"Where did you get two flamethrowers?" I demanded.

"Annalyn can occasionally change her weapon like I can. Come closer to us!" Simone screamed at both me and Sam. I scrambled to get to them and huddled up at Annalyn's back. Sam stood next to me, and we wildly slashed our swords at anything that came near us. Severed grass flew in the air, and the number of field

folk finally started to decrease. Without warning, Annalyn jumped in front of Sam and me and lit the grass like Christmas Eve. We were surrounded by a ring of fire.

"Fly! Now!" Simone ordered, turning us into birds. We launched into the air as high as we could get. A field folk jumped and grabbed my tail. I screamed, the little bird-like shriek echoing pathetically.

Just as I was being brought down by the weight, it disappeared. I actually jumped up because of it. I had been fighting so hard to stay in the sky. I didn't look back, I just beat my wings against the air to follow the others.

Chapter Twenty-Five

Knowledge (Well, Technically an Arm) is Power, Especially in a Monster's Mouth

WE flew for a long while. I had no idea what time it could be. I saw the roofs of several marble buildings, one much larger than the others, and Simone swooped down in front of us to land on the ground in front of the large building. She turned us back into humans, but she did Sam and me just a little too early, and I tripped and fell on my face while Sam just barely caught his own balance.

"Hey!" Sam complained as I peeled myself from the ground. I dusted dirt from my face and my shirt.

"Sorry," Simone said hastily. "Come on, it's a library, and those are marble doors that haven't been opened in centuries. You two push on that side, Sam and I will get this side. Sam, can you count us into pushing?" she asked, already walking up the marble stairs in front of the building. The pillars that held the outstretched roof up were perfectly pristine, as was the rest of the building. Only the steps had the smallest cracks, the only hints of moss. Still, something about this building felt ancient to me. Above the twelve-foot-tall double doors was a carving of an owl.

I braced myself next to Annalyn.

"On three," Sam instructed. "One, Two, Three!" He groaned with effort as he shoved against the door with Simone. Annalyn and I pushed too, the smooth marble beneath our fingers barely giving way. We stopped, heaving in the cool night air. Goosebumps riddled my skin, and I shivered as a wind passed.

"This is a bad idea, we won't be able to close the doors anyway. Let's just sleep outside." Sam crossed his arms, still breathing heavily.

"Well, for shelter for one, and warmth, I'm getting chilly out here." Annalyn rubbed her arms with her hands as if to warm them.

"We can just bundle up really tight, besides, we'll be protected from any weather under this roof," Sam argued. A fair point, that lacked one solution for our most pressing problem: monsters.

"What about the monsters?" I whimpered.

"It's not like we've slept without walls before," He had a point there too, but after Ada, I wasn't sure I could justify that thinking anymore.

"Alright, how about this, if we can't get those crappy doors open within the next six tries, we can sleep out here or break in through a window or something. Deal?" Simone suggested.

I couldn't see him very well, but Sam must have rolled his eyes. "Fine, let's keep banging on the stupid doors."

We got to our places again, and after three tries, the doors had just barely started to budge. Then, it hit me.

"My powers!" I said excitedly.

"Huh?" The others all said simultaneously. Simone turned to me, her glowing eyes full of confusion.

"The wind power! I think I might finally have it in me to not start a tornado!" I exclaimed, practically jumping with excitement.

"Yeah, that's because you had it traumatized out of you," I heard Simone mutter, though she sounded more proud than annoyed or sarcastic. "That's a great idea, Klotho. When we push, blast this thing with air like there's no tomorrow."

"If we don't get these doors open, there might not be," Annalyn added.

"Yeah, thanks, Annalyn, no pressure."

"Alright, Klotho, you count us in now." Sam braced himself against the door.

I took a breath. "Three, two, one!" I blasted the doors with wind so hard that it slammed the others in. With the small gap that I was able to create, I used the air inside the building to pull the doors open. Finally, I got it a foot open and had to stop. I huffed and puffed like a factory in 1910.

"That's good, Klotho, come on," Annalyn put her hand on my shoulder and led me to the door.

When we got inside, I coughed on the scent of dust. Simone's lantern glowed from behind me, illuminating bookshelves. Many of the shelves were completely empty. Some had scrolls that looked as though they would disintegrate if they were touched.

"It's a library," I said quite obviously.

"No, really? I thought it was a morgue," Simone replied, then her face went a bit more serious. "Actually, it might be an unofficial one. Come on, let's get this door shut." She set down her lantern, and with Annalyn's help, she managed to get the door shut again.

"Klotho must have loosened the hinges when she opened it," Sam concluded, plopping down against a bookshelf.

"Careful! We don't know how old that is. I don't want you to take the whole thing down on top of us," I cautioned.

"It's not coming down because I leaned on it. Really, Klotho, have some faith in dead people's engineering," Sam waved away my concern. "Can we just sleep now? I didn't get any before the ground dissipated last time."

Simone turned her lantern back into her ring as an answer. I heard rustling feathers and then silence. I lay down next to an empty bookshelf on the cold, hard floor, put my arm under my head, and lay there for way too long. The floor pressed into my hip and my ribs, and I was cold. I curled up tighter, hoping to draw some warmth. I heard shifting and shuffling.

"Aww, screw it. Simone, do you have some matches? I'm cold," Sam called. His voice echoed eerily in the used-to-be library.

A bird swooped up, and Simone turned back into a human. She gripped a handle on the ceiling. She opened up the skylight, one that I hadn't even noticed, and then turned back into a bird and swooped down.

She started making a fire, and I slid over to it, curling up next to a bookshelf closer to it for warmth, but still shivered.

"Does anyone have some blankets?" I asked.

"I might have a couple. But I know I have a tarp, so if I can't find a blanket, you can use that," she started rifling through her bag. After a few minutes of cursing under her breath and aggressively yelling at her bag, she tossed the tarp at me.

"That's the best you're getting. Now, if you would excuse me, I'm going to sleep." She proceeded to turn into a small bird I didn't recognize again and flew up into the bookshelves.

I wrapped myself in the stiff tarp and curled up, deciding that further complaining was a bad idea. I fell into a fitful sleep, lighter than I've had this entire trip. It was almost as though I wasn't even fully asleep, just stuck in the part halfway there.

I woke up to screaming. I kicked my legs, but found myself caught in the tarp and hanging off the ground as if I were in a makeshift sack. I screamed with whoever else was doing it and managed to get my head and shoulder out of the tarp enough to see what was picking me up. A massive black dog with deep red eyes and horrific breath was holding the tarp up with me inside.

Its gaze shifted, and it was looking right at me. Fear, that had now become much more familiar since being on the island, ripped through me, and my swords appeared in my hand. I was able to get my arm out of the tarp, and the dog shook me, causing me to promptly drop my only weapon.

'Now, Klotho', you may say, 'Why don't you just blast that furry beast with air? It would leave you alone eventually.' If you are, in fact, thinking this right now, I would have to advise you to go outside for about ten minutes and feel what normal wind actually feels like. No amount of wind short of a tornado will stop this thing from eating me.

Where were we? Oh yeah, fearing for my life.

I grabbed helplessly for anything I could as the tarp rocked me. I got hold of something smooth with grooves like a hand. I yanked on it, and with a crack, it gave way. I pulled it closer to me, though it was fairly heavy. I turned my head and saw that it was a marble arm, broken off at the shoulder. The dog switched its grip on the tarp, pulling me closer to its mouth. I shrieked and swung. The arm made contact with the dog's ear, and it dropped me.

I rolled out of the tarp, kicking it away. I looked around frantically for my sword, but I couldn't see it anywhere. The dog bent its legs, and before I could react, I was pinned underneath it by one of its colossal paws on my chest.

"SOMEONE HELP ME!" I screamed. In response, I heard a snore. Great, I guess I'll have to do this myself. The dog opened its mouth over my face, and I shoved the severed statue arm right into the back of its throat. It choked and hacked, even tried to spit. It was no use; the arm was lodged tight in its throat.

I scrambled to get out from under it. I ran and hid in one of the empty shelves, shaking like a leaf.

"Sam? Simone? Annalyn? Where are all of you?" I heard a snore next to me, and when I looked over, Sam was curled up. "Sam? Sam! SAM! SAM WAKE UP!" I grabbed his shoulder and shook him. His eyes cracked open.

"Ten more minutes, Dad," His eyes began to slide shut again, but I smacked him in the face out of desperation. His eyes opened wider this time.

"Oh, Klotho? What was that for?" He rubbed his now slightly red face.

"Why were you screaming? And what is that sound?" The massive dog was now making choking noises and scratching the floor.

"A giant black dog attacked me. I was screaming like crazy, but no one heard me," I realized at that moment that besides being scared out of my wits, I was also vaguely annoyed. I was the least experienced person on this cursed mission, after all.

"Huh, that's weird, Annalyn and Simone are usually super light sleepers," Sam stood up, looked around, and proceeded to scream: "RISE AND SHINE, LADIES!"

"Samuel, if you wake me again, I will impale you on one of these statues!" Simone yelled back, sounding grumpy as ever with a dose of raspiness in her voice.

"Oh, speaking of strangling, I shoved a statue's arm down a massive dog's throat, and now it's choking," I blurted.

"What?" Sam, Annalyn, and Simone said at once. Simone poked her head out from one of the high shelves, Annalyn right beneath her. Sam sounded confused, Annalyn concerned, and Simone delighted.

"If this were battle lessons in Nikephoros Academy, you would have gotten an A for creativity. I'm going to take a look." Simone turned into that same bird I didn't recognize from last night and swooped over the bookshelf. I heard a bird shriek that I assumed meant happiness, then a sound like someone was in extreme pain.

I ran around the bookshelf to see Simone doubled over laughing.

"Okay, that is hilarious. Why didn't you wake us up?" she asked.

"I tried, but no one came." I put my hands on my hips.

"Huh, that's weird, if you were screaming, Annalyn and I should have heard you. Don't count on Sam though, he sleeps like a corpse," Simone replied.

"Is there anything you did that might have made you sleep deeper?" I questioned.

"Well, I couldn't sleep for a little while—" Simone glanced at Annalyn, who had just emerged from behind a bookshelf. "—and you made some tea, and drank some yourself. Maybe there was something in the tea that made us sleep harder. What did you put in it?"

"Just a tea bag I had lying around. I didn't think it was anything sleep-related," Annalyn said, rubbing her jaw. "Then again, my parents are fond of natural remedies, and my dad has insomnia."

"Well, in that case, remind me not to drink any more tea from your parents'." Simone waved it off. "Come on, we should leave in case there are more hellhounds running around."

I gathered the wind in the back of my mind and blasted the doors open with the help of Sam, Simone, and Annalyn's pushing. We slipped out and started to follow Simone down a path. Not a clear path, but one much more well-trodden than what we had been walking on previously. We were going uphill, not horrifically steep, but the incline made my thighs burn with effort.

"How many more eternities until we get to the underworld?" I called up to Simone, who was, as usual, far ahead of the rest of us.

"Actually, we're pretty close," she yelled back.

"What? Really?" I felt a grin spreading across my face. The journey would be ending? After eleven days of suffering, it was about time.

"Yup, once we get over this hill it will open to a kind of bowl in the earth. There's some kind of challenge to get in, but it changes every time someone goes down," Sam explained.

I felt color drain from my face. "What kind of challenges?"

"I have no clue, I've never been down there before, remember?" Sam grabbed my wrist and yanked me into a run after him. We crested the hill at a run, breaking through the trees and stopping right at the top.

Sam was right, it was like a massive bowl, the river flowed down into it and vanished underground, and every inch of the ground in the dip was blooming with flowers. Red, yellow, blue, pink, purple, and everything in between.

We walked down to where the river disappeared into the ground. I skidded down the hill, the dew-covered grass soaking my feet. Getting down there took a solid ten minutes, most of which I spent watching the river and admiring the flowers. I'd never seen them so densely in one place and over such a large area. The river water seemed to darken on its way into the ground. No fish went down there, no plants, just stone, also gradually darkening until at the mouth of the ground entrance, they were black.

"Do we go in through there?" I asked, not excited at all. The entrance was so low, going through would mean being fully submerged in foot-deep water for at least one god knew how long.

A cool summer breeze blew, colorful swirls around into the shape of a woman. She had hair the color of ripe wheat, braided into a crown around her head with live asphodels and narcissus. She had peach skin and a button nose. Her round, large eyes were blue as the midday sky. Thick golden eyelashes framed them, and her eyebrows were more of a dark blonde than any deep shade. It made her look soft. She was wearing a flowing dress of pale pink. The border at the straight neckline, the edges of the sleeves, and the hem were green with white flowers embroidered onto them.

"No, child," said the woman. "Hello, Simone, Sam, Annalyn. Klotho, you do not know me, so allow me to introduce myself. I am Persephone, and my husband has been waiting for you. To reach the underworld, you must pick the correct flower from this field. Hades wanted to leave it with few consequences for mistakes, but the spell he used was tampered with, and if you pluck the incorrect bloom, let us say that you will be arriving to the underworld the old-fashioned way."

I nodded because I had no idea what else I was supposed to do, and this seemed to satisfy her.

"Good luck, choose wisely." With that, she vanished in that same summer breeze.

I looked back out at the field of blooms. Simone swore with almost as much color as the carpet of flowers before us.

"Well, we're screwed," Sam announced.

Simone sighed, "Spread out, look for any flower that looks vaguely unusual. Call us over before picking it though." With that, she turned into a field mouse and vanished into a flurry of petals. I walked in another direction, the flowers putting up a resistance to my feet. Many were flowers that sprouted around ankle height, but there were a fair few that went up closer to my knees.

I bent over and started inspecting the flowers. For a long time, I saw nothing unusual. I saw a group of black flowers, with four petals that tapered at the ends and a blue line running down the center of each. The leaves were frosted green and somewhat fuzzy. When I bent with a knee to the ground for a closer look, the stems of each flower had knife-sharp thorns.

"Hey! Over here!" I yelled out, though the others were far away. Thankfully, my voice carried far enough for at least Simone in her field mouse form to hear me, and she blasted out her own order for Sam and Annalyn to get over here in the form of a violent shriek in a bird form that I couldn't see from this far away. She dropped down, and a field mouse popped up next to me so fast I shrieked and would have stomped on it had it not turned into Simone roughly six seconds later.

"Oh, you think it's the black ones?" she sounded disappointed.

"Yeah, is that bad?" I asked.

"No, it's not bad, just a bit obvious. Hades doesn't mess around with gifted ones like some of the other gods do, but he won't make it this obvious. Good thinking though," Simone encouraged, turning just as Sam and Annalyn arrived.

"Wait, what's this flower called?"

"Oh, that's Hellknob," Annalyn answered. "And Hades probably wouldn't have put it there for us to pick."

"Yeah, you're right," he said, stomping through a patch of daisies. He sounded angry at the suggestion, but I tried to put it off to hunger, which Sam had never really handled all that well.

I continued my search, and Sam called me over to a group of flowers he called Hellbore, saying that the name might be an indication.

"Yeah, but isn't that also too obvious?" I asked, remembering Simone's words and Persephone's warning.

"Yeah, you're right," he said, turning, and his eyes brightened. "Oh, look at that!" He ran over to it, a flower with six orange petals in sharp shapes. They had yellow dots and dark green stems. To my utter horror, he reached down and yanked the flower out of the ground.

"Sam!" I gasped.

"What? I can't pick a pretty flower? Oh my goodness, are you okay?" I must have looked as white as I felt.

"Not when you could die by picking it!" I argued frantically, but the ground shifted right behind him. In a second, an entrance complete with stairs had been drilled into the ground.

"Well, I'm not dead—wait, is that what Persephone meant? Oh wow, I guess I took the right one," he added, glancing behind himself. I didn't answer, just stared at the hole with my mouth hanging open.

Chapter Twenty-Six

Chairs Are Semi-Decent Hiding Places
(only from really busy gods,
don't try this with your mom.)

"You did *what*?"

Simone's hands flew to her hips. Her bag was stuffed with dandelions and shamrocks, which she told us were edible. Sam, being Sam, attempted to take some immediately, but first Simone made him repeat after her that when someone says "go to the underworld the old-fashioned way," they mean dying. Annalyn looked very nervous to be finally entering the underworld.

Simone handed out dandelions and shamrocks, and I stared at them.

"Are you sure these are edible?" I asked.

"Oh yeah," Her voice echoed as she stepped into the tunnel. "They actually taste okay, just make sure there aren't any ants on them."

I looked at one of my dandelions, blew on it though I didn't see any ants, and bit off the flower. It was strange, not bad, kind of sweet, and the petal texture was nice. When I ate the stem, it was bitter, but I swallowed it anyway. The shamrocks were better, a kind of sour taste, but not bad. Next thing I knew, I was done with both varieties of plants, and all it did was give me the contrast to realize that I was really hungry. My stomach rumbled for more, and I mentally shushed it.

We walked, and walked, and walked. Down, down, and down some more. Down until it was so dark that Simone's lantern only seemed to penetrate it for a few feet, and I was too far behind for it to be useful. Down until my ears popped, down until I tripped over my own foot and tumbled down the hard stone stairs like a sack of wet mice.

My elbow banged into the ground, and I slid. I stuck out my other arm, and it hit Sam's knees. His legs buckled underneath him, and he effectively sat on me, which stopped my tumble, but was also very uncomfortable.

"Ow!" I yelped, the sharp edge of the step digging into my cheek. Sam shifted, trying to get up, and my face slid across the step because of it. I felt the sting of a cut. Sam finally got off of me and helped me up. I touched my right cheek and hissed at the abrupt sting. I felt the warm wetness of blood.

"You okay?" Sam's voice echoed loudly from my right.

"Mhm, you go ahead in front of me, I won't fall again."

This prediction turned out to be demonstrably false, as I fell two more times in the span of thirty minutes. That may have been because the stairs became steeper, not like ladder steep, but not something I wanted to fall down again.

"Klotho, you should go in front, I don't want to land on you again." Sam's footsteps stopped as he waited for me to get in front of him. I felt along the wall with one hand as I walked, trying to prevent another fall.

"This tunnel should have handrails, or lights," I grumbled.

"Maybe he was counting on his guests being able to walk down stairs," Sam snickered in response. I whipped my head back to scowl at him, realizing: a) he couldn't see me anyway, and b) I do not have the balance to focus on anything other than walking. I promptly fell down the steps yet again, this time managing to roll right into Annalyn, who fell and knocked into Simone, and all three of us bounced down the steps until we hit solid, flat ground.

I blinked hard against the dust we'd kicked up and managed to get myself out from under Annalyn. I looked up at the space we were in, and my stomach did some turns. It was like a gigantic cave, so large and wide I couldn't see all the way across. There was no sky, just black stone. High above the ground, a man was tied to a burning wheel, which illuminated the space. We were on a kind of large hill that was cut off by the wall which the tunnel was carved into.

From my vantage point, I could see a gigantic field with floating spectors that looked like ants far away. I saw another barren land from which screams emanated, far away, a grouping of islands sitting in clear water, and around that, a meadow with scattered souls roaming. Trees littered the spaces between these fields – poplars, and in the very center of all this was a black palace, a colorful garden on one side of it. The five underworld rivers snaked through the ground.

I heard clattering, like hard sticks being clacked together. I looked towards the sound and shrieked. I jumped behind Annalyn and Simone out of fear for the armed skeleton running full speed towards us.

"Don't worry, it's just one of Hades's guards. It won't hurt us unless Hades wants it to," Simone reassured me. The skeleton guard reached us and gestured for us to follow it. The sword at its side swung around on its belt. Simone followed it without question, and after a quick look at Sam, I decided I was better off following them too.

The skeleton clattered us all the way to the black palace and led us into an open-air space surrounded by pillars and a gate. At the back of the space, on a dais that overlooked it, sat the man I'd seen next to Zeus at my choosing ceremony. He sat on a throne made of obsidian with bones set into it like a mosaic.

He somehow looked even more like the king of the dead than he had when I was up on Olympus – in a black chiton that seemed to shift in a phantom breeze, a crown of bones, and skin so white you'd think he'd never seen the sun in his life. The skeleton opened the gate and shut it behind him, leaving us outside. He went to the god, Hades, bowed, and I saw his jaw moving.

"Let them in," Hades said in a booming voice that couldn't have been more rulerly if he tried.

The skeleton guard opened the gate, letting us in, and it promptly ran off. I forced my legs to move towards Hades. Annalyn looked just as nervous as I did, and Sam only slightly less so.

Simone, as predicted, did not look even remotely afraid.

"Hello, Hades, nice of you to have a bunch of flowers try to kill us." She opened up her bag and started rifling through it, probably for her journal. I was staring at her dumbfounded. This man could lift a hand and kill her before she had time to blink, and she still had the guts to be sarcastic. "Not like that's the first time something like that has happened," she added, clearly referring to Blue Leaf Field and the ice lilies.

"I did not mean for the spell to be so high stakes. I'm sure Persephone told you as much," Hades replied with a frown.

"I'm just messing with you, I know you didn't mean to. Where did I put that book?" She stuck her entire, fluffy-haired head into her bag.

"I am very sorry that I couldn't come to you, but you know how the underworld is. I look away for one moment, and the ceiling cracks open, or my workers are abused, or my property gets stolen," Hades told us.

"Oh, it's alright, I get it. You know, when we get back to camp, I'll just be glad if no one's burned the place down," Simone's voice was muffled by the fact that her head was in a bag. "Or dumped paint remover onto the walls, or freaked out all the dragons, or flushed themselves down the toilet, again."

"Maybe you should turn it upside down instead of sticking your head inside it," Annalyn offered, possibly worried for Simone's lungs.

"Great idea!" Simone yanked her head out of the bag, took it off of her body, and turned it upside down. An avalanche of random objects fell out, leaving a two-foot-tall pile of random crap. "Huh. I need to de-clutter this thing. I could swear there's something else in there." She shook the bag, and an honest-to-gods instrument case fell out onto her right foot.

"Ay!" she yelled and jumped back. She proceeded to curse in a language I couldn't understand. "How did that get in there? I don't even play the saxophone!" She promptly dove into the pile in search of her book once more.

"Where did that thing go? Is it one of those cursed books that's enchanted to avoid its owner?" she griped.

"A cursed book?" I asked, though I totally believe it. The island was crazy enough for it.

"Yup, it's a pretty common prank. I hate it though," she explained.

"Maybe you should keep it in a pocket instead," Sam suggested.

"What pockets? Sam, I'm a girl. Our clothing rarely comes with pockets, and if they do, they aren't big enough for a whole journal. Besides, the thing would get soaked, set on fire, and wrecked seventy times over if I dared to have it in a pocket."

After a while, she raised an object out of the pile. "Success!" she exclaimed. She proceeded to throw everything else, including the saxophone, back into her bag and stood before Hades's dais as though this was an entirely normal occurrence. "Okay, what happened with the helmet thing? And if you say that you just woke up and it was missing, I will not hesitate to take a flamethrower to your tapestries."

Hades almost flinched. "I am well aware." That choice of words made me wonder just what went down the last time Simone was in the underworld. "The night it was stolen, I was asleep, and I heard a noise. I stepped out of my room and saw my skeletons chasing a cloaked figure. The person was shorter than my guards, but they slowed my skeletons and were able to leave the underworld, though, I know not how. I went back to sleep, thinking that all was well, but when I woke, I felt the urge to check my helmet, and it was gone."

"Do you have any other descriptions of this person? A specific height maybe?" Simone asked after jotting down what Hades had said.

"They were about your height, the cloak seemed heavy and was black, but that is it," Hades explained.

"Is that it?" Simone asked, clearly a bit disappointed.

"Yes, unfortunately," Hades replied, sighing. Sam's stomach growled like a monster. Hades's eyes fixed on Sam. "Do you children want something to eat? Food is important for growing children."

"Wouldn't the food of the dead trap us here forever?" I asked nervously, worried I'd offended him. I remembered the myth where Hades had trapped Persephone in the underworld, and sure as heck wasn't going to be eating any pomegranates down here.

"Ah, you're the new one. Klotho, I believe. I am a god, Klotho. I can snap my fingers and food from the land of the living will appear. I wouldn't feed you the food of the dead. I don't want any of you here until it is absolutely necessary," Hades replied. My face went red with embarrassment. At least he didn't seem offended. "Come, dead children are of no use."

With that, he stood up and walked through a doorway behind his throne, even Simone had to run to catch up with his steps. This led us to a dining room with a massive wooden table that included chairs we would probably have to stand on in order to actually see above the table. Hades looked at the size difference and snapped his fingers, which shrunk both him and the table.

"Sit wherever you like," Hades took the head of the table. When he snapped his fingers this time, food and plates appeared in front of us.

Simone sat down closest to him, then Annalyn across from her, Sam next to Annalyn, and me next to Simone. We ate gratefully, though I was too shy to take too much.

"Any theories as to where this thief may have taken it?" Simone asked before shoving what was, in my opinion, way too much rice into her mouth at once.

"Really, Simone, I have no idea where it could have gone."

"Have you searched your own palace?" I piped up, though my voice came out quiet. Hades looked right at me. I then realized that the camp had sent a group to do just that, and my face went pink.

"Yes, I checked the palace, as did a group of young gifted ones much like yourself. You are free to search as you like though, I suppose there isn't much left to steal from my palace," he said sadly. I highly doubted that, considering that he was not only the god of the dead but also the god of wealth, but after I was done eating, I scampered off with Sam trailing behind me and we started to work our way through the rooms.

Six sitting rooms, three offices, and a cup of caffeinated green tea later, we were back in the throne room. Not much to search there, but I bent over to check under the throne anyway. It was shadowed, but the floor was so dark it provided enough contrast for me to see a piece of paper lying on the ground.

"Huh," I murmured to myself. I reached a skinny arm into the space between the throne and the floor, my pointer finger just brushing the edge of the paper. I reached again, and pulled the slip closer to me, then I was able to get my nail underneath and I fished my arm out from underneath.

Looking at the paper in better light, I saw that it had writing in the same runes I'd seen basically all over the island. I couldn't read them, and I assumed that Hades had already checked there and decided the paper wasn't important, so I shoved it into my pocket for later.

"Have you found anything?" Hades asked hopefully from directly behind me. I shrieked and jumped.

"Oh, I'm sorry, you scared me. No, we didn't find anything," I responded. His face fell before he schooled it into a more godly expression.

"That is alright. Thank you for searching. I'll send you children on your way now. I do hope someone finds it soon. The Helm of Darkness is a dangerous thing in the wrong hands." He then asked Sam and I, "I suppose you don't know where to go, do you?"

"No," Sam answered. "Could you point us in the right direction?"

"Of course, follow me." Thank goodness the man had shrunken down because he walked fast enough at only six feet tall. I didn't want to have to sprint with him being 20 feet tall.

He led us through weaving hallways to a chamber with a gigantic chasm spanning ten feet across and 20 feet wide. The rest of the chamber was empty, only bare black walls and a lantern hanging from the ceiling. Annalyn and Simone stood waiting for us.

"Gorgyra should come along to give you her challenge soon. Thank you for coming, and I do hope you find the helm." With that, Hades shut the door behind him.

We just stood there awkwardly.

"So... how long does this usually take?" I asked.

"Not long, usually. Did you guys find anything?" Simone replied.

"No," Sam told her. I was about to agree with him when I remembered the paper I found under Hades' throne.

"Just this," I pulled the folded piece out of my pocket and handed it to Simone.

She opened it up, and read, "'I've had success in getting the helm from the underworld, a few gems from the helm's surface will suffice for the ritual. Hide it somewhere good and don't tell anyone where. When you get back to camp, tell our allies that it is time, meet at the southern tip of the island. Down with the gods and all who stand with them.' Signed..." she paused, and slowly looked up.

No, no, she's just looking for an idea, it can't be—

"Annalyn."

Simone's voice barely reached above a whisper, but the single word, the single name, filled the space until the air was too thick. The walls felt too close. Her name rang in my head, and suddenly I could see everything that went wrong.

And you made some tea, The tampered spell, The break-shaped wood chunk, The lightning strike while we were asleep.

"All of it..." I muttered, "All of it was you?" Everything that happened over the course of our journey flashed before my eyes. Even that first day, when I ate with her. Every time, and I couldn't see it.

Annalyn didn't look so pretty anymore. Her glossy brown eyes, always looking so innocent, were cold.

"It really took you that long to figure it out, I mean, you're new, but Simone, you know me."

Annalyn giggled, that was so wrong for the situation it made my skin crawl all over me. "And I tricked you. You know, I'll admit you came close, but you were always too loyal, you always think that those you care for won't harm you. Such naive thoughts for a leader. You should be ashamed of yourself."

"What ritual?" Simone's voice was deadly calm. She stepped forwards, her hand changed, and I realized what she was doing. Getting in front of Annalyn to protect Sam and I. Annalyn wasn't fooled.

"The one that told me our plan would start with Klotho and her arrival." Annalyn's hand was clenched in a fist. "If there is anyone to blame, blame her."

I stepped back, tears welled in my eyes. Was it my fault? Was I to blame for this? She said that I'd signaled the start of their movement. Was it because I was evil? Was I horrible and didn't know it yet?

"*No*, she is a fifth grader, she hasn't even started middle school! She hadn't even known we existed until weeks ago. You are at fault, *you are to blame.*" Simone shouted the last part. She stepped forward, and Annalyn opened her fist at the same time she backhanded Simone.

Thick grass shot out of the ground and slammed me in the side. Blades of it wrapped around my waist and yanked me away. The grass dragged me across the rough stone and all I could do was flail, but the grass wouldn't relent.

I skidded to the edge of the chasm, and with a cry I tumbled over, slipping into the crack. Tears filled my eyes, never on the mission had I felt such fear. I gripped the stones with my fingers sweating from anxiety. The grass had let go of me. I locked my feet into little shelves of rock and mentally begged for Annalyn to think I was dead.

I was holding on for dear life with my head just below the surface of the chamber when I heard Sam yelp and he fell over the edge himself, he grabbed onto a dead root, and I reached out to pull him away from it just before it shot out with a force and stiffness that would have killed him. He got a good hold just before my hand was cramped. I bit my lip so hard it split to keep from yelling in pain.

"What is she doing?" Sam whispered from a foot below my head.

I craned my neck, hoping Annalyn wouldn't see me. Simone had her dagger out and Annalyn was standing in front of her, mace out and ready, but she didn't look like she wanted to use it just yet.

"Just standing for now," I hissed down at him.

"Simone, listen to me. The gods don't care about us, they never have, you've seen it yourself. You have the most contact with them. I'm sorry that I misled you, I am, just come with me. They've made us feel weak, they've betrayed us with their horrid advice, make *them* feel weak for once." Annalyn said, her voice forged in anger.

"No, you didn't just mislead me, you misled all of us, betrayed all of us. Sam and Klotho are dead or close to being because of you. How could you? I thought you were my friend. I thought I knew you." Simone had never sounded so angry and had never sounded so sad.   "Why are you even doing this? What did they do?"

"Oh, you don't know, you don't?" Annalyn was seething. "What about Jaslene? And Diwata? Zeus gave them advice and now they're gone! You've seen what that swine does to his gifted ones, Simone. Fight with me. Down with the gods, raise Tartarus, and start a new age. We could be great. You could be great." Annalyn expected Simone to go with her.

Would Simone go with her?

"Bringing the fall of the world wouldn't make me great, it would make you a monster." She then told Annalyn exactly where she could shove her delusion.

"Very well," at that, Annalyn lunged forward, mace flying through the air. I make a meek noise of surprise and horror. Simone blocked the blow, her dagger turning into a shield. The clang of metal on metal was deafeningly loud. I cringed away from it.

Simone turned into a bird to dodge Annalyn's next strike. Her feathers transformed into the red scales of a dragon and she blew fire at Annalyn. Ananlyn dodged the fire blast by shrinking, but the flames nearly blasted my head off my shoulders. My screech made Simone turn back into a human.

"Klotho?" She started running towards me, looking relieved.

Annalyn grew back to usual size behind her. She ran up behind Simone, her slippered feet quiet as a mouse. She pulled her mace back over her shoulder.

"Simone, look out!" I shouted desperately.

"What's going on?" Sam yelled out from under me.

Ananlyn threw her weight into the blow, though Simone tried to lunge away. A sharp edge of her mace gashed open Simone's thigh. Simone yelped in pain and fell over. Almost the second she hit the ground; she vanished. Ananlyn froze in place, I strained my ears for wing flaps or footsteps, but I didn't hear anything other than my own beating heart.

Next thing I knew, Annalyn was barreling across the floor, propelled by an invisible force with such strength that Simone must have turned into something to throw Annalyn so far. Annalyn hit the wall with a gasp of pain that made me flinch.

"Get out of here Annalyn, get out of here! Leave!" Simone shouted after turning back to her human form. Her carrying voice boomed across the stones. "Get out or I'll kill you!"

I could hardly believe what I was hearing.

Simone can't do it, it would kill her. If I watched it would kill me.

Annalyn stood up, leaning against the wall. Staring at Simone like a prediction she had made was coming true.

"Tartarus will rise, Simone, join up now, before it's too late," Ananlyn warned.

"I told you already. No." Simone's voice carried that hidden threat of death.

"This means war." Ananlyn smashed a glass bead on the ground and vanished into thin air.

CHAPTER TWENTY-SEVEN

ATTACK OF THE GARDEN HEDGES

SIMONE helped me out of the chasms first, then since Sam was too low for her to reach bending over, she turned into a Pegasus and had him sit on her back. Her face had turned remote.

She reached into her bag, and I watched her bandage her leg.

"Can the challenge this Gorgyra lady gives us wait? I don't think any of us will be ready to do it now." Sam asked, sounding calm, but looking shocked. Maybe he couldn't process what had just happened.

"I'm sure she'll postpone it, assuming she knows what just happened." For once, Simone's voice was quiet.

Darkness swirled beside us, and a woman with smooth skin white as bone, waving hair of pale gray, and labradorite eyes reminded me—with a pang of grief—of Ada. The black spread out over her whole eyeball, not just her irises. The center of these eyes was a kind of shining bluish-green fade. Like the surface of a river, almost. Her dress was thin black fabric and a silver girdle shone at her waist. Her feet were bare.

"I am Gorgyra, and you have already succeeded in your task." She tells us, the only hint of emotion being a deep sadness in her round, pooling eyes.

"What do you mean?" I asked weakly. The events of the past—what was it? Fifteen minutes maybe? It couldn't have been so short, so much couldn't happen in that amount of time.

"My challenge was to find the traitor among you, it appears I didn't have to give you the challenge for that to come to pass." She told us. "I will drop you off at the next nymph. Good luck young gifted ones."

She didn't call us children, I noted. Gorgyra waved her hand and we were picked up by that same cyclone of wind that had taken me to Olympus on my first day.

When we were dropped back into the forest that covered most of the island, the whole of what had just happened rushed at me like a swarm of wasps, and tears burst from my eyes. I remembered everything that Annalyn had done for us and for me.

Sam and Simone sat down hard against a fallen tree and I sat with them, curling my knees to my chest. I tried to make the tears stop, but Simone and Sam didn't complain, so I let them fall. Simone put an arm over my shoulder and I heard Sam sniffle. When I opened my watery eyes, he was crying too, Simone's other arm over his shoulder.

Somehow, despite being the closest to Annalyn, and bleeding through imperfectly applied bandages, she was the only one of us not crying. Though, I can't say I didn't expect it. When Sam and I were done, she pulled us to our feet.

"Whatever nymph that's going to challenge us may want us to come to her. The first nymph I had to face after I came back last time was an old dryad, so look for a really big tree somewhere. No spreading out too far, if you can't see us, call out someone's name. If someone calls a name, we meet back at this fallen tree. Got it?" Simone then pointed us in different directions and set to work.

I walked slowly, examining each tree. Some were darker than others, taller, wider, some short and thin. I was sure each had a dryad in it, but Simone said that the dryad she remembered was really old, which meant an old tree.

Just my luck that all the trees looked young and pristine.

A branch snapped to my left. I screamed and whirled around, sword flying through the air—and decapitated a garden hedge. A squirrel darted off underneath it. I breathed a sigh of relief, and my face went red.

I just attacked a garden hedge, I thought. *That's ridiculous.*

"Klotho?" Sam called out, he came through the brush, "You alright?"

After Ananlyn I wasn't really, but he knew that.

"No monsters. Just a hedge." I kicked the chunk of hedge that I'd cut off. He looked at it with a puzzled expression.

"Why would there be garden hedges in the forest?" He asked. I shrugged in response, grateful for the distraction.

"Maybe Simone or..." I shut myself up before I even spoke her name. "Maybe Simone knows."

"Yeah," Sam's voice was thick. His brown eyes watered, he wiped them hastily, "I'm sorry. Shouldn't be crying. It's her fault anyway."

"No—I mean yes—I mean—it's fine." I scrambled for the right words.

"Klotho? Sam?" I heard Simone yell out into the trees. We ran back to the fallen trees.

"What is it? Did you find something?" Sam's breathing heaved in and out from running.

"I found this," Simone held out a chunk of a tree, cut roughly and badly, but done with something sharp. "Judging by the map, we're in a section of the island where no one's been for years. Decades, even. And this is a new cut."

"Was—" I had to swallow hard, but the lump in my throat hardly diminished. "Was it *her*?" I couldn't bring myself to use Annalyn's name.

"Maybe," Simone's face did that thing again. Where it showed nothing. She changed the subject hastily. "Did you guys find anything?"

"Yeah, Klotho? Wanna tell her?" Sam replied to me.

"A garden hedge that looks fairly kept up for supposedly being abandoned for decades." I still felt too stupid to mention that I'd decapitated it. "Do you know what that could be?"

"That might be a New Gift Garden." When Sam and I raised our eyebrows in confusion, she clarified, "If you do something selfless enough for the gods, they'll give you a fourth power, and make a garden in your honor. Let's check it out."

We led her to the garden badge and circled it until we got to an entrance.

"Oh, thank goodness you're here!" A dryad appeared right in front of us, making me jump and shriek. "She's hurt, the challenge was to find her in the center of this maze, without flying Simone, but that girl got to her, she's hurt. You have to go, now!" She ushered us into the entrance of the maze and the hedges shut behind us before I could even consider not going in.

The actual walls of the maze behind the hedges were pale beige stone, the grout white and the ground dusty.

"No pressure, huh?" I murmured.

"Come on, walk as fast as you guys can without exhausting yourselves. Come on," Simone practically jogged ahead.

"Simone, wait!" Sam called after her, I ran to catch up with both of them.

"What?" She asked, "If we don't get there soon, she'll die!"

"We can't run the entire way, and how are we supposed to know which turns to take?" Sam countered.

She opened her mouth a couple of times, then finally shut it completely and nodded. "Fair point, but we can't debate every single fork in the road. We need a better way to move."

"The dryad said no flying," I warned.

"Who said we had to fly? Klotho, you're the lightest, up the wall with you." Simone ordered. I glanced at the ten-foot-tall wall nervously.

"Are you sure? I'm not a very good climber..." I could just see myself slipping off the wall and falling onto my back like an idiot.

"I'll catch you if you fall," Sam assured me, which made me exactly zero percent less worried.

"More like he'll get you up. If you fall, there's a better chance that I'll catch you." Simone corrected. "Now as I said before, up with you."

Sam stood by the wall and made a step with his hands. I took a nervous gulp, grabbed a stone that was sticking out of the wall, and heaved myself up. I shoved my toes onto another sticking-out rock and was just barely able to keep from falling. My heart beat like crazy with the effort of keeping myself up.

I skidded to the edge of the chasm, and with a cry I tumbled over, slipping into the crack.

I gripped the stones with my fingers sweating from anxiety.

I banished the thoughts from my head as fast as I could. Freaking out now was not an option. I looked up, reached with my free hand, and felt along the wall for a rock to grab onto. I found a shelf-like dent that would suffice, and promptly felt with my foot for another hold, when I found one, I repeated the process.

Again, and again, and again.

It took what felt like hours, but finally, once my hands were hit with friction and felt like I had just ripped all the skin off my fingers, I was up on the maze wall. It was flat enough, about a foot and a half wide.

"How is it up there?" Simone asked.

"Flat, your turn." I sat down because the height made me nervous. With my luck, I would manage to step into the one place that it wasn't sturdy enough to hold me and plummet to a painful failure.

Sam managed up the wall much faster than me and grinned when he reached the top.

"Show off," I grumbled.

"Oh, Sam just did that because you showed him the way first. If he was getting up on the first try, he'd fall off the wall about six times." Simone then proceeded to fall off the wall twice, shrieking in what had to be the best impression of a dying bird I had ever heard in my life.

Sam snickered, and I was surprised to find that I giggled as well, even despite the heavy mood.

"Who's the one falling now?" Sam teased.

"Shut up," she promptly started speed walking over the stone and I was too afraid to catch up, so I was left behind. Thank goodness I could at least see them. I turned to my right to look deeper into the maze. I could see tall, green-leafed branches sticking out of the center. One problem that I noticed, some of the walls were stone, like this one, but the others were hedges. Now, I'm no plant expert, but I know pretty well that none of us can walk on hedges.

Maybe Annalyn could help with that, my mind burst before I could correct myself. *No, you idiot,* I told myself, *she betrayed you. Left you all. She didn't do anything for you besides try to stop you, and slow you down.* I remembered when she asked to take a break and I naively agreed with her. Was she the one that asked the nymph to change the place? To nearly kill us?

"Oh boy," Simone called out from in front of me. "We'll have to jump down." I saw what she was talking about a moment later when we hit a dead end. The wall stopped and gave way to hedges.

"Jump? Won't we hurt ourselves?" I asked.

"Not if you bend your legs when you land," Simone replied. She sat down on the edge of the wall and took a breath.

"As soon as you hit the ground, bend. It absorbs the shock." Sam explained.

"Alright come on," Simone muttered to herself. "Three, two, one," she pushed herself from the wall and her legs crumpled beneath her so that she was on one knee with her arms out to her sides. She stood back up, wincing, and I remembered that Annalyn had injured her. "You next!" She called up at Sam.

He tried to jump standing up and proceeded to have to roll to not break his ankle. When he got back up, he was dusty and I saw the beginnings of a bruise on his knee.

315

I sat down on the edge, with the sharp corner digging into the back of my thigh. The stone was rough, and I was sure that I would scratch myself on it. I sucked in a breath, counted down in my head, and failed to jump.

I realized that I was making a much bigger deal of this than I had to, and shoved myself off as abruptly as I could. I shrieked and a wind blasted up underneath me, which cushioned my fall, though it coated us all in dust.

"Hey, that worked!" And then I got punched in the face by a garden hedge.

My nose hurt, I felt blood dribbling down my face. Over my chin, onto the ground. The hedge reached out in two shaped like a ram and sucked me in. I screamed, the hedges had small branches, stiff and painful. They scraped against me. I hacked at them with my sword, but they were too strong, the space was too small for me to wield the thing without hurting myself.

The hedge slammed me into the earth beneath it, pressing down on me with a weight I'd never expected from a mere plant.

"Help! Help me!" My voice was hoarse and scratchy with fear. I elbowed the hedge as hard as I could and turned over so that I was facing up. What I was looking at was just a hedge, but with arms of its branches and leaves holding me down. Another arm grew out and punched me in the face again. Leaves broke off and fell into my mouth. When I spat to get them out, blood splattered onto the ground next to me.

I hacked upwards with my sword, hoping to stop this landscaping nightmare from doing any further damage. All my violent smacking accomplished was getting my sword absorbed into the garden hedge.

Oh no, now you've done it. That sword is the only weapon I have! My nose was smarting and I could taste the iron of blood in my spit. I whacked the hedge with one hand, and it punched my chest so hard I couldn't breathe. I frantically tried to get air in, but nothing would come. I reached up, the hill of my sword was vanishing into the hedge. Something snaked around my throat, I wasn't sure why, I couldn't breathe anyway.

My fingers closed around the very tip of the hilt and I yanked downwards. Mu Chet's finally expanded enough to take in air, and when I sliced upwards this time, I kept a firm enough hold to keep my sword.

The hedge weighed down on me again, pressing hard and painful. It let up for just a second, presumably to try again, when a pair of hands grabbed under my shoulders and yanked me out.

The ground scraped against me. I bearded heavily. It was Sam who had grabbed me out.

"Thanks," I barely managed to get the word out through how heavily I was breathing.

"I take it no powers are allowed," Sam said. "Simone, you got some tissues?"

I felt wetness on my upper lip, I touched it and felt a sticky, warm substance still flowing from my nose. Simone yanked an entire box of tissues out of her bag, which proceeded to explode in a flurry of soft paper. It whirled around us haughtily, obscuring our vision and smacking us with wads of tissues.

I yelped and ran. One wad of tissues hit my nose, which still throbbed, and carried a stain of blood right into Sam's neck. He quickly followed my lead, booking it away from the flurry of tissues. I grabbed Simone, who was battling it out against the remains of the box, and we just shot through the maze, hardly caring where we would end up.

The tissues followed us for a while, before falling limp to the ground behind us. We kept running as fast as our legs would take us just to ensure that there weren't any more hygiene products trying to kill us.

When we finally stopped at a corner, I fell to my knees and failed to breathe through my nose, though I desperately wanted to. My throat felt skinned and raw. Simone was resting her hand on her knees. Sam leaned against the wall.

"Well... good news is... we're almost there," Sam said between heaves of air. I nodded in agreement. The branches at the center of the maze were much closer and reachable.

"Well, we've hit a dead end. I'll go up the wall to see if there's another way close by." Simone pulled herself up one of the walls the best she could. There weren't any hedges around us, thank goodness, but I didn't want to know what the stone walls would do to us if one of us used our powers.

Simone stood to her full height on the wall while I pinched my nose between my fingers to stop the blood.

"How is it up there?" My voice was high and nasally.

"There's no regular entrance to the center of the maze. The ring around. The center is hedges, so we probably need to jump over them to get in." She looked strange, paler than normal, and her voice was strained. Her chest moved fast like she was breathing heavily.

"Simone? What's wrong?" Sam asked.

"Nothing—uh, the nymph, she's... bleeding, a lot. And her arm... um..." Simone turned her head to us. "Just come on, and Klotho, get your singing voice ready."

That poor nymph, I thought as I yanked myself up the wall behind Sam. *Annanlyn is horrible.*

"Klotho, you first. What you're going to do is get a running start and once you get to the edge, jump over the hedge. Don't hesitate, just go. Remember to bend your legs when you land." Simone shifted around me and pushed me forward. I dreaded running again, but I steeled my nerves.

I got ready and bolted over the stone. My feet pounded against the rock, and I was at the edge in what felt like a second. I closed my eyes and pushed off as hard as I could. The momentum carried me forward, the bottom of my shoes brushed against the garden hedge, which stayed still, thank the gods.

I held my breath and crashed hard into the earth. My legs crumpled underneath me and I smacked stomach-down into the cobblestone ground. I groaned in pain and pushed myself up with my elbows. A scream tore itself from my throat.

There was a severed arm in front of me. Cut at the shoulder with a bruise on the skin. A bit of bone sticking out of it, and blood Shades of green stained the pale gray stones. It pooled underneath the cut-off appendage and flowed through cracks in the stones. Bleeding *everywhere* was the woman to whom the arm belonged. She lay between the massive roots of a mighty oak tree, wider than me and much taller. She had green-brown skin, and a slim frame, and the side of her leaf-green dress was black with chlorophyll blood. She wasn't screaming she didn't even look awake.

I stood, got sick in a fanciful cut bush, and heard Sam screech as he landed right into the pool of blood. He shrieked once more when he saw what he had landed on. Simone landed more quietly and sprinted to the dryad.

"Klotho!" She said urgently, kneeling in the dirt next to the poor dryad. Short, straight black hair clumped and stuck to her neck with blood and sweat. Her eyes were shut and her face was pale.

"Twinkle twinkle little star," I sang right into the woman's ear, but nothing happened. No musical notes appeared.

Then blood dripped from the dragon's mouth as it chewed Ada.

My breath quickened. Simone called into the dryad's ear.

"Wake up, come on, keep singing!" She rifled around in her bag, found what she was looking for, and put it under the dryad's nose. A horrific chemical scent hit me, sour and spicy, and the woman's eyes dragged themselves open. I sang so fast the words were hardly legible, but the glowing music notes appeared, and the blood flow stopped,and then the skin started to grow back. Slow, like a layer of glue. Instead of pink, it showed up pale green.

"Oh, my dear," The dryad said weakly. She reached up and touched my face. "Thank you, thank you."

"You're welcome," I replied because I didn't know what else to say. I heard Sam hurl behind me. Landing on a severed arm couldn't have left his clothing un-stained. At least it was green blood, and not red.

"I will heal the rest of the way. Get the boy, and I'll send you off." She straightened, tried to lean on an arm that was across the yard, and ended up just leaning against the trunk of her tree.

"Sam," Simone called. He came over, looking a bit greener than is healthy. As expected, his shirt was stained with green chlorophyll.

The nymph waved her hands in the air, and the swirling green wind took us to our next torture mean challenge.

Chapter Twenty-Eight

Bees, But Worse

WE appeared on the very tip of a mountain with the wind nymph who had already saved me three times at this point.

"Again?" I asked, too tired to bother being polite. The air was thin and cold, and the gravely rocks crunched when I shifted my weight. Goosebumps rose on my arms.

"It appears so," she told me.

"What's the challenge? Sorry if we're being rude, we just want to get over with it all." Simone said, rubbing her eyes. Sam and I nodded in agreement.

"Of course, I understand. Your challenge is to collect a jar of honey from the Serpent Bees, without dying. The tree is right next to me, here's the jar, and best of luck." She handed a four-inch-tall glass jar to Sam and poofed away.

"What's a Serpent Bee?" I questioned. I did not like the sound of that name. I assumed it must be some kind of serpent-bee hybrid that only ate meat, and I was partially correct as you, dear reader, will soon find out. Simone's face was a staring into space version of: 'Oh boy, here we go.' "What's a Serpent Bee?" I asked again more urgently. I glanced at Sam, who had a similar expression on his face.

"They're like bumble bees, same size and fuzziness. The main difference is that these bees are obligate carnivores, much like snakes. This means they can't properly digest any plants. They will eat any meat they can get too, which includes the meat of living things." Simone explained. "Translation: we're screwed."

"How are we even going to manage that?" I whined.

"I have not a single clue. Sam? Got anything?" Simone replied.

"I've heard you can smoke bees out of their hives. Let's try that." He suggested, with no better thing to do, that we set to gathering supplies for a Smokey fire.

I went down the mountain to search through the short trees and managed to find some fallen leaves and sticks. My back hurt from my position, but I continued anyway. I was reaching for a branch when I heard a crunch and whipped upright.

A literal brown bear stood roughly fifteen feet in front of me.

Except, this bear had eyes white as milk, was a full six feet tall at the shoulder, and its black teeth stuck out at the sides of its mouth like fangs. I could smell it from where I was standing, a kind of wild must mixed with blood. There was a wetness around its mouth that looked suspiciously red. Brown fur grew all over it, sticks and leaves stuck on its stomach. Black and razor sharp. Its lips pulled away from its teeth in a sneer and it growled, low and deep.

I heard another little crunch, this one from behind. I had just realized what was going on when the bear lunged. I shrieked and chucked myself out of the way with the help of a truly powerful gust of wind. I hadn't even realized I was using my powers, and honestly, any punishments I may have faced for using them seemed unimportant compared to an *actual bear*.

This sent my hair flying into my face, and I curled up on the ground with my hands covering my neck. I was shaking like the trees around me, they swayed, left and right, from the wind I had summoned.

That should have been a sign of surrender to any person, but this was not a person I was dealing with. I hoped that the bear would see me and decide I was too pathetic to waste calories on.

If it's brown, lie down, if it's black, fight back, and if it's white, good night.

But that old saying might not have any weight here. If there was anything I'd learned about this island and its creatures, it was that they were unpredictable. I'd just done the worst possible thing to a bear and gotten in between the possibly magical beast and her cub.

Knowing this, I curled tighter.

The bear came through the low trees to me. She bent her head and sniffed me hard. I was trembling like nothing else. She nudged me with her paw, and I became very aware of massive black claws more like that of a raptor than a bear.

Come on, please. I'm just a kid, I'm just a kid. I mean take begged the bear to leave me alone, though I knew it was impossible that any thought could dissuade her.

She kicked me, which felt more like a punch with the paw, and I moved limply. My ribs ached at the force, but I didn't even dare to cry. For all I knew this bear would see me as a threat if I did anything other than lying there. I couldn't lie still, there was a good chance I would stop shaking for the rest of the day, but at least I could be semi-still.

The bear rolled me over and I shut my eyes tight, preparing to have my guts ripped out. I held my breath, even once my lungs burned. The bear snuffed my chest and my neck. That made me sweat in terror.

She moved up to my head and tears slid down my cheeks. I was shocked they were even able to get through my eyes when I was fairly certain that I'd never be able to open them again. Something wet and warm slid over my cheek. A tongue, as massive as the bear it belonged to.

Then, she was gone. I didn't dare to so much as open my eyes until a few minutes later, and when I did, she was lumbering off through the low trees, paying no attention to me.

I sighed in relief and scrubbed the remaining tears off my cheeks.

"Klotho? What are you doing?" Sam asked, coming over with some trouble. "Oh, these stupid—" he promptly tripped on a branch sticking out from a bush and fell onto his face. I let out a sudden laugh.

"Oh, I ran into a bear." I looked down where my collection of twigs and dead leaves had been, but my arms were empty. My hair was full of twigs, but other than that there was nothing.

"What?" Sam shoved himself up out of the brush.

"Yeah, I'm fine though," I told him. "Still have all my internal organs."

"I'll take that as a success." He promptly dragged me around himself. "No more bears, just making sure of that." He said and shoved a bundle of sticks into my arms.

We got back to the tree and set the fire.

"Now run!" Sam yanked Simone and me both behind a boulder. A torrent of buzzing erupted from the hive, which I was sure wasn't normal, but when had the island ever been normal?

"Bees get aggressive sometimes, and these aren't the kind you would want to annoy," Sam explained, peeking out the edge of the rock to check on our progress.

"Oh really? I never would have thought that we want to keep flesh-eating bees happy." Simone responded with her usual snark.

Smoke billowed from the fire directly up to the nest, which was a kind of orange-redish color instead of the usual honeycomb yellow. The bees swarmed out of the hive angrily. They flew up above their nest in a cloud of angry buzzing. I mean, I guess if I were being smoked out of my home, I'd be pretty upset too.

"Okay, showtime. Let's go in, get the honey, and run." Simone bolted out before Sam and I could argue, and we had to follow her assault on the beehive.

Simone put the jar into her bag for safekeeping and had Sam hoist her up so that she could get some honey. I watched the bees carefully. They didn't seem like they were going to attack, at least not yet.

Simone wobbled, though she'd braced herself against the tree. Sam's face was tight with conversation and his brow shined with sweat. Simone nearly fell over when he shifted his stance, which made him stomp to the side in an attempt to regain balance.

"Sam, hold still!" Simone ordered with a yelp. She nearly slipped out of his grip, just barely able to save herself by hugging the tree. She nearly fell over when Sam shifted his stance.

"You're heavy!" He complained in response.

"Well, I'm sorry Mr. Noodle arms, I can't control my weight!" She retorted searching for a handhold in the bark of the tree. She shifted her weight and Sam nearly fell over, she accidentally kicked him in the chest and he groaned.

I decided that was enough horsing around for them, we couldn't finish the rest of the challenges if the bees got annoyed at them for shaking around underneath them.

"I can help," I offered, deciding that Simone falling may start the bees to attack. Sam nodded frantically.

"Get her other foot. Simone, hold on up there," I linked my fingers together and braced myself. Simone stepped into my hand, and Sam sighed with relief. "Much better."

Eventually, Simone managed to grab into a chunk of rough bark and step off of us. She shimmied up right underneath the hive and stood precariously on a branch.

"Are you sure that's safe?" I asked. The fall would be around fifteen feet, and we'd survived worse for sure, but those worse times had been with help. I doubted that Sam and I would have been able to catch Simone if the branch snapped. I mean, I guess I could have used my wind powers, but I'd just barely been able to avoid causing another tornado during the last challenge, I didn't want to risk it with a hive nearby.

"Nope." She called back.

Slowly, she sawed off a chunk of honeycomb with her dagger and ran the blade across. Orange honey spilled out into the jar, but it wasn't enough to fill more than a quarter of the container, so she sawed off another chunk.

"How do you think that honey tastes?" Sam asked.

"I don't know, maybe meaty? What even is honey anyway?" I asked. I knew it came from bees, but I had no idea how it was actually created.

"I have no clue, but it looks a little weird, doesn't it? This kind seems to have blood mixed in," Sam replied. "You know, I've never actually seen Serpent Bees before."

"Really?" I asked, keeping my eyes on the things.

Simone coughed into her arm, which muffled the sound. The mass of bees bobbed, though I didn't know whether that was them noticing or not. I hoped not, if sound agitated them, it would be game over.

"Yup, they only live at high altitudes, honestly it's a miracle we didn't run into the things on our way through the mountains." Sam explained, "They move in groups, often hundreds of them will all be flying together to more efficiently strip their prey of meat."

"Well, it's just our luck that we have to steal honey from a full nest of these things." I picked at my lip with my fingernail, which had grown mostly back after the little raft incident.

The terrifying fuzzy bees hummed through the air and smoke floated up from our fire directly into Simone's face. This was a problem for a multitude of reasons, one of which was the fact that smoke doesn't always smell so great. This air quality problem could cause people to cough, and if those people are Simone, coughing is not a good thing while trying to be a bee burglar.

"Are you alright up there?" I called.

"Yeah, I'm fine so far. You know, I thought I liked the smell of campfire smoke until now." She blinked smoke-induced tears from her eyes.

"Do you think we could put it out?" I asked both Sam and Simone. I stepped closer to the fire and pulled some water out of a puddle.

"No!" They chorused, and I dropped the water.

"That smoke is all that's keeping the bees out of the hive right now. I don't know what it is that keeps them away, but I'd like my flesh, thank you very much." Simone squeezed more honey into the jar and wiped the stuff off of her fingers.

"Does it feel the same as regular honey?" I questioned.

"Yeah, smells the same too. I'd taste it but I'm not about to get sick if this crap has bacteria in it." Simone replied.

Air blew into the fire and fed the flames. The smoke wafted extra hard into her face with the gust of wind and Simone coughed so loudly it made me flinch, and the bees decided that was unacceptable. They swirled down at her in a massive ball of terror and she proceeded to scream and rapidly curl up on the branch. She swatted at the onslaught of bees, but nothing would deter them.

Sam and I shrieked. My heart raced in my chest just from watching.

Oh no, oh no, oh crap we're all screwed. My mind raced with panic. How could you even fight bees? A sword would be next to useless, a dagger even worse.

"WHAT DO WE DO?" I shouted, not really to anyone specific.

Sam was frozen in place, I could almost see the cogs turning in his head and I sincerely wished they would go faster. And Simone was too busy with getting small chunks of her arms and legs ripped out by the meat-eating bumblebee freaks to do much of anything.

In my need to not watch Simone get torn apart by insects, I grabbed a handful of dirt and threw it at the bees, which only served to make them angry. They didn't attack me, thank the gods, but they did double the ferocity.

"Sing! Maybe if you heal Simone she can get out her flamethrower or something," Sam yelled.

I had no idea what to sing, but I needed to come up with something fast, so I just went for 'Twinkle Twinkle Little Star' again. I saw the bloody bits out of Simone's arms and legs close, only to be ripped back open by the bees and shut again, creating a kind of infinite food source for the dang things.

And possibly torturing Simone.

But it was our best—scratch that, our *only* option. I was running out of lyrics in this one and I sure as heck wasn't about to bust out any other nursery songs, so I went with one I'd heard my mom sing once.

"*Why does thou sit
Upon my grave*

328

And will dead lips to speak?"

I'd never had the prettiest voice, but bees seemed to calm down, so I kept going. I prayed that they would at least leave us alone.

"Why does thou weep

Upon my grave

And will not let me sleep?"

The mass slowly peeled itself off of Simone and came back together in a blob of black and yellow. It bobbed up and down rhythmically like a dance. Bees dancing was much more terrifying than it sounded.

"My breast it is as cold as clay

My breath is earthly strong,"

I couldn't remember the next line and was horrified that my lack of attention to my mom's music would get someone killed. I'd never tell her to quiet down the radio again.

"And if you kiss my cold clay lips

Your days won't be long."

Simone came to her rescue, trembling with the jar in hand. She slowly reached up and ripped off another piece of honeycomb to squeeze in. Simone's voice was better than I expected from someone who'd just been breathing in smoke.

"How oft on yonder grave sweetheart?

Where we will want to walk

The fairest flower that ever I saw

Has withered to a stalk,"

I remembered the rest vividly. The bees came down in a swarm at me, but not as aggressively as they had with Simone. They seemed almost hypnotized. Maybe Simone's comment about Disney princesses wasn't unfounded.

"When will I see you again sweetheart?
When will I see you again?
When the autumn leaves
That fall from trees
Are green and spring up again,"

My voice shook with terror as the bees went around and lifted me in a chair of buzzing insects towards their nest. I dragged out the last section with as many long holds as I could get in there without voice cracks.

"How oft on yonder grave sweetheart?
Where we will want to walk
The fairest flower that ever I saw
Has withered to a stalk,"

The beating of thousands of little wings carried me, and all the friction heated my backside uncomfortably. Simone shoved the jar at me and I was just able to scrape the rest of honey the that we needed from the exposed section of the nest.

I started the song again, shaking so hard that my vision was affected. The bees carried me down and promptly flew back inside of their hive. Sam dragged Simone and me off while I screamed to keep the wretched bees happy and not eat our flesh.

We finally made it to the grassy ledge overlooking the river and collapsed to the earth. The ledge was only four feet over the water, so I wasn't worried about falling in just yet. The soft grass felt great on my burning legs. I laid back, heaving in the cool mountain air like my life depended on it. The sky was growing deeper blue, sinking low to the ground.

"With our luck, the next challenge will be a marathon." I blurted, then realized my grave mistake. "Oh wait, no, I just gave the universe ideas!"

"If that nymph... has us going to some new challenge... in the middle of the night... I'm going to be... so mad..." Simone said between breaths. She was covered in little spots of pink skin where I'd just barely healed her.

"You've jinxed it. Hear the wind?" Sam groaned and we all paused to listen. Sure enough, a torrent of wind announced the nymph.

She appeared in front of us in all her unscathed glory. "Well, that was certainly a creative method of avoiding imminent death. And your voice certainly isn't terrible."

"Thanks," I said because I was basically on autopilot and never wanted to see a beehive again.

"Who's the next nymph?" Sam asked reluctantly.

"A Nereid, I think her name is Cordelia." The nymph told us. I shut my eyes tight and tried not to groan. The ocean was my element, with the whole water thing, but my breath-holding capabilities were practically nonexistent, as I'd seen throughout this mission. I'd never spoken to a Nereid before, so I didn't know their temperament. For all the information I had in them, they could be psychopathic dolphin friends or the nicest mythical creatures to ever live.

"Do you know what branch of torture—CHALLANGE—" Simone rapidly corrected herself with a facepalm. "I meant to challenge—she'll fit us with?"

"No, unfortunately, I do not. But you will find out very soon." She lifted her hand as if to snap her when all three of us yelled:

"No!"

She froze with a puzzled expression on her face. "What?"

"We're exhausted," I told her.

"Yeah, can you give us like five minutes to take a breather?" Sam requested. She glanced between us.

The nymph eyes us, "Alright, I suppose you would be a bit over-exerted."

After what felt like less than a second, she had us all stand-up.

"Wait, we're dealing with a Nereid. They're spirits of the ocean..." I realized what she was going to do at the same time as Sam and Simone.

Simone opened her mouth, "Wait, please don't drop us into the—" and then the wind swirled around us and we were dropped into the cold ocean.

Chapter Twenty-Nine

Is That a Turtle or a Snake?

THE water hit me like a shock of stone. I sank, frozen (maybe literally) under the salty waves. Once I pulled myself together, I waved my arms blindly through the water. My sense of direction was so frazzled I couldn't tell what was up or down.

I opened my eyes and the salt burned so badly I felt warm tears on my cheeks after I shut them again. I let out my breath because the pressure was too much, and sank. With all my remaining energy, I pushed myself up, making the water propel me. I broke the surface with a giant gasp.

The night's cold air shocked my face and I had to blink hard to stop hot tears from falling out of my eyes. My leg stung from the initial impact of the water, which was utterly freezing. I spun my arms under the water to keep my head above the surface, though my arms ached badly.

I was shivering so hard I must have looked like a chihuahua. I waved my arms and kicked my legs to keep myself afloat. The waves pushed and pulled me up and down, left and right. I coughed out water and blew air through my nose. I tasted salt.

"SAM!" I gulped in the cold night air. The only light was the thousands of stars dotting the sky. The sun had set, but the blue light stuck around. My heart smacked against my chest despite the cold, and I breathed fast and hard. "SIMONE!"

I heard the sound of someone breaking the water about ten feet to my right and a loud breath in. "KLOTHO! SIMONE!" Sam called out hoarsely. His hair was plastered to his forehead, darkened with water.

"Here!" I swam over to the best of my ability. The waves beat against me, pushing me up and down in the water. Slowing me down. I heard the water surface break again and a deep breath. A pair of familiar glowing eyes opened and frantically whipped the head they belonged to around.

Simone spotted us. "Where's the Nereid?" She swam over, panting and shivering like both Sam and I. She spat water out of her mouth.

"We don't know. But we aren't going to be able to find her underwater." Sam's voice shuddered with the cold of the water.

"What is wrong with these nymphs? We'll freeze to death in this water!" I fretted. I think I was being reasonable, but we've been through so many other more terrifying things that I felt like I was being dramatic.

"It'll be alright, Klotho, we've been nearly drowning before. You got us out that time, I'm sure we'll be able to do it this time." Simone assured me.

But I couldn't have done it now. I was too tired. I was too shaken. Getting honey from those bees was a stupid challenge. It seemed so much easier than surviving the open ocean. It would be dark soon, and once it was dark we wouldn't know where we were going.

"That nymph better be coming around soon, or Klotho's right." Sam snipped, interrupting my train of thought.

With perfect timing, the Nereid chose to appear in the water in front of us. She didn't wave her arms and I couldn't see her legs. She seemed to just float there elegantly in the water.

"Hello there, young ones. I suppose you'll be asking about your challenge?" Her voice had not the slightest hint of a shake to it, which felt wrong in contrast to my trembling.

"Get on with it, please," Simone replied in a much shakier voice due to the cold. My teeth were chattering like nothing else.

The Nereid giggled, "Very well, then. You are to get back to your island without the use of any wooden raft or boat. Get to work." And she vanished into the depths of the ocean.

"We're going to die," Sam said with worrying calmness.

"No, we aren't, I have something that we can use." I think Simone searched through her bag (How in the world did she still have it? Oh my goodness that thing was more reliable than most people.) and yanked out some kind of tarp-like bag thing.

"What is that?" I asked through chattering teeth.

"An air mattress." She replied as a large wave carried us up and then dropped us back down.

"Aren't we not allowed to use a raft?" Sam asked, I found myself nodding, then got embarrassed because nobody could see me, and nodding was pointless.

"She said we couldn't use a *wooden* raft. And this sure as hell doesn't have wood in it." Her eyes turned down to what must have been the tag, "At least I don't think so. Do either of you know the wood content of air mattresses?" We both stared at her in silence. "Never mind. Anyway, it's better than freezing to death in the water."

"I guess so." Sam relented.

"Can you stabilize the water a bit? Make sure not to do too much if you can't manage, or you'll exhaust yourself."

"I'm already exhausted. I'll be fine." I closed my eyes and imagined the water stilling, the waves grew smaller, and finally, they stopped, leaving a circle of water with a diameter of about 10 feet still as ice. My remaining energy drained out of me, like a slow trickle. I was barely able to summon the force to keep myself floating. I heard the gentle claps of the water around us and Simone blowing into the air mattress. She breathed in through her nose and blew out again, the hollow mattress filling slowly.

After what felt like hours later, she shoved the stopper into place and we had a raft! Our main problem of drowning had been remedied. Now for the next problem: getting on the thing.

"Klotho?" Sam asked, "Water solidifying?"

"I can't," I said sheepishly, yawning while shivering. "I'm spent, I don't think I could move another drop of water if my life depended on it." *Well, it currently does, and the stilling effect has evaporated already.* I thought with a mental facepalm.

"Then we'll just have to do our best. I'll try to hold it in place, Sam, you first." Simone held the floating air mattress awkwardly while Sam grasped onto the edge and tried to get on. He managed to throw himself onto the air mattress with some kind of flopping fish maneuver, which pushed it off towards Simone, who went underwater to keep it from flying too far out. The mattress wobbled so badly that he had to cling to it, waiting for the mattress to quit shaking like the ground during an earthquake, before getting off to one side.

"Klotho... you next." Simone panted.

I kicked myself over and grabbed onto the mattress. My wet fingers got plenty of tooth on the sort of fuzzy surface, but the mattress was high up on the water compared to me, and I didn't have the strength to pull myself up. I threw my arms further onto the air mattress and tried to kick up. The air-filled monstrosity moved when I kicked. I tried to yank myself forward, but with nothing to hold onto, my shaking fingers slipped. My chest heaved to get in the cold night air.

I was freezing and tired and sore and utterly miserable.

"Sam... can you... help me...?" I managed to get out between heavy breaths. I couldn't feel my toes and my feet were unbearably cold.

"Got it." He stuttered and reached to grab my arm. With that hold, I was able to get into that mattress. The frigid air made it feel like my limbs were staticky, my teeth chattered so hard I wasn't even able to get out a thank you. Also, I needed to pee.

"Simone, I think you're allowed to use your powers so just like turn into a fish or something," Sam said, shivering.

The wind blew by, caressing me with its frosty torture. Why did I hate the summer heat so much? This cold was much worse, though I'd grown up in Minnesota. I'd never been wet so late at night. I don't think I'd ever felt so cold.

"No, you guys rest, I'll push this thing. Do either of you see the island?" She replied. I looked around and saw a black silhouette behind us. I groaned, the island was too far away to be looking that small. Those nymphs were testing us.

"There," I pointed.

"Ok, I'm turning into a dolphin, so don't expect me to reply to anything," Simone replied, turned into a dolphin, made a dolphin sound, and started pushing us toward the large black mass.

I laid down on the air mattress and curled myself up as tight as I could. Sam's weight shifted on the other side of the mattress. My sopping wet hair stuck to my back and shoulders with the freezing water. I'd never be able to brush it out again, I was sure. My clothing was soaked, I felt bad that there was a good chance it was ruined. It was likely that I'd never see Alona again, but I wanted to return the clothes to her at some point.

My arms and legs shook, so I wrapped my arms tighter around myself. I don't know how in the world I managed a nap while I felt like a half-frozen popsicle, but I did.

When I woke up, it was to the blackness of night. The only light around was the thousands of stars Hugh above, and I could just barely see the difference between the sky and the sea. The black mass of the island was also visible, and we were going much slower than I remembered from before.

"Simone?" My voice was creaky and shivering, then I realized she was still a dolphin. "You can come up and rest if you want, I can push the mattress." Though I was still shivering and probably would have looked endlessly stupid in full lighting, Simone jumped out of the water and landed on the air mattress as some furry creature without a single word of argument.

I imagined the waves taking us towards the island, which seemed to be moving all on its own. That was strange for sure. The last time I checked, the islands didn't move. I squinted at it trying to make out if this was just the darkness playing tricks on me.

A long appendage flew into the air, like a flipper. *Coming off of the island.* Oh, oh no, that wasn't the island at all. It was too small, I just realized, far too small to be an island. A pair of glowing yellow eyes the size of my head peeled open. Crap.

"Um, guys?" My voice trembled for an entirely new reason.

"What?" Sam asked, maybe looking at the black mass and seeing it shift and move. The current pulled us closer. "Oh boy."

I tried frantically to get us back away from the creature. Imagining my powers pulling the boat back, but that hour of sleep wasn't enough for me to reverse this creature's pull.

"Simone, Simone! What is that thing?" My breaths became quick and uneven. I whipped my head to where I could feel her weight on the mattress.

A pair of glowing eyes opened and that weight suddenly became much more pressing and had me desperately clinging to the edges of the mattress to keep from falling off.

"What thing?" She yawned, her eyes landed on the magnificently undefinable sea beast and she swore seven separate times. "Klotho, have you tried pulling us away from it?"

"It won't work. My powers aren't good enough." I didn't understand. I could do so much more on the island, why couldn't I come through now? Was it exhaustion? What was wrong with me?

"Then we wait and see what it does. Stay as still as you can. No sudden movements," Sam whispered. I watched the creature, shivering like crazy because no amount of muscle control could stop it.

The creature swam closer to us, the glowing eyes coming closer. Then, they vanished. The whole mass vanished under the water. I waited for a moment before I breathed a sigh of relief.

"That was close," Simone spoke. "Good that wasn't an aggressive one. I haven't fought any sea monsters before."

"We would have been screwed, huh?" Sam's voice had a hint of a grin in it. "Let's wait till morning, then we can check the map and find where we're actually going. Wouldn't want to run into another—"

The sea creature burst out of the water underneath us, sending us flying through the air. My scream was barely distinguishable from the whistling of the wind. I landed hard in the water and managed to get back up just in time to crash my head into something hard.

I grabbed into it, the creature swung around, and my fingers slipped. I hit something softer, with tough skin and I yanked myself back from it. The creature moved, and I was driven back under the water. I flailed, and my hands broke the water but I didn't. I kicked and had to take a breath and I ended up with a mouth and nose full of seawater. I coughed and choked and some burst of my power sent me rocketing up out of the water.

I landed hard on my side on what felt like a shell.

"It has a shell!" I heard Sam scream. Then he shrieked again. "And a long tail!"

I whipped my head to his voice and heard a great splash. That must have been him hitting   the water. Did the thing throw him with our tail? Was it some kind of snake mixed with a turtle? That was all the shell was telling me. Or was it a shell at all? Could it be plating? Like armor in nature?

"OW! Scales too!" Simone called back. The creature shook and moved and I slid around on what must have been its back. Ridges lined it, but not deep enough for me to grab. I wanted my sword, and my sword appeared. I tried to scrape through the shell, stupid, that was useless.

Light, I needed light. But there was none to use.

Then the world was turning and I was falling back into the water, cold and awful. The waves smacked me into the belly of my creature. My sword shifted and there was a sting in my shoulder, then it was a much worse sting, so bad I hissed and cried out hoarsely. I tasted salt, then my mouth was filled with it and the wet coldness of the water.

The creature was suddenly gone. Its absence left me unsteady in the water. My arms flew through the water, dragged down by my sword. A softer-bodied creature crashed into me with full force. A hard head covered in wet hair smashed into my lower jaw and I tasted blood. No time to figure out whether it was mine or not.

"Sam?" Simone asked breathlessly.

"No," I croaked back.

"SAM!" Simone shrieked. Then the creature was on top of us, yellow eyes slit pupils and glowing. A greater blackness than even that of its body opened in its face and there were glints of paleness.

"AAAAHHHH! TEETH!" Simone announced with a guttural scream. "SHARP TEETH!"

The creature made a sound like a mix between a growl and a roar and I heard Simone plunk into the water. What seemed to be the flippers lifted and slammed into the water. The waves that movement caused pushed me up and back then they crashed over me. Bubbles popped all over my skin. The foam sizzled and vanished off of me. The salty water entered my nose and my eyes stung so hard I couldn't see a thing even if there was any light to see with.

I crashed into the creature's shell again, my chest throbbing with the impact.

I kicked away from it, hard, pushing my legs through the water. The creature shifted, and the water pulled me towards it. I was sucked under the water and I was trapped under an immense weight. I tried to slide underneath, but a hard sting on my arm discouraged me. The scales. I had to get out or I would drown.

I pushed myself down in the water, and I was sucked forward by a current. I tried to break free, but my head hit a softly scaled underside. The belly of the creature. I tried to swim further, but I couldn't hold my breath.

Salty water filled my lungs, every thought became jumbled. My lungs hurt, and burned, my chest ached, my arm and shoulder stung. The salt seemed to grate on me. I was dying. I knew   I was dying. Sam was calm when he said we would die, but I wasn't calm at all. My heart was racing. It was the only sound I could hear and it seemed muddled by water.

Tha-thunk, tha-thunk, tha-thunk, tha-thunk.

I swung my arm up, trying to get down. *If I can get out underneath it, then I'll live.* The thought wasn't in words, more like a feeling. The arm I swung was the one holding my sword, and my sword stabbed into the creature. It rumbled, and though I couldn't hear much, it must have been roaring in pain.

I yanked my sword out badly, the blood warmed the water. There were spots in my vision, green and pink and blue and purple.

I kicked away, my brain was sleepy, and my arms were heavy. My legs felt like lead. My feet were frozen blocks, my nose was too. I was slapped into the air by that flipper. I was just able to get a breath in when I smacked back into the water.

I flailed until my head was back above water. I was sure I smelled awful, but I wouldn't have known, I couldn't smell a thing, and my nose was filled with snot and salt water.

"Sam? Simone?" My voice was weak with exhaustion. The yelling had done its number and the salt only made it worse.

"Klotho! Are you okay?" Sam swam over to me. The black mass of the creature was far enough away for it drowning me to not be quite a threat just yet.

"I think so?" I replied, "What about you? Where's Simone?"

"I don't know, the thing roared though, I think she stabbed it," Sam told me, and I was reminded of being stuck under the thing.

"No, I did. I stabbed it. Its belly is soft." My legs were too tired to live and my arms were sore, but I didn't dare to stop trying to float.

"Good, I'm going to go and stab it again. Stay here if you can." I reached out to stop him, but he was already gone.

"Sam, no!" I called out. "Sam! Sam!"

But no one replied. I had to go after him, there was no way he'd be able to survive. I had freaking water powers, surely, I'd been using them to help me unconsciously. I kicked off after him, though my muscles and my head all screamed in protest.

The waves pulled me down and up, towards the giant beast that I'd stabbed. I heard Simone scream. A blood-curdling, utterly horrible scream of terror, then, nothing. My breath quickened even more. My head ached. When was the last time I drank clean water?

"Please, come on, Sam," I murmured to myself.

Then the flipper of the creature crashed into me and I was sent skidding backward over the water like a boat. The creature let out a horrible scream and then vanished under the water. With a burst of strength, I had my powers push me towards where the sea beast used to be. The thing surfaced again, which had me on its back, the shell. I held on the best I could, then slid down to its head.

I raised my sword above my head and stabbed down. The sword slid to the side and I cut open my leg, not even making a dent in the creature. I hissed in pain, and the creature turned. I was thrown off it and I got stuck under its belly again. I swam downwards, but floated up and hit someone, Simone, or Sam, I couldn't tell which until my hand ran into the curtain of wet hair. I turned, reaching out my arm, and it ran into Sam's head.

It was pitch black, but Simone somehow managed ti grab my sword arm and face it up towards the creature's belly. I followed her lead and managed to get Sam to do the same by grabbing his wrist, the one with the sword hilt sticking out and turning it up.

Simone changed positions somehow and kicked both of us as a signal to stab. I thrust my sword up, then yanked it out. The water became warm with blood, so much so that a stream of it pushed against me. The creature's body vibrated, then stopped altogether.

The weight of it pushed us down, it was sinking, I realized. I grabbed Sam and Simone, Simone by the ankle and Sam by the wrist, and I used the water to pull us out from under the creature.

We broke the surface, panting and soiled and probably looking horrible.

"Where's that mattress?" Sam asked. "Or do you have another one?"

"Give me a minute, I'll check." She turned into some kind of bird and flew up into the air. Two minutes later, she came back in probably dolphin form. She turned into a small bird, sat upon something, turned back into her human form, and turned her ring into a lit lantern.

The light was shocking at first, but when my eyes adjusted, I was shown the image of a soaked twelve-year-old covered head to toe in blood sitting on top of a pristine air mattress.

I don't think I've ever been so annoyed.

Chapter Thirty

Introducing Our New Hobby: Kidnapping

"How in the world is this air mattress unscathed?" I demanded as Simone helped to yank me up onto the thing. Sam managed to get in all on his—no, I'm kidding, he was too tired to even make an effort so Simone and I had to haul him up while Simone had the lantern in her teeth.

Sam groaned. "Where do we need to go?"

Simone dug the map out of her bag and checked. It promptly flew in her face and she had to wrestle it back down with a shouted spell. She handed Sam the map, and lantern to me before curling up.

I pushed the raft with my powers as hard as I could without passing out.

The ride back was a blur. My head and throat hurt, and I blacked out until we were washing up on shore. It was blue side now, the sun not quite up, but coming. Sam practically threw the map back at Simone.

"Come on lady! Get us to the next horrid homework assignment!" Sam shouted at the ocean. Right on cue, the nymph appeared out of the water looking supremely annoyed.

"Well, I'll tell you I've never met such fed-up children in my life." She huffed. "But if you insist, I'll send you horrid creatures to the naiad. Some friend you have to be sending monsters after you." She lifted her hand.

"What?" Simone interrupted and the nymph lowered her hand. "Oh yes, I saw her earlier. She cast some spell to summon the thing, I hoped she was casting it away, but I suppose not." The nereid lowered her hand with a hint of satisfaction on her face.

"You didn't think to stop her?" Simone demanded, crossing her arms.

"Well of course not, I was afraid to go near her. I did hear what she did to Adoeete, I wasn't about to let her take my arm off. Unlike the trees, I cannot simply regrow limbs." The nereid scoffed.

"So, you knew she tried to murder Adoeete and you just let her summon a monster? I mean no disrespect, but what were you thinking?" Simone continued to press.

"Adoeete is not perfect, I assumed that your dear Annalyn acted in self-defense. She is a botanokenetic, I assumed she wouldn't hurt the trees without purpose." The nereid countered.

"What's a botan—a botanekine—botanokenetic?" I whispered to Sam, struggling with the pronunciation.

"Someone who controls plants, in the camp we separate the different powers into classes. Hydrokinetic, pyrokinetic, botanokenetic, aerokinetic, geokinetic, umbrakinetic, and photokinetic, to name a few. Most abilities don't fit those names exactly to the letter, but they're close enough." He whispered back.

"Well, she will, so if you see her talking to a monster, watch out. Thanks for not killing us." Simone didn't sound very thankful, but the nereid didn't seem to mind. "Now just please don't drop us into another body of—"

And we fell right into the raging river.

I was rolled forward, right towards a massive rock, I was about to crash into it head first when my powers kicked in and I had the water hurling me out of the river and right into a tree. I caught one of the branches and hauled myself into a sitting position. Sam had managed to grab onto a rock, and Simone had turned herself into a bear.

"Are you guys ok?" The water in the river was cold, and I know it sounds wimpy but all I wanted to do was get into a *warm* bath. Or warm blankets. I was freezing.

"Yeah," Sam's voice shivered with him, he jumped from one rock to another then onto shore. Simone lumbered through the water and shook off. "Hey!" Sam flinched away from the flying water.

"Sorry," Simone replied when she turned back into a human. I would have expected her to laugh, but I think we were all too tired and miserable for anything like that. Her leg was badly cut open, her shirt was bloody—well, most of her was bloody, but most of that wasn't hers. Sam's arm was bad, bruised, and painful looking, but the rest of him looked okay.

I felt awful, my leg and shoulder hurt. Stupid salt water.

"I'd feel better if you did some healing magic," Simone stretched her arms. "If you're up for it, anyway."

"I'm up for it, just... uh..." I realized that she was on the lowest branch of the tree and that branch was fifteen feet off the ground.

"I'll help," Simone turned me into a bird and I clumsily flapped my way to the ground.

"Wait, never mind Klotho's singing—no offense—Simone, I want to hear *you* sing again," Sam said with a mischievous grin. "Your voice isn't nearly as bad as I expected."

Simone rolled her eyes. "No. Klotho, mind closing some of these wounds?"

"Sure." I hummed loudly, not in the mood for a song, and the simple melody was enough to close all of our wounds, though not perfectly.

"Oh, come on," Sam pestered.

"No, I don't sing normally. That was a special circumstance in which I was under the threat of losing my flesh to bees," Simone stayed firm.

"Pleeeeeeeeaaaaaase?" Sam drawled out the word as long as he could and gave Simone puppy eyes.

"The next time I sing to you is the day you die," Simone growled back and Sam shut his mouth with an audible snap.

The naiad popped out of the water, and I recognized her from that time we went hurdling off a cliff on a raft. I shrieked and jumped back, the sun blasted into my eyes and I blinked hard to keep it out.

"Well, hello there." She said, looking us over. She frowned and quickly schooled her expression to a kind of concerned disgust. "You three are looking... in a bit of need of a shower."

"Yeah, we didn't have time for one while we were trying not to get murdered by a gigantic turtle snake thing," Simone replied with a sickly sweet smile and fists clenched together so hard her knuckles glowed bright white.

The poor naiad looked understandably intimidated. "Well, no time to waste then," she said rather nervously. "Your challenge is to capture a specific water dragon, with red eyes and white scales. Your Annalyn cursed him, and he won't stop lashing out at the other dragons. He should be coming upstream, best of luck, and keep away from his claws." She transformed into water and was carried away by the river.

Sam had never looked more livid. "A water dragon. *Known to be violent*. You know, she could have just killed us."

"Would have been quicker, too. Come on, let's get to work. Anyone got a rope?" Simone rubbed her temples. "Oh wait, *I* have a rope." She promptly fished out a thick coil of it from her bag.

"Do either of you know how to make a trap?" I asked.

"I can, but it's for land animals, not dragons." Sam took the rope and frowned. "I guess we'll just have to wait and let it come to us."

"Maybe make a slip knot? So we can pull it tight when we need to." Simone took the rope back and twisted it around her arm to make the knot, leaving a large loop at the end. She put the loop in the water, handed it back to Sam, and turned it into a bear.

"What's she doing?" I asked.

"Getting fish, we need some kind of bait to trap the dragon." Sam shrugged.

Fish splashed from the lake and Simone caught four in her mouth before lumbering back to the bank. She shook herself off, spraying us yet again. This time I was too tired to flinch away.

She set the fish down and wrapped three together with the tall grass from the bank, which she tied to the rope so that it wouldn't float away. The fish bled into the water, hanging limply. I remembered dimly that they would probably smell terrible later on.

There was a fourth fish left, the biggest one.

"What's that one for?" I asked rather stupidly.

"This is for us." Simone had Sam set up a fire and she shoved me as close to the fire as she could without burning me. "Your lips are blue," she offered as an explanation. Cold water dripped down my back, making me shiver.

"So are yours," I pointed out, then, looking at Sam, I found that he was a similar shade.

Simone opened her mouth, but with no argument, she just watched the fish, turning our makeshift spit when the skin got dark and crispy.

Sam's mouth was practically dripping with drool. "I'm starving," he said to Simone's scrutiny.

"Good news for you then," She took the fish off the spit and plotted it up, taking the head and tail for herself and splitting the body in half for Sam and me.

The fish was so hot it burned my fingers, so I had to toss it around in my hands to avoid it touching my skin for too long. I never thought that I would play hot potato so literally with a fish. I almost dropped it onto the ground.

"How long do you think it'll take the dragon to get here?" I asked without much better to do. I blew on my half of the fish hard while Simone crunched on the tail.

"I don't know, it could be minutes or it could be hours," Simone replied. She stole a small chunk of fish from my half and hissed in pain when it burned her fingers. Steam plumed off the small chunk where the white flesh was torn off. She blew on the chunk with a strange mouth formation, long and narrow.

"What are you doing?" I asked.

"Blowing on the fish—oh, you mean with my lips." She popped the little chunk into her mouth. "That's just my flute embouchure; I've been blowing on things like that since I started playing. It's pretty convenient—"

She froze with her eyes on the river. A white back fin covered in pearly scales snaked through the current. The dragon.

I yanked all the flesh I could off the bones and breathed quickly with my mouth open to cool it. Simone took hold of the rope end, waiting to pull. The dragon came closer, closer, and then its front leg went through the loop.

Simone yanked the end of the rope tight, and the dragon turned its red eyes towards us in rage. It reared back, spewing water right into my chest. I was blasted back by the force and rolled around on the bank to get back up. It blasted another torrent of water at Sam, but I reached out with my hydrokinesis and managed to stop it dead.

The blob of water wobbled, *please,* I thought, barely hearing it as my gear beat in my ears, *work.* I whittled it into an arrowhead-like shape and tried to throw it back at the dragon. The water then fell out of my control and plopped onto the ground.

The dragon looked down at its front right leg, wrapped with a rope. It walked backward, dragging Simone, who was unwilling to let go, along with it. I was rooted to the ground. I tried to move but couldn't muster it. I felt my heartbeat in my fingers.

No, I prayed it would do what I thought it would. But my prayers must have gone unanswered because it yanked itself back through the water with a flap of its wings and Simone got pulled along like she was on a water tube.

"Simone!" Sam shrieked and—lacking in good ideas—chucked his sword at the dragon. He missed by a mile, and the dragon continued to drag Simone around in the water, pulling her under and around rocks and logs. It jumped over one rock and Simone had to twist to avoid crashing into it head-first. The dragon paused for a second, giving Simone just enough time to take a breath before it resumed dragging her around. Water sprayed from the river, the current pulled Simone to the side and her hip cracked into a rock.

I heard a gurgling shriek of pain and the rope slid from her fingers. She grabbed onto the rock and reached out to catch the rope, barely managing to grasp the end. Her eyes were teary with pain and she was quite obviously avoiding using her left hip. I was reminded of the way my bruise felt from the dragon that killed Ada.

The dragon looked at Simone, glaring through those red eyes. It reared back in flight and heaved itself out of the water. Simone was yanked with it and plunged back into the center of the river when the dragon dove. It pinned her underneath itself.

"Do something!" Sam's breaths came in wild pants, he grabbed a rock and chucked it. "Klotho! KLOTHO!"

This snapped me out of my trance enough to run towards the river. I had no clue what I was planning to do, my powers weren't working correctly, and my sword fighting was still subpar at best.

But I stomped into the water, with my sword out, and immediately got yanked into a log that was lodged between two rocks by the current. My side scraped along the wet, spongy edge. I hooked my arm up around it and wrenched my head above water with a gulp of air. I coughed out water and kicked off the log to get to Simone. I made the current shove me towards her, glad that I could at least manage that.

All the sounds of struggle from above were muffled when my head dipped under the surface of the river. I opened my eyes, the debris floating made it hard to see, but the dragon's white scales shone even in the murky water. I rocketed towards them with a blast of water and crashed into the dragon's scaly side.

I pulled back my sword but realized that if I drove it in A: We were supposed to catch it, not kill it, and B: there wasn't a chance that I would be able to do any harm to the dragon without getting drowned by whatever energy I'd leave it.

Then there was the matter of Simone, who was trapped underneath. I breathed in water with panicked thought, my nose and throat burned, and I choked. I threw myself up, gasping in the air and just barely managing to get enough down before the dragon smacked me with its wing.

I skidded over the surface for half a second before the current dragged me back under. I thrashed hard until I hit the log, I clung to it and forced my eyes open under the water. I watched Simone struggle, and in a scattered bit of thought, willed a swath of water to pass under the dragon. It dislodged Simone, who couldn't have kicked herself away fast enough.

The dragon turned towards me, its eyes glowing with hate.

Oh *no*—

And it launched itself towards me. I screamed and grabbed for the top of the log. I hooked my elbow over and tried to swing myself up, but I slipped on the wet wood and the dragon crashed nose-first into my side. It dragged me underneath the log, I willed the water to throw me to the right. To get me away from this dragon.

My arm skimmed a rock under the water, there was a hard sting of pain. Then I crashed into the other rocks holding this log into place. The force knocked the air out of my chest and my lungs demanded air. I threw myself up, head first into the log. The top of my skull cracked right into the washed-up wood.

I grasped the wood and pushed myself out. The air froze my lungs, my nose, my cheeks. The sun blasted into my eyes and burned on my forehead. I snorted out water and coughed out splinters.

"Klotho!" Sam ran over the log, feet more agile than I'd ever seen them—oh no, he slipped hard, fell into his hip, and smacked onto the dragon's back. The dragon snarled from under the log and whirled under the water. Sam held onto its horns, face scrunched up in concentration as it tried desperately to shake him off.

Simone managed to swim over the rope still in her hand, tightening and looking as the dragon shook and spun.

"Klotho, do you remember when you practiced making water more solid? When you shape it? Do that, ropes, this one isn't enough," she said so rapidly it came out more like a bunch of spit.

Sam clenched his teeth, if he opened his mouth he would bite off his tongue—I willed the splashing water to elongate into ropes. Now for the tricky part, actually getting it to stay around the dragon. I imagined it creating a floating cage, criss-crossing all around.

"SAM, LET GO!" Simone bellowed.

"Are—" Sam managed to get out with a lull in the dragon's thrashing, "—you—" the dragon barely paused again, "—INSANE?"

"YES! NOW LET GO!" Simone screamed back in what had to be the most unassuring- yet-reassuring pep-talk I'd ever heard.

Sam decided that Simone was being ridiculous because he didn't let go.

"Oh, just tighten the ropes," Simone yelled with a gesture.

I imagined them pulling tight, and they did as I asked. Only two of those ropes disintegrated on the dragon's muzzle, leaving it able to bite and thrash its head. The rest went to plan, pinning the dragon's wings and tail down and around the log. Simone dropped the rope. One more problem, Sam was now trapped on the dragon's back.

Simone stared at the dragon for a moment, then paled. "Sam, can you wriggle out?" He was flat on its back like a badly flipped pancake.

"No," he tried to say, but with his face half down it came out more like, "Mhpho,"

"Klotho, this is going to sound even more insane than I am," Simone said, "You need to wriggle new ropes under Sam. Which is going to likely be very awkward,"

I pulled water noodles out of the river, "I think I've got it."

I shoved a water rope under his chest, under his legs, under his torso again. That looked like enough, but considering my luck I shoved in two more just for safety.

"Okay, now release the three holding him down," Simone told me. I did as she asked, and the water left wet stripes down Sam's clothes. He scrambled to get off, slipping twice like an old cartoon character, and crashed right into the water next to me.

"Ugh," Sam groaned and dragged himself along the log and onto the bank. He then collapsed in the dirt.

Simone and I quickly followed his example, I sat against a tree instead and Simone leaned on a rock. That Naiad better come soon, or I was probably going to fall asleep and never wake up. My eyelids dropped, my heart hummed in my hands, and heated my ears. The sun peeked through the leaves, and I let my eyes close just for a second...

Sam shook me hard, "Wake up! Wake up! It's the Naiad, she's getting us back!"

"Wha...?" I looked up through my blurred eyes and saw the naiad standing in the water.

"Well, after you do one little thing for me." She raised a finger as if to tell us to wait.

Oh, please, *please*, I couldn't handle another task, the last four should have killed me. I was only alive because of luck, I couldn't handle this. Why had I gone in the first place? Why didn't I reject this? No... I just wanted to go home, to go home.

"Let the dragon go," she said simply. "All you must do is release the dragon, and you are free to go back to camp."

I sobbed with relief and was just about to do it when Simone stood up sharply.

"Are you telling us that we just spent the last however long trying to trap this darned dragon, only for you to *let it go*? Did you not tell us half an hour ago that this one was violent?" Simone demanded.

"Well, yes, but so are many other things on the island. Let it go, and you can go home," The Naiad told us remarkably calmly.

Simone reached out a hand for Sam and I to hold, I felt the swirling wind around the edges of my body, and I released the ropes tying down the great dragon. I heard an earth-shaking roar, and then I was sitting on the soft grass of the Camp Myth field.

Simona C. Huska

Chapter Thirty-One

Dinner Declarations

ANNE found us sprawled on the grass. She quickly looked us over, and her eyes caught on the open space next to us. Her face crumpled.

"Annalyn...?" her voice broke with the question. I realized what we must look like, soaked and exhausted with bloodstained clothes and limbs. All are bruised up and barely working correctly. The wind blew and I tried not to shiver, but Anne spotted it anyway.

And I looked harder at her, dark circles under her eyes, her knees trembled ever so slightly. What would I do if I had a friend going on a mission like this? Would I be able to sleep? Be able to have anything but nightmares?

"No," Simone said, "Annalyn isn't dead." Her face was cold.

"What?" Anne's expression crossed into confusion and that mess in the chamber came back to me with full force.

"She betrayed us," I croaked. I covered my face with my hands. "She's trying to wake Tartar or something," I breathed in through my nose, then out through my mouth. In, out, in, out. Then I was crying. Hot tears licked my face.

"Tartarus," Simone corrected, "She's trying to destroy the gods by waking Tartarus." She rubbed my back.

I lifted my face out of my hands in time to see Anne pale. But she nodded.

"Do you want me to... spread the word?" She asked, but her voice was choked, and I remembered that Annalyn was her friend too.

"No," Simone said, "I need to talk to Medea first. I'll... I'll announce it at dinner today,"

I couldn't imagine ever announcing news like that.

"I'll get Medea, but before that... I should tell you that campers have been disappearing, not dead, just vanishing into thin air. The camp's been cut in half." Anne told us.

Sam stared at the grass underneath him. "Their allies," he murmured. Anne just nodded painfully. She turned and practically ran off, and her shoulders shook with a sob. How many more of her friends had vanished? How many more betrayals was she facing?

Medea came running a few minutes later, her clay-red dress billowing around her, "Anne told me you have grim news, I must hear everything—" She took one look at us and stopped dead in her tracks.

"Hey, Medea," Sam said, I waved pathetically and wiped tears off of my cheeks.

"You three should come with me," she said, looking over at Simone. "We will speak in my office."

Simone hauled Sam to his feet and we lumbered off to Nikephros Academy. We walked up three flights of stairs to get to Medea's office in the northwest tower. The room was lavishly decorated with a rug showing colorful scenes of roaming animals and a hardwood desk. In front of the desk were three plush chairs in red brigade and behind the desk was Medea's matching one. Three steaming ceramic mugs stood on the table, the scent of green tea wafted through the air. A jar of honey sat in the center.

"Sit, speak when you are ready." Medea sat down across from us and waited. I picked the middle seat, Sam was to my left, and Simone was to my right. With the quiet environment and the bad news we were about to bring, it felt like we were about to get suspended.

I picked up my mug, leaving the saucer on the table. The tea was still too hot to drink, so I blew on it and looked over at Simone. It seemed like she should speak first, she was the one who fought Annalyn.

Simone took in a breath, "Annalyn is trying to wake Tartarus and destroy the gods."

Well, not exactly the most gentle delivery but we'd have to start somewhere. Medea's expression didn't change, but she went very still. She watched Simone with hawk eyes, waiting patiently for more.

"She betrayed us in the underworld when Klotho found her note, we still have it, but we don't know to whom it's addressed. Annalyn escaped before we could get more information." Simone drizzled honey into her mug, the simple action harshly contrasted with the brutal truth of her words.

Medea sat and seemed to stare somewhere far into the past, "May I see the note?" Medea asked, reaching her hand over the table in request.

Simone nodded and reached into the bag, pulling out the folded-up letter. Crisp and clean. She slid it towards Medea, her fingers tightened on the paper, and then she released it as though she'd been burned.

No fair, I thought with a scowl, *that chunk of paper is in better shape than me!*

Medea carefully unfolded it and looked it over. Then she read it again, and again. She folded it back up and set it on the table.

"Tartarus and his allies have set up a base at the southern tip of the island, I see," Medea reminded us.

When you get back to camp, tell our allies that it is time, meet at the southern tip of the island.

I heard it in Annalyn's voice, even though it was Simone who had read it. *This is serious,* I realized, *they're going to do it.*

"What does that mean for the camp?" I whimpered.

What would my parents think? My dad always told me he would protect me at all costs, my mom even more. They would never let me fight in this... this... I couldn't bear to even think about it. If I said it, even in my mind, it would make it real.

"It means that we will need to have some long conversations." Medea glanced down at my untouched tea and I sucked it down. The tea was a bit bitter, even with the honey. But the warmth trailed down into my chest, fell into my stomach, and warmed that too. It made me feel a little better.

Sam hadn't even picked up his cup. "How are our schedules looking?" Speaking of appearances, he looked sick.

"You are to shower and *rest* until dinner." Medea emphasized 'rest' with a sharp look at Simone, who quickly dropped her gaze to the table. Medea kept speaking to her, "At dinner, you will be the best to announce this new development, as you were there, but we will speak about that privately. You three may use the school showers, Anne reported to me that a pair of girls got into a fight and one bled all over the camp shower floors, so they are currently being cleaned. I've had Anne set up clothing for each of you in the Flameheart showers instead."

Sam stood up, with Simone and I quickly following.

"Thank you," I murmured. Medea just nodded.

Sam led us to the Flameheart showers. Each was completely separate, with a door that left a dry half of the seven by seven-foot space to change in. I found the same clothes that Anne had given me on the first day, the striped shirt, and the straw hat. Hopefully clean underwear and socks.

I scrubbed my scalp, the sudsy water ran brown into the drain and washed off my body with water so warm it was almost uncomfortable. I rubbed in the conditioner, detangled it the best I could, rinsed, and got out. I was sick of being wet. I dried myself off with the towel, though my curls dripped onto the tiles, I looked up into the mirror and stared. I hadn't seen my reflection for most of the mission, but I'd seen glimpses of my filthy hair, which shone bright red. My skin was still peeling from sunburn.

The most notable difference was in my body, I was less muscular when I came to the island. But now, my thighs were more powerful, my biceps were slightly defined. I no longer looked like a gangly stick. My cheekbones seemed to stick out more, though maybe that was just my cheeks being more hollow.

When I came out, the hat pulled firmly onto my head to avoid getting *more* sunburned, Sam was already waiting. He stood in the hall, leaning on an emerald green locker. He was dressed in a clean white shirt and blue shorts. His shoes were the same ones he had been wearing in the quest, and they were so beaten up it prompted me to look down at mine, which were similarly depressing.

"What do we do now?" During the mission it had been simple, get up, walk, fight a giant thing trying to kill us, eat something, keep walking, fight another thing trying to kill us, maybe eat again, sleep, and then wake up and do it all over. Not having to do anything like that was both calming and... boring. Yeah, it was awful and terrifying, but we were always doing something. We always had a distraction.

"I guess we'll just go about our day, I'm going to sleep. Simone's probably going to kill whoever got into a fight in the camp showers, terrorize whichever kids have been sneaking out past curfew, you know, the usual." Sam shrugged with his attempt at casualty.

"Sleeping sounds like a great idea, as long as I don't roll off the bunk again," I replied.

"You guys just go!" I heard Simone shout from one of the showers, "I'll be in here a while!"

Sam and I glanced at each other, he shrugged and we set off to our cabins. Along the way, we were hounded by campers. Each congratulated us, though with noticeable tenseness.

I nodded and uh-huh'd along until the head of the Persephone cabin told everyone to cut it out and let us go to sleep.

"You two look like you've been up before the sun," She said in her Scottish accent, "go to sleep if you know what's good for you."

She then escorted us to our cabins, murmuring about incessant campers the whole time. I managed to kick off my shoes and climb onto my bunk before passing out. I was too tired even to dream.

Sam came to shake me awake at dinner, he looked like he'd just woken up.

"Dinner?" I asked groggily. I sat up and rubbed my eyes. My hair was still damp and was probably a disaster.

"Yeah, in like fifteen minutes," Sam replied.

I swung my legs over the side of the bunk and climbed down, a hair brush had been laid out for me on the bottom bunk and I managed to get most of the snarls out before the bell rang. I grabbed the mat and walked over to the pavilion. The rest of the campers were just chatting and running around as usual, with no idea of the news they were about to receive.

I came to sit down with Anne and Vega. Vega waved to me, her bright eyes dreamy and unfocused as ever.

"Hello curly duck," Vega said in greeting.

I looked at Anne in confusion, she shrugged and gestured for me to sit down. I plopped far too hard onto the picnic blanket, which made my butt hurt. A plate appeared right in front of me, chicken, rice, and broccoli. The fork sat on the edge of the plate. My stomach growled and I didn't even bother to blow on the still-steaming chicken before shoving a chunk in my mouth.

Of course, it burned my tongue and I had to open up my mouth and breathe quickly to cool it.

Anne giggled, "Hungry?"

I nodded aggressively.

"The duck traveled far, she should be hungry after her journey." Vega's long fingers lifted a mini carrot to her lips. She crunched on it while Anne and I stared in silence, unsure what to make of this comment.

Our attention was snapped away when two hard cracks sounded in the pavilion. Simone stood up on the platform with a grim expression. I shifted on the blanket, the quilted surface suddenly felt too hard, and my stomach filled with rocks.

"Children of Camp Myth," Simone announced, "I regret to inform you that we are at war."

"What's going to happen—"

"Does this mean—"

"What happened—"

"How will we fight—"

The whispers carried for a few moments, before quieting naturally. Simone's face was stone cold, but I thought I saw her gulp before speaking again.

"On our mission to the underworld, we were betrayed by Annalyn Dulfo and found that she and the campers who have been disappearing are attempting to wake Tartarus and destroy the gods." The resulting gasp had Simone pause. "All those over the age of ten who do not want to fight or cannot fight should leave the island within the month. If you have nowhere to go, Medea and I would arrange housing. Children ten or younger may stay here if they have older siblings who are fighting, but if the Island becomes too unsafe, they will be sent back to the mainland.

"If you don't want to fight or stay here, come to Medea and I after dinner to discuss. If any over the age of ten want to fight, and if any ten or under want to stay here, come to Medea and I tomorrow morning and we will discuss that." Simone's eyes roamed over the crowd. "Thank you for your time."

Then she vanished into thin air.

The pavilion exploded into chaos, almost like when the fire dragon came to camp. Only a small percentage of the campers who were eligible to fight chose to leave, and most of those kids were the ones who couldn't fight for whatever reason. I was torn, my parents would be so worried... but I brought this war here, I was the signal that the time was right.

I couldn't just leave.

"What about you, Klotho?" Anne asked, and I realized that she and Vega were talking about the fighting. "I'm staying, I can't leave the island in a time like this."

"I need to call my parents," I told them and left for my cabin.

Inside, after the sunset, I tossed and turned while mulling it over. My legs tangled in the blanket and I threw it off of me, suddenly too hot. I wasn't able to sleep for most of the night, but I managed to shut my eyes and pass out for a good two hours.

I was floating inside of the lagoon. Poseidon floated in front of me. The clear, ocean water flowed gently like wind. Colorful fish swam in the near-sunrise light.

"Hello, Klotho," he said. His voice reverberated in the water, deepening it, expanding it, until it was more than human. It reminded me that he was a god and one of the ones Annalyn was trying to destroy.

"Um, hi." I waved. Bubbles burbled out of my mouth, warping my words and making me sound kind of stupid. "I'm sorry that there's a bunch of people trying to... uh... kill you." There was no way to make that sound apologetic with bubbles coming out of my mouth.

Poseidon blinked at me, "You know about the choice that must be made, then."

"Yeah," I murmured.

Poseidon nodded, "Choose wisely."

I woke up falling from the bunk, I panicked for a moment before I hit the floor. Reaching my hands out and clutching for anything, expecting to hit the rock. But I hit wood and that brought me back to reality.

The wind was knocked out of me and I had to wait what felt like forever to breathe in properly again. I felt tired, but staying up all night let me reach a decision, at least.

I got up and walked outside, Medea and Simone stood at the pavilion. I came up to them and cleared my throat, bringing them out of their conversation.

"Klotho? Have you decided?" Simone asked. Her voice sounded strange, stiff if that makes sense. Nasally, as if she had a cold. "Whatever you decide, I know what your parents will say. I'll wipe their memories if I have to. It's your choice no matter what."

"I need to call my parents," before I could change my mind.

"We don't have phones, but you can mirage them. Just take this orb, and say the full names of the people you want to call. It should make an illusion pop up of their faces." Simone handed me a palm-sized, pearlescent pale blue orb.

I walked to the edge of the forest for privacy and took a deep breath.

"Keiran and Cara Marina," I said to the orb, feeling kind of stupid for talking to a crystal.

An image wobbled into place just like a mirage, and my mom and dad were sitting at the kitchen table. My mom's under-eyes were dark, and my dad's too. His red stubble had grown out more than I'd seen it before, and his curly red hair was a newly-woken disaster on his head.

"Klotho!" The two of them called out at once. My mom lunged over the table to get closer, leaving her sprawled over it, kind of like a fish. She pushed herself up on her elbows.

"Are you hurt?" My mom fretted.

"Did you get enough sleep?" My dad asked, glancing me over.

"Are you eating enough?"

"What about friends—"

"Is everything going well—"

"Yes, guys, I'm fine," I cut in. "But there's some stuff happening, I don't know if you've heard about—"

"We know about the war." They chorused. My mom took a deep breath and looked at my dad. His eyebrows drew down and my mom's scrunched inward. They seemed to have a silent conversation before my dad sighed.

Wait, would they *make* me come home? Was that what Simone meant when she said she would wipe their memories for me? For some reason, that thought had never occurred to me. I couldn't blame them, if I had a kid I would probably do anything to get them off of this island. Do anything to get them away from the fighting. I knew what this could be, I knew. Or did I?

"Ms. Medea told us about the mission, and the outcome, and the war. She explained our options," His next breath shuddered on the way in. "She said that it may be safer for you to stay since you can't fight monsters as well as the other kids yet. But since you're eleven, you would have to fight in the battles, or become a nurse at the least." *And that could kill you too.* The unspoken words echoed in my mind.

"She told us that staying or leaving is your choice. Understand though, if you choose to stay now, you stay on the island for the school year. And you won't be able to go home for more than a month per year." My mom's voice cracked.

Leave, the scared little voice in the back of my mind whispered. *You can't fight here, you know you can't. You'll die, or get kidnapped, they take you and—*

No, they won't. I stopped myself at that line of thinking. *If I keep thinking like this I'll never get anywhere.* I let the silence drag as I turned around the pros and cons.

If I left, no one would ever forgive me. We needed numbers, I knew it. Numbers brought victory.

"Will there even be fighting? What if they just give up before we can even start?" I asked, but my mom shook her head.

"That Simone girl told me that your Annalyn is doing this because her older sisters died. All hate comes from love, and her love for her sisters has turned into hate for the gods. She will fight, even if her comrades don't." My mom told me. "If you need more time to decide we can wait till tomorrow—"

"No," I stopped her. "I've already decided."

"Yes?" Her eyebrows tilted up in worry, even as her lips turned into a small smile. My dad wrapped his arm around her.

I took a deep breath. "I'm staying."

EPILOGUE

THE picture felt frail in her slim-fingered hands. A lock of Annalyn's softly curling hair fell over her shoulder. Jaslene and Diwata stood on either side of a smiling nine-year-old Annalyn. She caressed the photo, brushing her thumb next to Diwata's long, straight hair. Jaslene's crooked teeth showed brightly in her grin.

She could almost feel it again, she could almost feel the joy of the picture in her veins. The day they'd first arrived at camp. She could practically feel Diwata's hair brushing her elbow. Could almost feel Jaslene's shirt under her arm.

"If only it was someone else," Annalyn whispered, "Anyone but Zeus," but of course she'd been picked by Demeter, while her sisters faced Zeus.

"You are very lucky, Annalyn, Demeter has a mother's wisdom," *Medea assured her as she led Annalyn out of the forest.*

"But I wanted to be with my sisters!" Annalyn sniffled and wiped her *eyes.*

Medea patted her back, "You will see your sisters other times, they are *smart, and they will survive."*

Oh, how wrong the sorceress had been. Oh, how wrong. Annalyn shouldn't have believed her anyway. Shouldn't have believed Medea, the woman who had let her own children die for some petty revenge.

"Annalyn," Ji-Min called from outside and knocked on the door. "Are you up for dinner?"

"Of course," Annalyn folded the photo again and slid it into her pocket. Her bed creaked when she stood. She walked through the narrow hallways with Ji-Min.

"I get it, they were your friends," Ji-Min comforted.

Annalyn just nodded. "How is the move-in going?" She asked after a short silence.

"Everyone's still getting into their guard rotations, so it'll be sloppy these first few weeks," Ji-Min said, her brisk steps gently patting the wood.

"So, we'll be vulnerable," Tartarus wouldn't be happy about that.

"For now, but we'll get ourselves together quickly, we have more adaptable campers on our side. More resilient too. This will be quick," Ji-Min told Annalyn. Annalyn smiled, she always appreciated Ji-Min's confidence.

"What's our plan for offensives?" Annalyn asked.

"If everything goes well and the weather's in our favor, we attack both Islands on August sixteenth." She and Ji-Min just came upon the dining hall.

A smile played on Annalyn's lips, "Perfect."

Acknowledgements

Thank you to my wonderful parents and little sister who helped me get this book published. Great thanks to Amna and Saanvi, who tolerated all my talking about this book and gave me ideas. Maryam, who also tolerated my non-stop yammering. Shetha, who's taught me more about grammar than school ever has. Apurva, who inspired me to get better at grammar so that I wouldn't have to use Grammarly (long story). Medha, who was delightfully unhinged enough to lend me some ideas as well. To Panchi, who like everyone on this list tolerated my incessant yapping. To all the people who edited the first draft (I am truly sorry). Thank you to Ms. Katzmarek (my fourth-grade teacher) for bringing Emily and me together so that Emily had the opportunity to get me into writing.

I have some choice words for Google Docs, which stopped allowing me to use the 'find and replace' feature. I am not going to write those choice words here, but know that I am watching you, Google Docs. Thank you to Autodesk Sketchbook, which allowed me to draw the cover for this book. Thank you to my own need to be satisfied with my art before putting it anywhere, and thank you to all the people who opened up this book and fell off of several cliffs to get here.

Author's note

I got the idea for this series in fifth grade and I started writing it (very badly, I might add) immediately. I got into writing because of one of my friends, Emily- so naturally I shared the doc with her hoping she would have something cool to add. I mean this next part with no shade, but Emily changed the personality of Klotho to the point where I no longer knew how to write her, and completely re-wrote the admittedly terrible throne room scene.

Now, I tend to be very particular about my writing and my reading. One of my greatest pet-peeves is when a character is very inconsistent, and trying to fix Klotho's new personality so that I could write it just wasn't worth the effort for me. So, I scrapped the idea until sixth grade came around and I found the idea in the deepest crevices of my google docs.

I braced myself for torture, knowing that my writing from fifth grade was abhorrent. My grammar was terrible back then, honestly it was terrible in sixth grade too, if the opinions of my friends can be trusted (they can). But I did what any twelve-year-old would do. I re-read the doc, cringed myself half to death, and decided that the idea was good enough to pursue further.

The end (or should I say beginning?)

ABOUT THE AUTHOR

SIMONA IS A THIRTEEN-YEAR-OLD storyteller and illustrator who has been creating imaginative worlds since she was very young. Under The Throne is her debut novel. When she isn't writing or sketching, Simona enjoys arts and crafts, music, and outdoor adventures like tennis, rollerblading, and biking. She adores history, particularly fashion history, and even sews her own outfits.

With a global perspective shaped by her Slovak heritage and travels to many places, Simona's love for exploring new cultures and climbing mountain ranges inspires much of her creativity. She can often be found with a book in hand, searching for her next great read or chatting about her favorite stories with friends.